D0363851

READER'S DIGEST

CONDENSED BOOKS

FIRST EDITION

THE READER'S DIGEST ASSOCIATION LIMITED
25 Berkeley Square, London W1X 6AB

THE READER'S DIGEST ASSOCIATION SOUTH AFRICA (PTY) LTD.
Nedbank Centre, Strand Street, Cape Town

Printed in Great Britain by Petty & Sons Ltd., Leeds

Original cover design by Jeffery Matthews A.R.C.A.

For information as to ownership
of copyright in the material in this book see last page

ISBN 0 340 22366 9

READER'S DIGEST
CONDENSED BOOKS

EXCELLENCY
David Beaty

CHASE THE WIND
E. V. Thompson

THE BADGERS OF SUMMERCOMBE
Ewan Clarkson

OVERBOARD
Hank Searls

COLLECTOR'S LIBRARY
EDITION

In this volume

EXCELLENCY
by David Beaty (p.9)

A white diplomat, a black dictator, a young pilot and a pretty girl; as the African state of Kajandi plunges from one disaster to another, the lives of these four people become entwined in surprising ways. An exciting story of power and intrigue, of adventure in the air and on the ground.

CHASE THE WIND
by E. V. Thompson
(p.139)

This sweeping family saga of young love and class hatred marks the arrival of a masterly new storyteller. Set in the Cornwall of the 1840s, against a background of the smouldering trade union movement, it is the story of Josh Retallick, an ambitious young copper miner hellbent on reform, and the wild and beautiful Miriam Trago.

THE BADGERS OF SUMMERCOMBE
by Ewan Clarkson (p.313)

The badger's way of life has
remained unchanged for thousands of
years, though now it is being
endangered by modern man. Here, in the
evocative style which has
captivated so many readers, Ewan
Clarkson follows one badger,
Borun, from infancy to parenthood,
penetrating deep into the
enchanting world of nature.

OVERBOARD
by Hank Searls
(p. 389)

Mitch Gordon's wife has fallen
overboard from their ketch in the
South Pacific. Not knowing where
or when she fell, Mitch knows only
she cannot survive for long.

As he searches for Lindy, he
recollects the ups and downs of
their marriage and the stormy
moods of the seas they encountered
on their voyage: a voyage which
was meant to fulfil all their dreams.

This dramatic story will leave
you aghast at the fury of the sea,
and respectful of those who dare
to challenge it.

EXCELLENCY

a condensation of the book by
David Beaty

Illustrated by Stuart Bodek.
Title Page by Cecil Vieweg.
Published by Secker & Warburg, London

In the aftermath of a bloody military coup in the African state of Kajandi, Bill Rutherford, a commercial airline pilot, finds himself reluctantly at the very centre of a web of danger and intrigue. He is unable to escape. On one side stands General Gawaka, the terrifyingly unpredictable new ruler, on the other a diplomat of the old school—His Excellency the British High Commissioner, whose very cool, attractive English secretary has her own mysterious part to play as events in Kajandi move towards an explosive climax.

David Beaty has written many best-selling novels based on his own expertise in the world of flying, but none so full as this of excitement and suspense, or so remarkable for its uncanny topicality.

ONE

"Sah . . . *sah!*"

The twin sounds punctured Bill Rutherford's uneasy sleep. He opened his eyes and saw, luminous in the twilight from the small bedroom window, the frightened black moon of the hotel-boy's face.

Automatically he glanced at his small clock, saw it was not yet six, then looked outside, searching for the glow of fires, alert for the crackle of gunfire. But everything was quiet.

"Yes, M'Wanga?"

"Sah, peoples downstairs to see you."

"What sort of people?" Rutherford's blood chilled. "Police?"

"No, sah, no!"

"Who, then?" Rutherford checked his wristwatch with the bedside clock. In another two hours he would be taking off from this benighted country, thank God. What a way to run an airline, and a one-man band of an airline at that. Bang slap in the middle of yet another bloody African coup. "*Who?*"

M'Wanga shrugged his shoulders, waved his hands. "Sah, sah, I do not know. Not once have I seen these peoples before!"

Rutherford sat up and swung his legs over the side of the bed. He ran his hand through his thick, dark-red hair. He was wide awake now and smelling danger. In the aftermath of a coup, "peoples" didn't come to see you with any good intent.

"Then why did you let them in, M'Wanga?"

"Me, sah? No, sah! Not me let these peoples in!"

"Who did then?" Rutherford stood up and stretched to his full lanky height. Frowning, he lit a cigarette and, walking over to the window, stood staring down at the road. There were no lights, for the electricity had been cut off nine days ago when the coup started. He could see, however, that the road, usually crowded, was ominously empty.

It was almost with relief that he heard the sound of a vehicle approaching. The relief turned sour when the vehicle turned out to be an army Land-Rover which screeched to a stop a few doors down the street. Doors slammed dramatically. Out of the back jumped three African soldiers, jack-booted and swaggering like SS men. They stood back, staring up at the windows, and instinctively Rutherford stepped back and ground out the red target glow of his cigarette.

"So how did they get in, M'Wanga?" As he spoke he heard the soldiers hammering on a door, below and to the left. Rutherford saw M'Wanga flinch.

"I do not know, sah. Very great mystery."

"I'll say!" Rutherford went to the washbasin and scooped cold water over his face. "What do they want to see me about?"

"Sah . . . they will not say."

Rutherford snorted. "M'Wanga, you know when I'm in Kajandi there's no one I want to see. And no one except the oil company wants to see me." He began rubbing his face dry, looking at M'Wanga in the speckled mirror. Beside the African's, his own face, tanned as it was, looked pale and bony. "Well, what are you waiting for? Go down and tell them to go away!"

"But sah . . . that is not possible."

"M'Wanga!" Rutherford said in his most deadly and level voice, "in two hours' time I will be taking off from Joro airport. I have my flight plan to make out, my load sheet to check. Many, *many* duties, M'Wanga." He shouldered his way into his white uniform shirt. "I mind my own business."

"Me too, sah. Always mind my business."

"M'Wanga, you're a liar! And a meddler!" Carefully Rutherford tied the knot of his black tie. "And one of these days, you, too, will hang from the gallows in Independence Square."

"Sah, sah." The palms came together as if in prayer, the eyes rolled heavenward. "No, sah! Me good boy! Me Gawaka boy!"

"You lie, M'Wanga." Rutherford smiled grimly at the African's sweating reflection. "Moto fellah, that's you!"

"No, sah, no!" The hotel-boy brought out from his pocket a badly printed handbill of the kind that had been distributed daily since President Moto's overthrow. On it was a photograph of General Gawaka, the new leader, a smiling big black daddy resplendent in braided and bemedalled uniform. The same picture which now beamed from hoardings and television screens replacing the cadaverous features of Moto. Fervently M'Wanga pressed the handbill to his lips. "Me Gawaka fellah!"

"And how many Moto fellahs did they hang this afternoon?"

"Five men and three women, sah. All ver' bad peoples."

Rutherford said nothing. Faintly through his sleep he had been conscious of the brass band and the drums blaring out the National Anthem—always the prelude to an execution. Now he felt ashamed of teasing M'Wanga. He had to live in Kajandi, poor bastard. All the same, Rutherford had to operate in and out of the place. And in his job, pity was a luxury he could rarely afford. He had to keep his eyes locked on the beam. That way, you landed, did your business and took off again safely. Letting your eyes stray in this sort of territory was as lethal as letting them stray off the panel on an instrument let-down.

He turned to slide his uniform jacket off its hanger, and eagerly the African boy rushed over to help him into it. Like General Gawaka's, it was unique. The one and only Rutherford's Airline uniform worn by its one and only owner (heavily mortgaged) and pilot. It was, in fact, a simple navy blue blazer with the four gold-braid bars of a captain and a pair of wings.

Rutherford folded his pyjamas and tucked them carefully with his clock and his shaving kit into his small bag, then shut and locked it. "Take it downstairs."

"Sah, the peoples . . ."

"Tell them to go away. Is the telephone working this evening?"

"Yes, sah."

"Then get me a taxi for the airport."

The African shook his head, sighed heavily and reached for the bag. It was the only expensive thing Rutherford possessed. Of brown leather, and emblazoned with a yellow sticker of a Kajandi crested hornbill round whose head was lettered in crimson *Rutherford's Airline*, it was the gift of the Anglo-Kajandi Oil Company with whom he did almost all his business, and his trademark was designed as a tribute to Kajandi from whose government he had managed to obtain (with much tramping of government corridors and the inevitable passing over of tokens of esteem) a licence to operate.

The hotel-boy left with the bag. The bedroom became suddenly darker, for night had come down like a sword. But it was still stifling and going over to the window, Rutherford pushed it wide open. Uneasily, he watched two of the soldiers from the Land-Rover emerge from a building across the road. One of them put a whistle to his lips and sent a shrill note into the night.

As though in answer, from beyond the hot tin roofs of the market, came the howl of sirens. A brassy bright lance stabbed round the corner as an armoured gun-carrier with a searchlight on the roof approached from Independence Square.

The light pierced the window and flung Rutherford's shadow against the wall. Immediately, he ducked. They'd got all their Dinky toys out tonight and that spelled trouble. In a moment maybe, some playful little hand might press one of those new machine guns. In the past days such scenes had become almost commonplace. Though the military coup had been successful, General Gawaka was still searching out the president and his followers. Moto had simply disappeared, the newspapers said to neighbouring Tomalia where he was busy whipping up Soviet support for his return.

The coup could only be calculated by Rutherford in terms of business risks. His profit margin had already been sliced by the nine day closure of the airfield. But now it was open again things might well be settling down. A stable government—left, right or centre—was all he asked for. An unstable government meant burning and looting.

The thought of his precious Skytruck defenceless on the ramp at Joro airfield made him sweat. He had visions of it being riddled with holes by some slap-happy machine gunner, or worse still burned. But no, Wahindi, the mechanic who looked after Echo X-Ray, had telephoned at lunchtime to say that all was well and that everything would be ready for a departure at eight that evening.

The new government in the end might be an improvement. Moto, who came from the biggest of the five Kajandi tribes, the Assangi, had reputedly been fanatically anti-British, and though that had not interfered too much with Rutherford's one-man band, an even mildly pro-British government could mean more business. He had provided a quick efficient service to the Anglo-Kajandi Oil Company and these things got around. What he must do now was play it cool and hang on.

Fate had never exactly given him any big handouts, but he had no sense of deprivation. His father, a night-fighter pilot, had been killed with his mother when a buzz bomb had flattened their cottage near RAF Gittisham. His pram in the garden was untouched, and he had been brought up in the North by a grandmother. He'd got a job as a mechanic after leaving school, studied every evening and finally got a scholarship to a flying training school which had given him his commercial pilot's licence at twenty-four. He applied for jobs, but it was a time of recession and the big airlines were full. But one evening in December, coming away from an unsuccessful sortie to a small outfit at Aberdeen airport into blinding rain, he took shelter in a derelict hangar at the far end of the aerodrome.

Idly sorting through a lot of junk, he came upon three quarters of a Skytruck. Propped against the wall, he found both wings and one of the engines under a tarpaulin. From the peeling paint on the exterior he puzzled out the letters AN--- KAJ-N-- O-L.

In the telephone directory he found an entry *Anglo-Kajandi Oil* and by ten the next day he had established contact with a man called McKaig, a high executive in the company. Yes, the Skytruck had belonged to them. It had been used to ferry spare parts and technicians out to experimental rigs belonging to the company in Kajandi. But it had cracked up landing two years ago and was now the property of an insurance company who didn't know what to do with it.

The upshot of the interview was that the pilot was put in touch with the insurance company and introduced to an Aberdeen bank to whom he paid over every penny of his savings. He got a job with a garage where he did nightwork and weekends, and worked most of the day on the broken aircraft. Within nine months the Skytruck was flying again, and *Rutherford's Airline* was born.

That was four years ago. There followed a strenuous period of building up—taxi work, ferrying staff and spares and mail for the oil company, bringing in to booming Aberdeen early fruit and vegetables and exotic flowers.

Eventually it had seemed that the best way to expand was to move nearer London. It so happened that the old RAF station at Gittisham was now a small civil aerodrome with plans for development. A number of charter companies had already put up their signs. With the backing of Kajandi Oil, Rutherford joined them. He duly set up a tiny base in a wooden hut with a large sign saying *Rutherford's Airline*, leased hangar space, took on a room in the old pub, and engaged a maintenance engineer called George Stokes, who doubled up as base manager and storeman.

The oil company was now drilling successfully in north Kajandi, the transport of spares and mail and personnel trebled and Rutherford had organized himself in Joro, where his benefactor McKaig was now the manager of Anglo-Kajandi Oil. The pilot had paid back two thirds of his mortgages. By the end of next year, if the Kajandi government kept reasonably stable, he would be out of the red and the Skytruck would be completely his property.

Down in the street, the soldiers were banging on the building next door. The sight galvanized Rutherford into action. He walked out onto the shadowy landing. A single oil lamp, smoky and untrimmed, lit the well of the staircase. The treads creaked. Some creature skittered across his feet.

Down in the lobby, M'Wanga was waiting. Still clutching the bag, he beckoned Rutherford towards the gloomy corridor leading to the back of the hotel. "Taxi . . . at the back . . . not come to the front. Soldiers, sah."

Quickly, Rutherford followed him past the dining room, and down two steps into a kitchen that stank of *matoke*, or banana porridge. The room was dimly lit by a turned-down gas jet under a saucepan. He heard a movement, glanced sharply round and saw a hand stretched towards him, ghostly and disembodied.

"Captain Rutherford . . ." The voice breathed so low he could hardly hear it.

Peering into the blackness, he saw the shadow of a thin body and the top of a head covered in what looked like a turban.

"Who are you?"

The head shook. "It does not matter."

"Like hell it doesn't!"

"Listen, sir, please! A man's life is in danger. We need your help!"

Rutherford clenched his fists. All he asked was to go about his business. "Look, Mr . . . it's not on. I don't know you. I can't even see you."

But his eyes had got used to the darkness. He saw a face now, brown-skinned and small, two miniature gas jets alight in two large grey eyes. By the look of the pale skin he was one of the Asian community that all Africa these days apparently wanted to get rid of. Well, he was sorry for him. But what could *he* do?

Then just behind the Asian boy, he saw someone else. Taller and broader, an African, black as the ace of spades, with a small pointed beard and wearing a kaleidoscopic sports shirt.

"You saw those soldiers." The Asian youth spoke urgently. "You know what they are doing? Searching for this man. And if they find him—" The voice broke off dramatically.

"That's nothing to do with me." Impatiently Rutherford began to move away.

Thin fingers encircled his left wrist like wire. "But it is! You are leaving tonight! You *will* help! *We* will get him on board your Skytruck."

"Like hell you will!"

"No one will see. In England he will be met."

"You've done your homework! Or M'Wanga has done it for you! But one thing you didn't learn, chum. I'm no illegal

15

immigrant runner. If I was, I'd be either bloody rich or behind bars." The thought of it made him break out in a drenching sweat.

"Please, sir. Help us, I beg you!" The voice touched a nerve Rutherford didn't know he possessed. But it didn't move him to pity. Contrariwise, the very pain of it moved him to fury. With his right fist, he punched the fingers off his wrist, and shouldered the youth aside. Caught off balance, the Asian stumbled backwards, knocked the saucepan off the gas, spilling the *matoke*. Almost simultaneously from the front of the hotel came a banging on the bolted main door.

Some unknown emotion stamped that scene on Rutherford's mind: the smell of scorched *matoke*, the sudden flare up of the gas jet illuminating the dirty dishes stacked in the sink, the terror in the African's face, and the contempt in the young Asian's curiously hypnotic grey eyes.

Rutherford left them—contempt notwithstanding—pushing his way through to the back door. No one tried to stop him. The taxi was waiting, his bag already loaded. Within seconds, he was being swept through the city towards the South Gate.

Joro, capital of Kajandi, was a fortress—half natural, half contrived, effectively bounded on the north and east sides by the Ruanga river that fed into Tissa Lake, and on the south and west by a turreted wall. Four gates, named after the primary compass points, controlled all traffic in and out. They were now heavily guarded.

At the South Gate, the taxi was stopped. First the driver, then Rutherford were waved out by two soldiers with fixed bayonets. A third one examined Rutherford's papers, his passport, his licence, shining a torch in his eyes, as if he didn't believe he was the same man as the one in the photograph. They then turned their attention to the taxi interior, ransacking the boot, opening up the bonnet, squatting down and peering underneath.

Rutherford watched them grimly. How those people in the kitchen had expected the wanted African to be smuggled through, God only knew! He drew a long sigh of relief as the soldiers waved him back into the car. Not just for that moment—but also for playing it safe in that kitchen.

16

It was a five-mile ride from the South Gate to the airfield and every mile eased Rutherford's spirit. The airfield was on its emergency lighting system, and he could see the pricked out runways like open arms. At the gates, the taxi was stopped again, but he was not ordered out. He felt at home. Airports, thank God, were orderly places full of familiar buildings and aircraft. At the passenger hall he paid off the driver, and hurried up the steps. Through the plate glass windows he searched for the red and silver of his Skytruck. Though he could not see it, he could rely on Wahindi to get it there on time.

African Airways were his agents and they had his papers ready in the office. The manifest and load sheet had been made up— four unserviceable Lowry pumps, a couple of dozen valves, six crates of assorted rock and mineral samples for analysing, and a cracked borer were in position, strapped under tarpaulins in the optimum position for the aircraft's centre of gravity. The flight plan to Gittisham was ten hours and forty minutes with a following wind. He checked it carefully. The weather was going to be cloudless.

Cheerfully he signed up at the African Airways counter. The cafeteria was open. He suddenly remembered he hadn't eaten all day. He bought a pile of ham sandwiches, some apples and a can of lemonade for flying rations. Then just as he was walking towards the doors to the ramp, Wahindi came up. Rutherford hailed him with real pleasure.

Wahindi was a small man, darker-skinned than most Asians, highly conscientious and expert at his job.

"Everything is on the top line, Captain Rutherford." He spoke in a musical sing-song way quite different from the slow Kajandi slur.

"Good! Then shall we—"

"Do you mind, Captain? A DC-4 has gone sick on us. Skytruck is ready on ramp now. Could you see yourself off?"

"Sure." Clearly the mechanic was in a hurry. So Rutherford went through customs and immigration, showed his pass to the helmeted guards at the gate, and walked across the crowded ramp to the waiting Skytruck.

The old familiar smells were there—the warm sweet scent of

petrol, the smell of parched earth and cooling tar, and a whiff of scorched rubber.

A DC-6 was leaving, its propellers chopping a long shaft of yellow light into pineapple chunks. The light was coming from the control tower—the usual revolving searchlight, Rutherford thought, until it came purposefully towards him. It fingered him all over, then having identified him, moved on.

Rutherford carried on with his external inspection, removed the chocks from under the wheels, opened the rear door and put them on board. Switching on the cabin lights, he clambered inside. Methodically as always, he began checking the cargo. He was just inspecting the reserve fuel tanks when suddenly he smelt something alien.

He stood up, puzzled. A curious combination of smells, but familiar. A sort of sweaty African odour combined with—yes, now he knew, that boiled banana porridge they called *matoke*.

His eyes fixed on a black tarpaulin covering a dozen containers by the door on the starboard side. It moved. He got hold of the end and ripped it away. From behind the wooden crate, two bulging eyes rolled up at him fearfully.

Rutherford saw the little black beard, the nose squashed wide across the brown face. His surprise was swamped by fury. So the Asian boy had smuggled the man in. That was the meaning of the searchlight on top of the control tower. Some hint had reached the authorities, and they were searching.

In total silence, the two men looked at each other. Neither moved. Then suddenly the Kajandi made a great spring through the still open door onto the ramp and, a frantic shadow, zig-zagged into the night, trying to reach the cover of a cluster of aircraft. Just behind him came the long yellow spear of light. He reached a port wheel of a 707, and huddled down behind it.

Inches away now, the searchlight began fingering the fuselage. The port leg blossomed a brilliant silver. The light wavered. Then all at once it stopped dead—on two shoes and a pair of ankles jutting from behind the 707's tyre.

Immediately there was a scream of sirens. A fire engine came hurtling forward. Soldiers began rushing towards the spotlighted

707. The Kajandi crawled from behind the wheel, ran to a small Apache, jumped on the wing. The searchlight followed and behind it came the soldiers.

The Kajandi stood by the starboard engine, helplessly looking all ways. Then he slid down the propeller and now ran wildly in ever-decreasing circles, in and out of undercarriage legs, dodging behind fuselages—while all the time, relentlessly, the fire engine circled and the soldiers closed in.

Rutherford was just turning away, not wanting to see the end, when a jeep skidded to a stop by the plane door. Two soldiers carrying submachine guns jumped up into the Skytruck and gripped his arms.

"Here, what the hell . . . ?"

A Kajandi lieutenant waved a revolver under his nose. "Get down!" They pushed him out onto the ramp.

"There's been some mistake. I'm a British subject."

"You . . . Moto fellah!"

Rutherford shouted, "He was inside my aircraft. He was a stowaway, I tell you!"

The soldiers bundled him into the back seat. The lieutenant jumped back behind the wheel, swung the jeep away.

From behind a fence of guns in the back seat, Rutherford went on angrily, "I don't know the man! He was a stowaway! I found him on board. I—"

"You was helpin' that fellah!"

"I wasn't! I wasn't! I was—"

"You was helpin' that Moto fellah to escape!" The lieutenant put his foot hard down and joined the chase, pulling clear of the fire engine and recklessly scattering the pursuers on foot.

Just ahead now—psychedelic shirt flapping, arms and legs pounding like pistons—the refugee ran. Then, as suddenly as if he had been shot, he toppled—caught by the hot blast of jet engines as a DC-9 taxied out for take-off.

As the jeep raced towards him, he struggled to rise. The jeep slowed and stopped. The lieutenant got out and the next moment there was a flash like silver lightning as the blade of a *panga* knife was caught in the searchlight.

No cry. No calling out. A red fountain of blood spurted up into the glittering beam. There was a thud as the body fell, then a great shout of laughter.

"That is what happens to Moto fellahs!" The lieutenant grinned as he got back into the jeep, let in the clutch and accelerated towards the airport buildings.

Here Rutherford was manhandled into an office and made to stand in front of the lieutenant's desk.

"Moto fellah!" the lieutenant screamed, hitting him with his revolver butt. "Moto fellah!"

Blood began running down Rutherford's face. His left eye swelled. "I'm a British subject," he repeated. "A friend."

The argument went on, in Swahili, in Kajandi and in English. Eventually they took him to Ndole jail near the market. Built by the British on the lines of a Norman fortress, it had high brick walls, a round tower at each corner and windows that were long barred slits in the shape of crosses. By candlelight, Rutherford was led through tiled corridors reeking of urine to the yard in the centre of the prison. It was already filled with dark shapes. There was just room to sit on the ground, but deliberately Rutherford stood by the door to the main building, hoping to speak to an official.

His head was beginning to swim. There was a thumping ache behind his eyes. Dully he was conscious that he had been framed, he had been sucked into something that was none of his business.

Now desperately he tried to think straight. He was in danger. Nobody knew he was here. He could be eliminated without trace. The new government would deny all knowledge. He would simply be regarded as one of hundreds who had disappeared in the coup.

Over in the far corner of the yard, an ominous hammering had started. Torchlight flickered on the sweating black faces of carpenters, busy with wooden beams, iron rungs and ropes.

Grimly, Rutherford watched the scene. He recognized that his only hope of getting out of this hell-hole was the British High Commission. And he had to contact them fast before that multiple gallows in the far corner went into business.

But *how*?

TWO

On the top floor of the British High Commission, Tom Bancroft had lit two candles and placed them on either side of the decoding table.

The candle flames flickered on the grey paint of the filing cabinets, burnished to gold the brass bars of the grille leading out onto the landing, and put a fuzzy halo on the still silent teleprinter.

As duty officer, he was quite alone. In the candlelight, he looked younger than fifty-three. The streaks of grey in his thick hair were invisible. The loose-fleshed cheeks and ample body took on the dignity befitting a diplomat with thirty years experience in the Foreign Service. There was no sign in this kindly illumination of his being a re-tread given a job with other unwanted colonial civil servants when the British Empire collapsed after the war, of his present dogsbody role of consul cum administrative assistant cum cypher officer. No sign of the lines on his face etching the disappointments of a career broken by circumstances and—deeper and more ineradicable—the death of his wife of plague in India.

He had been sitting beside that damned teleprinter for most of the last nine days, waiting for communication from outside Kajandi to be resumed. For five days the British staff and their families had been brought inside these thick Victorian walls, while outside the battle had raged. Kids all over the place—up and down the stairs, in and out of offices. The strain had been made worse by the high commissioner's insistence that everybody in the building should go "dry" during the emergency. Bancroft, however, had had the foresight to replenish his own personal whisky supply in the locked bottom drawer of the decoding table just before the emergency started. Fortunately, with the victory of Gawaka and the resultant comparative peace outside, everyone had been allowed to return home before his cache gave out.

He had been passing the hours of the night by reading the troubled history of Kajandi from the registry files next door—the catalogue of events since a regiment of the Buffs had settled a series of inter-tribal wars by occupying the place in 1875. Then had come the missionaries, followed by schools, hospitals, ministries, courts of justice, parliament. But Kajandi had remained more a collection of tribes than a country. The Assangi in the north had always given trouble. Certainly the British had had more than their bellyful—culminating in King Zazu leading a march on Joro thirty years ago, which had finished up with the king being exiled to England, where he was still living in obscurity. Independence from Britain had been granted five years ago. Only a few days before the coup, Moto had declared his intention of leaving the Commonwealth.

Revolts, wars, coups, blood—those were the waters that had flowed under the Kajandi bridge before the events of nine days ago.

Bancroft was at present reading the copy of the high commissioner's dispatch to the Foreign and Commonwealth Office about Gawaka's coup. The original still remained in the diplomatic bag waiting for the British Airways VC-10 to come in after the nine-day closure of the airport.

"To Her Majesty's Secretary of State for Foreign Affairs. Sir . . . on the morning of 18th May, Nigel Naylor, my first secretary and head of chancery, was walking to work alongside the south entrance to Government House when there was the sound of machine guns and five Centurion tanks wheeled round in the road just in front of him, broke the iron gates and proceeded up the drive, firing heavy mortars. At the same time, six bombers swept at low level just overhead with their bomb doors open. Mr. Naylor threw himself flat and crawled under a parked car. A series of explosions came from inside the grounds of Government House. During a lull, Mr. Naylor managed to telephone me. I immediately set off the signal for Operation Sanctuary. Within half an hour, our staff with their wives and children were inside the walls of the High Commission. I sent one brief message off to you, but then two mortar shells landed on the roof and destroyed our aerials and the leads to our generator. Mains electricity had been cut off. Our teleprinters went dead.

"A wave of hysteria swept the town. . . . A dusk-to-dawn curfew was imposed. Jet fighters flew regularly over the city. Bombs were dropped . . . shell and machine-gun fire continued sporadically. . . .

22

A huge crowd gathered outside the High Commission and began to hurl bricks through the windows. . . . I was beginning to have fears for the safety of our women and children.

"Then on the morning of the fourth day, all firing stopped. The hostile crowds outside the High Commission dispersed. Looking out from my office window towards the railway and the river, I saw a train had stopped on the track and the driver was giving the Victory sign in morse code on his whistle. There were people on top of the carriages, and they began waving at us and singing 'Land of Hope and Glory' which is the school song of the Catholic High. There was no more firing that day, or the next. And on the evening of the fifth day, we held a short prayer meeting in my office and gave thanks to God, and then all shook hands with each other and dispersed to our homes."

It was typical Hugh Fortescue stuff—dry and pious and praise-the-Lord. From bitter experience, Bancroft took a more realistic view. Praise the Lord certainly—but at the same time pass the ammunition. And ammunition was what the High Commission did not have.

An enormous explosion suddenly shattered the silence. Bancroft dashed out onto the landing and grabbed a pair of binoculars that always hung beside the window. He looked outside.

There was a flickering of light round Ndole jail, but there was no sign of fire and nothing but darkness everywhere else.

He was turning to go back into Chancery when, just as unexpectedly as the explosion, on came the lights, and, as if by magic, up came the city of Joro—the street lights of the main avenue leading to Independence Square, the ghostly whiteness of Government House, the battlemented walls. Now Bancroft methodically began searching from east to west. The American embassy was still there. So was the parliament building. So were the ministries, and the apartment block where Bancroft lived with other staff of the High Commission: Nigel Naylor, head of chancery, Peter Evers, commercial secretary, Dermot Harmer, defence attaché, and Sarah Harris in charge of aid. So was the British Residence where lived Hugh and Priscilla Fortescue.

Bancroft lifted the glasses a little and was trying to see beyond the South Gate and the shimmer of Tissa Lake to the small bungalow where Virginia Lacey, H.E.'s personal assistant, lived, when behind him a metallic chattering started.

The teleprinter had suddenly come to life. The High Commission was back in communication with the outside world.

He returned to Chancery, blew out the candles, switched on the lights and settled down to decode the messages beginning to come in, reporting the actions of various African states to the recent events in Kajandi.

. . . TOMALIA HAS DENOUNCED COUP AS AGGRESSION PREPARED BY THE IMPERIALISTS AND THEIR LACKEYS . . .

This was typical and to be expected. Tomalia was where Moto was reported as taking refuge. Bancroft reached for another message.

. . . UGANDA DEMANDS THAT THE BRITISH HIGH COMMISSIONER IN KAJANDI BE TRIED BY INTERNATIONAL COURT FOR HIS COMPLICITY IN THE PLOT AND FOR HIS CRIMES OF RAPE COMMA INFANTICIDE COMMA AND MASS MURDER . . .

Even the Foreign and Commonwealth Office might manage a frugal smile at that one in connection with His Excellency Mr. Hugh Fortescue, CMG. Perhaps, one day, His Excellency Sir Hugh Fortescue, KCMG. But doubtful, in Bancroft's view, for this was Fortescue's last posting before retirement after a singularly undistinguished diplomatic career.

Suddenly the telephone shrilled out, drowning the clacking of the teleprinter. Bancroft swore and grabbed the receiver.

An English voice said unsteadily, "Look . . . quick . . . give me the British high commissioner!"

THE EXPLOSION had shaken Ndole jail to its foundations. Momentarily the yard became as light as day. There was a sound like a mountain falling. Immediately panic broke out amongst prisoners and guards.

Then back came the darkness, and Rutherford saw his chance.

He dodged through the door and ran down the corridor. This could only be an attempt by Moto fellahs to rescue their own supporters by blowing a breach in the walls—if only he could find it in time. He mingled with the shadowy guards who were rushing up and down, also searching.

The north and south walls were intact. He tried the main gate, but that was locked and guarded. He had just dodged into the entrance to a corner turret, when the lights came on and all the corridors were flooded with light.

At least the turret was dark. He dashed up the twisting staircase, hoping to find an exit. But all the way up were only narrow slit windows not remotely big enough to climb through. At the top, feverishly, he thumped rafters, searching for loose tiles or skylights.

Nothing. This was a dead end trap. He wound his way down to the ground, peered round the doorway into the lighted corridor. It was empty. No guards. The panic appeared to be dying down.

Crouched in the archway of the turret, Rutherford waited for twenty minutes, then put his head down and ran down the corridor to the administration offices. He dashed inside the first one he came to, grabbed the telephone, and dialled the number of the British High Commission.

An intermittent buzz, then he heard the receiver being lifted. Immediately he asked for the high commissioner.

Agonizingly slowly the voice at the other end said, "He's not here at present."

"Who are you?"

"Consul. If I could help, Mr . . . ?"

"Rutherford . . . of Rutherford's Airline."

"Oh yes." At least the man appeared to have heard of him.

"I'm in Ndole jail."

"I'm on my own at present, Mr. Rutherford. But as soon as His Excellency—"

The line went dead. Normal in Kajandi, even when there wasn't a coup. Rutherford dialled the number twice more. No luck—just a high-pitched buzzing.

He was trying for the third time when he heard footsteps. An official was walking down the corridor, carrying papers. He disappeared around the corner without seeing Rutherford. But if he stayed much longer, he knew he was bound to be caught. He made a dash for it back to the yard and stood by the gate again, weighing his chances. The explosion had not apparently breached the walls, but at least the High Commission knew he was being held in Ndole. They were bound to make inquiries. The new Kajandi government could hardly pretend they knew nothing about him. It would be embarrassing if he simply disappeared.

Above him, the black sky began to turn grey—another Kajandi day had dawned.

WITH THE DAWN came the West's reactions to the coup in Kajandi.

There was nothing from Britain, but clearly the USA, France, West Germany, were in no hurry to recognize the Gawaka regime. That being so, Bancroft had a bet with himself that when eventually the FCO's instructions did arrive, they would simply be the three words, "maintain low profile".

Intermittently with decoding, Bancroft had tried Ndole's number to try to get more information about the Distressed British Subject but with no success. Now he could hear movement in the streets. Soon the high commissioner and other members of the staff would be coming in.

There was a sudden pinging sound. Instinctively Bancroft ducked. Then he heard another shot. He went out onto the landing and picked up the binoculars, focusing first on the long expanse of High Commission lawn then shifting his gaze along the street to the left.

His eye was caught by a little knot of people gathered round an ancient black Austin Princess, on the front of which he glimpsed three tiny blobs of red, white and blue.

It looked as though someone had had a go at the high commissioner's official car, and Bancroft was just about to rush downstairs to help, when he saw the bonnet push forward like the prow of a ship, parting the crowd to either side like a bow wave, and move sedately onward towards the High Commission. Bancroft smiled. No doubt Fortescue had given a sermon to the black chaps about the danger of firearms, and now he was giving them a demonstration of the white chap's cool.

As he turned away, he heard the sound of high heels clicking up the stairs. "What's the excitement *now?*" a girl's voice called.

"Someone took a potshot at the Austin Princess but missed. H.E. has restored the peace."

Virginia Lacey, Fortescue's personal assistant came to the window. She had dark hair and grey eyes, high cheekbones, a pointed chin and a small well-bred nose.

Bancroft smiled warmly at her. "Situation back to normal in here as well. Electricity. Teleprinter."

"Anything through from the FCO, Tom?"

"Not yet. But lots from everywhere else."

"H.E. will want to see." Miss Lacey began walking towards the high commissioner's office.

"I'll bring them in. And would you tell him we've got a DBS? Chap called Rutherford phoned."

"What's the trouble?"

"Don't know exactly. He says he's in Ndole, but we got cut off. Anyway, tell H.E. I'm pursuing." He hesitated. "Did you hear the explosion?"

She stopped and looked back at him. "What explosion?"

"Big one. About four this morning. Clearly you didn't."

"One of the advantages of living outside the city."

"Maybe. But you're too isolated. Why don't you move into our apartment block?"

"I like it by the lake."

A metallic chattering interrupted them. A message was at last coming through from the FCO. As he began decoding, Bancroft was saying to himself at least he'd won his bet: ". . . MAINTAIN LOW PROFILE . . ."

UNDER THE stone portico of the High Commission, the car stopped. The driver opened the door, Hugh Fortescue slowly emerged and walked up the nine steps into the cool gloom of the hall. He was rather a small man with a high bony brow, a sandy moustache, a precise mouth, and a skin stained mepacrine yellow from a lifetime spent in the hottest and most insalubrious of Her Majesty's possessions. From under pepper-and-salt eyebrows, his blue eyes focused on the receptionist, a pretty Kajandi girl.

"Good morning, sir." She smiled.

"Good morning, Mary-Rose."

The High Commission interior was unalterably Victorian—high ceilings, a large hall from which climbed a heavy mahogany staircase to a landing lined with shelves of leather-bound books. There was a faint smell of mothballs and mildew.

Fortescue went upstairs to the second floor, then along the corridor, past Chancery, to his office at the far end. "Good morning, Virginia. Teleprinter working?"

"Yes, sir." She looked up from her typewriter and waved a sheaf of flimsies. "Tom's just brought you these."

"Good show!" After being incommunicado for so long, it was a relief to be back in business.

"And there's a DBS in Ndole. A man called Rutherford."

"Ah yes, the airline chap. What for?"

"Tom's not sure. They were cut off. Tom said he'd take care of it, sir."

"Good!" The high commissioner sat down at his desk and put on a pair of half-moon spectacles. "Now let's have a look at those flimsies."

She passed the messages over to him. She was the only British secretary in the High Commission. True to Fortescue's belief in Africanization, the others came one each from the five tribes of Kajandi. His political philosophy was simply that the white chaps had had a head start over the black chaps, the benefits from which the white chaps had a sacred duty to pass on. Since the premature rushing through of independence for British colonies after the war had been a severe blow to this philosophy, it was now up to the white chaps to redouble their efforts to see the black chaps had cottoned on to the hang of things.

That the western way of life was the best, Hugh Fortescue had no doubt—as indeed neither had the people of Kajandi, who saw in cars, television sets, aeroplanes and refrigerators the symbols of that superiority.

Fortescue finished reading the flimsies, then picked up the last message and read the three words aloud. "Maintain low profile!"

He gave Virginia a wry smile. "In other words, do nothing. What about recognition of Gawaka?" He paused. "We'd better get another despatch into the diplomatic bag."

Virginia brought over a chair, flipped open her dictating pad and took out her pencil.

"To Her Majesty's Secretary of State for Foreign Affairs. Usual courtesies." His voice was crisp. "Further to my previous despatch . . . all is quiet. Curfew has been lifted. The airport is open. General Gawaka appears totally in control.

"The coup was not unexpected. Moto was a dedicated intellectual who ruled Kajandi with a ruthless authoritarianism and made many enemies. On my arrival, he kept me waiting nine months to present my credentials. He could hardly bear to be civil to me— and the American ambassador fared little better. Moto hated Britain and was about to withdraw from the Commonwealth. The armed forces were to be re-equipped with Russian and Chinese weapons. In addition, word leaked out that certain senior Kajandi officers trained in Britain were to be invited to a banquet at Government House, and there shot.

"General Gawaka saved the bacon by arriving for the banquet in a tank at the head of his crack armoured brigade. Within three days, he had moved into Government House. Moto had disappeared, the Russians had shuttered their embassy windows, and the general's tanks and police were rounding up all Moto supporters.

"We know little of the general, except that he has a long service record in the Kajandi army and was trained in Britain. As for Anglo-Kajandi relations, I would have thought we had reached the bottom with Moto. Surely things cannot get any worse. If things get better, there could be a very real opportunity for us here—"

"Sir!" Tom Bancroft appeared round the door. "Sorry to interrupt, Excellency, but this DBS. I've at last got through to the prison governor—"

"Could you go to Ndole, Tom, and see what it's all about?"

"I offered. But the governor wants you, sir." Bancroft paused. "I'm afraid it's a capital charge. Rutherford got involved in helping Nakungu, Moto's foreign secretary, to escape."

Hugh Fortescue stared out of the window. Some of these white chaps, when would they ever learn?

"RUTHERFORD . . . *RUTHERFORD!*" An African captain in khaki uniform came into the exercise yard. "Come this way."

The pilot was escorted to a room on the first floor furnished with a rickety table and two steel-framed chairs.

A rather small man, dressed in a fawn tropical suit, was standing by the barred window.

"Good morning, Mr. Rutherford. My name's Fortescue . . . the British high commissioner."

They shook hands. The high commissioner's blue eyes studied Rutherford minutely from under pepper-and-salt eyebrows, but all he said was, "Shall we sit down?"

"The governor has filled me in with the background of your case." The voice was precise and rather gritty. "What I want now is your side of the story." He listened in silence as Rutherford told it. "And that's the whole truth?"

"Yes."

"I see." The high commissioner paused. "You were taking oil-pump parts back to England?"

"That's all."

"Do you ever take passengers?"

"Sometimes. But only oil company employees."

"Have you had a stowaway before?"

"Never."

"The trouble is, Rutherford, your stowaway was Moto's foreign secretary. And you were discovered with the goods on you, so to speak."

"But as soon as I found him, he—"

"Yes . . . but the guards say *they* found him."

"Then they're lying."

"That's what *you* say, Mr. Rutherford."

Suddenly the pilot realized that this dry husk of a man was all that separated him from the gallows in the yard.

"And they're not just liars, they're murderers!"

"Mr. Rutherford," Fortescue said sharply, "this country is

30

emerging from a revolution and is still under military law. I cannot emphasize too much that we must proceed *diplomatically*."

"I'm in the airline business. That Skytruck is my only asset. Do you think I'd risk everything by breaking the law?"

"That is what you're accused of, Mr. Rutherford."

"It's nonsense!"

The high commissioner stood up. "Then we must try to convince the authorities."

The interview was over. Outside on the landing, the army captain was waiting to escort them downstairs.

"You'll get me out?"

As the pilot was led back to the yard, echoing down the corridor came Hugh Fortescue's voice. "You are being held under warrant, Mr. Rutherford. My hands are tied."

So are mine, Rutherford thought. Behind my back, while they slip the noose round my neck.

THREE

Fortescue returned from the jail preoccupied. He told Virginia to cancel his lunch engagement and asked for a look at all papers relating to Rutherford and the Kajandi Oil Company.

She took him the files, and left him undisturbed for two hours. Then she knocked on his door. "Shall I get you a sandwich, sir?"

"Thank you, Virginia . . . but no, I'm not hungry."

She hesitated. "Sir . . . this DBS. What was the trouble?"

He went on reading. "You probably don't know, but Nakungu was . . . well, executed is the word being used . . . at the airport last night. He was on Rutherford's aeroplane."

"It was on the radio. They mentioned something about an escape organization. Did Mr. Rutherford say anything about it?"

Fortescue shook his head. "Knows nothing. That's his story. The prison governor told me an Asian mechanic working at the airport is involved. Wahindi, I think the name was."

"Have they got him?"

"Not yet. But they're confident they will."

"Will Mr. Rutherford be all right?"

"I hope so, Virginia." He looked at his watch. "Good heavens, two thirty already! I'd better be off to Government House."

"About this Rutherford business?"

He nodded and got up. "No time to mess around. There could be a misunderstanding. I shall have to go straight to the top."

"Shall I telephone?"

"No." From a cupboard he took a helmet with sprouting ostrich plumes and a white ceremonial uniform. "I shall simply arrive. But you can get my medals and sword from the safe in Chancery."

The African, he was always saying, liked a leader to *look* a leader, as gorgeous and powerful as a god. By the time Virginia returned, he had nearly done all he could. Most high commissioners were reluctant to don ceremonial dress. Hugh Fortescue had no such inhibitions. In his view, it was all he had left—no more gunboats, no more companies of Marines.

Virginia pinned his few medals on his left breast. Then he buckled on his sword. She handed him his plumed helmet. The car was summoned.

With the minuscule Union Jack fluttering on the bonnet in front of him and in full ceremonial rig, His Excellency Mr. Hugh Fortescue, CMG, set off for his first meeting with General Naji Gawaka, Possessor of Almighty Power and Knowledge, Lord of the Tribes and the Land, the Father of all Twins, the Blacksmith's Hammer, the Cook with all the Firewood, the Smelter of Iron, the Power of the Sun, the Good and Everlasting.

FORTESCUE caught his first sight of the general as the car approached Government House. He stood framed in the portico, wearing a dark blue uniform covered with gold braid and medals, arms outstretched in welcome, seeming as big as that colonnaded pile itself and as black as it was white.

"Your Excellency . . . id is a pleasure to meet you."

General Gawaka spoke in slow careful English, slightly Africanized with a hissing of the s and an occasional d sound instead of a t. He led the way into the hall. "It is ver' beautiful here . . . but you have been before, of course?"

No, Fortescue had to admit that he and Priscilla had not been included in the guest list of Moto's parties.

"You have not seen the grand lounge? Or the banqueting hall?"

So first of all, it was a tour of the great house, with the general displaying an almost childlike pleasure at showing off his new home, and the high commissioner holding off the reason for his visit, anxious not to crack his good humour.

But when it came to sitting in the huge library, sipping tea and declining chocolate cake, Hugh Fortescue was aware that time was running out. "General, there is a matter—"

"Excellency, I did not show you my treasure, my cat. Puss, puss—"

"General," the high commissioner interrupted firmly. "This matter is most important. There is an Englishman being held in Ndole jail."

In the silence, a Persian cat came mincing over the gold Chinese carpet. The general leaned forward and tickled its arching neck. "Dat matter has already been reported to me, Excellency."

"This morning I visited the jail and he told me his story."

"Dat story, too, I know. He was caught red-handed!"

"Nakungu was a stowaway on the plane."

"There is only Rutherford's word on dat!" Suddenly, the general rose to his feet. "Excellency, what is id you wish of me?" The cat, halfway up his leg, toppled back onto the carpet. "Are you telling me what to do?"

"Of course not, General, I was simply—"

"Are you asking me," the general's voice ricocheted off the book-lined walls, "to interfere in de course of justice? Now, at dis time? Wid reports that Moto is across the frontier, and de Tomalia army is mobilizing? Wid Kassilolo, Moto's crooked chancellor, still in Kajandi? Wid Moto's tribe of the Assangi in de north refusing to swear allegiance? Wid an organization running an escape route for Moto's men? Wid Moto fellahs setting off a landmine at Ndole jail?" The general was shouting now, sweat pouring down his face. "Is dis your message for me? Open your jails! Let de traitors and de murderers and de rapists and de looters and de thiefs go free!"

Hugh Fortescue sat, right leg over left, balancing his cup and saucer on his knee. "Clearly there are problems, General. But many of these, if I may say so, you have already overcome. The bombing and shooting have all but stopped. You have established law and order. You are now in charge."

The general stood quite still, his anger cooling. Then he said very softly, "You came to me, Excellency, because you want something."

"On the contrary, General, I came here to *give* you something."

Good humour flickered back into Gawaka's eyes. He sat down. "And what is that?" The cat climbed into his lap.

"Information."

"What information?"

"The information that we have checked our files. Rutherford is purely a businessman. There is nothing that could connect him with the escape attempt last night."

"In that case, Excellency, what has he to fear from a court of justice?" The general's black eyes and the cat's amber eyes stared fixedly into the high commissioner's blue ones.

"Of course, nothing . . ."

Suddenly the general threw back his head and laughed, a gusty noise as low and deep as the wind through the mahogany trees. An arm the size of an ebony branch came round Hugh Fortescue's shoulders.

"Hugh . . . Hugh! You and I . . . we are men of the world, yes? Rutherford is a businessman, as you say . . . and dat is de heart of de matter. All men have their price. Nobody does nuthin' for nuthin'. Rutherford thought he had found a cargo more precious than gold." The general smiled with satisfaction. "But now he has had his fingers burned. There is much foolishness done by your people and by mine. But you and I, we see, we know . . . yes?"

"We hope we do," said Hugh Fortescue cautiously.

"Hugh, Hugh . . . we do see, we *do*! And we must act together, yes? Kajandi will be a great country. But only if you and I stand four-square, yes?"

That Fortescue could certainly agree with. "Yes, General."

"Naji—you must call me Naji. Naji . . . it is a funny name to you." The general laughed again. "Hugh is a funny name to me."

And then, just as suddenly as before, the general rose to his feet. The cat toppled onto the carpet, and the interview was over.

Hugh Fortescue got up and in silence, side by side with the general, moved forward out of the library into the hall and down the steps to the car.

The waiting film and television cameras recorded the solemn moment of their handshake, before the high commissioner climbed into the back seat and the car glided away.

AFTER DINNER that night, Hugh and Priscilla Fortescue sat together on the veranda of the Residence. In the garden fireflies were twinkling. From the grass came the crackling of crickets. A cool breeze rustled the bougainvillæa, and Priscilla had draped a cardigan over the shoulders of her dinner dress.

"It was, Priscilla, *the* most extraordinary meeting with a head of state I have ever had."

Hugh Fortescue patted her soft plump hand. At fifty-eight she remained the most beautiful woman he had ever seen. Though childless, she was comfortably maternal. White haired, full figured, well groomed and sweetly scented, she was the personification of what one day he hoped she might be—the lady of the manor of some Hampshire village.

"The whole time I felt his eyes on my face. He was weighing me up. And then he suddenly made up his mind about me." Fortescue snapped his bony fingers. "Gawaka laughed. And as we walked out he put his arm round my shoulders. A black chap and a white chap walking forward together." He was deeply moved.

"I'm very glad." She drew in a long breath. She felt bitterly that her husband had never had the success in his career that he deserved. No one seemed to recognize or value his selflessness, his integrity and his true excellence. These last years under the Moto regime had been especially difficult. Now, faintly, there seemed a light at the end of the long tunnel.

"And this man Rutherford?"

"I have a hunch that the general took my point. I think he might well make a gesture and free Rutherford."

In fact, Rutherford was already free, and back at the Hotel Afrique. Dead tired, hardly believing his luck, he had tumbled into bed and gone straight off to sleep.

And while he slept, the main press in Joro was printing the morning edition of the *Kajandi Times*. There on the front page was a large photograph of General Gawaka and the British high commissioner shaking hands on the veranda of Government House under the banner headlines: GREAT BRITAIN RECOGNIZES GENERAL GAWAKA. BRITISH HIGH COMMISSIONER WELCOMES OUR NEW REGIME.

A copy of the *Kajandi Times* lying on Mary-Rose's desk was the first thing Bancroft saw when he went inside the High Commission hall. He grabbed it and went up the stairs two at a time, hurried into Chancery and practically crowned Nigel Naylor with the newspaper.

"Have you seen this?"

Naylor was a willowy ex-Etonian, Fortescue's Number Two, responsible for the post's morale and discipline. Cautiously he admitted that he had. "Well, Tom . . . you know H.E. went to see the general about that pilot character."

"But surely even he didn't tell him we'd recognize?"

"No, of course he didn't. But the conduct of *any* official business with a new regime can be construed as an act of recognition."

"H.E. must know that. What I can't understand is why he's jumped in with both feet. As the problem child of the EEC, we shouldn't lead the way. Our position's with the also-rans."

"A cynical view, Tom . . . if I may say so."

"You may say anything you like to me, Nigel. But when it comes to saying anything at a diplomatic cocktail party while unspeakable things are going on in the prisons outside, you'll talk about the weather like we all have to do. That's our job. Passing by on the other side."

"H.E. doesn't see it that way."

"But the FCO does. Play the invisible man . . . those are their instructions. They're going to have a fit when they find they've recognized. Couldn't a denial be issued?"

Naylor hesitated. "Only make matters worse."

"But Nigel . . . you've seen the signals. Nobody else is going to be in a hurry to recognize Gawaka."

"H.E. formed a favourable opinion of him."

"So he swapped recognition for Rutherford's neck!"

"If he hadn't, there might have been a nasty diplomatic incident."

"Now there'll be an even nastier one."

"You never know." Naylor smiled bravely. "Things might get better."

At ten o'clock, Bancroft went into Virginia's office. "Well . . . what do you think about it?"

"About what?"

"You know perfectly well." He regarded her morosely. "Oh hell, Virginia . . . what's H.E. gone and let us in for *now*?"

She pointed out quickly, "He got Rutherford out of jail."

"How do *you* know?" When she didn't answer, he went on. "At any rate—" with a certain satisfaction, he gave her a flimsy "—I bring tidings of great joy from Central Africa Department."

The FCO had again spoken—prefix Flash, classified *Top Secret*.

. . . HAVE RECEIVED YOUR DISPATCH WHICH HAS BEEN READ HERE WITH INTEREST STOP SYMPATHETIC WITH YOUR ORDEAL BUT GLAD OF HAPPY OUTCOME STOP CONTINUE TO MAINTAIN LOW PROFILE STOP UNDER NO CIRCUMSTANCES MUST WE RECOGNIZE GAWAKA TILL OTHERS PRECEDE US . . .

"If that pilot character *is* out of jug, Virginia," he said as she read it, "ring him up and book us both a passage home!"

RUTHERFORD woke at noon. Outside, everything appeared normal. The only evidence of the night before last was his bruised face. He examined it in the mirror. The lefthand side had swollen. His kit was still in the Skytruck, but he kept at the hotel spare clothes and toilet requisites. Now he shaved, put on a clean shirt and slacks and went downstairs for a late breakfast. Smiling as usual, M'Wanga brought him the morning paper, iced paw-paw with limes, bacon and eggs, toast and coffee.

Now he was out of jail, what was he going to do? His first

thought had been to get the hell out and stay out. But now he read in the *Kajandi Times* that Britain had recognized the Gawaka regime. That was an indication of stability. There might be golden opportunities in staying here and being in on the ground floor.

As he drank his second cup of coffee, he weighed up the risks and the rewards. He would be at Gittisham for a week. By then presumably a clearer picture would have emerged, and he could then decide whether it was worth while to return.

He telephoned to Wahindi at the airport, but couldn't get hold of him. Finally, he left a message for the mechanic, saying he would be on the ramp in an hour and asking that the Skytruck should be ready for immediate take-off. Then he collected *all* his belongings, cancelled his room and paid his bill, while M'Wanga took his stuff out to a taxi.

The search by the South Gate guards was more thorough—but otherwise the trip to the airport was the same as usual. Rutherford got a porter for his baggage and went over to the African Airways counter. There he told the clerk that his delayed flight to Gittisham would now be proceeding.

But the clerk was new and didn't understand about the message left for Wahindi. "Nobody here, no Wahindi, sah."

With rising irritation, Rutherford stumped across to the big glass window looking out onto the ramp. There was no sign of his Skytruck. Where his aeroplane had been two days ago there was only a smudge of oil being pecked at by two crows.

He was seized with the fear that it had been destroyed. Brandishing his pass at two hesitant guards, he pushed through onto the tarmac and hurried round to the maintenance hangars. Where the hell was Wahindi, and where the hell was his Skytruck?

Every time he saw an overalled man, he stopped him and asked for Wahindi. Nobody knew him, let alone had seen him. Impatiently, Rutherford went into the main hangar office and demanded Wahindi and his Skytruck.

Nobody knew anything about either. Nobody had ever seen either. Nobody seemed to believe they had ever existed.

God, Rutherford thought, putting his hand to his bruised face.

Maybe the blows had been harder than he realized—and now he couldn't distinguish between nightmare dream and nightmare reality.

Fifteen minutes later—hot, thirsty and exasperated—he glimpsed through the window of a small corrugated iron hangar at the back of the maintenance area a flash of red and silver paint. There she was, his Skytruck, corralled inside along with two Comanches and a Dove. He rushed round to the front, only to find the door padlocked.

In a surge of relief, he rushed back to the hangar office and demanded the key.

They had no key. No authority to open, even if they had a key. Furious now, he returned and began pulling on the door. Then he felt a hot hand on his shoulder. A big black policeman with breath that smelled of beer and who appeared to know only two words of English: "Government property".

It was no use getting steamed up, Rutherford told himself. He must keep his cool. Clearly nothing could be done at the airport itself. He located his porter and his belongings, relieved that at least they were still there, picked up a taxi, and drove back to the Hotel Afrique.

If M'Wanga was surprised at such a quick return, he didn't show it. Within minutes, Rutherford was re-installed in his old room. He told the boy to bring up a lemon squash with lots of ice. Then he rang McKaig. The girl at the Anglo-Kajandi Oil office said quickly that he was out.

Rutherford did not wait for his drink. He took a taxi to the oil company building and went straight to McKaig's office.

From above a newspaper, McKaig looked at him warily before simulating surprise and saying, "Bill!"

"I didn't go to Gittisham."

"So we heard."

"There was a spot of trouble."

"In coups, these mix-ups happen." McKaig didn't want to hear any more.

"God knows when I can get those Lowry pumps to the UK for you. You see, they've stolen my Skytruck."

40

McKaig put the newspaper down slowly. "Sorry to hear that."

"Locked it in a hangar. And my maintenance chap, Wahindi . . . he's scarpered."

"These characters, so *bloody* unreliable!"

"Can you get my aircraft back for me?"

"Doubt it, old lad. Don't see, to be honest, how we can help at all. Your best bet is to ask the high commissioner." It was obvious that in the present situation McKaig preferred to have as little contact with the pilot as possible.

"I didn't want to trouble him." He had almost said "again".

"That's what he's there for, old lad."

IT WAS OVER a mile from the office to the High Commission, but Rutherford walked through the heat to give himself time to think. The high commissioner must have pulled some pretty powerful strings to free him. Perhaps now he could be persuaded to act as quickly for his livelihood.

He turned in through the High Commission gates, went down the drive and up the steps into the hall. At the far end through a wide window, he caught a glimpse of a lawn and the river beyond, smelled water and sandalwood. Turning, he saw an African girl sitting at a desk. He walked towards her.

"I want to see the high commissioner, please."

"Have you an appointment, sir?"

Rutherford shook his head. "Not an actual appointment. But I know he'd want to see me."

"And what is the name, sir?"

"Rutherford."

"He's very busy, sir."

"But I insist I see him!" He gave her a faint smile to soften the sharpness of his tone.

The receptionist hesitated, then plugged a wire into a telephone board and picked up a receiver. A minute later, down the carved mahogany staircase came Fortescue's personal assistant. Her small nose was held ominously high, Rutherford thought, as he took a couple of paces to meet her.

Sunshine from the staircase window spotlit his face. He saw

her grey eyes catch sight of his bruised cheek. A strange expression momentarily ruffled her composed features. But when she spoke her voice was calm and formal.

"Mr. Rutherford? I'm afraid it's not possible for His Excellency to see you. He's very busy."

"I appreciate that," Rutherford smiled ingenuously. "But I'd only keep him for half a minute. You see, he was very helpful to me the other night and I'd like to thank him."

"I'll give him your message."

"I feel I should give it to him in person."

She hesitated.

"It must be a helluva job at a time like this." Rutherford took one step towards the staircase and then another. "For Mr. Fortescue, I mean. More kicks than halfpence. So I thought," he shrugged, "a thank-you wouldn't come amiss."

She looked at her watch and sighed. "Well, just for a couple of seconds then, Mr. Rutherford." She gave him a sweet-engaging smile. "As you say, His Excellency doesn't get many bouquets."

She preceded him up the staircase, slim bare brown legs twinkling distractingly in his vision, to the first landing, up another staircase and through a door marked *Miss Virginia Lacey* into a large airy office with tiger lilies and cannas a mass of colour on the window sill. She knocked on the door at the far end of the room and then opened it, leading Rutherford in.

"Mr. Rutherford just wants to thank you for your efforts, Excellency."

The diamond-bright eyes lifted from a mass of papers on the desk. "Oh, that's all right, Rutherford. Glad things worked out." The eyes were already returning to the papers. "Good of you to come . . . bit busy myself just now."

"There's one other thing," Rutherford interposed quickly. "Now they've stolen my aircraft."

Miss Lacey was standing by the door deliberately keeping it open. He heard her outraged indrawn breath, and it wasn't outrage at his Skytruck being stolen.

"My Skytruck, sir, they've stolen it. They've locked it up in one of the hangars."

"Impounded, Rutherford . . . that's the word you mean. Mmm." The high commissioner bit his lip. "Clearly there's been some misunderstanding. Well . . . you'd better sit down and tell me about it."

For the next fifteen minutes they were closeted together. Before Rutherford left, he had extracted a promise that the high commissioner would "do something".

Outside, Miss Lacey went on typing and did not look up. As he passed behind her chair, on a sudden impulse he bent down and touched the shiny sweet-smelling top of her head with his lips. "Thanks."

Miss Lacey continued typing. "Good-day, Mr. Rutherford," she said icily. "Will you please see yourself out?" She smoothed her hair as if an annoying insect had alighted there.

It was a little cooler outside. Rutherford walked briskly to the Hotel Afrique. At least he had achieved his object, which was to place this urgent problem squarely into someone else's lap. He felt no guilt whatever at the way he had achieved it, though he didn't care to guess what Miss Lacey thought of him.

FOUR

. . . THE ACTION REGARDING MR RUTHERFORD WAS PERHAPS IN THE CIRCUMSTANCES A TRIFLE PRECIPITATE STOP NOW RECOGNITION HAS BEEN CLAIMED BY GAWAKA IT WOULD BE EMBARRASSING TO DENY IT STOP . . . ONE CAN ONLY HOPE THAT OTHER COUNTRIES PARTICULARLY RESPECTABLE AFRICAN STATES WILL SOON RECOGNIZE STOP IN THIS CONNECTION NO DOUBT YOU ARE SEEKING THE INTENTIONS OF THE UNITED STATES. . . .

Bancroft, decoding, thought to himself at least one could rely on Central African Department at the FCO to see sense. Polite, understated as always, nevertheless this was a rocket for the high commissioner—and in Bancroft's view, richly deserved.

The rest of the Western world remained uncommitted. None of the African States had recognized, and Tomalia, Mambia and Mozambique had broken off diplomatic relations. A resolution condemning the general's coup in the Organization of African Unity at Addis Ababa had only narrowly been defeated. It was clear that Moto had powerful friends.

The only friend Gawaka appeared to have was Hugh Fortescue. With the flimsy in his hand, Bancroft waylaid him as he came up the stairs after attending the swearing-in ceremony of ministers of state (all army officers) where he had been the only foreign representative present.

"Signal from the FCO, sir."

Bancroft followed him into the inner office, where Fortescue sat down behind his desk and put on his spectacles. He read the signal in silence.

"Of course it's difficult for London to appreciate the situation here," he said at last.

"Difficult for us, too," Bancroft suggested. He was suddenly seized with the fear that Fortescue simply couldn't recognize a reprimand when he saw one.

"I don't think so, Tom. We can use our eyes. Joro is back to normal. It is our practice to recognize *de jure* when a government has control of the country and the obedience of the people, both of which the general has."

"Appears to have," Bancroft corrected.

"He seems a straightforward friendly chap. He has humour. Puts you at your ease. I had lunch at Government House with him and the Lady Damina."

"Would she be his fourth or fifth wife, sir?"

Very slightly, Fortescue's eyebrows lifted. "He's a Muslim, Tom. They're allowed four, you know. He was talking about his plans. There's going to be a lot happening in Kajandi soon."

Bancroft did not know whether to say "Good!" or "Oh, God!", so he said nothing.

"Gawaka isn't the usual African dictator. He's quite open about the fact that stringent measures are needed at present. When the Moto opposition dies he's going to hold free democratic elections to parliament. He's also stopping all this nonsense about leaving the Commonwealth."

"But what about other countries recognizing?" Bancroft tapped

44

the flimsy on the desk. "That's what the Department is worried about. Our total isolation."

Fortescue regarded him over the top of his spectacles. "Once they see how Gawaka is shaping, other countries will recognize soon enough. America amongst them."

"So that just leaves the one thing unresolved, sir."

"What's that, Tom?"

"Rutherford's Skytruck," said Bancroft sourly.

THE ARCHITECT, in Bancroft's opinion of their present predicament, was at that moment out at Joro airport, pursuing possible contacts who might help him and keeping an eye on his still imprisoned aircraft.

An American 707 from New York had been refuelled and its departure for Johannesburg announced. As its passengers filtered back onto the ramp, one of them left a yesterday's *Washington Mail* lying on a seat.

Rutherford picked it up, but as he opened it out, it was snatched roughly away from him. Startled, he looked into the bloodshot eyes of a Kajandi soldier.

"What the—"

The soldier tucked the newspaper under his arm. "Government property," he said, and walked away.

"HAVE YOU seen the *Washington Mail*, Hugh?"

"No."

"Not surprising." The American ambassador passed a copy across his desk to the high commissioner. "Gawaka has banned it. Read the lead story and you'll understand why."

Fortescue put on his spectacles and studied the headline. The two of them were sitting in Craig Ogilvie's office in the American embassy—a concrete pile complete with bullet-proof glass, armed guards and television cameras watching all comings and goings.

Fortescue read the article slowly. In highly-coloured detail, it was the story of how twenty Assangi had been lined up one behind the other and each forced to batter in the head of the man in front of him with a rock. The last in line had been clubbed to death by soldiers. The executions had been carried out because the men were relatives of Kassilolo, Moto's chancellor, and had refused to take the oath of allegiance to Gawaka. The account was written by two *Mail* reporters from "somewhere in Northern Kajandi".

"Well?"

Fortescue folded the newspaper and handed it back. "No pictures."

"You don't believe it?"

The high commissioner shrugged his shoulders. "Journalists are always on the look-out for stories of violence."

"The State Department are worried." Ogilvie indicated the newspaper on his desk. "There's so much we don't know about Gawaka."

"In the course of the last few days, I have got to know him well. He is a man of vision."

"Glad to hear you say that, Hugh. But of course, the State Department wants proof." Ogilvie hesitated. "You can't blame them for being cautious. Gawaka wouldn't be content with recognition. He'd want our material support—they always do."

"In the circumstances, a good investment, Craig."

"Even if Moto happens to be alive and makes a comeback with MiG fighters and Russian tanks?"

"I don't think you need worry about that, Craig. In the next few days, I'm sure you'll have evidence enough even for the State Department of how firmly the general is in the saddle and how democratic he intends his rule to be."

"After which," the American ambassador smiled and stood up, "we'll recognize."

AT 9:00 A.M. on every alternate Saturday—always provided there was no revolution, earthquake or thunderstorm—the wives of the four married staff of the British High Commission, led by Priscilla Fortescue, and accompanied by Virginia, and Sarah Harris who was in charge of aid projects, would go about their duty of Good Works. It might be teaching the native women sewing or English or hygiene. Or it might be organizing the listless youths into

46

teams of shoe-blacks, or looking after homeless boys, like the project at the old Indian embassy which Virginia had made her own.

Through the landing window Bancroft watched Priscilla get in behind the wheel of the Fortescues' fawn Zephyr, and close the door. The other five ladies were all arranged inside like brightly-wrapped fruit bon-bons. Slowly the car moved away and out of the gates.

In their own way, Bancroft thought, they were wonderful. Not that there wasn't another side. For instance, they were often accused of being snobbish and stand-offish by the wives of visiting technical assistance officers. But they did get things *done*. Which was more than he was able to do these days.

Bancroft left the window and went back to Chancery where a mountain of applications to get out of Kajandi into Britain—particularly from Asians—awaited him. He opened the bottom drawer of his desk, extracted the bottle and measured out the necessary dose to keep his pecker up.

At one o'clock the telephone rang. It was Fortescue inquiring whether he knew Virginia's whereabouts.

"She's at the old Indian embassy, sir. The Boys' Home."

"Yes, of course! I wonder if you could contact her, Tom. I've got a couple of reports I'd like to dictate."

"They're not on the telephone, sir. But I could go round and collect her."

"Thank you, Tom. I'll be in after lunch. Round two thirty."

He was glad of the excuse for a break. With a bit of luck, he might finally persuade Virginia to have lunch with him. He went downstairs, got into his old Vauxhall and followed the route of Priscilla's Zephyr out of the main gates and up the newly-named Gawaka Avenue.

This was the best part of Joro. The street was well-paved and wide and lined by flowering flame trees. It soon deteriorated and became a dirty, deeply rutted lane. Bullock carts, bicycles, mammy-wagons, crowds of shouting pedestrians slowed the Vauxhall to a crawl.

Eventually, close to the city wall, Bancroft turned left down a cobbled alleyway, past a tavern and a pottery factory. In a cul-de-sac at the far end was the old Indian embassy—a dilapidated house with peeling pink stucco.

Six bare-footed boys were sitting on the steps eating their lunch of *matoke* and pancake. They watched him warily as he got out of the car. One of them called out, "Miz Lacey!"

Before he reached the front door, it opened, and there she stood, incongruously fresh-looking in the cobwebbed frame.

"Hello, Tom?" It was a question.

"It's all right, Virginia. Just H.E. wants you this afternoon for dictation."

The relief showed in her eyes. "Oh, I see."

"What else were you expecting?"

"Nothing."

"*Who* else then?"

She smiled. "Nobody." She began to walk down the steps. "Thanks for coming to collect me."

"Pleasure." He paused. "Oh Virginia, would you like to have lunch with me today?"

"Better not keep H.E. waiting." She was already opening the door of the Vauxhall. "Some other time perhaps."

He got into the other seat behind the wheel. "That's what you always say." He started the engine up, and gave her a crooked little smile. "But H.E.'s not going to be in for an hour."

"*Touché*, as they say."

The Vauxhall bumped out of the courtyard.

THEY ARRIVED back at the High Commission after lunch in the Club promptly at two thirty. But H.E. had already preceded them. So had someone else. A Rolls-Royce was parked by the steps, and the drive was full of motor-cycle police.

The two of them walked up the stairs together. The high commissioner's office was empty. Below the wide window looking onto the long lawn could be seen two backs—one thin, one fat. Four hands were clasped behind them—one a freckled knot of bony fingers, the other a black bunch of bananas.

"They look very pally," Bancroft observed. "Wish I wasn't

irresistibly reminded of Laurel and Hardy. What d'you think they're talking about?"

"Amongst other things, Mr. Rutherford's Skytruck."

"Another . . . misunderstanding?"

"So H.E. says."

Moodily Bancroft watched the two figures right about turn smartly and begin walking back. "They look very pleased with themselves. Can't be just Rutherford's Skytruck, surely?"

"These days, H.E. is always cheerful."

"Why, Virginia, *why?* Doesn't he realize how isolated we are?"

"He is very sure of General Gawaka's qualities."

"How can he be so soon?"

"Don't ask me, Tom."

The garden was empty now. The sound of footsteps could be heard coming up the stairs. Bancroft moved to the door.

"If you won't tell me anything else, Virginia, at least let me know what part of our shrunken Empire H.E. has swapped for Rutherford's Skytruck."

THE TELEPHONE rang in the Hotel Afrique.

"Mr. Rutherford?"

He recognized the studiedly neutral voice. "Yes, Miss Lacey."

"I have some news for you."

Bound to be bad—that was his first reaction. There were shortages of everything in Joro now—meat, milk, petrol, liquor, even fruit. Only an abundance of dust and exhaust smoke and the reek of sewage, and long queues of cars waiting at the city gates to be checked as the search for Moto supporters intensified. There was nothing to do but work out, as each day went by with no revenue-earning trip, the probable date of his bankruptcy. And all the time, the fear of the tap on the shoulder from an armed guard.

"Your Skytruck is being released."

"Oh thanks . . . thanks a lot."

"Don't thank me, Mr. Rutherford. His Excellency made all the arrangements."

"Then I'll come over and—"

"No, Mr. Rutherford." The voice had taken on the slightest

edge of humour. "Not again! I'll thank Mr. Fortescue for you."

"Well, thank you for being so—" What was the word? He gave up and came down to brass tacks. "I'll get a taxi to the airport. The sooner I take off for Gittisham—"

"There are still certain formalities."

"Oh, I see." He did not want to spoil things by probing too deeply into diplomatic niceties. "When can I go then?"

"Tomorrow. You are to report to the clerk at the African Airways counter tomorrow at eleven p.m. You'll find your bag and papers still on board. The aircraft will be just as you left it. Your load sheet and met. report and flight plan to Gittisham will all be made out ready. Have you got that, Mr. Rutherford?" The voice sounded anxious. "At eleven p.m."

"Don't worry . . . I'll be there on the dot."

"And . . . have a good trip."

"Well, thanks, Miss Lacey." He was genuinely touched. "And thanks again for being so—"

"England should be lovely now."

"Well, at least it'll be a change from Joro. 'Bye, Miss Lacey."

Although he couldn't leave until the following night, he immediately began his preparations. He telephoned the airport meteorological office for tomorrow's weather forecast. Carefully he worked out his courses, calculated his ground speed, plotted Gittisham's position and gave it two haloes for luck.

Then he rang McKaig. "I've got my Skytruck back."

"Wonderful, old son!" McKaig appeared particularly anxious to be pleasant. "You'll be taking our Lowry pumps then?"

"Right. Leaving tomorrow. Preliminary flight plan ten hours with half an hour refuelling at Zurich, if you'd send a signal."

"Delighted, old son."

There was nothing else to do but hang around and keep his fingers crossed. Next day, he had an early dinner, then lay on his bed dozing on and off till M'Wanga called him to say the taxi was waiting.

Bright stars and a cold wind greeted him. Through deserted streets, the taxi moved to the South Gate. Two enormous Kajandi soldiers materialized out of the shadows.

Rutherford and the driver were told to get out and were searched by one guard. The other went over the taxi, opening the boot and his luggage, pulling at the seats, even taking the cap off the petrol tank and shining a torch inside. Finally, they were allowed back into the taxi, waved through the gates. Again there were guards at the airport gate, but these ones knew him. No cars in the park. Passenger Reception was a sheet of neon light without any passengers. Nothing moved. Only the searchlight on the top of the control tower restlessly circled, momentarily picking out the silent silhouettes of aircraft.

Rutherford paid off the taxi, picked up his luggage and pushed open the glass door. It was one minute to eleven.

None of the airline counters was manned, except that of African Airways. A clerk raised his head, and, without asking who he was, uttered one quick breathless sentence: "Mr.-Rutherford-sah-is-gennelman-to-see-you-sah-in-Mr.-Mullah's-office."

Mullah was the airport manager. Rutherford sensed trouble.

He swore under his breath and bounded up the steps towards the control tower, knocked sharply on Mullah's door, and went in.

The room was in darkness, and his first reaction was that there was nobody there. Then in the light thrown from the corridor he saw the silhouette of a man half blocking the far window. A husky voice said softly, "All yu pilots are jus' like me, Cap'n Rutherford. Yu jus' want to stand quietly in de darkness and watch de stars in de sky."

In through the open window came the night smells of an airport —grass, kerosene, tar, a whiff of exhaust smoke. An African was leaning out, one huge eye gleaming startling white in a black profile.

"Come over here, Cap'n Rutherford. Do yu know who I am?"

Blacker than the darkness around it, the face had disappeared. Then slight as a butterfly wing, it was brushed by light from the revolving beacon. Dominating it was the melon-smile that shone down benevolently from half the hoardings in Kajandi.

"Yes."

"And as yu see, Cap'n Rutherford, I know yu . . . oh, yes, and your company, too. It is a good company, yes? Obeys all the rules, yes? Had Moto government contracts, yes? Had money paid into your bank account here, yes?"

"Yes, but that was for—"

"Oh yes . . . we know what it was for! We know all dat . . . oh yes! Yu have an Asian mechanic, Wahindi, yes?"

"Well, I *had*. But he's gone!"

"Where, Cap'n?"

"That's what I'd like to know."

The smile disappeared, the eyes had become unblinking. So he had been released simply to be caught again. Rutherford looked round the room for soldiers. The man at the window was wearing grey flannels and a double-breasted blazer. But the two of them were quite alone.

"Yu like it here in Kajandi, Cap'n Rutherford?"

"Yes, General."

"Yu have done business for Kajandi's good?"

"I think so, General."

"But good for yu, too, eh?"

"If I didn't make some profit, I'd be out of business."

The general nodded sympathetically. "And never have yu had trouble, eh?"

The pilot hesitated. There was a sudden bellow of laughter. A huge hand struck him on the shoulders. A breath like a hurricane, full of coconut oil and cigar smoke and that sweat-soaked earth African smell, roared over Rutherford's face.

"Dat little business de other day!" Another aromatic gust swept over the pilot. "Never mind! Yu were paid for it, what business is all about, eh? Dose fifty thousand shillings paid into your account, eh?"

Rutherford said stiffly, "That was advance payment for air cargo from Kajandi Oil. The same pumps which today I'll be—"

"Never mind! A business deal, eh? It was just a liddle misunderstanding . . . But it has all come right in de end, eh, Cap'n? Everything now is straight, as yu British say, and above de board. All right for everyone, yes?"

"Well . . . I hope so."

Rutherford felt a thick arm come round his body and pinion

him in a bear hug. "I like yu, Cap'n Rutherford! Yu are British. I like de British. Who were de ver' first to recognize my government? De British! Who is my ver' best friend? De British high commissioner! I tell yu something, Cap'n. Dere is ver' few people I can trust. Can I trust yu, Cap'n Rutherford?"

"Of course, General."

"I hear voices. I trust dose voices. Dey tell me many things. Do yu know what dey tell me, many years before I became president?"

"No, General."

"Dey tell me dere is gold in de Assangi country beyond the hills. And oil, uranium, chemicals, diamonds."

"Oh yes, General?"

"And now I tell yu something I have told only one other person . . . my ver' best friend Hugh Fortescue." Gawaka cocked his head sideways. "Dose voices spoke de truth. Surveys now show it. Dere is everything up dere. Kajandi will be rich." He paused. "All dat means much more business, Cap'n. Business for de British. Business for Kajandi. Fair shares all round does no harm to nobody, eh, Cap'n Rutherford?"

"No harm, General."

"And now, Cap'n, jus' to show yu how much I like yu and trust yu . . . I have a liddle business for yu."

"I'd be glad to do it, General."

"Yu go to Zurich, yes?"

Rutherford nodded. "I refuel there, General."

"It is just a liddle cargo, yu understand. Will yu take a liddle cargo to Zurich for me? Nothing ver' much . . ."

"Certainly, General. Where is it? We'll get it loaded."

A big smile and a bear hug. "Forgive me, Cap'n Rutherford . . . I have anticipated yu. It is already loaded." The general took the pilot's arm and began walking him towards the lighted corridor. "Dere is jus' one small thing. Dere is no need to look around . . . like last time." He stopped in his tracks and gave Rutherford the melon-smile. "All is correct! Jus' take it to Zurich. And dere yu will be met by my second best friend . . . a dark man in a blue uniform called Johnson. He will see to de refuelling and de removal of de cargo. He will come up and say his name to yu. . . . Johnson, he will say. I am Johnson. Leave everything to him, Cap'n Rutherford . . . and then continue on your way."

"That seems simple enough, General."

"Yu will be well paid, Cap'n." A large right hand came up and captured Rutherford's. "And now—" They had reached the door. "Go, my dear Cap'n . . . go about your business." Rutherford was pushed into the corridor. "Leave me to watch de stars in de sky."

The door closed. Rutherford went thoughtfully downstairs. On the African Airways counter, all his papers had been laid out. He studied the load and trim sheet—all up weight at the maximum of 11,000 kilos, trim 0.2 feet behind the centre of gravity. He looked at the maintenance form—signed up, correct. He scrutinized the signature—indecipherable. Not Wahindi's. He took out his pen, hesitated, then, mindful of Gawaka's warning, signed the forms one by one.

Once outside on the tarmac, he could just make out the familiar lines of his Skytruck, sandwiched between a ghostly Fokker Friendship and a battered DC-4.

He hurried towards it. Coming up under its nose, he tapped it affectionately as though the aircraft was a huge horse. Under his fingers, the fuselage trembled in the wind from the north.

He called, "Anybody around?"

Nobody. He switched on his torch. The light flickered over the tyres, up into the wheel wells as he inspected hydraulic lines and electrical wiring. He climbed up onto the starboard wing. Halfway through dipping the tanks, the tower searchlight stopped on him, followed him as he went over to the port wing, then back onto the tarmac, pulling away the wheel chocks, opening the door and putting them and his case inside, then clambering in himself.

Even then, it did not go away. The yellow light peered at him through the portholes as he looked over the compartment.

The cargo looked exactly the same as ten days ago—same lashings, same tarpaulins. Only right at the back had there been an addition—the general's cargo, covered by green canvas fixed securely to the floor.

He hesitated. All his pilot's training whispered to him . . . make

54

sure, trust no one. But the light was still on him. Gawaka's words echoed in his ears. The memory of that previous horror stirred.

He turned his back on it, and walked up to the flight deck. He switched on the master-switch, and sat down in the lefthand seat. This was his home, the only thing in the world he could trust.

His briefcase was exactly where he had left it on the righthand seat. His bag was on the floor behind. He did not even trouble to look inside. He knew that everything would be there—and that everything would have been gone through with a fine-tooth comb.

He picked up the celluloid check list, and went through the items one by one. Then he selected tower frequency on the VHF and asked for taxi-clearance.

"Runway Zero One, Echo X-Ray. No other traffic."

He switched on the landing lights, pushed the throttles forward. Sluggishly, the three wheels of the Skytruck began turning. As he taxied to the end of the runway, the searchlight followed him.

"Echo X-Ray ready to roll."

"Echo X-Ray cleared take-off. Cleared to climb on course."

Ten degrees of flap. Throttles right against the stops. Brakes off. Sweetly and slowly, the Skytruck moved.

Nosewheel still on the ground. Twin landing lights charging the darkness. The needle on the airspeed indicator crept up— forty, fifty, sixty knots. Through his fingers on the control column, Rutherford could feel the aircraft coming alive. Very gradually, he began easing back.

And then suddenly, the nose reared, tipping the pilot right back in his seat. The engine note became laboured. He could feel the braking effect from the high angle of attack.

Using both his hands, he tried to push the stick forward. Useless. The nose still soared.

Now the aircraft became menacing, the spears of the landing lights rose higher in the night. The Skytruck had gone berserk.

He fought back with all his strength, trying to get the nose down. He caught sight of the speed—ninety knots, the needle stuck solid on the indicator.

Three more runway lights left. And then the red boundary. In this nose-high begging attitude, he'd never get off.

He took his right hand off the stick, grabbed the trim wheel to push it forward. But immediately, the nose rose sharply higher. He let go of the trim.

The last runway light came drifting towards him.

He lifted his feet off the rudder. Straining hard, he managed to get one pressed against each spectacle of the control column. Then with all his might, his back dug deep into the seat, he pushed.

The nose quivered, slowly began to dip, dipped further. The starboard wheel lifted off the ground. On one leg, the Skytruck hopped over the threshold lights, tottered unsteadily up into the night.

He was still flying the aircraft with his feet. He pressed with his right foot to level the wings. At two hundred feet, he managed to get the flaps up. Gradually, the nose gave up the struggle against him. The climb flattened. As soon as he dared, Rutherford grabbed the elevator trim wheel, and wound it full travel forward. He lowered his legs back on the rudder, put his hands on the stick, and brought the engines back to climb power.

He swore out loud at that bloody African loader, putting Gawaka's stuff right back at the rear. Wahindi would never have allowed that to happen. What the hell was the cargo anyway, that made the tail so heavy?

He cursed himself, too, for not checking it. He was going to have a look right now. . . .

He centralized the controls and engaged the autopilot. Immediately, the Skytruck started weaving. He slammed the autopilot out, and tried again. Still no good. With the aircraft so badly out of trim, the autopilot refused to cope. He would have to handfly all the way.

So there he sat, imprisoned again, this time in the seat of his own Skytruck. The stars had disappeared behind high cloud. The night was pitch black. The hours passed, and the effort of instrument flying began to hypnotize him. All the little phosphorescent figures on the dark instrument panel wove weird patterns in his mind, as he flew northwards across the Sahara and over the Mediterranean.

The tail-heaviness had been deliberate. Instead of a judicial execution, this ingenious way of getting rid of him had been decided. Hadn't Gawaka hinted that he had taken money for Nakungu's passage? But, if that theory was right, how did Gawaka's cargo fit in? Why would he incriminate himself by coming out to the airport to talk to him? Why did he seem so anxious for Rutherford to be his friend?

Zurich tower came up suddenly. "Visibility six hundred yards in heavy rain. Echo X-Ray cleared for approach on runway One Six."

More likely to be the work of that damned escape organization. That bloody Asian boy having his revenge for the last time.

The Skytruck bucketed around in heavy turbulence and he became preoccupied with his immediate survival. Through ragged stratus at four hundred feet, he caught sight of the runway. He put down full flap, throttled right back. Two minutes later, he was down and taxiing to the ramp.

No sooner were his engines stopped than a truck appeared. The fuselage door was opened. There was the sound of footsteps coming up from the cargo compartment. A strange man appeared on the flight deck. Just as Gawaka had forecast, he said, "Captain Rutherford . . . I am Johnson."

He was a dark man in a blue uniform certainly, but it was difficult to tell his nationality—certainly not a Kajandi, but then not Indian or Asian either. A mixture probably.

Rutherford said, "The stuff's right at the back, Mr. Johnson. Bloody nearly killed me!" He climbed out of the seat. "After unloading and refuelling, I want everything checked. Otherwise I won't sign the load sheet."

Johnson said soothingly, "It'll be all right after we get the rear cargo off, Captain."

Rutherford collected his briefcase and walked to the back of the aircraft. The cargo door was wide open and the truck backed right up against the fuselage. There was no identifying name on its side—just an anonymous three-tonner, grey under the film of early-morning rain.

When Rutherford returned twenty minutes later after checking with met. and doing his, flight plan, the truck and Johnson had vanished. Now his cargo was simply the pumps—still positioned as Wahindi had ordered. Rutherford started up, taxied out, then lifted off easily. The trim was again normal.

The weather cleared halfway up France. For the rest of the flight, it was bright sunshine. From fifty miles away, he saw the white cliffs of England. Just inland was the double cross of the runways at Gittisham, ringed by rusty old hangars. Even before he landed, he could see the figure of George Stokes, the other half of the staff of *Rutherford's Airline*, standing on the ramp.

Stokes marshalled him in, shouted up, "What's kept you? Prowting's been ringing twice a day from the Lowry factory about those pumps."

Rutherford clambered out of the aircraft. "A little matter of a military coup."

A tractor hummed in the fields beyond the perimeter. A blackbird sang. The air held an almost unbearable sweetness. It was like coming back into another world.

"Pour me a large whisky, George. I'll have that for my breakfast." Rutherford breathed in the scents of new mown hay and honeysuckle. "I have at last realized how lucky I've been and never known it. And I want to drink to Merrie England . . . bloody government, falling pound, rising prices, economic crisis . . . the lot!"

FIVE

In Kajandi, at soirées and embassy receptions, the view expressed was that at the very end of his career Hugh Fortescue had brought off a diplomatic coup. Kajandi was going to be rich and therefore powerful, and Britain had been the first country to recognize the new regime.

Every day the relationship between the British high commissioner and General Gawaka grew firmer. If Naji Gawaka was uncrowned king, Hugh Fortescue was mentor and father confessor. It was in relations with the Assangi that Fortescue's influence was most evident. The general's first priority, the high commissioner urged, must be towards unifying Kajandi. Clearly now there would be wealth, but only if the tribes worked together. And the black chaps must work side by side with the white chaps. Such was Hugh Fortescue's philosophy.

Quite what was Naji Gawaka's philosophy remained something of a mystery. There were still dark pools there, fears of omens, juju and taboos inbred in the general's childhood.

When in the grip of such superstition, Gawaka would become withdrawn and childlike—as happened on the second Friday in June. Hugh and Priscilla Fortescue were invited to tea at Government House. It was a family affair, at which the Lady Damina presided. The conversation was on domestic matters. Four of Gawaka's children came in and ate cakes and played.

The general had appeared thoughtful. Fortescue's invitation to a garden party at the High Commission, to be held on 10th July with the express purpose of introducing British businessmen to Kajandi ministers, failed to arouse more than perfunctory approval.

When the tea things were taken away, the general suggested to the high commissioner a stroll in the gardens. Walking on the lawn by the banks of the Ruanga in the pink glow of sunset, he said suddenly, "Hugh, I have ver' bad news."

Fortescue tensed himself, but he gave no sign of anything except polite sympathy. "I'm very sorry to hear that."

"My rule, dey say, Hugh, will only last a hundred days." The general stopped, and clenched his fists and glowered at the red half orb of sun. "Only sixty-six more sunsets, dey say!"

For a second, Fortescue was bereft of words. Then with the briskness of a nanny he asked, "*Who* says, Naji?"

"A soothsayer. I have not talked with him myself. But he tells many people. Gawaka of a Hundred Days dey are calling me."

"A silly story, Naji! Politically motivated."

"Put out, yu think, by Moto's men and dose American reporters of de *Washington Mail?*"

"Well, I don't know about that," Fortescue said diplomatically. "But such stories are *not* anything for you to worry about. When the tribes are working together, Moto's men will be *your* men."

"But where is Moto, I ask myself. And Kassilolo? Dese voices," he cupped his ears, "dey tell me, find Moto! Find Kassilolo!"

Fortescue said gently, "Either dead or fled the country."

"How fled? How could dey go? Ah, yes!" Gawaka pressed his hands tighter on his ears. "De voices say de escape organization. Dey say de escape organization is run by Asians."

"That's not very likely, Naji."

"Why not? An Asian boy with grey eyes was seen with Nakungu. De day he was killed resisting arrest." He walked on a few paces in silence. "Dere is pressure in my Cabinet for severe action against all de Asians."

Fortescue's heart sank. "That would be most unwise! They are a valuable part of a technical economy."

Fortescue's vehemence appeared for the moment to reassure the general. "Perhaps you are right."

"Besides, you must win them over to you. As you must win the Assangi. Then there is a great future for all."

Twilight came down softly. As they turned back towards the house, a comfortable companionship again settled upon them.

"I do not know if you have seen the Michelangelo painting of the Creation on the ceiling of the Sistine Chapel, Naji. Two hands stretch out to touch each other."

"Dat is interesting."

"It is all there, Naji, everything we have talked about. Maintain. The word comes from the Latin *manu* meaning in the hand and *tenere* meaning to hold. Hold in the hand. Holding hands."

"Holding hands. Main-tain."

"That's what we must do, Naji. That must be our policy."

"I like dat. I like dat ver' much!" The big smile was back. In the half darkness, the high commissioner felt a tug on his sleeve. "Here is my hand, Hugh."

Fortescue could just see it, held out in front of him. "And here is mine, Naji."

They walked like that—gripping each other's right hands— over the lawn and up the steps and into the hall.

"Holding hands," the general repeated. "Main-tain."

THAT WEEK in his room at the King's Arms in Gittisham, Rutherford did some thinking about Kajandi.

"It's pretty hairy out there, is it?" George Stokes asked him when they had dinner together on the Wednesday. He had brought the news that the pumps would be ready in four days time.

"Bloody's a better word," Rutherford said grimly. "The regime's rocky. You know what these military dictators are."

"Cadillacs, Rolls-Royces, their own jets, wine and women." George Stokes nodded mournfully. "The lucky sods!"

"They can run the country into the ground in no time and then where's our Kajandi connection?"

"Up the creek."

"Not to mention broke. That last trip," Rutherford paused, "cost *us* money. Skytruck hung up doing nothing for three weeks." But he had plans. He was going to drum up local business. The Skytruck was adaptable. Business should come rolling in!

But that was one of the snags of Merrie England. Business did *not* come rolling in. Credit was tight. His bank manager could not increase his overdraft, and the only business that rolled in was a not very profitable charter to Jersey to bring back tomatoes and new potatoes.

Even before he reached the ramp after he landed from that trip, he saw the smile on Stokes's face. He unbuttoned his jacket and scowled. "And what have you got to be so happy about?"

He learned ten minutes later in the office. George had laid out the morning papers beside a freshly poured cup of tea. The *Daily Mail* carried a huge headline: KAJANDI—THE NEW ELDORADO. Even *The Times* gave it a front page column, and referred the reader inside to the parliamentary report and the business news.

Rutherford sipped his tea and read the accounts slowly and carefully. According to both papers, gold, uranium and diamonds as well as oil had been discovered. Everything the general could possibly want for a rich and booming economy was there in his treasure chest. Now it seemed that everyone wanted to help him

61

get it out. British consultants were being sent to Kajandi. Shares in Anglo-Kajandi Oil and other companies had rocketed on the Stock Exchange. Other countries besides Britain had recognized Gawaka's regime, though the United States and Israel, France and West Germany, still held aloof.

"Looks like we could be in on the ground floor, eh, Bill? Not many firms have got a licence to operate in Kajandi."

"True." Nor had many firms carried a mysterious load for the president himself into Zurich. Or had their pilots clapped in jail on a capital charge.

The pumps from Prowting would be there that evening. The question of whether he was going back with them to Kajandi absorbed Rutherford's mind for the rest of the day. He weighed the pros and cons carefully. He could get someone else to freight the pumps. But if he did, that would be the end of the Anglo-Kajandi connection. Just when apparently things were on the up and up. He couldn't afford to be too choosy, or too chicken, come to that. It was a vital decision and he intended to sleep on it.

The night was warm and still. Rutherford lay on his back with his hands under his head, while through his mind flickered all the unanswered questions. What had happened to Wahindi? What was the cargo under the green cover? Was Gawaka stashing stuff away in Zurich? Was he genuinely seeking Rutherford's help? He had spoken the truth about the rich potential of Kajandi, perhaps he spoke the truth about that too. Gawaka probably couldn't trust his own pilots farther than he could throw them.

Rutherford turned his face towards the cool air drifting in through the window. The questions trooping through his mind all merged into one. *What was in it for him?*

He suddenly had a vision of Virginia Lacey's face, heard again her half-wistful words over the phone, "England should be lovely now." So it was, but he went to sleep immediately, his decision made.

He got up at eight and had a quick breakfast. Then he went out into the lobby to phone Stokes. "George, have the pumps come?"

"Yes."

"Then load them. I'll take off at eight. Organize a route forecast and flight plan to Joro, would you?"

It was still bright sunshine outside, but the forecast all over Europe was thunderstorms and high cloud. With full tanks, the flight plan was direct to Kajandi in eleven hours.

Rutherford signed the load and trim sheet in the office, and walked out to the waiting Skytruck—impatient now to be away.

He had actually begun taxiing when Stokes appeared, waving something.

Rutherford stopped, throttled back. Stokes opened the rear door, scrambled up to the flight deck. "Thought you'd better have the morning's mail." He threw half a dozen letters into the pilot's lap. "Take care now!"

The pilot glanced down at his lap. Nothing but bills and circulars. "I will."

The weather was even worse than forecast. Five minutes after take off, heavy rain and turbulence enveloped the Skytruck. For the next four hours, the tossing and tilting were too much for the automatic pilot, and he had to handfly on instruments. It was not until he was over the Mediterranean that he broke cloud.

Rutherford breathed a sigh of relief. His arms were stiff. Now he engaged the autopilot and checked in over Tripoli. Looking down, he saw the letters still in his lap. He sorted through them, not opening any till he came to the last one, an ordinary white envelope with his name and address typewritten. One Swiss eighty centime stamp on it with a postmark of the day before yesterday.

He opened it. Inside was one sheet of notepaper on which was typed a single sentence: *Matthew Kassilolo gives heartfelt thanks for his safe deliverance, and may God bless you and keep you always.*

WHAT DID he do now?

Back again in Joro, Rutherford asked himself that question a dozen times a day. All the time, he was haunted by the fear that there might be a tap on the door and M'Wanga might come into his room to say again, "Peoples to see you."

And once again, there would be the dim gaslit kitchen and the shadowy figure of the Asian boy with the grey eyes. But this time he was not pleading with him to smuggle others out of Kajandi, but telling him to. For now he was one of them, had been sucked into the escape organization and become part of it—so how could he refuse?

Get out while you can, an inner voice whispered. And yet there were other voices. The voice of the bank clerk informing him that a cheque for 80,000 shillings from the Kajandi Government had been credited to his account. The voice on the BBC foreign service radio describing the rich prospects of Kajandi. The voice of McKaig assuring him that "the future is gold-plated, old son."

The inner conflict inside himself had not yet been resolved when on Tuesday evening, just before dinner, the reception clerk handed him a letter. Inside was a gold printed invitation card: *The presence of Captain Rutherford at 11.30 a.m. on Wednesday 6th July at Government House is commanded by Generalissimo Naji Gawaka.*

"SO WE MEET again, Cap'n Rutherford. . . ." The billiard-ball eyes, sparkling black, protruded more than ever.

Rutherford had been kept waiting in the hall for half an hour. The omens were evil. The general did not smile. He made no offer to shake hands. "Come dis way."

Rutherford followed Gawaka into the garden, through the rose garden towards the river. On the banks of the Ruanga the general stopped and cupped both hands over his ears. "Cap'n Rutherford."

"Yes, General."

"Do yu hear de voices?"

"No, General."

"Dey are saying something to me. But dey are ver' faint."

Rutherford stood in silence.

"Yu remember dey told me of Kajandi's wealth?"

"Yes, General." Rutherford stared fixedly at the muddy waters of the Ruanga.

"It is something about flying, dese voices are saying. Yu are a flying man, Cap'n. What is id dey say?"

"I don't know, General."

"There! Can't yu hear?"

"No, General."

Then Rutherford did hear something—the crackle of a twig. He turned his head.

An African was running over the grass, holding up a thin-bladed *simi* knife. "Look out, General!"

Rutherford rushed forward, tripped up the man, threw himself on top of the writhing brown body, and grabbed his right wrist.

Kicking and panting, still holding the knife, the African wriggled from under him. He was small, but had muscular arms and a wrist like steel. He knew judo, got a half-nelson on Rutherford's left arm. First one, then the other managed to get on top. Rutherford got his knees hard into the African's body, heard him groan. The next moment, a hard blow on the back of his neck made him momentarily senseless. In that second, the man had him pinioned on his back, the knife within inches of his throat.

Slowly and relentlessly, the blade came lower. He could hear the thunder of his heart and his own heavy breathing. His struggling became feebler. His grip slackened. Now the African pushed his chin right back, baring his neck.

Rutherford watched the silver blade rise against the blinding blue of the sky, poised for the *coup de grace.*

And then suddenly, there was an enormous bellow of laughter. The knife was thrown aside. The African released his hold on Rutherford, and stood up. From the depths of a bamboo grove came Gawaka, still laughing.

"My dear Cap'n Rutherford. Well done! Well done!"

The pilot got up from the ground, dusted himself down.

"Don't look so down-hearted, Cap'n! Yu put up a ver' good fight! Allow me to introduce yu." He motioned towards the grinning African. "This is Major Ghinza, commander of my armoured brigade. Champion wrestler of the Kajandi army."

The African held out his right hand. "No offence, Captain."

Still in a daze, Rutherford took it. Gawaka put an arm round each as they shook hands. "My ver' good friends . . . Cap'n Rutherford and Major Ghinza."

Still holding onto them, he began to walk back towards Government House.

"Yu must understand, Cap'n, that I have many enemies. I have ver' few men I can trust. That liddle job yu did for me last month was in the nature of a test. That test yu passed. But my voices are ver' careful. Would this man protect yu, dey say. Can yu trust him wid your life?"

They were back in the hall. A servant opened the gilded door into the dining room. At the far end of the long table were laid three places.

"And now, gentlemen, yu must both be ready for your lunch. Major Ghinza on my left. Cap'n Rutherford at my right hand."

The meal lasted two hours. Turtle soup, fresh salmon, venison steaks, ice-cold fruit salad washed down with French wines. Throughout that time, Gawaka talked only of his development plans for Kajandi, his need for foreign investment.

It was when they were drinking brandy that Gawaka came back to the point. "Now that yu have earned your colours, Cap'n, I have something to ask yu. Will yu be my personal pilot?"

"WHO DID you say, Virginia? Rutherford? Oh yes, the pilot chap!" Hugh Fortescue gave her a slight smile. "Must invite him."

The two of them were making out the guest list for the garden party. There were, for a change, many people to ask, but regrettably, there would be several important absentees.

"I'll ring Craig Ogilvie now, Virginia . . . and get it over with."

She dialled the number of the American embassy, then handed over the receiver. "The ambassador's on the line now, sir."

"Craig, it's Hugh Fortescue. We're having a garden party here on the tenth. Just wondering if by that time—"

There was a long pause while the high commissioner sat listening.

"The *Washington Mail* must have found such stories good for circulation to continue them," eventually he said, a trifle grittily. "Unpleasant incidents no doubt continue in Kajandi as they do in your country and mine . . . and have done for hundreds of years. But to exaggerate and embroider and attribute them to Gawaka,

as your two journalists are doing, Craig, is frankly mischievous. Particularly as Joro, as you can see for yourself, has never been quieter or better governed."

There was another long pause.

"Well, I'm sorry we won't see you on the tenth. Some other time perhaps."

The invitations to the chosen were duly sent out. Rutherford opened his as he might a letter bomb. He had not yet made up his mind whether to accept the general's invitation to be his personal pilot. There were, after all, his Anglo-Kajandi Oil connections. But Gawaka was not pressing for an answer and had suggested that he consult his business friends and the High Commission. So the garden party would be an opportunity to do that.

He arrived late. The screeching of sirens outside announced that the general was hard on his heels. He was rushed down the reception line, then into the garden where the white-helmeted band of the Kajandi Armoured Brigade was playing the "Londonderry Air". He walked slowly down the path to the far wall. There, from the vantage point of a small grass bank, his eyes travelled over the gathering.

It looked, he thought, like some Victorian do—the long dresses, the tables beside the blossoming bushes, the red-sashed, white-gloved servants, the parasols, the music, the scent of flowers and perfume, the clink of glasses, the jingle of medals. While in the background stood the nineteenth-century High Commission—terraced, porticoed, wide-windowed. From this distance, you could think you were back in the good old Empire days.

He watched the general emerge from the French windows, escorted by Fortescue and other members of the High Commission like tugs docking a huge blue liner.

Rutherford strolled through the rose garden, and finally threaded his way to a white-clothed table. He picked up a plate and was just helping himself when McKaig came across. "Congratulations to the general's personal pilot."

"I haven't accepted yet. I wanted to ask you about my Anglo-Kajandi commitment."

"Oh, we'd fit in with the general, old lad."

"What about the repair runs to Gittisham?"

"As and when you can! Anything we're pressed for can go scheduled airline. In any case, apart from a trip to Bakhari to pick up oil pumps from the Gulf, there's nothing urgent."

"When'll that be?"

"About three weeks time." He suddenly peered over the pilot's shoulder. "The high commissioner seems to be summoning you." He gave Rutherford a slight push forward. "Be seeing you!"

Rutherford walked across the lawn to where Fortescue chatted to the Lady Damina and Virginia Lacey. "Ah, Rutherford! The general has just been asking me," the high commissioner said briskly after presenting him to Damina, "if you have accepted his offer yet?"

"No, I haven't, sir. I've a business commitment to Anglo-Kajandi, so I had to have a chat with McKaig first."

Fortescue nodded understandingly, and having asked what had been the outcome, said, "Do I take it that now you accept, Rutherford?"

Before he replied, Rutherford turned to face Miss Lacey. Shaded by the brim of a demure straw hat, the large grey eyes held a disturbing mixture of expressions—partly hostile, partly amused, but altogether challenging.

"Yes, Excellency," he heard himself say. "I accept."

"Good, good." Hugh Fortescue nodded. "I'll tell the general your decision." Then, the matter settled, he escorted Damina away to the tables where iced coffee was being served. Rutherford found himself alone with Virginia Lacey, and unable to think of anything to say to her.

"Does that decision call for champagne?" she asked him, crooking her finger towards a waiter.

"I'm not sure." He took a glass. "How about you?"

She hesitated. Then she took a glass, and raised it. "I think it might. Good luck! Happy landings!"

He laughed nervously. "I'll need them."

"Will you be flying a great deal, Mr. Rutherford?"

"That's rather up to the general."

Miss Lacey nodded. "Most things in Kajandi are."

He looked at her sharply. He heard a mocking inflection in her voice. He felt himself lumped together with all the self-seekers bowing down to the new Messiah on whose head glittered that halo of treasure in the Northern hills.

"Will the flying in Kajandi be difficult, Mr. Rutherford?"

She was only trying to break the silence, but suddenly he saw a chance to improve his position with her. "Not at all."

"But surely there are hardly any airfields?"

"There don't have to be."

With satisfaction he saw her eyes widen. "All I need to put my Skytruck down is a piece of flat land." He looked round. "Say from where we're standing now to the end of the lawn."

"That's amazing!" She smiled. "But how about taking off?"

"A little longer. To the far wall."

"You must be a very clever pilot, Mr. Rutherford!"

Once again his ear caught that mocking inflection. "I have a nasty suspicion you don't believe me, Miss Lacey."

"Oh, but I do, Mr. Rutherford!"

"One of these days, I'll surprise you. Next time I'm invited to a reception here, I'll come in my Skytruck. And I'll put her down exactly as I said."

She laughed. "I doubt if you'd get invited again if you did. Besides, our best receptions are at night."

"No problem there either. Just give me three lights. A green one where we are now. A white one half way down the lawn, and a red one near the wall."

"Just a green, a white and a red?"

He saw her amused expression. "I'm sorry. I don't usually shoot a line." The mocking expression faded. Encouraged, he went on, "Maybe one day you'll let me take you up and show you."

"Some day, that would be nice."

But it was all very vague. He was about to suggest taking her out to dinner or somewhere into the country. But he didn't possess a car and taxis were unreliable. And while he was thinking how to cement their tenuous relationship, the consul chap Bancroft came over, reeking of whisky. He rested his hand possessively on Miss Lacey's arm and asked when Rutherford was going home. "To the UK, I mean, *not* of course from this party."

"Not for some time. My next trip's in about three weeks to the Gulf. But talking of going home. . . ." Rutherford looked at his watch, smiled and excused himself.

He walked back to the Hotel Afrique. He had a nagging feeling at the back of his mind that he'd made a couple of wrong moves that afternoon. He'd clinched a bargain that maybe shouldn't have been clinched, and he hadn't clinched a date with Virginia Lacey. The latter fact irritated him more than the former.

He drank a few beers in the bar, watching the cockroaches climb up the wall, and went to bed. He woke late. M'Wanga was knocking urgently on his bedroom door. He handed him an envelope with the presidential crest and then beckoned him to the window. Drawn up outside was a huge, custom-built red Buick station wagon with *Rutherford's Airline* and *by Appointment to the President of Kajandi* in gold letters on the side. Inside the envelope was a gilt-embossed card on which was written: *A small token of esteem and friendship from Naji Gawaka.*

While his unbelievable luck lasted, and before he even tried the Buick, Rutherford hurried to the telephone and rang Virginia.

SIX

"The general is very grateful for the gift from the British government, though of course he would prefer it was much larger."

A small titter, led by Nigel Naylor, began circulating round the table via consultants and experts from England and the High Commission staff and stopped abruptly at Tom Bancroft who sat gloomily staring at the table.

"I explained to the general that in no way would we wish to influence him but that he should prepare his own shopping list for the loan." The experts nodded in agreement with the high commissioner. ". . . But of course, now you have had a chance to look round here and talk to ministers, we all want to hear your ideas."

He turned his head in polite invitation to the white-haired expert on his right.

". . . Oil, put the money into prospecting, drilling, extracting."

Bancroft began doodling on his pad, as Sarah Harris cleared her throat. ". . . Agriculture is Kajandi's first priority. The cattle-breeding project at Ruanwela. . . ."

". . . The real wealth of a country is in its young. Education is the key." The man from the British Council spoke with missionary zeal.

". . . Mining potential. . . ."

". . . Manufacturing industry. . . ."

The words floated through Bancroft's mind as though in a dream: "Cost-benefit analysis . . ." "Local costs . . ." "Manpower studies. . . ."

"Have you any ideas, Mr. Bancroft?"

"None, sir."

"Well, then," Hugh Fortescue said, "now everyone's had their say, perhaps we should look at the general's shopping list." He raised his eyebrows in Virginia's direction. "We have it now, I take it, Miss Lacey?"

She held out a thick envelope.

"Thank you, Virginia." Fortescue opened the letter. "Let's see what he says." In his rather gritty voice, he began to read out the items, one by one: "Twelve Saladin armoured cars. Twenty Centurion tanks. Ten vertical take off Harrier fighters. Six Strikemaster light bombers. Two hundred Bren guns. Twelve Vickers anti-tank guns. Twelve four point five inch mortars. One hundred Blowpipe surface-to-air missiles. Two hundred Swingfire surface-to-surface missiles. Ammunition, bombs, rockets etcetera."

There was a complete silence when Fortescue finished. Then the high commissioner said, "The general has got hold of the wrong end of the stick. Aid rules forbid, of course, the buying of weapons. We must ask him to think again."

From around the table, immediately bubbled up again the experts' ideas.

". . . Mining. . . ." ". . . Chemicals. . . ." ". . . Agriculture. . . ."

"THE GENERAL was asking after you the other day. He's puzzled, Craig."

"What about?"

The British high commissioner was again sitting in the American ambassador's office. Outside, the noonday sun turned Joro's tin roofs to silver.

"Why you still don't recognize."

Craig Ogilvie sat back in his seat. "Well, Hugh, he must be aware of the continuing stories of disturbances and worse amongst the Assangi."

"According to the general, those *Washington Mail* journalists are telling lies. The north has never been quieter." Fortescue paused. "Last week, the general made a proposal. You may know that he has his own personal pilot—a chap called Rutherford—and he flies around the country doing what you call whistle-stop visits."

"I did know."

"All part of his Unify Kajandi campaign. What he suggested is that you and I accompany him when he is addressing the Assangi over next weekend and *see for ourselves* just how quiet it is."

The American ambassador shook his head. "Sorry, Hugh."

"The general will be sorry, too. Pity! I'm very much looking forward to it."

THAT SATURDAY, dead on the dot of nine, Rutherford lifted the Skytruck off the main runway at Joro, and went into a screaming turn to port.

He had been kept so busy flying the general all over Kajandi that he hadn't yet managed his date with Virginia Lacey in his new Buick station wagon. He was always being called out at a moment's notice, but at least now he knew his new employer's tastes. Gawaka was an aviation enthusiast who loved panache in his flying.

"This pilot of mine, Hugh!" The general looked round from the right hand seat. "He is mad fighter-boy!"

"So I see, Naji."

"He tries everything to make his passengers sick. 'Go ahead,'

I tell him, first time I fly. Loop de loop, spin. Everything . . . he try everything to make Naji sick. And then he says to me, 'Excuse me please, General . . . I feel a liddle sick myself!'"

Even above the shrill whistling of the engines, as the Skytruck came out of the tight climbing turn and levelled off over Tissa Lake, could be heard the roar of Gawaka's laugh.

"How, 'bout yu, Hugh? Yu feel all right?" Fortescue managed a nod and a green smile. "Dat's my boy! Now we really going to enjoy ourselves, eh?"

Behind Fortescue an Assangi tracker called Jumo was being quietly and decorously sick into a flamboyant red and green handkerchief. He was there to look after the black *chop* boxes, cases of whisky and gin, oil stoves, safari tents, beds, Thompson lamps, rifles, cartridges, recorders and amplifying equipment.

Their first destination as they flew north was the village of Poda, a collection of brown mud huts with beehive thatch around a dozen larger buildings made of the local stone. Rutherford put the nose down, scaring a herd of Thomson's gazelle off into the forest. Then he put the wheels down and set the aircraft onto the school playing fields opposite a waving crowd.

Jumo opened the door. General Naji Gawaka in his blue uniform burst out of the Skytruck, both hands high above his head.

They all gathered round him in a half circle—men in army overcoats and rain-matted felt hats; in filthy mackintoshes and monkey-skin cloaks. The native chiefs wore their feathered headdresses, gold earrings hanging from the long lobes of their ears. Most of the women were in bright orange or green cloths, but some were naked, carrying babies at their breasts, while the children ran around in scraps of string and cloth.

Of what the general said to them, Rutherford had only the vaguest idea—recognizing only the odd word, *jambo* (hello) and *pombe* (beer), Kajandi *moja* (one Kajandi) and of course *uhuru* (freedom).

Then it was back into the aircraft. That first day, they visited three large villages, a small town and a co-operative settlement. On each occasion, the drill was the same. On the last stop of the

74

day, Fortescue stood beside Rutherford under the starboard wing. The sun was disappearing in a blaze of scarlet and green. A full moon, white as milk, had risen above the forest. A quiet congregation sat on the ground, listening to General Gawaka.

Fortescue said, "Have you seen anything so peaceful? He's telling them that great riches will be theirs. For down inside the ground—this is where he stamps his feet and digs in his heels—there are jewels and oil and all manner of wealth. And their white friends with their great technical skills will show them how to unlock this treasure-house."

They took off and flew just above the dark forest. Fifteen minutes later, they found a flat clearing with a stream beside it. Rutherford landed on the short grass.

Then, in the general's words, "Ever'body mucking in together", the pilot helped Jumo erect the tents, while Gawaka and Fortescue armed with *pangas* and axes went into the bush to cut down thorn bush and bamboo.

Within an hour, they were sitting in front of a crackling fire. Behind them, a kerosene refrigerator was making ice and cooling drinks. The menu was lamb chops and yams which the general insisted on cooking himself in billy-cans. "Dis shop stuff," he complained. "Id is not the same. Tomorrow, Jumo, we will shoot something tastier."

Savouring cool whisky and warming his tired limbs, Rutherford stared at the fire and listened to Gawaka's plans. Where they were sitting, he would build a safari camp with a game reserve around it. Over to the west would be the uranium mines.

It was past midnight before the general decided it was time for bed. Rutherford checked over the dark Skytruck before turning in. He seemed hardly to have laid his head on the pillow of his camp bed than there was a roar from outside. His tent was jiggling in the half-light above him, and Gawaka could be heard shouting to grab a towel and come down to the river.

The general naked looked even more enormous than in his uniform. He was standing in mid-stream when Rutherford arrived, his trunk as thick as a mahogany tree, a rippling of rapids being stopped dead in their tracks by the twin brown rocks of his vast backside. Beside him, Hugh Fortescue looked as silvery and slender as a eucalyptus tree.

The water was icy—fresh-melted snow from the mountains. The three of them splashed around. By the time they emerged, Jumo had bacon and eggs ready and steaming hot coffee.

They ate hungrily before setting off through the bush with Jumo leading. They saw wild pig running. Twice they came across the platter dents of elephants' feet, and heard the roar of lions.

Then a herd of Thomson's gazelle, golden in the sun and with snowy white underbellies, went mincing delicately towards a thicket of yellow thorn trees. The general raised his twin-barrel shotgun and fired. From six hundred yards, he dropped the leader dead in his tracks. Startled, the rest of the herd bounded off into the forest.

Jumo went forward to skin the deer, taking the tastiest meat and leaving the rest for the vultures. As they made their way back to camp, Gawaka was saying that he could not bear to kill. For food, yes. But even now, he had been assailed by sadness for "dat fine beast".

At Akarda, capital of the Assangi country, a crowd of thousands had assembled at the airport. All the chiefs were there. There was total silence as the general spoke—they appeared to be listening intently to every word. Before he left, he had them laughing with him. He grabbed a large Assangi woman in a red cloth and a polka-dotted blouse, and began doing the High Life dance.

The general remained on the top of his form for the rest of the trip. His energy was enormous. After making speeches all day, he could still talk half the night.

There was only one slightly discordant note. That was on the way home to Joro. They were flying at 5000 feet in the clear. Gawaka was in the righthand seat, talking to Fortescue behind.

Suddenly, a couple of miles ahead, Rutherford caught sight of what appeared to be a hole burnt in the middle of the foliage. Grey wisps of smoke shimmered upwards in the hot sunshine. Through his open window, he could actually smell scorching.

His first thought was that it was a forest fire. Then he saw crumbled mud walls, blackened thatch, a pattern of round holes.

He was putting the nose hard down to take a closer look when suddenly it lifted sharply.

The general's conversation with the high commissioner had ceased. He had his hands on the co-pilot's controls and was pulling hard back.

The Skytruck shot upwards.

"Now it is my turn to fly!" Gawaka turned his head back again towards the high commissioner, a huge smile on his face. "Watch out, Hugh . . . I am real kamikaze pilot!"

BACK IN HIS office at the High Commission, Hugh Fortescue sat dictating a dispatch to Virginia.

". . . We spent the entire time in the middle of the Assangi country with no protection. There was not the slightest sign of disturbance or opposition. This peacefulness was powerful ammunition for me in pointing out that Gawaka's concentration on weapons on his shopping list was misplaced. He was not entirely convinced, but I think I made some headway. He has become very aviation-minded, and this enthusiasm might be channelled away from jet fighters into the possible provision of a Starjet as a start for his own civil airline. . . ."

"HERE! Turn off the road here!"

Virginia Lacey pointed to a track that ran to the left off the red laterite road. "It's all right," she smiled at Rutherford's expression. "The surface is quite good. It forks farther on and one part leads to Owitara village. It won't damage your beautiful Buick."

The date with Virginia had eventually materialized. The general had become grounded in a Planning Conference, and Rutherford was released. Now he swung the Buick onto the softer shaley surface. She was right. The track surface was firm. Already through the open windows he could smell the lake. Jacaranda and eucalyptus, acacia trees and banana palms sent a dappled shade which was a relief from the unbroken sunlit glare of the road.

They had driven along in holiday mood. She had peeled him fruit. They had pointed out to each other sights such as the sausage trees with heavy fruits shaped like giant loofahs, marabou storks flying low overhead. Slowing down for a family of monkeys to cross the road, Rutherford thought he had not felt like this since he was a boy.

And then, as the road wound gently downhill, he suddenly caught a shimmer of the lake through thick leathery leaves. "This it?"

"Yes. Round the next curve you fork left again and then you'll see it. The right fork leads to the village. Go slowly, then you'll get the full effect."

Obediently, he took his foot off the accelerator and followed the bend in the track. As he did so, the whole vista of the lake burst upon him. It was shaped like the head of a spear, the edges a steely shadow, the rest blazing with burnished light. There was a narrow skein of pale sand just below them. And at the far side, coming right down to the lake's edge blossomed shrubs of pinks and reds and oranges and yellows.

Rutherford stopped the Buick and switched off the engine. Jungle sounds—the screech of birds, the cry of wild animals in the forest—underlined the quiet. The visual beauty moved him profoundly.

But something moved him still more. Virginia was watching him intently. And the expression on her young face was that expectant eager one of an adult offering a child something rare and valuable.

"Well?" she asked him.

"Breathtaking," he said. "I couldn't begin to describe it."

She sat back with a contented sigh. The place for the picnic had been her idea—Owitwara Lake up in the northern hills. She had provided the picnic basket, and bottles clinked invitingly as they bumped the last hundred yards down to the strip of sand.

Here, the heavy scent of tropical blossoms mixed with the smell of the water. Rutherford had a sudden irrational feeling of danger. Not this time from sudden death and search and prison. But from her. And his awareness of her.

He stopped the car in the shade of a sandy overhang. She got out before he had time to open the door for her, kicked off her

78

sandals and walked towards the lake, a slim figure with the breeze ruffling her hair and whipping her checked cotton skirt against her thighs.

He hauled out the picnic basket and then strolled towards her. At first he thought she was simply staring at the opposite bank, then he saw she was staring down at the sand. Tyre tracks had bitten into its damp surface.

"Land-Rover, by the look of it," he said. "Forestry chaps?"

"Could be," she nodded. "Or someone taking the long way round to the village."

He felt oddly reassured by the presence of other people. As if he wasn't quite Adam in the Garden about to make man's first irretrievable mistake. "I suggest we swim first and then eat."

She nodded and undid her skirt and blouse. Underneath she wore a very brief bikini. Her legs were long and tanned.

Though he'd not led the life of a monk, women had always been secondary to his job, and egotistically, he supposed, he could take them or leave them. With the accent on leave them. Now he wasn't so sure of the philosophy.

For the first few minutes they stood up to their waists in the water, watching a goliath heron coming down onto the lake in a rush of water, with its legs thrust forward to brake.

"Couldn't have done better myself," Rutherford smiled, unconsciously dropping his hand onto Virginia's shoulder. She said suddenly, "Let's swim, I'm getting hungry."

She struck out into the lake, keeping parallel to the shore. Then she turned over and lay on her back staring up at the sky. He trod water beside her. "Weaverbirds." She lifted a dripping arm and pointed to a flock of yellow and brown birds flying excitedly to and fro. "If you like to afterwards, I can show you some of their nests in the trees."

Her grey eyes reflected the cloudless blue of the sky. He leaned forward and kissed her wet mouth lightly. "Anything you say. I'm in your hands."

Just for a second the clear grey eyes reflected something darker than the sky. Then expertly she flipped herself over and swam for the shore.

Half an hour later, they had eaten their lunch and were sipping ice-cold chablis. It was all very civilized and intimate. Too intimate. Rutherford leaned forward, and pulled her to him, sliding his hands down her back, feeling the smooth skin of her warm breasts against his bare chest. He fastened his lips over hers, kissing her properly for the first time.

She returned his kiss. She didn't draw away. It was he who pulled back from the cliff edge.

"Come on," he said, getting to his feet, and pulling on his trousers over his swimming trunks. His voice even in his own ears sounded over-casual and hearty. "Those weaverbirds' nests, I'd like to see them. We don't want to head for home too late."

"It's quite a way."

"Suits me."

There was a rough track leading into the forest with just enough room for them to walk side by side. For the next half hour they said little. There were thorns and bamboo thickets to cope with. Farther on, they passed through a deserted *shamba*, the houses crumbled, the fields neglected and full of weeds.

This was the village that Virginia had mentioned. Now they began looking up into the trees for the weaverbirds' pendulous nests. Suddenly Rutherford stopped. "Isn't that one?"

He pointed at a shadow hanging from the crook of a mahogany tree in a little clearing to the right of the path.

Pushing aside the elephant grass and bamboo, he began walking towards it. And then he saw. He turned quickly, trying to stop Virginia.

But it was too late—he could tell that by the sudden freezing of her body. He took hold of her hand, began pulling her back to the path when a weird horn wailed out, followed by the sound of footsteps.

From the direction of the deserted village came a troop of Kajandi soldiers guarding a line of African men and women— Assangi by the look of their high foreheads—connected by a long rope round their necks.

Rutherford pushed Virginia behind the bamboo. Seconds later the little procession passed within a few feet of them, moved into the clearing and stopped at an upright piece of limestone rock in the centre that had been roughly chiselled into a pillar. Instead of being grey with lichen it was stained dark red-brown.

Rutherford knew what it was—a juju stone. He knew what was going to happen, and he recognized their danger. He pulled Virginia down on the ground under the camouflage of the waving elephant grass.

There was an uncanny silence. No birds called, no chattering of monkeys. Nothing moved. The sun was high overhead, and a hot damp smell was coming from the steaming earth.

Then the horn rang out again. Another procession came into the clearing. These men and women walked together in loose formation, led by a man whose wizened black face was marked heavily with grey *wamba*, feathers over his white woolly hair, a monkey-skin coat over his shoulders and rows of brass bangles round his wrists and ankles.

Some of the soldiers had taken out *panga* knives and were cutting down thorn bush and scrub. Underneath that same mahogany tree which had first attracted Rutherford's attention, they lit a fire, and a thick cloud of aromatic smoke came curling upwards, mercifully covering the disembowelled corpse that hung by a rope high in the trees.

RUTHERFORD drove down the red road back to Joro like a bat out of hell. He kept his left hand on the wheel and his right hand on Virginia's cold ones. His eyes were fixed dead ahead on the road. He was programmed as though for an automatic landing. Get the hell out of this nightmare, and get Virginia home.

Rutherford pressed his foot harder still on the accelerator, as though if they only could go fast enough, they could escape those terrible pictures. There had been a hideous oath-taking. But an oath to whom? To Gawaka? Those Africans who were not bound had been allowed to go then. In their place from under the mahogany trees came those linked by that dreadful rope necklace. The medicine man had chanted higher and louder, had begun dancing in front of them in a convulsive ballet.

Rutherford half closed his eyes. He could not bear to think

about it. He tried to concentrate on his driving, but up it came, above the roar of the Buick's engine, the shrieks and screams of the tortured Assangi women.

Then it had been the men's turn. They were arranged in a line, one behind the other. A rock was put in the hands of all except the first man. . . . Half an hour later, nothing remained in the clearing but the acrid smoke and the corpses and the vultures circling in the sky.

Rutherford's grip on Virginia's hand tightened. But she didn't respond. She kept her eyes lowered, her hands clasped desperately together, as if holding them like that she held her whole body, which might otherwise fall apart like a stringless puppet. Under her light tan, her face was drained of colour.

"Virginia?" He shook her rigid hands, and she turned her head and looked at him, her eyes so darkened that he couldn't see the irises.

If only she'd shout and scream and even have hysterics! His foot was still pressed hard down on the floor, and the red dust flew up from under the Buick's wheels. The sun had set by the time they arrived at her place. He leapt out and opened the door for her. She stepped out quietly.

"Key?" He held out his hand. She opened her bag and dropped the key into his palm. As he walked the two steps up to the door, he asked, "Where's your boy?"

"He's got a place at the back. He finishes at five." Her voice was steady but she slurred her words like someone who'd been drinking.

"Want me to get him?"

"No." Then she turned to Rutherford and managed a vague unfocused smile. "Thanks. . . ." She raised her hand as if saying goodnight.

"I'm not leaving."

She didn't argue. She wandered into the comfortably furnished room where she'd offered him a drink when he picked her up a lifetime ago. She sat like a stranger on the edge of a chair.

"I'm going to run you a bath. Then you're off to bed. But first I'm getting you a drink. Where d'you hide your liquor?"

82

"Over there in the corner. The bathroom's the other side of the hall."

On a government-issue table was a silver tray laden with bottles and glasses. He half-filled two glasses with brandy and carried them over to her.

"Come on! We both need this." He waited till she lifted the glass to her mouth. He heard her teeth rattle against the rim. "Down it in one!"

He tossed his own back, poured her another and then walked across the hall, found the bathroom and turned on the water. Then he went in search of the bedroom. The boy had pulled down the blinds and it was in darkness.

Rutherford switched on the bedside lamp, turned back the bed. A nightgown was already laid out on it. He picked it up, opened a wardrobe full of clothes, found her housecoat and returned to the sitting room.

She looked less taut. A faint colour, the brandy probably, had come up in patches on her cheeks.

"Bath," he said, standing over her and thrusting her nightgown and housecoat into her hands. "Don't stay in it too long. Five minutes. I'll time you."

She tried a feeble joke as she stood up. "Are all pilots bossy?"

"They are. And don't lock the door! You might feel faint."

"You know, I'm really all right."

"But you'd be better if you'd let go. Don't bottle it up. Howl."

She shook her head and disappeared into the bathroom. Five minutes later she emerged, her face flushed, her hair clinging damply round her forehead.

"You've been awfully kind, Bill. But go home now."

"I'm tucking you into bed before I go." He shooed her into the bedroom, and quite dispassionately watched her take off her housecoat and climb into bed.

He sat on a corner of it, and touched her damp hair.

"You've been so good, Bill. . . ."

Then suddenly her face crumpled, broke like a plaster cast. She buried her head against his chest, and flung her arms round him, rocking and sobbing.

He moved with her. The rocking slid imperceptibly into a different rhythm. He stretched himself on the bed beside her, kissed her full and hard on her mouth. "Virginia, I love you." He was not sure then whether he did nor not. But it was his way of warning her what was going to happen.

It was release. Release from horror and pain and thinking. Release in a velvet trap. Release and imprisonment.

RUTHERFORD woke suddenly.

The bedroom was still dark. He was drenched in sweat. Not with the heat, but the nightmare. God, it was vivid!

He let out a long sigh. Virginia had drifted off to sleep with her head resting on his arm. Yesterday's horror had caught them both off guard. They had clasped each other for comfort like sole survivors from some global catastrophe.

He had whispered that he loved her. Just as he had whispered the old-fashioned endearments he remembered from childhood. He had been touched when, apparently soothed, she had gone off to sleep. But love was an alien word. It was a bit in your mouth. And once it was over your tongue, you were bridled and broken.

Yet Virginia, he would have sworn, was not the girl to make love mechanically or without feeling. He turned his head and brushed her hair with his lips.

"I'm not asleep," she whispered suddenly, raising herself onto her elbow.

"Then you should be. Try to go to sleep again."

"I can't." She leaned across him and caught hold of his left hand. "What time is it?"

He looked at the glowing of his wristwatch. "Twenty past three. Do you want me to scarper before your boy comes?"

She hesitated. Rutherford felt a little twist of jealousy and suspicion. He wondered if her boy was used to seeing men here. But almost immediately, he dismissed the thought. Perhaps because he wanted to.

"I'd like you to stay. You make me feel . . ." she broke off and shivered as if memory of the picnic suddenly flooded in. "If you want to stay, that is."

84

"If I want to! Of course, I want to!" He pulled her down against him and buried his face in her hair. "You never know what they'll do next. Why don't you come and live inside the walls? You'd be safer."

"Things like that go on in the city, too. *You* should know."

"But I didn't know it was as bad as that. . . . Does Fortescue know?" he asked her after a heavy silence.

She shrugged her shoulders. "He knows and doesn't know. He's got to filter out what he *daren't* see."

"That's being a diplomat!" Rutherford exclaimed bitterly. He felt a wave of nausea sweep over him. Then anger. Not just at *what* he'd seen, but that he *had* seen it. It was unfair. Monstrous! A threat to his independence and isolation. "Fortescue should speak to Gawaka," he said, laying the blame with relief at the high commissioner's door. "It's up to him. They're buddies."

She gave an exasperated little sigh. "It's not as easy as that. He does his best. But things are, well," she hesitated, "precarious."

His anger gave way to a sense of foreboding. "They wouldn't turn on foreigners, would they?"

"I wouldn't think so." But she didn't sound sure.

"You shouldn't go driving round on your own," he muttered irritably. "I'll wait and drive you to the office."

The eagerness of her acceptance surprised him—as if it were all part of some pre-ordained plan. But it was Saturday, her day at the old Indian embassy. She would like him to drive her there. It would be a good opportunity for her to show him around.

SEVEN

Rutherford parked the station wagon outside the old Indian embassy. A dusty eucalyptus tree rustled above them as they got out and hand in hand, walked into a bare hall. A group of Kajandi boys stared at Rutherford curiously.

"A friend," she still held his hand, "Captain Rutherford. He flies aeroplanes." She pointed upwards. Their big eyes followed her finger politely.

"How many boys do you usually get in?"

"Thirty or forty. We don't actually turn any away. In there," she pointed to a large room beyond, furnished with some tattered armchairs, "is their day room."

In the kitchen a fat mammy with a yellow scarf tied round her head was busy over a charcoal stove. Upstairs the rooms were furnished only with mattresses on the floor.

"And how is it all supported?" He felt like a sightseer asking questions of the guide.

"We run bazaars and collections. The government leaves us alone. We have an Asian, Joseph, who is caretaker. This is his office here."

She unlocked a door and led the way inside a tiny office in which were two chairs and a desk. She locked the door carefully behind them. "He's not here today."

Rutherford stood at the door uneasily. Something of the oneness that he had felt with her had fragmented. She said to him suddenly, "Come in here, Bill."

He had not noticed there was another door leading off the office. He followed her down two steps into not so much a room as a big, windowless cupboard. There was a mat of rushes on the floor, a chair and a bed beside the right wall.

A man was lying there, an Asian in shorts and singlet and plimsolls.

"This is where Joseph sleeps," Virginia was saying in a matter-of-fact way, when the man turned his head.

At first, Rutherford didn't recognize him. He had lost weight and skipped the rest of his middle years into old age.

"Wahindi! What are you doing here?"

But he already knew. An inescapable chain reaction of terrifying proportions was beginning in his mind. Again he could smell banana porridge. He was back in the kitchen of the Hotel Afrique.

That figure whispering in the gaslight had been no Asian boy.

Suddenly he grasped Virginia by her loose hair and jerked her head back. "Grey eyes!" he said. They looked back defiantly into his. "You!" he said softly. "So it was you all the time!"

"Yes."

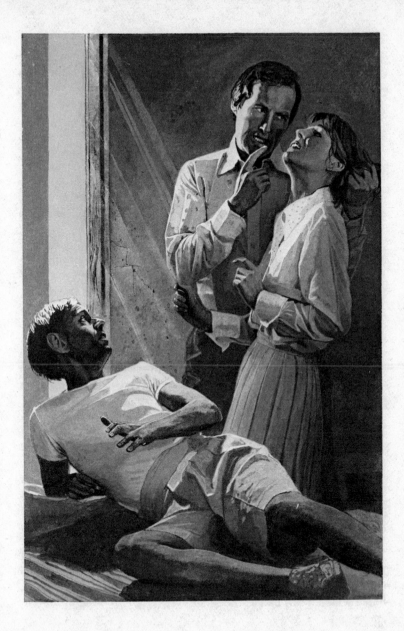

"Seeing all, hearing all, saying nothing!"

"They will kill me, Captain Rutherford, unless—"

Rutherford ignored Wahindi. He had not yet taken in the magnitude of the disaster that had befallen him. All he could think of was what a fool he had been. He had been taken for a ride. He had fallen for the oldest whoremongering trick in the world.

He pulled her head hard back. But she ignored what he was doing. "I've got to get him away," she said. "Will you take him?"

"So you want the Nakungu and Kassilolo exercises repeated?"

She nodded. "There's no other way."

"Why do you bother to tell me? In case this time I *did* look?"

The big grey eyes stared calmly back at him. "No. Because I didn't want you to be simply used."

"I see." His voice was bitter. "I was to be given the privilege of making the choice?" For a full minute, he said nothing. He released her hair. Her head jerked forward, her eyes were still on him. Shadowy in his corner, Wahindi lay silent.

Rutherford closed his eyes. Choice? He gritted his teeth. He had been given no choice at all! After what he had seen yesterday, how could he leave Wahindi?

How the hell had Virginia got mixed up in this? And why? He wanted to shake her till her teeth rattled, make her stop, pull out of this suicidal game. Yet some deep wound inside refused to allow him. She had cold-bloodedly exploited his feelings for her.

"You're going to Bakhari next week. Will you take him?" Virginia asked.

"I'll have to, won't I?" Rutherford replied. "After all, you paid me last night in advance."

It gave him some strange perverse comfort that she lifted her hand and slapped him hard across his face.

FIFTEEN MINUTES later, they sat alone together in the little office. A hopeful Wahindi had been sent to get his lunch.

"How the hell did you get involved in this? You of all people?" Rutherford's anger had cooled to bitterness. "You've got no interest in Kajandi politics. . . . Politics are the same here as home. One lot's as bad as the other."

She shook her head. It was difficult to explain.

"Try!" Rutherford folded his arms across his chest. "We've got nothing else to do at present."

She said, "The escape organization began in Moto's time."

"Moto heap bad fellow, too?"

"It's not funny!"

"Christ, it's not! That was just the condemned man wise-cracking to his executioners." He glowered at her. "All right, I get your point, there was oppression then."

"But nothing like this."

"And when did you decide you'd do something about it?"

"I didn't. I just got involved. Through this Home. About a year ago, our Indian manager helped one of the boys' fathers to escape over the border into Nigeria. He brought him here. There were others. Then, when the real terror began, people began coming here to hide. I was contacted by an organizer. I was told Wahindi would help at the airport."

"Through Wahindi that first poor bastard was put on my Sky-truck? Don't you care that I've got him on my conscience?"

"But there was no alternative. He was too well known to try any other way."

"You'll soon be saying, at least he died quickly."

"I'll say it now." Her face flushed. "You *saw* those others."

Rutherford said nothing for a moment. "And you, my friend, also lumbered me with Kassilolo, and let me almost kill myself?"

She said nothing.

"Someone tipped you the general was organizing a nest-egg in Switzerland. That he wouldn't trust his loot to a Kajandi pilot. And that no one naturally could be allowed to look at the cargo. So that, too, was worth a try?"

"It was, yes." She looked up at him defiantly.

"After all, if I had killed myself, what's one expendable bush pilot compared to your Scarlet Pimpernel racket?"

"We didn't realize about the loading."

"I'd die nice and quickly. And who knows, the general might have another shot at exporting his . . . what was it? Gold, by the weight of it."

"Gold and ivory."

He eyed her bitterly. "It's a wonder you didn't ask me to knock that off as well." And then, as an odd expression flickered in her eyes, "Or is Mr. Johnson one of your band of brothers?"

She was silent.

"*Is* he?"

"He must be, though I don't know for sure. I know very little about individuals. It's a sort of grass-roots effort, passed by word of mouth. Because people are frightened, for themselves and their families. You get asked and you do something. As," she added slowly, "I'm asking you now." When he made no answer, she went on, "Yesterday . . ."

"I've had enough of yesterday," he interrupted. But he wasn't altogether referring to the massacre. Yesterday he had been used by her. "It might well have been an isolated incident. Kajandi is just a bunch of warring tribes. It *could* have been some sort of private feud."

"It wasn't. I *know*. Though this is the first I've seen." She pushed back her chair and began pacing up and down the little office. "There is a bridge," she said in a low voice, "over the Ruanga, just north of Joro, where executions take place every Saturday. Not for any reason. Just because they are Assangis. Then the bodies are pushed over the parapet to float downstream."

"But Gawaka wants peace with the Assangi."

"If they're all dead, there will be peace."

"I heard him talking to them. Quite unarmed."

"Because," she stabbed a finger at him, "in the forests behind were units of Gawaka's old brigade, and thirty tanks!"

"Have you proof?"

"Didn't you see bombed villages when you were flying over?"

Rutherford suddenly remembered the black scar in the forest, and Gawaka pulling back sharply on the stick. He held his head in his hands. What a bloody mess! Why in God's name hadn't he stayed where he belonged in Gittisham? Why had he ever returned?

The silence dragged on. Then Virginia said, "Do you still blame me for involving you?"

90

"Yes."

She paused. "Shall you take Wahindi to Bakhari?"

"Yes. I go next Friday." He got up. "That all?"

"Yes." She licked her lips. "Except to ask you, if . . ." Her voice trailed.

He walked to the door. "If I'll ever forgive you?"

She nodded.

"The answer's no." He turned the handle. That dreadful stench of banana porridge drifted up from the kitchen. "Like the smell of *matoke*," he threw over his shoulder, "I'll hate you till the day I die."

It struck him as he hurried out that that wouldn't necessarily mean he would hate her for very long.

A FEW DAYS later the telephone rang in the British High Commission. It was the American ambassador.

"Hugh . . . we're leaving."

"Craig, whatever . . . ?"

"You probably know that the Kajandi reports in the *Washington Mail* abruptly stopped. We now know why. Those two journalists are dead."

Fortescue said slowly, "Have you proof?"

"The best. Their heads were sent to the embassy. In a parcel."

There was a horrified silence. "Craig . . . I'm sorry. Are you sure there hasn't been some mistake?"

"No mistake."

"Look, Craig, I'll take it up with the general."

He did straightaway, going round to Government House. The general could not have been more concerned. What had clearly happened, he explained to Fortescue, was that some of his overzealous supporters, no doubt mad with anger at the reporters' misrepresentations, had taken it upon themselves to dispose of these men. It was very wrong of them, and those who had done it would be sought out and punished according to the law.

That conversation Fortescue reported to Ogilvie. But by that time, the Americans were already packing, and within two days, their embassy was shuttered.

"HERE! *Quickly!*"

Rutherford drove the station wagon onto the pavement, and opened the passenger door. A dark shadow leapt forward, and Wahindi scrambled into the back and stretched himself prone.

Rutherford slammed down the aluminium floor, bundled two bags, a packing case and his briefcase on top of it, let in the clutch and went bumping forward over the cobbles of Ararat Street. His mouth felt as dry as road dust, his heart hammered louder than the Buick's engine. But so far, so good. Pick-up had gone according to plan. "About our date," Virginia had telephoned the Hotel Afrique. "Could we meet at the corner of Ararat Street at seven?"

It was a precaution against linking his Buick with the old Indian embassy. But no precaution now could stop linking him with the escape organization. He was in it up to his neck.

With his foot pressed hard on the accelerator, he drove sharp right to the west end of Gawaka Avenue, and into Independence Square. His foot eased off the accelerator, and with his right hand he touched the Luger in his trouser pocket. He had bought it yesterday with a government permit along with a rifle and some game equipment in the gunsmith's on Palace Avenue. If the guards found Wahindi, he was going to bloody well shoot it out, and make a run for it.

He swung the wheel of the Buick hard left. Ahead now was the South Gate. The queue of cars waiting to be searched had already started. The guards were being particularly thorough now the Americans were leaving. Rutherford slowed behind an ancient green mammy-wagon, and wound down his window. In front of him, the engines of the other vehicles throbbed and smoked. God, what a way to go, he thought. What a way to run an airline! Rutherford's ruin. To get chopped to pieces in an African blood bath.

There was a revving of engines. The procession moved up another five yards. He counted the vehicles. Six to go.

Suddenly a commotion started. Torches flashed. Guards shouted. A cry of triumph. A scream. They'd got someone—an Assangi by the look of the high forehead and the long neck. There was the flash of *panga* knives. It was like a dress rehearsal for Rutherford.

It was now or never.

Rutherford switched on the blue blipper roof light, swung the Buick round the mammy-wagon, then with the headlamps fully on and his thumb on the horn he accelerated past the waiting cars into the jaws of the guarded gate.

There was the running of heavy boots and the gleam of fixed bayonets as a line of guards came up to meet him.

He braked to a shuddering stop and wound down his window. "What the bloody hell's going on?" he yelled. "Why are you keeping me waiting?" A dozen soldiers swarmed round the Buick, led by a surly officious sergeant. "Don't you know who *I* am?"

The commotion round the Assangi died down. Ringed round with *panga* blades, the prisoner and his escort stared at Rutherford wide-eyed.

The pilot took out his torch, focused it on the Buick's side: *by Appointment to the President of Kajandi*.

He roared at the surly sergeant, "Can't you read? You are holding up the business of the State! I will report you to General Gawaka. You . . . you sergeant fellah, what's your name?"

Then he caught sight of a familiar face—a guard he knew. "Awoli, my friend! Tell this stupid sergeant who I am! It is very urgent! Open up the gates and let me through!"

Awoli began haranguing the sergeant in Swahili. Muttering started amongst the rest of the guard. All except the sergeant began smiling at him—uncertain, sheepish.

He put his thumb back on the horn button. He revved the engine up to full power and down again, up again, down again. Then he let in the clutch and began to move forward.

The line of guards skipped out of the way. Awoli and the sergeant raced each other to be the first to open the gate.

Blue light blipping, horn still full blast, Rutherford put his foot hard down on the accelerator, and shot out of Joro.

He kept his foot down all the way to the airport. There the guards knew him, and let him through without question. He left the Buick in the car park, sauntered to the African Airways counter, picked up his papers and told the clerk he'd be leaving for Bakhari in ten minutes.

Then he drove out to the ramp. He stopped on the other side of the Skytruck to the ever-circling searchlight, backed the Buick up to the door. Then he scrambled up into the aircraft.

The cargo had been loaded, but there was no sign of any maintenance workers. Deliberately, he was early. Yet haste now could be fatal. He waited till the finger of light had touched the Skytruck and travelled on before lifting the back of the station wagon, then the floor.

Out in the wink of an eye flitted Wahindi and was aboard and under the tarpaulins before two overalled maintenance workers arrived.

Rutherford swore long and loud at them for not being there before. All his pent-up tension exploded over them. He slammed down the back of the Buick in anger that was in no way simulated. But it was with himself he was angry. He dropped the car keys into the senior worker's hand and told him to drive it to the car park, lock it, leave the keys at the African Airways desk. The other man stayed to see him off.

He couldn't get away quick enough. Kajandi tower seemed unbearably slow. "Echo X-Ray . . . cleared for take-off. Cleared to climb on course to Bakhari. Report at cruising altitude."

Seconds later he was pelting down the runway and climbing into the tranquillity of the star-filled windless night.

"WE'VE DONE IT!"

Thirty minutes later at ten thousand feet, they crossed the Kajandi frontier and headed northeast over the desert.

"We've done it, Wahindi!" Rutherford felt foolishly, wildly elated as the engineer slipped into the righthand seat. He had snatched Wahindi alive from the madmen with their *panga* knives. He had done it for a mixture of motives maybe, the strongest of which was that there didn't seem any way out, but he had done it by choice. He had evened up the score, blurred the memory of Nakungu.

"How did *you* get involved?" he asked Wahindi as the mechanic sat gazing up at the arch of stars. "Did you mean to?"

"No indeed, sir." Wahindi shrugged. "But events involved me.

94

I have an uncle who needed to leave very quickly. He went to Nigeria in the cargo hold of a Bristol freighter. Then recently things are worse. They ask me to help more."

"Who's *they?*"

"Just people. We do not mention names. People letting a man stay the night and not asking questions. Letting him walk with you and your cattle towards the border and not crying *stranger.*"

"Who directs?"

"I do not know. It is only very small. There is no headquarters. Help is like bush fires. . . ." He hesitated for the right word.

"Spontaneous?"

"Something like that."

"And Virginia Lacey?"

"Miss Lacey sees many boys that are in trouble at the Boys' Home. Then after a little while, they tell Miss Virginia their real story. Help me, they say, or I die."

"And that is what Nakungu said?"

"And Kassilolo. With Nakungu, it was very difficult, they had almost caught him. The only hope was by air that night. This was when I told Miss Virginia about you. I told her that you were an honourable man."

"I refused to take him," Rutherford said.

"I do not blame you," Wahindi said. "It was so sudden. But the plan for Nakungu . . . it had to proceed whether you agreed or not. They got him to the airport strapped under Miss Virginia's car. I kept the Skytruck in the hangar waiting. When I saw you that night, and asked you if you would see yourself off, that was what I had done. We got Nakungu hidden as best we could. Then the Skytruck was towed out to the ramp. And I left."

"You had to be away to escape suspicion?"

Wahindi nodded. "But once Nakungu was discovered, that was it. They knew I must have been involved."

"What will you do at Bakhari?"

"I have friends, Captain. A car will be waiting for me."

For the next two hours, they flew on mainly in silence. The weather remained clear, and they could see Bakhari over fifty miles away. Rutherford came straight in for a landing.

95

On the ground, Wahindi said, "I thank you, Captain Rutherford. I am so grateful that—"

But Rutherford cut him short. "It was just your turn, that's all, Wahindi. It may be my turn next, who knows?" He shook the engineer's hand. "It's a rich life. Good luck in it!"

As Rutherford headed south again next day for Kajandi, for a man going back to hell he went with extraordinary lightness of heart. For no longer did he ask himself how Virginia could have involved him. He asked himself how in fact she could have not.

THE SUN had gone down in a blaze of red before Rutherford arrived back in Joro. Through the fast-deepening dusk, the runway lights glimmered like candles. The airport was quiet enough. Too quiet. Not another soul was around when he taxied up to the hangar. And very soon, he thought, with a lift of his spirits, he would see Virginia.

There were few people in the terminal building. The African Airways clerk took his flight papers and gave him the Buick's keys with a courteous smile. He felt the man's eyes on him as he walked echoingly across the marble floor, and the skin on the back of his neck crawled.

"Good night, Cap'n Rutherford." The guard gave him a perfunctory salute, and put out his hand. Rutherford almost jumped, but the raised hand was only to stifle a yawn.

The Buick was there in the car park. Rutherford forced himself to walk round it like some suspicious dog with a bowl of poisoned meat. He switched on the interior light and looked carefully around. He sniffed, alert for an alien scent. He lifted up the floor at the back in case someone else was hiding there. Then he started her up and accelerated away. The airport road was unnaturally quiet. No cars, just the odd bullock cart. Just when Rutherford should feel safe, he felt uneasy. Now he was obsessed with the fear of what could have happened in Joro while he was away. What if something had happened to Virginia? Relief that Wahindi's escape was successfully accomplished now turned into anxiety for her.

He trod harder on the accelerator, glancing from time to time in his driving mirror, expecting to see the flare of following lights. Christ, he thought, if anyone had told him six months ago that he'd come to this. Rutherford, the loner who never got mixed up *in* anything or *with* anyone. In it up to his eyeballs and sweating it out because of the girl who'd got him into it all!

He took the turn to the right towards Virginia's bungalow. A car came towards him. He decelerated to a crawl, waiting till it had passed before turning in through her bungalow gateway. Quietly he eased the Buick up the little tree-lined drive. With immense relief he saw her Escort parked outside the door. Still with his headlights on, he turned the car full circle, searching. Not a leaf stirred in the still air. The garden was empty. As far as he could tell no one was watching the bungalow. *Yet.*

He switched off everything and got out. A light burned behind the lowered blinds of the sitting room. He slipped like a shadow up the two steps. Before he put his finger on the bell, Virginia opened the door.

Till that moment, he hadn't considered how she would react to him. His last words to her at the old Indian Embassy had been that he hated her. So he did, in a way. Unfortunately, he felt other contrary emotions which were more difficult to express.

As he hesitated, she flung out her arms in a gesture of unfeigned relief. They stood for a moment, locked together. Then she drew him in, closed and bolted the door.

"How did it go?" she asked softly.

"Piece of cake."

"No one stopped you? Asked awkward questions?"

"Not a soul." He followed her into the sitting room. "Only thing was," he perched on the edge of the sofa and rubbed the back of his neck. "I didn't like the quiet when I got here."

"There's a reason for it." She poured three fingers of Scotch, and handed it to him. "King Zazu has died."

Immediate relief that the reason didn't involve her made him smile. "King Zazu? Who's he? Oh, yes, some old Assangi chief who fought the British and lost. Exiled, wasn't he?"

She nodded, poured herself a drink and sat beside him.

"The quiet is because everyone's scared stiff now of what's

going to happen. There's powerful juju attached to the body of the dead king. The Assangi will want his body. Gawaka will try to do it due honour. To be chief mourner. So *he* can assume his mantle. Become Lord of the Assangi."

Rutherford sipped his drink slowly. The drink or being with Virginia or both gave him a dangerous lift. "The corpse is still in London, I presume?"

"Yes. The British government are allowing the body to return to Kajandi. The general has said he will send his own personal pilot with the two empty coffins to collect it."

"Two?"

"That's part of the Assangi burial rites. A silver coffin inside a mahogany one."

Rutherford drained his glass, and held it out for a refill. "I came here," he said, watching her face tenderly as she turned back towards him, "to reason with you. To implore you. If necessary to take you by the hair of your head and *make* you," he paused, "get the hell out of here!"

"I know." She smiled apologetically. "I thought you might."

"But . . ." He took the glass. "*Two* coffins, you said?"

"Two."

"Two *empty* man-size coffins?"

She nodded.

He grinned and lifted his glass.

KING ZAZU'S DEATH had already started off a chain of signals between London and Joro. Both Houses of Parliament heard the news of his death with feelings of distant sorrow tinged with guilt. The reasons for his exile now looked trivial and flimsy.

The transport of the body back to Kajandi, its reception at the airport, the service in the cathedral and the interment in the Royal Tomb had all been precisely organized.

"The British who exiled him, the new government of General Gawaka, the Assangi whose leader he was, the other four tribes of Kajandi shall all be there side by side in united brotherhood, silently to pay respect and homage when King Zazu returns to the Land of his Fathers."

98

So wrote Hugh Fortescue to Central African Department. "The dangers and difficulties of crowd control, of the introduction of differing tribes within Joro can be imagined. It gives a measure of the stature of General Gawaka that he accepts the risks and calmly makes his preparations."

Four London police inspectors had already arrived to give lessons in crowd control. The streets of Joro were packed with soldiers rehearsing, and Ndole jail was packed with potential trouble makers. Other preparations had also been made with especial care. The royal coffins were fashioned in a small workshop on the south side of Joro.

Before Rutherford collected them, with the Buick's windows draped in black curtains, he had gone to a street close to the old Indian embassy. There an Assangi chief and a young Kajandi known to have helped the escape organization slipped in under the floor.

At the workshop, Rutherford saw that the coffins were placed side by side up against the rear door to leave enough space for the floor to be tilted up. As the car proceeded through the streets, behind the drawn curtains, the two men climbed into the coffins. Rutherford drove the Buick at funeral pace through the South Gate.

At the airport, Rutherford backed the Buick right up against the doors of the Skytruck, then moved the coffins himself into the cargo compartment on rollers.

The trip to England was uneventful. Once airborne, the two passengers came out of their coffins. They talked little, both seemed stunned. Once over England they relaxed, took Rutherford's hand and smiled.

It was dark when they arrived at Gittisham. He landed, went round the far taxi track, stopped at a break in the hedge. Within seconds, his passengers had jumped out of the rear door and disappeared into the night. Arrangements had been made for their reception, and they had been instructed on how to get to London.

It was a rather different journey back. The body had been put in the silver coffin which was then placed in the mahogany coffin. Made fast to the floor of the cargo compartment, it was covered by a Kajandi flag on which eight good-humoured young Coldstream guardsmen propped up their bearskins.

Just before he started descent to Joro, Rutherford felt a slight unexpected shimmer of the wings. Two fighters of the Kajandi air force were escorting him in.

Carefully, with the fighters sticking like leeches, Rutherford descended, landed, taxiied towards the ramp. Even above the sound of the engines, he could hear the ululations of the crowd. Prostrate on the ground, they beat the earth with their hands, moaning with grief.

A dais had been erected on which stood General Naji Gawaka with the British high commissioner at his right hand. From two flagpoles flew the Kajandi flag and the Union Jack, at half mast.

The door of the Skytruck was opened. A military band began playing the Kajandi National Anthem. Then the sky was rent apart by a high concerted cry, as the guardsmen, staggering a little under the weight of the multiple coffin, brought King Zazu back to the Land of his Fathers. Now the coffin lids were removed. The body was dressed in the dark blue uniform of a Major-General of the Kajandi army, an exact replica of the one worn by Naji Gawaka. The king's stars and decorations were arranged on his chest, above the red roundel of his cap. For two hours, the crowd filed by to pay their last respects.

Then the coffins were again closed, placed on a gun-carriage and draped with the Kajandi flag. Very slowly six white horses pulled the gun-carriage through the streets to the cathedral. Immediately behind came the state gold Rolls-Royce with the general and the British high commissioner, followed by a procession of cars, twelve tanks, ten armoured cars, trucks of soldiers wearing black armbands, then the crowds of weeping Assangi.

Two clergymen in black robes stood on the cathedral steps, heads bowed, hands clasped. From inside, as the gun-carriage approached, came the sound of the organ playing the Dead March from *Saul*.

As the service in the cathedral proceeded, Bancroft looked around him and thought, the living are as blind as the dead king. Here we all stand, and has anyone any idea what's going on and

100

what *really* this is all about? Virginia, for instance, kneeling beside me now, in official black, eyes lowered to her prayer book, what is she really thinking? Under the calm of the perfect PA, what turmoils, aches or loves? And why, as if I need to ask, has Rutherford got himself into the pew on the other side of her?

Bancroft saw them all, lifting up their heads and singing—Hugh Fortescue loudest of all, Naji Gawaka standing stiffly to attention, eyes big with sadness. God, Bancroft thought, what game is who playing with whom?

EIGHT

Through the open window came the evening scents as the high commissioner sat at his desk, dictating to Virginia.

". . . The ceremony in the cathedral moved all by its simplicity and dignity. Even though it is evident that Gawaka needs the support of the Assangi for the unification of Kajandi, this was certainly not political manoeuvring. Naked expediency is not a trait of General Naji Gawaka. . . . I and the other foreign representatives accompanied the body to the graveside with the Assangi elders. When the president stepped forward and took the prerogative of heir by placing the traditional barkcloth over the body, before the coffin lids were closed, there was no word of protest. . . . Peace has descended on a unified Kajandi. Furthermore. . . ."

Suddenly the telephone shrilled. The high commissioner lifted the receiver.

"*Fortescue.* . . ." The words echoed round the darkening office, like a cry of anguish from the depths of the jungle. "Moto is here, amongst de funeral crowds! Id is true! Id is *terrible!* He has been seen by de guards at the South Gate, trying to get out. . . ."

NEXT DAY, Hugh Fortescue sat at his desk dictating another dispatch to Central African Department.

". . . One must appreciate and make allowances for the shock to the general when he was told that Moto had been seen actually

102

inside the city. It was past eleven at night when he rang me. He was almost incoherent. At first, he began yelling at me. I deduced that for some reason or other he was blaming us. It was no use speaking to him on the telephone. I immediately went to Government House, and was received courteously and shown into the library. The general was alone, sitting at his desk. He said nothing, did not even look at me. I stood by the side of his desk, waiting.

"I am sure he was not being deliberately rude. He was far away, lost in his own thoughts. Then suddenly he said, very quickly and with deep emotion, 'You have betrayed me, Excellency . . . you, my best friend!' He clenched both his fists and began banging them on the top of his desk. He shouted, 'The burial of Zazu was a British plot! You knew Moto was in Joro! In the crowds at the funeral, with the Assangi all around, that was the perfect time and place for him to make his escape. Do this, Naji, you say, to unify Kajandi. We will help. And all the time, you were saying we will get rid of this man Gawaka. He rules with too harsh a hand. . . . He is not intellectual, like Moto. He is only a poor plain soldier.'

"I said nothing. My silence appeared to surprise him. He dropped his voice to an ordinary conversational tone. He asked, 'Why do you not speak?'

"I saw my chance then. I quickly probed him for the full story. It emerged, as I expected, confused and with little foundation. Two guards at the South Gate had sworn they had seen Moto, pursued him over to the western end of the city, then lost him. But when interrogated separately as to why they were sure it was Moto, their answers were contradictory. It was clearly a matter of mistaken identity.

"I went on talking to him querying, questioning, and he became quieter. He suddenly said. 'The guards are stupid fellows.'

"I then played my trump card. I had heard from your dispatch in today's bag that thanks to you the Kajandi air force crew was fully trained and that the promised British Starjet airliner would be delivered to Joro airport within two weeks.

"The change that came over him was electric. He got up from

his desk and his normal big good-humoured smile returned. He began calling me Hugh. He saw me personally to my car, promised a big ceremony at the airport. I know that I can rely on you to make absolutely sure the Starjet arrives at Joro airport on schedule . . ."

IT STOOD THERE, glittering in the sun like a vast tropical bird. The Starjet's wings were scarlet, the fuselage brilliant gold, the underbelly green, and the undercarriage legs silver—the colours of Kajandi.

On the dais where the general and his wife, Hugh and Priscilla Fortescue sat, there was movement. Up on his feet now, General Gawaka stood, holding up his hands for silence, smiling.

At last, he began speaking. He payed tribute to the marvellous engineering that the Starjet represented. He spoke of his plans for a Kajandi international airline service. But the very first flight of course would be within the boundaries of Kajandi itself, to Akarda, capital of the north, carrying himself and all his government. A wonderful step forward to unity had been achieved with the burial of King Zazu. He had had a message from the Chief of the Assangi saying how much they had appreciated the universality of the homage and respect.

"Now when I and my government arrive in Akarda tomorrow in our wonderful bird, we will say to our Assangi brothers, 'Come, let us embrace! Let us forget de past, de water under the bridge!'"

The blood under the bridge more like, Rutherford thought from his place below the dais.

"This is a present from Britain, let us not forget dat. From de very beginning of my government, de British are helping us, giving us what it is we need. . . ."

Now the general was gesturing to his pretty wife, beckoning her forward. Hesitantly, Damina got up and walked towards the champagne bottle, hanging by its neck on a thin rope from the aircraft's nose. She took it in her hands and, in an agony of shyness, she half-whispered into the microphone, "I name this aircraft General Naji Gawaka."

104

Loud and clear over the heads of the crowd, the brass band began trumpeting the Kajandi National Anthem. All rose to their feet, uncovered their heads.

Damina released the champagne bottle. It tinkled against the golden nose and swung back, unbroken. The brass band stopped dead.

Three times Damina threw the bottle at the side of the aircraft, then dissolved in tears. There was no smile now on the face of the general. He walked across the dais, took the champagne bottle in his hands, raised it high behind him as though it were a beheading axe and flung it against the side of the Starjet. There was an immediate loud explosion as the champagne frothed white and brilliant over everything, in a shrapnel spray of glass.

The christening of the aircraft *General Naji Gawaka* had been accomplished.

AT SEVEN that evening, just as Rutherford was halfway through dinner, M'Wanga came to tell him he was wanted on the telephone.

"Who is it?"

A shrug of the shoulders. "Sah . . . I do not know. They would not say."

Rutherford went up to his room to take the call. He did not want the publicity of the open telephone in the vestibule.

"Cap'n Rutherford?"

He recognized the voice immediately. "Yes?"

"The Skytruck . . . is it serviceable and fuelled?"

"Yes."

"Yu will be at the airport tomorrow morning at eight, where we met that first time . . . yu understand, Cap'n Rutherford?"

"Yes, General, I understand."

"Oh, and Cap'n Rutherford . . . tell *no one*."

THE PASSENGER HALL at Joro airport that morning was thronged with ministers, permanent secretaries, members of the cabinet who were accompanying the general in the Starjet to Akarda. The Kajandi pilots, still in their air force uniforms, were talking to

105

four pretty Kajandi girls dressed in scarlet, gold and green stewardess's uniforms.

Speak to nobody, Gawaka had ordered. Rutherford threaded his way to the control tower stairs and went up them to Mullah's office. Even in broad daylight, there was something sinister about the door. Would the room this time be full of soldiers?

He turned the handle, pushed the door open.

"Come in, Cap'n Rutherford."

Only the general—no one else. He was standing well away from the window this time.

"What do yu think of our Starjet, Cap'n?"

It was drawn up right outside. Rutherford could see the tops of the vivid wings.

"It's a good aircraft."

"Dat's what my voices tell me, Cap'n. And dese voices, dey also tell me Cap'n Rutherford would like to fly dat aeroplane. Who better to be de big boss of de big, big Kajandi Airways than Cap'n Rutherford . . . my ver' best friend?"

Keep close to Gawaka, Virginia had said. For your own safety and maybe ours. He's dangerous—that's why the Americans went, why the French and Germans are leaving. But be careful!

"That would be a great honour, General."

"We will see, Cap'n." Gawaka smiled and tapped his nose. "For de present, dere is dis important flight today. It is not right, dese voices say to me, for de president to arrive wid de others, all packed together like in a mammy-wagon. It befits de president to arrive at Akarda in his own aeroplane, flown by his own personal pilot."

Rutherford thought—scared stiff of his own Kajandi aircrew.

"You see what I mean, Cap'n?"

Rutherford said shortly, "You're not going in the Starjet after all."

Gawaka raised his voice. "It would not be *right* for me to go, dese voices say! Now I tell yu, Cap'n, I do not want to spoil de spectacle. It will be your privilege to take de president and his briefcase to de garlanded passenger steps in your station wagon. Dere I will shake hands with my friend, Hugh Fortescue, and de

106

other foreign dignitaries who have come to see the Starjet leave. Four African servants in white overalls will precede me up de steps, scattering rose petals, and den down de aisle to de special president's room at de front. I will go inside and lock de door. I have given strict instructions dat I am not to be disturbed. Yu will take your station wagon to de other side of de aircraft, to de steps away from the crowd. From my briefcase, I will take a white overall and put it on. Before anyone else boards de aircraft, I will come out of de president's room, lock de door, come down with my briefcase to your station wagon. Den as behind us de crowd cheers and de band plays, in all de excitement, we will drive away to your Skytruck. Yu will get clearance from de tower for local flying. And den, before de Starjet leaves, we will be on our way to Akarda." The big smile had returned to Gawaka's face. "De president will land first in his own aeroplane. Dat will be big surprise, eh, Cap'n Rutherford?"

Rutherford nodded.

It wasn't particularly difficult. Everything went like clockwork. Rutherford drove the general slowly up to the Starjet while the band played more frenziedly than ever. The guard of honour clanged their rifles in salute as the general solemnly shook hands with the diplomats, headed by the British high commissioner.

Then, preceded by the overalled servants, stepping on rose petals all the way up to the open door of the Starjet went General Gawaka. Just before he disappeared inside, he turned, saluted. While the crowd went wild, Rutherford moved the station wagon to the steps to the door on the starboard side of the aircraft.

Three minutes later, down came a white overalled figure carrying a briefcase, got in, closed the door. Rutherford pressed his foot on the accelerator and shot round the perimeter track to the other side of the field. Unnoticed, the two of them walked to the Skytruck. Gawaka stayed in the cargo compartment while Rutherford started up the engines, got tower clearance, taxied slowly to Runway 27. He glanced to the left, saw the colourful junket still going on, tiny pinheads still ascending the miniature passenger steps.

"Echo X-Ray." The controller's voice was excited and urgent.

"Please clear the runway quickly for the president's Starjet!"

Rutherford smiled wryly. "Wilco," he said, and opened up both throttles. At two thousand feet a minute, the Skytruck soared into the glittering blue sky.

Gawaka came up front. He had discarded his white overall. Like so many planets over his heart, the row of medals on his dark blue uniform reflected the sun. He sat down in the right-hand seat, craned round for one last look at the ceremonies still going on round the Starjet then threw back his head and laughed. He was in high good humour.

"Gawaka plans . . . and it is so! We will beat dem to Akarda, Cap'n?"

"We might." The pilot shrugged. "But the Starjet's much faster than us."

"Then let us have a liddle fun wit' dem! A race, yes?"

Rutherford kept at maximum cruising. The plates of the old Skytruck shuddered in protest, but at least the airspeed indicator registered 250 knots. And Gawaka could hardly have been friendlier. All the time he was talking about the future, telling the pilot of his grandiose plans for his world-wide air network.

Even though it was still only nine o'clock, the flight deck was unbearably hot. Now Gawaka was straining forward in his seat, staring ahead over the endless plains for the first sight of Akarda.

"It's some way off yet," Rutherford warned him. "You won't see anything for another twenty minutes."

What Gawaka did see, high above them, were the vapour trails of the Starjet crawling across the blue sky. "They are catching us up, Cap'n! Go faster!" He jumped up and down in his seat as if astride a horse. "We must reach Akarda first!"

To humour him, Rutherford pushed the throttles wide open, flipped the switches forward to maximum rpm. The needle on the airspeed indicator inched forward another fifteen knots.

But above them the vapour trails slowly moved ahead. Now the aircraft could be seen more clearly. From their height, the Starjet pilots had seen Akarda ahead. Already they were on the descent.

"More power, Cap'n!"

Instead, Rutherford began pulling back on the throttles and reducing the revolutions. He tapped the needle on the engine temperature gauges. "We've been flat out too long."

"Call up on your radio! Tell dem not to land yet!"

Rutherford had actually lifted the microphone to his lips, when, above and slightly ahead of them, the parrot-coloured aircraft seemed for one split second to swell in beauty. The gold and red and green cross became brighter still, then suddenly burst into one huge full-petalled blazing blossom. A giant chrysanthemum firework exploded in the blue sky. Glittering pieces shot about like sparks. Then just as abruptly, all colour was snuffed out under thick black smoke. Half a wing, an engine nacelle, bits of tailplane went spiralling down to earth.

Clear above the engines came the rolling roar of sound. The Skytruck bucked and bounced in the impacted shock waves. Rutherford throttled back hard and struggled to keep level.

Even after the air had steadied, Rutherford's hands still gripped the control column tightly. The windscreen ahead now showed only clear blue sky, and below them, slowly rising from the dense green forest, a pillar of dark cloud.

Rutherford let out his breath in a long, shuddering sigh. He pushed the Skytruck's nose hard down, clicked on the microphone.

But before he could say anything, Gawaka had gripped his wrist. The microphone clicked off.

"Cap'n Rutherford . . . turn the plane round!" He grabbed the controls himself. "We go home!"

"But, General—"

"Do as I say!"

The whites of Gawaka's eyes had gone bloodshot. He was in a paroxysm of fury. "Low down so dey do not see us! Quickly! *Quickly!*"

Rutherford headed south. For minutes, neither of them spoke. Then suddenly Gawaka went wild. He began pacing up and down the flight deck, stamping and shouting.

"You saw! You saw id with your own eyes! Id was a British plot to destroy me! His Excellency came with advice, help, gifts. Do dis, do dat. Make peace with the Assangi. Here is big beautiful aeroplane. De British are giving id to yu, General! Take a liddle ride! See how well id flies!"

He started banging the side of the Skytruck with his fists. "De British say Moto is better than this man Gawaka. We will keep Moto safe in Joro. So proud will Gawaka be of his present dat he will bring inside with him his government and fly north to show de Assangi. Inside also will be another liddle present. And den—" he waved his hands "—dat is de end of General Naji Gawaka . . . *or so they think!*"

Rutherford had taken the Skytruck down to a hundred feet, was skimming over the tops of the trees. He was trying to concentrate, while all the time the flight deck was filled with Gawaka's shouting and stamping.

"And dese were my friends! Dese were de men I trusted! Fortescue . . . liar, cheat, thief, traitor . . . murderer!"

Rutherford kept quiet, trying to think. The situation had become totally dangerous. Behind him, breathing heavily, Gawaka had slumped into the jump seat. ". . . Major Jerezoah, Captain Pieta, Colonel Sattala, Lieutenant Kasara . . . oh my comrades, my brothers!"

He was calling out the people on the aircraft in a roll of honour, rocking to and fro, holding his hands tight against his face, his shoulders shaking with sobs.

"All . . . all gone! Murdered by de British!" He threw back his head and yelled to the sky. "But believe me, brothers. . . . Gawaka will revenge yu! An eye for an eye! A head for a head!"

Over the trees could now be seen the minarets and walls of Joro. Rutherford shifted the Skytruck round towards the airport. Just by the bridge over the Ruanga, the general suddenly seized his right hand. "Do not land at de airport! Go to the barracks of the Armoured Brigade!"

Rutherford did as he was told, turned over the east walls and circled the red brick buildings at the end of Gawaka Avenue. The parade ground was perhaps just big enough if he came in very low and practically on the stall. As he landed he stood on the brakes, and the Skytruck shuddered to a stop in front of an astonished bunch of soldiers.

110

General Gawaka did not immediately move. He was quiet now. "Yu, Cap'n Rutherford, can still be my ver' best friend." He paused. "But what happens now?"

Rutherford looked back at him, saying nothing.

"Yu do not know. I tell yu something. I do not yet know either."

Silence now. "But *dey* know, Cap'n." Gawaka tapped his head with his fingers. "Dese voices . . . dey say to me, do not listen to others. Do not listen to dat man Fortescue. Listen to *us!* We tell yu. And now, dey are louder and clearer than ever. Do yu know why I did not go on the Starjet, Cap'n? Because dese voices, dey say do not go. Something terrible will happen."

Silence again. Gawaka was staring fixedly into Rutherford's eyes. "And now, id is as they say. But because of dem, Gawaka is alive. Gawaka, the deathless one! And now I must ask dem . . . what shall I do?"

The general cupped his ears with his hands like an R/T headset, and sat very still, listening intently. Outside, news of their arrival had spread. A guard of honour was quickly forming up. Two officers were moving smartly across the parade ground towards them. Rutherford recognized the one on the right as Major Ghinza.

Gawaka dropped his hands from his ears. He stood up and smiled. "Dey have spoken. Gawaka shall live! Gawaka's rule shall last not a hundred days but a hundred years! It is dey—" Shuddering, he closed his eyes. "De deceivers. De murderers. It is *dey* who will die!"

NINE

"Played, sir!"

Hugh Fortescue sat back in his seat and lightly clapped his hands. Around him were his protegés, his family—the four officers of the British High Commission, their wives and their children. The Saturday afternoon tennis party at the Residence was in full swing.

111

"The departure of the Starjet went very well, I thought."
Fortescue was addressing Peter Evers, his commercial secretary.
"The general was in excellent form."

"He was pleased with the Starjet. The first of many, he told
me."

"Wonderful plans! Tremendous imagination! Tries to jump the
gun, of course." H.E. sipped his lime juice thoughtfully. "We
must never let ideas get out of hand. It's all got to be paid for."

"But now the economy's bound to improve enormously! The
wealth is there!"

"Of course, but wealth is nothing without the stability of the
country. Unity . . . peace. As I've often told the general, that's
his number one priority. And give him his due . . . that first
priority he has consistently pursued. That safari trip of ours. The
bringing back of Zazu. Now this flight to meet the Assangi chiefs."

"You think the meeting will be a success, sir?"

"I see no reason to suppose it won't be. The general has a
way with people. That send-off of the Starjet this morning,"
Fortescue screwed up his eyes, seeing again all the colour and the
majesty, "wasn't it moving?"

The sound of the tennis balls had ceased. Nigel Naylor followed
his wife and Bancroft and Virginia off the court.

"How went it, Tom?"

"Lost, sir." Bancroft could not help saying, "As usual."
Bancroft, the born loser—he nearly added that as well.

"Ah, well, it's the game that counts."

He'll be telling us about the Great Scorer next Bancroft thought.
But the high commissioner simply suggested a lime juice.
Bancroft was actually reaching for the glass which Priscilla had
poured when beyond the walls of the Residence came the sound
of screaming tyres and sirens.

"What's that, I wonder?" Hugh Fortescue stood up. "A fire?"

"Soldiers, I think, sir."

"Tanks now," Naylor said. "There goes an armoured car!"

"Whatever . . . ?"

A servant in a white coat came hurrying out of the house. He
approached Fortescue, began speaking in agitated Swahili.

Fortescue said nothing, showed no emotion. Speaking as slowly as usual, he said, "I'm sure you ladies are ready for tea. What are the sandwiches today, Priscilla?"

"Cucumber, banana, tomato." She knew her cue and was already leading them inside.

Fortescue said nothing till they had disappeared, then he addressed the four men around him.

"There's some news . . . some sad news. It may be just market-place gossip. We must hope and pray it is."

Bancroft downed his lime juice, screwed up his face. Bloody awful stuff!

"There is a story circulating Joro that the Starjet has crashed."

There was a moment of silent horror. Then "No!" from Naylor and Evers. Dermot Harmer, the defence attaché, said, "How did it happen?"

"Any survivors?" asked Bancroft.

"I know nothing more. Until there is confirmation, there is no point telling the ladies. In my experience, I've heard stories like this numerous times that turned out in the end to be baseless. Yes, Fedaya?"

The same servant had come up. "Telephone, B'wana. Government House."

"Oh . . . oh, I see! Well—" he waved the others on. "You'll all be wanting your tea. I'll join you in the drawing room later."

It was fifteen minutes before the high commissioner reappeared. He came and stood in the middle of the drawing room.

"There's no point in beating about the bush. There's been an . . . accident. The Starjet has crashed. Nobody knows for certain where. Nobody knows why. That was one of the general's secretaries in Government House on the telephone—"

"The general?" asked Naylor.

"That's just it. There are two points on which there is *absolute* certainty. First, the Starjet has crashed. And secondly, there are no survivors."

The horror in the room was intensified by the laughter of the children upstairs.

"Now I am going to Government House. One can imagine the

113

scene there. Damina and the children . . . I doubt if they've dared to tell them. . . . That is what they will want me to do." He paused, then became brisk. "But clearly we must also think of ourselves. The situation is likely to be extremely tense. Nigel, will you please organize Operation Sanctuary. All British staff and families inside the High Commission. And contact the remaining British residents. Advise them to fly out immediately. It may blow over very quickly. But we must not take any risks. Everyone understand?"

They nodded.

"And, Tom. Send a message to the Department. Top Secret."

"I will."

"Right then." He gave a little smile. "Sorry for breaking up the party. I'll see you all back at the High Commission."

Priscilla accompanied him outside. Just before he got into his own car, the Zephyr, he put his arm round her and held her very tightly for such a dry emotionless man. Then he drove out into a street filled with armoured cars and tanks.

Government House seemed deserted. Fortescue knocked, called out, "Is anybody there?"

A servant materialized out of a veranda door. "Yes, sah?"

"Will you tell the Lady Damina that the British high commissioner has arrived?"

The man seemed puzzled. "The Lady Damina?"

"The general's secretary who telephoned me then."

"I do not know any secretary."

"Surely there must be *somebody* here?"

"Yes."

The man led the way to the library and opened the door. Thick curtains were drawn across the windows and the interior was as black as night. The leathery scent of old books mingled with the sharp smell of a cigar. Fortescue could just make out a burning red dot. Then, as his eyes became more accustomed to the dark, he saw the outline of a figure.

All at once, the library was flooded with light.

"Why, General—"

"Surprised, Excellency? Yu cannot believe it, eh? Why so pale? Do yu think yu see a ghost?"

"General, I'm—"

"Speechless, yes! Fortescue, yu stand condemned!"

"Naji, I am so glad! So *glad!* You are alive! You are well!"

"Gawaka is eternal! No one can kill Gawaka. Dat is where yu made your mistake!" The African rose from his desk, and pointed. "Yu are filled with horror that Gawaka is still alive!"

Fortescue said quickly. "I do not know what you mean."

"Yu lie! Yu have always lied to me. Yu have led me by de nose. Be friends, be brothers, yu say. Bring back de body of de Assangi king from British exile. Pay homage . . . Now yu say to me yu have done wonderful job, you have unified Kajandi. Now we will help yu to be rich, be powerful. And all de time, yu have been plotting wid de Assangi. Yu have whispered we are giving him big aeroplane. He is coming up to Akarda for big celebrations wid all his government. Let us put a bomb inside this gift—"

"That is not true!" Fortescue spoke very quietly. "It doesn't make sense. . . ."

"It makes big sense man!"

"We do not yet know the cause of the accident."

"No accident, man!"

"The facts will be established at the inquiry. We will send out British experts to help, if you wish."

"I do not wish! I will not have another murderin' British person here!" the general roared. "I have no time to *inquire.*" He mimicked Fortescue's dry precise tone. "Gawaka must be seen to act. To pounce on dese murderers. Wherever dey are. Whatever high place dey hide demselves in."

Fortescue said nothing. He was conscious of an electric hatred emanating from Gawaka as palpable as body heat. In the jungle, his father used to say, talk softly and carry a big stick. Today, there was no big stick, but one still talked softly. One communicated. Continued dialogue. Maintained.

"Is dat not right, Excellency?"

"If an atrocity has been committed, then of course the guilty must be brought to justice."

"Justice!" Gawaka crashed his clenched fist on the desk, swatting invisible enemies.

Fortescue kept quiet.

"If yu are my friend yu will help me. When my enemies smite me," Gawaka struck his left breast, "yu will feel it there."

"I do, General."

"Then prove it! Stand side by side wid me!"

Fortescue narrowed his eyes. Gawaka's anger was abating. A pleading note had crept into his voice.

"It has been a terrible tragedy, General. Of course we will stand by you, as far as we are able."

"What does dat mean? As far as able?"

"Just that, General."

A faint smile hovered on the general's lips. It contrasted eerily with the anger still smouldering in his eyes. Though he spoke more softly, he still kept Fortescue standing. "How many British staff in your High Commission, Excellency?"

"Four men and two women."

"All married, de men?"

"Except one. He is a widower."

"And children?"

The high commissioner paused. "Let me see, four. No, five," he replied.

"All here?"

"Yes." Within the walls now, thank heaven. Operation Sanctuary would be well under way.

"So, Excellency," Gawaka's smile broadened, "Yu have, as dey say, wid your wife and yourself, sixteen souls on board?"

"Yes, General. But I do not see the relevance."

"You will, Excellency. Take your mind back to your Aid Mission. Give us a shopping list of things yu need, yu said. Dat shopping list I gave you. Oh, but no, *no*, you say to me then. Tanks, armoured cars, rockets—you cannot have such things, Naji. You proposed mining equipment for de north. An agricultural station. Technical training schools. And—" the eyes glittered malevolently, "—a civil aeroplane. And now what has happened? From Akarda, the Assangi chiefs saw the aeroplane explode. Dey have declared I am dead and there is great rejoicing. Dey are massing to attack."

The high commissioner said nothing.

"And now, Excellency, you will understand dat after all it was *my* shopping list dat was de important one."

The high commissioner kept his eyes steadily on the general's face.

"Yu have a pen?" Gawaka pushed over a pad. "Here is some paper." There was a pause. "Let us begin. My shopping list is a liddle bigger this time. Ten vertical take-off Harrier aircraft, twenty-four Centurion tanks, three hundred surface-to-air missiles, forty Lightning fighters . . . am I going too fast for yu, Excellency?"

Fortescue had his head bent, writing it all down.

"Two hundred surface-to-surface missiles . . . have you got that, Excellency? With nuclear war-heads."

At last, the high commissioner spoke. "You know that is out of the question!"

"I know no such thing!" Gawaka glared across the desk. "Id is very much *in* de question! In dat ver' important question . . . are yu my friend? If yu do not get my shopping list for me, how can yu be my friend? And if yu are not my friend, den yu," he dropped his voice to a hiss, "yu are the snake in my bosom!"

"I do not follow your logic, General."

"Den again I explain." Gawaka's voice rose. "I give you one last big chance! One more only!" There was a long silence. "Give me what I need! Now, in my hour of danger!"

Consciously Fortescue played for time. "I will of course, have to consult London."

"Consult . . . certainly consult!" The general lowered his voice almost to a whisper. "How many souls yu say yu have on board? Ah yes, now I remember! Sixteen." He leaned forward. "I hold yu all in de hollow of my hand."

Fortescue bit back the politically dangerous words on the tip of his tongue. Time. The number one priority was always time. Time to pacify, time to unify, time to educate.

Aloud he said, "You must understand, General, that this will take time."

"Time, Fortescue? Time I have not!" Gawaka looked at his watch. "I will give you till midnight to agree to my shopping list. Otherwise—" His right hand clenched.

TEN

"Another brandy, Captain Rutherford?" Major Ghinza leaned courteously across the table, picked up the pilot's glass.

"Not for me, thanks," Rutherford looked at his watch. "Time to go!" Go where? And with whom?

From the window seat of the Officers' Mess bar, he could see his Skytruck drawn up to one side of the parade ground—bedded down with chocks under the wheels—while in the centre, columns of soldiers accompanied by armoured cars and tanks were moving off to the barrack gates and turning left.

To the north. The bomb on board the Starjet must have been planted by the Assangi. Waiting at Akarda, the Assangi chiefs would have seen the aircraft explode, and Gawaka would know that now he had a major revolt on his hands. That was the reason why he had insisted on landing here in the barracks—and the reason for all these troop movements.

"Major Ghinza, my professional soldier. Captain Rutherford, my professional pilot," that was how Gawaka had re-introduced them after they had landed an hour ago. "Both my ver' good friends. Look after him well, Major."

Look after him well was right. Ghinza had hung on to him like a friendly leech. Rutherford stood up. "Thanks for the lunch. Now I'd better get back to my hotel!"

"Not so soon! I will show you what we have here."

Rutherford ached to get away. That scene on the Skytruck—Gawaka rampaging like a mad elephant on the flight deck, shouting about a British plot, roaring vengeance, vowing to kill. Virginia, Fortescue, all the High Commission probably were in danger.

How do you cope with a madman in power? What do you do?

Getting out of here was the first thing. And his best bet was this friendliness with Ghinza. He must encourage it, all the time giving the impression of being led—and all the time leading.

"Thank you, Major. I'd like to see the barracks." He paused. "You know, I can't go on calling you Major. What's your first name?"

118

"Aleko."

"Mine's Bill. Lead on then, Aleko. I'm interested."

Not that there was much to see. Most of the stuff was on its way north against the Assangi.

Here was a lone, ancient tank standing in an empty shed. Aleko explained it in detail. They were getting on famously. Sitting in the driving seat, Rutherford appeared to be totally absorbed in the knobs and switches, "This the starter, Aleko?"

"That's right, Bill."

"And the gears?"

"Four forward, two reverse."

The next moment, with a low rumble, the engine had started.

"All right if I see how she handles, Aleko?"

The major nodded and smiled. The old tank lumbered forward onto the parade ground. Rutherford took the tank right up to the front gates, but they were closed. Clearly the friendship had not yet developed sufficiently for a trip outside. Nevertheless, it was progressing well. It was burning hot inside the tank, but Rutherford joked and laughed, spoke most warmly of General Gawaka.

Beside him, the major said reverently, "Our immortal leader."

It was past five when the tour of inspection was over and together they walked into the deserted ante-room for tea. It was all very civilized, just like Sandhurst, the major said.

When the conversation began petering out, the major walked across to turn on the television, then resumed his seat beside Rutherford. A High Life band—execrably loud, then suddenly a flash—the general would speak to the Nation at eighteen hundred hours.

Rutherford stirred uneasily. The first ideas of an escape plan had begun to crystallize in his mind. He hoped to God the general wasn't going to thwart it. . . .

More High Life band. The garish music clanged against Rutherford's nerves. Then that damned Kajandi anthem again! And now, the general himself, in full uniform and wearing all his medals.

For two whole minutes, the smouldering eyes stared out of the screen, but the lips did not move. Then he spoke—in English. "Brothers and Enemies, I speak to you both!"

Another long silence. All the major's attention was riveted on his superior officer.

"My enemies amongst yu will be very surprised to see me here. But my brothers will rejoice. Some of yu will have heard that a most dastardly deed has been done. The British aeroplane that many of yu saw me off in this morning has been destroyed by a bomb. All on board, all my government, all my ver' good friends are dead. How is it den that here I am alive?

"Because Gawaka is immortal! Nobody can kill Gawaka! But, brothers, traitors have tried! Ever since de voices spoke to me, told me that I am de real ruler of Kajandi, I have done all things possible for your good. I have talked friendship to all. Especially wid de Assangi. I have tried to make dem my brothers in a united Kajandi. And everybody said dat is right, de British, de United Kingdom, all de tribes of Kajandi, even de Assangi."

The major stirred on the sofa, spat out the word, "Assangi."

"But all de time, de British have been plotting wid de Assangi. De British have two faces. We bring gifts, dey say, equipment, technical help, everything. You want to make Kajandi rich. Here is big British aeroplane! And brothers, behind their hands secretly to de Assangi . . . *here also is a British bomb!*

"I have spoken to de British high commissioner. Oh, my brothers, you should have seen his face when he saw dat I was alive! How pale he went! How he trembled! A little man, a coward, shivering with fear before de eternal Naji Gawaka! Naji, he cries . . . id is not true de British have put a British bomb on board dat British plane!

"Show me it is not true den, I tell him! Show me yu are my friend! De Assangi are massing in de north. Dey are coming down to attack Joro, happily shouting Gawaka is dead! Show me dat yu are not a Moto fellah! Give me dose gifts dat now I want! Tanks, fighter planes, guns . . . nuclear rockets!

"Excellency, I say to him, is your answer Yes? He tells me he must get in touch wid London. Very well, I tell him, I am a reasonable man. I will give yu till midnight to say Yes.

"And if at midnight, dere is still no answer?

"Oh, my brothers, what can I say? Already yu will be going to the British High Commission in your thousands. You will be shaking your fists and shouting 'Traitors!' I say to yu . . . keep calm. But in your hearts, oh my brothers, is dis terrible ache." The general closed his eyes. "I am remembering my comrades, murdered! I know dat yu will be remembering dem, too. If de British do not say Yes by midnight, what can I do to restrain your righteous wrath?"

God, Rutherford thought—five and a half hours left—a deadline. He would have to work something out quickly. But it seemed he was not to be classed with the perfidious British.

"You are not like the others." The major was speaking. "You are one of us, Bill. That is what the general said to me. Never fear, you and your aeroplane will be most carefully looked after."

That was it! That was the real reason why he wasn't identified with the British. He and his Skytruck were clearly very precious indeed to Gawaka. If all else failed, if Gawaka's rule collapsed and his head was in danger, off he planned to go in the Skytruck to Zurich, to live in luxurious safety on the gold and ivory.

The major had risen, smiling. "Drinking time, Bill."

"I should be going back to my hotel."

"No." Sharply. "You are staying here tonight. A bed has been put in my room."

A prisoner, as he suspected all along. The plan he had been evolving would have to be stepped up. After seeing that madman on the screen, he'd have to move faster.

"But what about my things? Pyjamas, shaving gear—!"

"We will—"

"No, I'm sorry." It was Rutherford's turn to be sharp. Honoured guests have their privileges. "I want my own things." He appealed to the African's fastidiousness. "I mean, Aleko, if you were in my place. . . ."

It worked. As they walked down the corridor, Rutherford laughingly suggested he should continue his military education by driving over to the Hotel Afrique in an armoured car.

Aleko smilingly agreed. Fifteen minutes later with the major beside him, Rutherford drove off in a Saladin. A word at the gates from Ghinza, and they were through.

Down Gawaka Avenue, left past Independence Square, past Ndole jail. The market place was deserted. But there were lights on in the British High Commission. They will all have been brought inside, another Operation Sanctuary as Virginia had called it. But how much sanctuary was there against a madman? A large crowd had already collected outside the closed gates.

Into the winding back streets now and up the hill to the Hotel Afrique. Rutherford parked the car outside the front door. The two of them climbed the steps into the reception hall.

"Won't be long. My room's just at the top of the stairs."

No, the major would come up "to help".

It was then that he saw M'Wanga's head popping out of the kitchen doorway.

"Ah," Rutherford pointed. "That's M'Wanga . . . my batman, really. Excuse me, I'll ask him to rustle a few things in a bag for me. There's the bar. Order us a couple of whiskies, eh? Join you in a second."

Even before he reached it, the hotel kitchen brought him back to that other night. The smell of *matoke*, the darkness lit by the sputtering gas jets.

"Bwana—"

Rutherford whispered urgently, "M'Wanga . . . ring the British High Commission." The telephone would be tapped. He'd have to be careful. "Don't give your name. Say simply . . . green, white and red."

"Green, white and red, Bwana?"

Rutherford nodded, now saying loudly, "Pyjamas, shaving things . . . put them in that small tartan bag. And quickly, M'Wanga! the major and I can't wait all night."

M'Wanga was down with the bag before they were halfway through their whiskies. Rutherford drained his glass. "Better be on our way, Aleko."

M'Wanga followed them down the steps to the armoured car. The boy couldn't have telephoned yet. His face looked blank. God, Rutherford thought, I hope he understood! All the pilot could do as he got into the passenger seat was to say, "Thank you, M'Wanga. Put the bag here on my lap. Goodnight!"

"I AM GOING to be perfectly frank."

Hugh Fortescue sipped his cup of coffee, and dabbed his lips in the prissy manner which got on Bancroft's nerves. The entire British staff sat round the table in Chancery. H.E. had chosen Chancery not only because it was the centre of their communications, but also to avoid the occasional bullets and stones that broke the odd window. A present from the crowd at the gates.

"In grateful thanks for your agricultural project, Sarah," Bancroft said, as a tinkle of glass came from the other side of the house. "Or was it for the students' scholarships?"

"Oh, belt up, Tom!" Sarah's skin had a greyish tinge under her suntan. Everyone with the possible exception of H.E. was scared, himself included. Gawaka was going to slice them all to pieces and talk afterwards. Give them a state funeral, Bancroft wouldn't wonder. And a ritual execution of some odd people in the crowd presently outside the gate. Always good for an afternoon's Kajandi entertainment. Then after a while, if Gawaka held onto his hat and the riches really were as big as they seemed, the Foreign Office would kiss and make up.

"Isn't that so, Tom?" Bancroft was aware that Fortescue was addressing him. "Central Africa Department have advised us to play for time. I have pointed out that this time President Gawaka appears temporarily deranged. The shock, of course . . . coupled with his own escape. Clearly he cannot have been in the Starjet but in Mr. Rutherford's Skytruck that we saw take off some time before."

And *that* had been the conjuring trick of all time, Bancroft thought—beats sawing the lady in two any day. He looked in the direction of Virginia. She had her hands clasped on her knees and was staring down at them. He bet himself she was wondering, as he was, what in hell had happened to her boy friend. If it hadn't been for that roughneck, Gawaka might well be resting in that small bit of jungle that was for ever Kajandi. Gathered to his blood-letting forefathers.

Just across the corridor from Chancery, Bancroft heard the wives bedding the children down for whatever sleep they were going to get.

Midnight, that raging madman had said. The British government's agreement by midnight. Otherwise, he would have their heads. No, he had put it a little more cleverly than that. Otherwise, his soldiers and tanks which now surrounded the British High Commission would not be able to hold back the crowds from the violence of their anger and grief. They'd be even now whipping that crowd together. Then, at midnight, if nothing was forthcoming—over the wall. The *panga* knives flashing, and the soldiers coming in behind to see they made a good job of it.

"I take it that there is no chance that HMG will agree?"

"To such blackmail, Tom?"

"What about pretending?"

"They're thinking of every possibility."

"Meanwhile, we just sit it out?"

"We do. As we sat it out before. You and I, Tom, have seen this sort of thing happen a number of times."

"In slightly less glorious technicolour."

H.E. smiled approvingly at the attempted jocularity.

"And the scene is not entirely without hope. We—" he nodded at the military attaché, "—have had a little discussion. Fortunately all British residents managed to get off before the airfield was closed. And negotiations have been initiated by the Kenyans to send a plane. Though it is unclear," Fortescue added wryly, "how we could reach it through our noisy friends outside."

Sarah said, "I assume sending the RAF would be considered a show of force?"

"It would be considered an act of war."

"What about holding us hostage?" Bancroft put in. "Isn't that an act of war?"

"The president hasn't actually said that he's doing that. He has said HMG have till midnight to make up their minds. The troops and tanks are for our protection."

"Ha, ha!"

"Yes, well, Tom . . . ha ha maybe. But there is a nice difference. It also leaves the way open for a change of heart by the president."

"How likely do you think that is?" Virginia asked. H.E. looked at her regretfully. "Who knows?" He glanced at the silent telephone. "We may suddenly get a call from the general. Or London may come up with a bright idea."

"Even less likely," Bancroft said, and this time H.E. did not smile.

"One must take into consideration," Fortescue went on carefully, "the general's position. The Assangi are marching against him. He needs the weapons he has demanded if he is to survive. On the television screen, he had to play it up . . . to encourage his friends and frighten the Assangi."

Virginia looked at her watch. It was ten minutes past seven, and nearly eleven hours since she'd heard anything about Rutherford. What had happened after the Starjet crashed? She had listened intently to Gawaka's television broadcast, but he had simply made his arrival safe in Joro a miracle. Rutherford must have brought him. Had Gawaka then killed him in a fit of fury? If Rutherford were alive surely he'd have telephoned. Death to the British had been the last market gossip she'd heard. Had it begun with death to the first Briton close to the general? Rutherford himself?

There was a sound of breaking glass—another brick through the window. Across the landing, a child screamed. Virginia felt the chill of panic creeping up.

Half past seven. Fridays were usually early finishing days in London. Most of the FO staff would have gone home, but Central African Department could not have done. What were they doing? Had the United Nations been contacted? What was today's procedure for dealing with a mad ruler?

"So we simply leave our lines open and wait." Fortescue smiled at them all, and pushed back his chair. As he did so, the telephone rang. Eagerly H.E. reached out. Then the caller spoke and a frown of concentration appeared between his brows. "Would you repeat that? Slowly, please."

A slurred African voice could be heard faintly in the total silence of the room.

"Who is that?" Silence.

Then Fortescue said simply, "I have your message. Thank you." He put down the receiver. "Nothing very helpful, I'm afraid. Just four words. From an unknown Kajandi. Green, white and red."

ELEVEN

"I enjoyed driving that armoured car, Aleko."

"You were very expert, Bill."

"And one good turn deserves another."

They were sitting in the bar after dinner. It was past ten o'clock. All through the four courses, Rutherford had urged speed, but the major liked his food. He also liked his drink. He was refusing to be hurried over his coffee and brandy.

". . . so now I will show you my Skytruck, Aleko."

The major's face brightened. "That I would like very much. But first let us have another brandy."

"Not for me." Rutherford watched him sipping the stuff. Above their heads, the pointer on the electric clock clicked to one minute past eleven. Less than an hour left.

"Boy . . . bring us some more coffee." The major was signalling to the barman. "This is cold."

The major drank two more cups. Eleven sixteen. At last, he stood up. "Let's see that aeroplane of yours now, eh Bill?"

The major led the way outside. It was a bright clear night. The parade ground as always was floodlit. There was a guard standing on the corner.

Rutherford walked over to the Skytruck, opened the door, and led the way inside. He settled the Kajandi in the righthand seat and he turned on the flight deck lights. Methodically he explained all the instruments. All the time he was talking, he was measuring with his eye the length of concrete in front of the aircraft.

"Now there's so much to remember, Aleko, that we have check lists."

He took out the Before Starting Engine check list, began reading each item, guiding the hand of the Kajandi so that he did everything. "Push that button there . . . that's it! . . . Switch on! . . . Now the port."

Both engines were turning. Aleko was delighted. Five hundred yards, Rutherford had decided. No wind. That barrack block to get over at the far end, but it should be all right.

126

"See the handbrake? Take hold of it and release it."

"Is that right?"

"Perfect! Brakes off, engine started." He turned to the major. "You let me drive an armoured car and tank. Now it's your turn to drive an aeroplane. Only fair." He smiled. "Just taxiing round the parade ground, of course. Put your hands on the throttles . . . that's right. Ready?"

"Ready, Bill."

"Move them forward a little." The engines note increased, but the aircraft stayed where it was. Rutherford threw up his hands. "Oh damn and hell!"

"What is the matter, Bill?"

"The chocks, Aleko! The bloody chocks are still in position!" He drew back the throttles. "Jump out, there's a good chap, and pull them away from the wheels."

"Right!"

The Kajandi got out of the seat. Rutherford heard the rear door open, feet touching the ground, the slamming shut of the door. Then he heard Aleko pull away the chock on the starboard side. Through his side window, he watched him remove the chock under the port wheel.

The second both the chocks were away, Rutherford opened the throttles to take-off power. He caught a momentary glimpse of the major's face, mouth open, shouting, as the Skytruck moved forward.

Gathering speed over the concrete—fifty, sixty, seventy knots. Eighty-five knots—he pulled the nose wheel off the ground. Ninety, ninety-five—the barrack block loomed up like a cliff dead ahead of him.

He heaved back on the control column. Inches above the tiled roof, the Skytruck roared up into the night.

AT ONCE . . . Bancroft watched the high commissioner write the words on the telegram form—even in extremes following traditional practice.

What was going to happen to them? The department had made every sort of suggestion, after they had got over their first reaction of what has old Fortescue got himself into *this* time. They had tried cautiously using the telephone, knowing it was tapped, but then all overseas calls had been suspended.

Bancroft looked at the telegram on his way up to Chancery to send it off. WE WILL CONTINUE TO PLAY FOR TIME. Well, it was now eleven thirty. They had exactly half an hour of time left.

When he got up to Chancery, two messages had come in and been decoded.

The first read: A COMPROMISE ON THE SUPPLYING OF ARMS HAS BEEN SUGGESTED STOP BUT SURELY THIS WOULD EMBROIL US IN THE GAWAKA MOTO STRUGGLE STOP IN NO CIRCUMSTANCES COULD WE PROMISE NUCLEAR WEAPONS.

The second was longer. WE WERE THINKING OF IMMEDIATELY BREAKING OFF DIPLOMATIC RELATIONS BUT ON FURTHER CON-SIDERATION. . . .

That would really cook everyone's goose. Outside the crowd were becoming more violent. All the lights in the front had been switched off. There was only a heavily shaded table lamp on the high commissioner's desk. No other illumination.

Except for those three lights down there in the garden—the green, white and red torches that had been set out in a line on the lawn, Virginia's interpretation of that strange telephone call from the African. From where he was standing, he could see them gleaming like glow-worms in the darkness.

The message had come from Rutherford, she had insisted. With the aid of those lights, he would be able to land his aeroplane. All the High Commission staff must be in readiness for immediate evacuation.

. . . WE ARE ALL DEEPLY WORRIED FOR YOUR SAFETY STOP AT THE SAME TIME COMMONSENSE DICTATES THAT GAWAKA MAY WELL BE BLUFFING STOP IF YOU CAN POSSIBLY HOLD OUT . . .

As Bancroft put the flimsies on the high commissioner's desk, he looked at his watch. Eleven forty. He didn't mind for himself. Re-treads had little rubber left on them.

Fortescue read the telegrams slowly. "Well, they don't take us far, Tom."

"Nowhere."

RUTHERFORD skidded the Skytruck round to the west, following the river low down on the water.

Pitch blackness around him now. And to help him land—if M'Wanga had got the message through, if Virginia had remembered, would be three lights—the green threshold, the red boundary and a white one in the middle for luck.

A ten foot wall to descend over. If he undershot, he'd wipe his wheels off. If he wasn't dead centre, he'd put a wheel in a flower bed and slew round in a ground loop. If he came in a knot too slow, he'd stall. If he came in a knot too fast, he'd overshoot the lawn and go straight into the rockery. And to guide him, three little lights—if he was lucky!

Through his open side window, he peered anxiously into the darkness.

There they were now! Beyond the glimmer of the Ruanga, in front of the bright lights along Gawaka Avenue. He swung the aircraft right round to port to line up with them. There was no wind. He would land from the river so as to be close to the High Commission building. Then all the staff could board immediately and be away.

Gear down, throttles right back. A hundred feet, descending. Eighty feet. He could make things out now. No lights on in the High Commission. Some sort of commotion outside the main gate.

Fifty feet. The airspeed dropped right back to eighty-five knots. The Skytruck hovered on the stall. Through the open window, the night air blew in cool and scented.

Twenty feet. The dark water of the Ruanga just below him. The railway line coming up, a train steaming leisurely along it.

Ahead now, the horizontal line of the High Commission wall. Just as he put down full flap and began to level out for the landing, he heard the whistle of bullets.

"WOULD YOU like a cup of tea, sir? The girls have brewed up again."

"No, thank you, Tom. I'll . . ." The telephone shrilled. Into the blue eyes again came hope.

"Fortescue . . . yu are unmasked! I know all!" The words came out in a torrent of furious abuse. "Inside your High Commission you have Moto!"

"General, that is not true. He is not here. He has never been here."

"Moto has broadcast to the Assangi! He has told dem dat here in Joro he awaits dem. Dey are to come quickly, for as de sooth-sayer prophesied, the Gawaka regime is over."

"General . . . there is a noisy crowd of several thousand outside our gates. I would be greatly obliged if you would kindly ask your guards to disperse them!"

"Excellency . . . when will my nuclear weapons arrive?"

"If we could talk over this matter quietly together . . ."

"Quietly together! Fortescue, are yu mad? De Assangi are descending on us. De people who surround your High Commission are my very loyal subjects. Dey *know* dat all along yu have been protecting Moto! Dey demand your blood, de heads of everyone in de British High Commission! I have tried to pacify dem. I have told dem dat yu are giving us all sorts of tanks, guns and nuclear weapons and we will wipe de Assangi from de face of de earth!"

He stopped. There was silence. "Fortescue, do yu understand?"

"I hear the words you use, General."

"Fortescue, yu have five minutes left! Five minutes before . . ."

Faintly at first, and then rapidly swelling above the torrent of abuse over the telephone came the sound of engines. The building rattled. Bancroft rushed over to the window. In the light of the green torch below in the garden, he could just make out the gleam of an aircraft wing.

Fortescue covered the mouthpiece, "Rutherford?"

"Yes, sir."

"Quickly then, Tom! Evacuate!" He uncovered the mouthpiece, and spoke slowly. "No, General, you have got things wrong. There is . . ."

A bellow at the other end interrupted him. Again he covered the mouthpiece. "Naturally, I shall stay, Tom. But everyone else must leave. See Priscilla goes. Tell her it is my wish."

He resumed his attempted telephone conversation. "If I may put in a word of explanation, General. . . ."

130

Bancroft dashed out of the office. But everyone had heard and was already moving. Rutherford had got the Skytruck down neatly near the main door into the garden.

But the aircraft had been seen from the gates. The soldiers hesitated. They recognized the aircraft used by the president. Had General Gawaka arrived like a god again, personally to begin the slaughter? Midnight, their commanding officer had said. They held their fire. A squad saluted.

Then one of the crowd high on the wall spotted the little square group, like rhinos at bay, women and children in the middle, men on the outside, as it moved stealthily but fast down the veranda steps.

There was a shout. A hand grenade exploded in the shrubbery.

"Quickly!" Rutherford shouted as they began to scramble up inside. "We can't wait any longer!" There was the sound of engines being opened up. Only Priscilla and Bancroft remained on the ground.

Bancroft took Priscilla's arm and shoved her inside the aircraft. In the glimmer from the green torch, he saw the expression on her face. Almost with thankfulness, he slammed the door shut, ducked against a hail of stones and ran for the veranda door.

As he ran, the Skytruck turned, the wind from its propellers whipping his sweat-soaked shirt against his body. He stood, holding his breath, as the aircraft pelted towards the red light at the end of the garden.

Suddenly it made a leap. For just a second the top of the wall burgeoned upwards, the shadow of the aircraft a black blossom above it. Then they separated, and the aircraft had merged into the night.

The crowd screamed. The soldiers began firing. Red tracer bullets streaked up like phosphorescent pilot fish.

As Bancroft groped his way upstairs, there came the crash of glass from the dining room windows. H.E. was still on the telephone. He raised his hand as Bancroft came in. He did not seem surprised to see him back. The two of them, after all, were the old hands, the expendables.

Bancroft wrote in block capitals ALL AWAY SAFELY, and

131

passed it across the desk. The high commissioner saw it, nodded. A curiously youthful smile came over the dry, desiccated face.

". . . Fortescue, id is almost midnight. Give Moto up! Give me de weapons I need!"

"General, I think perhaps you do not fully appreciate . . ."

"Fortescue," the general interrupted, roaring louder than ever. "You have exhausted my patience! My people can wait no longer!"

There was the sound of the receiver being banged down at the other end of the line. Suddenly there was silence. The firing and shouting of the crowd outside had ceased.

"Strangely quiet, Tom."

"Ominous, sir." He went outside to the spy-hole on the landing. The crowd was still there, bigger than ever. But now the street lamps spotlighted figures clambering up the railings, beating down the gates.

He hurried back. "They're coming over the walls, sir!"

"Then I shall have to go out and speak to them."

"I shouldn't, sir."

But he had already got up and gone over to the cupboard. Opening it, he brought out his ceremonial white uniform. "They must not invade sanctuary!"

"Sir . . . they have guns!"

Already he had pulled on the trousers, done up the buttons on the white uniform jacket. Then he sat down and put on his shoes. He smiled. "I shall talk to them, Tom. Explain that Moto is not here. That we are all friends." Not a glimmer of fear in the blue eyes as he stood up again and put on his helmet.

He walked out onto the landing, Bancroft following.

"What are you doing, Tom?"

"Coming with you, sir."

"No. You stay here. Lock Chancery and burn the files."

Through the front window, Bancroft saw now that the courtyard was a seething, swarming mass. The gates had been broken down. Carrying sticks and spears, the yelling crowd were converging on the closed High Commission door.

As Bancroft watched, that door was opened. Directly below him he saw the feathered helmet and white uniform emerge. Out onto the top steps came His Excellency Mr. Hugh Fortescue, white chap, CMG.

He held up both his hands, he started to speak.

Then suddenly there was a hiss, a silky swish singing in the air. As though in slow motion, Bancroft saw a spear rise above the broken gates, watched it soar, quivering, begin dropping.

He saw the white uniformed body stiffen, sway, fall. Now came a volley of bullets. And then, triumphantly leaping over the body, came the crowd.

Bancroft ran up to Chancery, locked the doors, got out all the files and began piling them into the incinerator. He could hear them downstairs, screaming themselves into a frenzy. Doors banged. Tables overturned. Glass and china shattered.

"Moto!"

Now the rush of feet on the stairs. They were on the second floor, hundreds by the sound of them. The acrid fumes of the burning files made Bancroft cough. The crowd heard, smelled the smoke, came bounding up. Finding the gate of Chancery locked, they banged frenziedly on the brass bars.

A soldier came thrusting through. He saw the figure behind the grille and raised his revolver. Just for a moment, Bancroft thought he was going to shoot the lock. It was almost with relief that he saw the aim was at him.

There was suddenly an enormous explosion of bright light all round him, then velvety darkness.

It was the soldier's second bullet that shattered the lock. The crowd poured screaming in. They smashed chairs, tables, radios, threw everything they could lay their hands on into Bancroft's fire till the whole landing was ablaze, all the time yelling for Moto's blood and the heads of his British friends.

But gradually it became clear even to the mob that Moto was not here. Just as the chief in the big hat with the ostrich feathers had told them.

The fire and smoke drove them downstairs. The noise died down. Outside, they began slinking away, edging past Hugh Fortescue's body where it still lay—not unlike their own Kajandi crested hornbill, the white feathers now blood-stained. The leader in all his finery had been killed—the unspeakable deed done. They feared the powerful juju of the dead thing.

The crowds and the soldiers vanished. Within the walls there was no sound but the crackling of fires.

Night went by. The fires burned themselves out. The smoke thinned to grey wisps through broken windows.

The northern horizon was coloured by the flash of heavy guns. But from the east a pink light had begun to stain the scarred walls of the High Commission, the dawn of yet another African day.

And inside the High Commission, there came a sound. The damaged teleprinter started chattering, stopped, began again, stuttered, managed just one word in plain language . . .

MAINTAIN.

David Beaty

"Fortescue was one of those very few men who play a straight bat in a crooked world. Having read my book, you will realize that its title is not meant to be in the least satirical. To me Fortescue is 'Excellency'. Pre-eminent in his own way and possessed of a simple old-fashioned goodness, he stands head and shoulders above all the other characters."

David Beaty was talking as he led me on a conducted tour of his twenty acres of Kentish fields and woodland. We were stretching our legs after a delicious lunch prepared by his wife Betty, who is also a novelist.

David went on to say that in contrast to Fortescue, Rutherford epitomizes the ordinary person who thinks he can get on in the world minding his own business.

If some of his judgements sound a little idealistic, David has earned the right to make them, for he has spent most of his life serving others. After distinguished wartime service in the RAF, he became a BOAC pilot. His first novel was published in 1949 and he took up full-time writing in 1953. Books such as *Cone of Silence* and *The Proving Flight* established his reputation and brought their due monetary rewards.

In 1963, David suddenly decided to study for a post-graduate degree in psychology. Afterwards he was appointed to the Overseas Development Administration. For the next seven years he administered British aid in various parts of the globe, including several African and South American states.

"A novel is an extension of the author's personality and experience, and after twelve years of being purely a writer, I felt that both were in need of refreshment," David told me. "Studying psychology and spending a period with the ODA provided exactly that."

Clearly it also provided a lot of background material for *Excellency*, although David was at pains to point out that all the characters were strictly fictional. He also denied that the story was based on the present situation in Uganda. "I could name you another dozen countries in the world—by no means all black—where my story could have taken place."

N.D.B.

CHASE THE WIND

a condensation of the book by
E. V. THOMPSON

Illustrated by Keith Richens
Published by Macmillan, London

Cornwall in the 1840s wasn't all pretty fishing villages. There was fishing certainly, but there were also copper and tin mines where Cornishmen worked—and often died—in pathetic squalor far below the springy moorland turf.

The miners, led by dedicated men like the ambitious Preacher Thackeray, were in turmoil. And young Josh Retallick, a miner's son educated —some might say—beyond his station, was caught up in that turmoil. Torn this way and that by his idealism and his love for the reckless Miriam, he was to be drawn inexorably into the seething conflict.

It was an age when the threat of deportation hung over every man who dared question the doings of his betters. The scene was set for violence, and violence and love each play their part in this remarkable first novel.

Chapter 1

Ninety fathoms below grass, in the darkness at the bottom of the main vertical shaft of Wheal Sharptor copper mine, Joshua Retallick stepped from the ladder onto the ore-strewn floor. The boy took a couple of shaky steps, his legs trembling from the long climb down.

Above him, so far up that the clean, star-studded sky could not be seen, was a small, square hole. Through this was hoisted the copper ore that would make one man rich and send fifty more to premature graves.

Josh moved to one side as boots scraped on the wooden rungs overhead. The night shift was coming down after him. As each man stepped onto the floor he would flex his arms, easing his shoulder muscles, muscles knotted by the prolonged fear of falling.

The miners passed through the openings into the tunnels that sloped gently away from the main shaft. Once inside they paused to light the yellow candles that each man relied upon to give him light to work and warning of foul air.

Josh followed one of the miners along the tunnel where he knew Ben, his father, was working. At first, the tunnel was narrow, with water oozing from the walls. Then, suddenly and dramatically, it opened out into a huge vault, eighty feet wide and thirty high, lit by flickering candles. Here there had been a seam of near-pure copper. Now it was a rock-walled emptiness, the ore long since fed into the belly of a Swansea smelting house and disgorged as gleaming blocks of metal, to be shipped in tall-rigged vessels to a world eager for high-grade Cornish copper.

A dirty, sweating figure, stripped to the waist and pushing a laden wheelbarrow, appeared in the vast chamber. Seeing the new arrivals he rested the wheelbarrow, and called back down the tunnel. "Time to finish, Ben. Night shift are here."

The call was taken up by unseen men in other tunnels, "Knock it off! Night men are here!"

Men cramped in unnatural postures gratefully eased their way back from exploratory borings and headed towards the main shaft to begin the long climb to air and home. The young miner who had first signalled the arrival of the relief shift grinned at Josh. "Has Preacher Thackeray given up trying to learn you? Does he think you should be working below ground wi' us now?"

"No." Josh grinned back. "Lessons ended early. There's a meeting of the benefit union at the St. Cleer chapel tonight."

"I wouldn't mention anything about it to your dad. He's not too happy wi' talk about Thackeray's 'union'."

Budge Pearn towelled his body with his rough-spun shirt. At eighteen he was four years older than Josh. His mother had died in childbirth. His father had been killed in a mining accident when Budge was seven years old and he had been taken into the Retallick household.

"When are you coming up to see my Jenny and the baby?" He pronounced it "bebby". "Little Gwen's right handsome now."

"I know. Jenny brought her down home today. That reminds me. You'd better not be late home. Mother gave Jenny some boiling bacon for your supper."

"I'll be up on the moor before your dad sets foot on the ladder. Give my love to your mother." And, with a cheery wave, Budge was gone.

FARTHER ALONG the tunnel, Ben Retallick crawled back over a heap of newly-dug ore. He was one of the most experienced miners on Wheal Sharptor. But at thirty-five years of age he was reckoned an "old man" by mining standards. The 1830s were an

140

era when a miner who had seen his fortieth birthday below
ground was something of a rarity.

Outside, in the wide tunnel, Ben stood upright slowly and saw
his son. "What are you doing down here, Josh?"

"My lesson finished early. I thought I'd meet you."

Ben saw Budge Pearn's half-filled wheelbarrow and frowned. It
was time the lad learned that a man always emptied his own
wheelbarrow below ground. Then he smiled at his own thoughts.
Budge had plenty of time to learn. With a pretty wife and baby
daughter waiting for him at home, there was more reason to be
on the surface than trundling another man's ore down here for
three pounds a month.

"Come on, son. Let's go up top and taste some fresh air."

At the ladder there was a great deal of good-natured banter and
jostling between the men. Ben stood back. At the end of a shift he
had neither the energy of the youngsters nor patience with them.

Another man also lacked patience. Moses Trago elbowed his
irritable way through to the ladder. Broad-shouldered and brutal,
Moses cared for no man. Behind him, walking in his brother's
shadow, the quieter John Trago loomed just as large.

The arrival of the two men put an end to the miners' good
humour and Ben and Josh shuffled quietly forward with the
others.

This was the part of mining that Ben found more difficult with
each passing day. From ninety fathoms down there were five
hundred and forty ladder rungs to be climbed before a man's head
rose from the hole in the ground. There had been a time when
Ben would count them. But no more. These days he gritted his
teeth, and climbed blindly.

Once on the ladders all talking ceased. A man would regret
each mouthful of wasted air when he arrived, lungs roaring for
oxygen, at the top of the shaft. Josh was aware of this and he
climbed steadily and carefully ahead of his father.

Never a pleasant experience, tonight the climb suddenly
became a nightmare. Josh and Ben were on the fourth ladder,
almost fifty feet from the bottom of the shaft, when there was a
blood-freezing scream from high above them.

Josh had no idea what was happening, but it was a sound Ben had known many times. His "'Ware below!" rang out and he used the same breath to clamber up to share a rung with Josh. "Swing behind the ladder," he hissed. When the boy obeyed, Ben closed his arms about his son and held him tight against the ladder with arms and knees.

Most times a falling man would mercifully smash his head against the side of the shaft and know no more. This one was not so fortunate. The scream had died to a low, inhuman sound as he flailed past Josh and his father, but he remained conscious until he crashed onto the floor of the shaft. Josh would remember the sound of it for as long as he lived.

For two full seconds there was silence. It was broken by the clattering of boots as the men on the lower ladders scrambled back down.

"Ben! Ben Retallick!" the cry went up.

"I'm here. Who was it who fell?"

"Budge Pearn."

"Oh my God! His poor maid." Suddenly Ben felt old and tired. "Wait for me at the fifty fathom level," he told his son. "There's nothing you can do here."

Josh turned and climbed numbly, not sure whether the lump in his throat would make him cry or be sick. Budge Pearn had been as a big brother to him.

BEHIND HIM, down on the floor of the shaft, Ben looked at the smashed body and thought of the young wasted life. "Poor maid!" he repeated. Though only a few weeks past her seventeenth birthday, Jenny Pearn was now a widow with a baby to support. Like Budge she was an orphan, her father having died in an identical accident.

Tom Shovell, the shift captain, swung off the ladder and bent down over the body. Then he looked sympathetically at Ben. "You get on home. We'll do what's necessary here." Ben nodded. "I'd be obliged if you would take it on yourself to tell Jenny. You —or Jesse." Jesse was Ben's wife. "I needn't tell you how sorry I am, Ben. He was a well-liked lad."

"There's little comfort in that for poor Jenny."

He began the climb to the surface once more. At the fifty fathom level Josh joined him. On the surface, the miners clustered round the top of the shaft murmured their sympathy.

There was a chill March wind blowing on the moor. Ben and Josh took the path that wound over the shoulder of the tor, towards the small cluster of slate and granite cottages huddled in a shallow depression on the east-facing slope.

"How . . . how do you think it happened?" Josh asked, speaking for the first time since they had left the shaft.

"I expect Budge was in a hurry. Probably trod on a loose rung. I've seen it happen too often."

He stopped talking as they heard a woman's light footsteps running and stumbling along the path towards them.

"Ben! Is that you? Oh thank God you're safe! Thank God!" Jesse Retallick clung to her husband, shaking violently. "They told me there'd been an accident. Was anyone hurt?"

"It was Budge." Ben felt her stiffen in his arms. "He fell from the ladder."

"He's dead then." It was a statement of fact, not a question.

"Yes," said Ben gently, "Jenny hasn't been told yet. I was going to see her but it might be better if you did."

Jesse was silent for a long time. Then she burst out, "Why? Why did it have to be Budge? The two of them had found so much happiness together. It's that damned mine. Worn ladders, frayed ropes . . . ."

"Enough now, Jesse. It gives us our living."

"Try to tell that to Budge—God rest his soul." She sobbed once, a long, uneven breath. But she slipped from Ben's arms when he tried to comfort her.

"I'll go to Jenny now. Before she hears the news from someone else." She moved away along the path and her voice came to them from the darkness. "Ben?"

"Yes?"

"I'm not forgetting to thank God it wasn't you."

As she hurried off, her words reminded Ben of the disconcerting, impetuous girl he had married, and he loved her for it.

143

IN THE KITCHEN of their small granite cottage on the outskirts of Henwood village, Josh ladled stew from the cooking pot on the fire into two bowls while Ben eased his boots off. They sat, eating in silence. Small but spotless, the kitchen served as dining and living room. In the one other downstairs room all the "best" possessions were housed.

Suddenly the door banged open and Jesse Retallick bundled Jenny Budge inside, a thin, pale girl with little Gwen clutched wailing to her. Jesse took her straight through into the best room.

A minute later Jesse was back. "Josh, make yourself a bed on the floor in our room upstairs. Jenny will be moving into yours. Ben, bring some fire in here . . . . She hasn't started crying yet. When it comes it will be all the worse for the waiting."

Josh left his father filling a bucket with live coals from the kitchen stove, and made his bed up in a corner of his parents' bedroom. He was lying in it when his father came into the darkened room.

Ben saw the glitter of tears on his son's cheek. He said nothing but walked to the window and looked down the valley. There was light shining from the large windows of the chapel and he guessed the body of Budge Pearn had arrived there.

Then he heard the sound from the room downstairs. Starting as a low moan it quickly swelled and expanded until it burst out as a sob. Then Jenny began crying. Painful as it was to listen to, Ben felt a sense of relief. Now, Jenny was someone to comfort, a young girl who had lost her man. Before, she had been unapproachable, locked away where no one could join her.

Ben went downstairs, put on his boots and coat and let himself out of the house. Despite the chill east wind he found a great many villagers gathered in the Henwood chapel. There were inquiries from all sides about Jenny as he strode in the door. The women in the crowd knew that tomorrow, or the next day, it might be their turn. The mines were notorious widow-makers.

The inside of the small chapel was clean and stark. Ben was surprised to see the preacher inside. The Reverend Wrightwick Roberts was not a resident preacher. He rode the North Hill Methodist circuit. Only the larger communities like St. Cleer, where Josh went for his lessons, could support a resident preacher.

The North Hill circuit minister was himself an ex-miner, his shoulders almost as broad as Moses Trago's, but when he spoke his voice was soft. "It's a night for grieving, Ben. The Lord's ways are beyond the understanding of mortals." He nodded towards a closed door at the end of the chapel. "Budge is through there. Mary Crabbe is with him."

Mary Crabbe had been taking charge of births and deaths in the district since before Ben was born. He nodded his acknowledgment. "It's been a sad day, Wrightwick." He sat down on the end of a bench. "You'll see to things? Take the service for him? I'll be paying."

"And what about Theophilus Strike? Won't he give anything?"

Ben managed a faint smile. "That sounds like Preacher Thackeray talking. Theophilus Strike is a mine owner, Wrightwick. He pays wages. Jenny will collect whatever was due to Budge— and a guinea or two besides."

Wrightwick Roberts frowned at the mention of William Thackeray. The fiery young St. Cleer preacher was fast establishing a reputation as a miners' champion and the younger men flocked to his sermons on Sundays, packing the large St. Cleer chapel.

"Why do you let Josh stay at Thackeray's school, Ben? He's not a good influence."

Ben shrugged, "His lessons are cheap—and good."

"But Thackeray teaches things that you won't find in any schoolbook. He feeds his ideas to young miners who know no better. Telling them to band into a 'union' and demand more money is dangerous talk, Ben."

"All I've heard is rumours. None of them from Josh," said Ben, standing up. "But I do know the boy is learning things I would dearly love to have been taught. Josh won't have to go down a mine because he knows nothing else, Wrightwick. And he won't end up in your chapel with Mary Crabbe straightening his broken limbs." He stopped and drew a deep breath. "I'll be away now before I say more than I should."

"We've been friends too long for me to take offence," said the preacher. "And I'll walk up with you. I'd like to see Jenny."

BUDGE WAS buried on a day as grey as the occasion. Wrightwick Roberts, not a preacher to cut corners at a man's funeral, sent him on his way to the hereafter with as good a reference as any man could receive. In the same sermon the preacher damned a mine that allowed a man to fall to his death and then failed to send a representative to his funeral.

In all fairness, Theophilus Strike *had* delegated someone—his senior mine captain. But Herman Schmidt could think of better ways to spend an afternoon than listening to a sermon in praise of one of the workers he regarded as little better than animals.

Instead, Schmidt was shut inside his house in the nearby town of Liskeard. He was already in a state of alcoholic stupor. He spent much less time at the Wheal Sharptor than Theophilus Strike was aware of, but once a week he carried out a full inspection of the mine. And from this weekly visit the mine captain was able to compile his reports and direct the operations that kept Wheal Sharptor a profit-making mine.

Herman Schmidt was a brilliant mine captain. He was also a foreigner, an atheist, and a drunkard. The miners hated him.

"WELL DONE, Josh. Your reading is greatly improved. Keep it up."

Josh looked down in embarrassed pleasure. The Reverend William Thackeray was not given to handing out unearned praise to his pupils. Starting these classes had been one of the first tasks he had set himself upon taking up his appointment at St. Cleer. A slight, stooping figure, he had accepted many years before that he was no physical match for his fellow men. So he had chosen words as his weapons. Sent to Cornwall, he saw the appalling rigours of work below ground. It was inevitable that he should become a social reformer. With his power of oratory he quickly earned the enmity of the mine owners and "adventurers"—those who held shares in the mines. But he cared little for any of them.

He spoke to Josh again. "Yes, young man, you have it in you to become as educated as anyone in these parts." He suddenly stopped and jabbed a long finger at the air an inch from Josh's nose. "But that is only the beginning. What are you going to *do* with that education?"

146

The question took Josh by surprise. "I don't know, sir—but I think I would like to be an engineer."

"An admirable ambition." The menacing finger was lowered and the preacher glowered at the class. "How about the rest of you? You are all the sons of enlightened men. Miners who are determined their sons will not have to go underground simply because they are unable to do anything else. Does any other boy know what he would like to be?"

The hands rose hesitantly and sporadically.

"Hmmmm! We seem beset by uncertainty." He looked around the room at the tousle-headed, ragged boys and sighed. "For all my teaching, I have no doubt most of you will waste your knowledge, using it to count barrowloads of ore."

He shrugged. "At least you won't be cheated by a dishonest mine captain. All right boys, school is over for today. I will see you at the same time tomorrow."

THE TRACK from the school in St. Cleer wandered aimlessly in the general direction of Sharptor, skirting the Caradon mines and dipping down to where the great shaft of the Wheal Phoenix yawned deep in the shadowed valley. Josh ignored it and went straight across country, toiling up onto the high, lonely Bodmin Moor.

This was the place he loved above all others. It was a vast landscape of sweeping emptiness, its stunted bushes, bowing to the east, evidence of the prevailing winds of winter. Now the gorse was a tangle of yellow blossom. Here and there a lacework of streams left the turf soft and sponge-like underfoot. Above it all, blunt-winged buzzards circled remorselessly in search of prey.

On the moor Josh could think. Create his own future. He had told Preacher Thackeray he wanted to be an engineer. In truth, he knew little about mechanical things. He had looked at the steam-engines in the Caradon and Phoenix mines and had been impressed with their size and noise, but he knew nothing of their workings. He decided he would like to find out.

Josh was on the high moor proper now. He paused to watch a buzzard which had strayed into the territory of a pair of crows.

The large black birds were working as a team. While one harassed from close range, the second climbed high above them, dropping into the battle area with wings closed. The buzzard, sure of its superiority, continued unhurriedly on its course. Only occasionally did it roll onto its back to meet the threat from above with outstretched talons. Then it was the turn of the crows to take evasive action.

Josh liked to see the buzzards. They enjoyed complete freedom of the great moor, a freedom he would dearly love to possess. But, except for long summer evenings and occasions like this, there was little time for exploring. In the mornings he worked at the mine, dressing the ore at the surface with the women and other children. In the afternoon he attended school at St. Cleer. Most evenings he would help with household chores before settling down to more schoolwork. The evening schooling had become more difficult since Jenny and the baby had come to live with them. Baby Gwen had begun to cut her teeth and she cried a lot.

Josh could see the small group of cottages well down on the slope. Another ten minutes and he would be home. But first he had to pass the Tragos' home—and Morwen Trago was sitting astride a long, rounded boulder outside the entrance.

The Tragos were a strange brooding family and their "house" very much in keeping with their image. It was comprised of gigantic slabs of rock, the back wall buried in the hillside. The doorway was a crevice between the rocks with an odd-shaped wooden door seven feet high. Here lived Moses Trago and his wife and two children, together with his unmarried brother John.

The "house" had not been built by the Tragos. Superstition had it that it had once been a burial-place for the "old men" whose shallow diggings scarred the moor.

Morwen Trago, Moses' son, was almost two years older than Josh. Sliding from the rock, he took up a position straddle-legged across the path. Josh approached warily, stopping ten feet away.

"What do you want, Morwen?"

"What do I want?" The bigger boy feigned surprise. "I live here, Josh Retallick. There's nothing says I can't stand outside my own home if I want to."

"Then you'll let me pass?" Josh's face felt taut.

"Of course I will—once I've seen what you have in that bag."

Josh's grip on his canvas schoolbag tightened. "It's only schoolbooks. They belong to Preacher Thackeray."

"Do they now? A preacher's books! Religious nonsense, that's what books are."

Morwen was echoing his father's words. They had been accompanied by a stinging cuff on his ear when Morwen had asked whether he could take reading lessons with Preacher Thackeray. That had been when Morwen was working on the surface with Josh and some of the other boys. Since then Moses had found work underground for his son.

"Books are only nonsense if you can't read them," Josh retorted. "And they are staying in my bag."

"We'll see about that . . . !"

Morwen began to advance towards Josh. He stopped when Josh stooped and picked up a broken piece of granite.

Morwen Trago looked at Josh standing with the piece of stone in his hand and weighed his chances of tackling him. Just when it seemed he might ignore the odds, a barefoot girl with tangled long black hair ran between them.

"Stop it, you two! Josh, put down that stone."

"No. Not until I'm past Morwen."

She turned to the other boy. "Let him go, Morwen. Ma wouldn't like it if I told her you were bullying."

Miriam Trago was the same age as Josh, but her shrill young voice carried the air of authority that came with being her father's favourite. With a scornful shrug, Morwen Trago said, "Keep your books. Only cissies and preachers read books." He turned and strolled away towards the rock house.

Josh dropped the stone and mumbled, "Thank you, Miriam— though he wouldn't have stopped me."

"I don't care about that. I didn't want to see Morwen's head split open. That's all."

With a look almost as scornful as her brother's she too turned away.

"That's not true, Miriam Trago," Josh called after her. "You just don't want people to think you're nice. But you stopped us from fighting because you thought I might get hurt."

Miriam swung round and glared at him for perhaps five seconds. Then she bent down, took hold of the bottom of her ragged dress and raised her hands above her head.

She was wearing nothing beneath it.

Josh's face went scarlet. He turned and fled down the path with Miriam's derisive laughter chasing him most of the way.

Chapter 2

The wet, cold days soon gave way to warmer ones as spring advanced into summer. For Josh, the longer days meant he was able to spend more time on the moor. He avoided the Trago home as much as possible, but would often see Miriam in the distance. She had wandered the moors from her earliest days and knew the whole wild area better than any. She worked a full day shift with her mother on the grading floor at the Wheal Phoenix, but her evenings were spent out on the moor. There she felt free.

Although Josh and Miriam would occasionally see each other on the moor, the next encounter between the Retallick and Trago families occurred at a more senior level. It was a brief and violent meeting.

The Sunday evening was warm and pleasant. Ben, Jesse and Josh, a few paces ahead of the shift captain Tom Shovell, Jenny and baby Gwen, were taking a slow walk homewards from Henwood chapel, making the most of an opportunity to feel sun on their faces. At the edge of the village the Reverend Wrightwick Roberts caught up with them. They spoke together of the new corn laws.

"Unless something is done soon a month's pay won't buy a bag of flour," said Jesse.

The two men nodded agreement. "It's a bad law," said Ben bitterly, "that prevents corn from entering the country, then sends half our own corn elsewhere. Unless Parliament does something we'll see the troubles of twenty years ago with us again."

They reached a steep part of the track and, taking baby Gwen from Jenny, Tom Shovell tucked the infant into the crook of one arm. He made light work of the gradient, despite the extra pounds that Gwen had put on in recent weeks. In sharp contrast, Jenny was thin to the point of frailness now and her skin had developed a translucent paleness. She had been a pretty girl before. Grief had changed her into a woman of unusual, haunting beauty.

When they arrived at the cottage, Ben, Jesse and Jenny went inside with the baby. Josh stayed outside with the preacher who was talking to Tom Shovell.

They had not been there for many minutes when a bellow from the direction of the moor brought their conversation to an abrupt halt. They turned to see Kate Trago, the wife of Moses, running wildly towards them, her long hair streaming behind her. Fifty yards behind her Moses lurched unsteadily with a wide-legged gait.

Kate stumbled and fell in front of the startled group. As Wrightwick Roberts went to help her she heaved herself up. They saw that one eye was swollen with an ugly graze beneath it.

Taking the preacher's arm, she pulled him towards the cottage. "Hurry, all of you!" she pleaded. "Moses is mad-drunk. Get inside or he'll kill me—and you!"

The preacher freed his arm. "Take her in and you go with them, Josh."

"Let me try to reason with him," said Tom Shovell. "I know him, Wrightwick. He'll listen to me."

"He won't listen to anyone in his state. Get everyone into the cottage. Quickly!"

The door banged at his back as the preacher turned to face the drunken miner.

Moses was steadying himself on the path. "Get out of my way," he said. "I want my wife."

The preacher's voice was pitched low and coaxing. "Leave her be, Moses. She's inside talking to Jesse Retallick."

"I don't care who she's talking to. She's a lazy idle slut. No, she's worse than that. She's a thief. A thief!" Moses lurched

151

forward and Wrightwick Roberts winced at the gin fumes the drunken miner belched into his face as he spoke.

"You know what she did? Do you want to know what that bloody woman did?" He screwed his mouth up. "She took money from my pocket. That's what. Took it when she thought I was asleep."

"I expect she had need of it." The preacher's voice was still calm and even.

The miner's unshaven upper lip curled back in a sneer. "I'll tell you what she has need of. I don't have to go to chapel to learn how to run my life. I'll do it my way. And so will she."

He lunged towards the door but Wrightwick Roberts was too quick for him. He stooped under the other man's arm, put his shoulder beneath his armpit and heaved. Moses Trago took eight or nine uncontrolled backward paces before crashing to the ground.

Rolling over quickly he looked up at the preacher. Sheer rage sobered him momentarily. "I'll kill you for that!"

He came up from the ground with unexpected speed. Quick as he was, someone else was faster. The door behind the preacher was jerked open and he was thrust aside as Ben Retallick took the head-long rush of Moses Trago with outstretched arms, closing them around the drunken miner as the two men came together.

Moses was no stranger to fighting and he was not to be overwhelmed so easily. He staggered around until both men fell heavily to the ground. Ben's grip slackened for an instant. It was enough. Flinging his wide shoulders back Moses broke the encircling grip and scrambled to his feet.

Ben was still on his knees when Moses' boot took him on the shoulder and knocked him rolling down again. Then the other miner moved quickly around him. Kicking him in the ribs. Aiming for his head. It was one of Moses' wilder kicks that proved his undoing. It missed completely. Ben was quick enough to grasp the foot and with a twist he sent his opponent crashing to the ground once more. As Moses began to rise Ben crashed a rock-hard fist against his temple. The force of the punch dropped him backwards to lie prostrate with arms flung wide.

"Now there's as fine a punch as ever I have seen," said Wrightwick Roberts. "It would have felled a bullock."

"It needed to," replied Ben, rubbing his knuckles.

It took three bucketsful of water, flung unceremoniously over his face, to make Moses Trago stir. He twitched, shuddered, rolled from side to side and then slowly sat up. Head between his hands, he let out a loud groan.

"You may think you are suffering now, Moses," the preacher told him. "One day you'll have to answer to the Lord for your misdeeds. This drubbing will be as a gentle tap on the hand compared with what will happen on that day."

Moses' reply was an oath accompanied by another groan. He got unsteadily to his feet and stood swaying and glaring.

"You'll live to regret this day, Ben Retallick," he said. "So will you, Preacher." He raised his voice to be sure it carried into the house. "You tell that woman of mine if she dares show her face inside my home I'll break every bone in her body."

He turned and staggered away towards the high moor.

"You best be careful of him, Ben," said Tom Shovell from the doorway. "Moses is a dangerous man."

"Tom is right. You keep clear of him." Kate Trago came from the house, peering painfully through her one good eye. The other had closed completely.

"He'll be all right when he sobers up," declared Ben. "We were boys together, Kate. I know Moses Trago as well as any man."

"No!" Kate shook her head. "Moses is not the man you once knew. In the last few years he's changed. Oh! I know he's always been rough, but there's more to it now. He's turned sour inside. He envies you more than anyone else, Ben. You've got all the things that Moses hasn't. Respect. A house. I know it sounds stupid but he hates you for having things he's scorned to have all his life."

She stopped abruptly. "I've said far too much. Take heed of it and I'll have thanked you for helping me. I must go now."

"You can't go yet!" Ben protested. "Moses is raving drunk. He'll kill you if you go near him."

154

"He won't." She shook her head. "He'll go home, stumble onto his bed and sleep until morn. Then he'll get up and go to the mine. That's all there is in his life. Drink, sleep and work. But he won't hurt me any more." There was the gleam of a tear in her eye. "Besides, I'm his wife. I've got to go to him."

She went on her way without looking back.

THREE DAYS after the fight Miriam Trago waylaid Josh on his way home from the St. Cleer chapel school. She stepped out from the tall fern into his path when he was on the high, flat moor, hidden from the cottages on the other side of the tor.

"Hello!" It was a casual greeting.

"Hello!" Josh's reply was more cautious. His small feud with Morwen Trago had exploded into something far more serious now that their fathers were involved.

But Miriam had not sought him out to extend the feud. "Have you been to the chapel school?" It was an unnecessary question. They both knew it. "What do you learn there?"

"Oh, lots of things. Reading. Writing. Sums."

"I wish I could learn to read and write."

"Why don't you ask your dad to let you go?"

She shook her head. "I did ask him. He says there's no need for such fancy ways for girls." The mention of Moses Trago brought about a long, uncomfortable silence.

"My dad's not all bad, you know," she said at last.

As she spoke she looked down at her bare feet. They had long been a subject for disapproval among the villagers of Henwood. But Miriam enjoyed feeling the springy turf of the moor beneath her feet.

"He doesn't hit me often. When he does he's always sorry afterwards."

Josh said nothing. He was anxious to avoid a clash.

"He works hard. Even your dad says he's a good worker."

"So he might be. But he gets very quarrelsome when he's been drinking."

Her head came up and her dark eyes met his. "That's his way. He doesn't mean anything by it." Then the challenge subsided.

She touched the corner of one of the books that protruded from his canvas bag. "What's this?"

"It's a writing-book."

"Writing? Show me. I want to see what your writing looks like. Please!"

Josh hesitated. Despite Miriam's apparent interest he was still wary of her. "All right." He extracted the book and opened it and held it out to her, disclosing handwriting that was small but not very neat.

The untidiness meant nothing to Miriam; she was impressed. "There's such a lot of it. Did you write it all?"

He nodded, absurdly pleased at her praise. "There's lots more. Almost a whole book full."

"What does it say?"

He turned the book up the other way and began to read. ". . . He said unto him, the third time, 'Simon, son of Joseph, lovest thou me? . . .'" Josh read two pages before closing the book. "That was from the Bible," he told her.

"It was beautiful!" Miriam's expression was full of wonder. For the first time he noticed that she had very dark eyes, fringed by the longest eyelashes he had ever seen.

"Could you write my name—Miriam?"

Josh nodded, "Yes." He rummaged in his bag and came out with a scrap of paper. "I need something to rest this on."

"I know just the thing. It's in a secret place. Nobody but me knows of it." She took his hand and, full of excitement, pulled him after her as she left the path and plunged into the ferns.

When they reached an apparently impenetrable barrier of gorse, she released his hand and dropped to her knees. "Follow me."

She disappeared into a low, dark, gorse tunnel which twisted and turned for twenty feet before coming out into sparkling sunlight once more. Thick bushes were all around, but here in the centre was a large flat rock. Two others, leaning against one another, formed a small triangular cave. When Josh stood up he could see the whole of the Phoenix valley through the thin top branches of the gorse bushes, but it would have been impossible for anyone to see the two children from below.

"Here, rest the paper on this rock."

She sat cross-legged on the granite, her skirt tucked between her legs, her calloused knees as brown as a gypsy's. Josh unslung his bag and, taking out a book, placed it on the rock. Then he smoothed out a piece of paper, laid it on the book, knelt down and carefully wrote the letters with a thick-leaded pencil.

"M-I-R-I-A-M. Miriam. There you are!"

She had been watching him, hardly daring to breathe. Now she took the paper as though it was a magic formula for all the riches of the world. "This really is my name? It says 'Miriam'?"

"Yes." Her reaction was most satisfactory.

"Can I keep it?"

"Of course you can. It's of no use to me."

"This is the first time I've ever seen my name written down. I'll keep it for ever and always."

"I'll teach you to write it yourself if you like."

She dropped down beside him and gripped his arm. "Oh, please!"

He first had to show her how to hold the pencil. Then how to form the letters, with his hand clenched over hers. It took a long time and the result was far from satisfactory, although Josh insisted it was fine.

"No," Miriam said, clutching the piece of paper with Josh's effort on it, "this is much better. But I'll do it properly one day if you'll learn me."

"I don't know," said Josh uncertainly.

"You can use this place as your own," she persisted.

Josh wavered. "All right," he said. "I'll teach you. Meet me on my way home from the chapel and I'll give you a lesson. Not every day though."

They finally settled for three days a week and Josh set his bag back on his shoulder. "Are you coming?"

Miriam shook her head, "Not yet. There's a full moon tonight and I want to watch it from up there." She pointed to where the great rock mass that was Sharp Tor rose stark and grey above the moor. "Why don't you stop and see it with me?"

"No, I must get back. Mother will be wondering where I am."

"If you come up Sharp Tor with me I'll let you kiss me."

"I don't want to." He turned his back on her and walked away.

"You will one day, Josh Retallick. You will one day!" Her voice mocked him as he set off home across the moor.

NOBODY NOTICED how late Josh was. The house was full of people, among them most of the miners from Ben Retallick's shift, and Tom Shovell and Nehemeziah Lancellis, the mine ostler.

It was Wrightwick Roberts's booming voice that met Josh's ears when he went in. "I am not happy about this trip into Bodmin. To go to see a public double hanging is shameful enough. With it taking place on a fair day there will be all manner of sinful things to entice our young men."

"But it's a holiday," argued one of the men. "A hanging of miners from the Kit Hill mine. Some of us know them."

"There's nothing to be proud of in knowing convicted murderers," retorted Roberts.

"From what I hear others were more to blame than them for the killing," said Jesse Retallick from the kitchen doorway. "A militia man, wasn't it?"

There was a growl of assent from the miners.

"There can be little excuse for killing a man, Jesse," said Roberts. "A man's life is sacred."

"And so is a man's family!" Jesse retorted, hands planted firmly on her hips. "Didn't the shareholders, the adventurers, lock the men out? Stopped them from working, then wouldn't give them the money they were due? It's not surprising the miners got angry. But even then the adventurers wouldn't stand up to them like men. They called in the militia."

"These are things you don't understand, Jesse," said Roberts. "The men wanted a charter. They spoke of uniting all the miners in the district. It's dangerous talk, Jesse."

"I may not understand about charters and uniting the miners, Wrightwick Roberts. I do know how a man would feel if he saw his family starving, and him knowing the adventurers owed him money!" Red-faced, with eyes flashing angrily, Jesse slammed into the kitchen.

158

Ben Retallick chuckled. "I could have told you it wasn't wise to tell Jesse she 'didn't understand'. Not when she feels so strong about something."

The preacher ran a handkerchief around the inside of his collar then held up a big hand for silence, "All right, men. Now we've decided to go to Bodmin . . ." He paused until the spontaneous laughter died away, ". . . we'll get down to details. Nehemeziah, how many wagons will we have? . . ."

THE DAY of the execution dawned bright and clear. The sun rose on the wagons loaded with miners and their families being pulled by the toiling horses up the steep track from the Sharptor mine. Chapel folk had possession of the front half of the convoy, while the last two wagons were filled with the younger miners— including Morwen Trago—among whom bottles of gin were already being passed.

Most of the older children were riding together. Josh found himself sitting close to Miriam. But this was a different Miriam to the one he met on the moor for her lessons. True, she still wore no shoes on her feet, but her hair had been brushed back tidily and the dress she had on was made from new calico. As always, however, she kept up a steady stream of chatter. The embarrassed Josh said little in reply. But when someone called that Bodmin could be seen up ahead, he knelt up beside her, looking between the straddled legs of the driver on his high seat. The hooves of the horses struck sparks from the teeth-rattling cobbles as the wagoner held them back down the steep approach to the town.

Now there were new sights aplenty. The slanting rays of the morning sun woke a million window-panes and the streets were at times so narrow that the upstairs of the houses leaned towards each other as though sharing a secret. Here and there the streets opened out into squares where stalls and sideshows, tinkers' carts, and livestock of all descriptions tangled together. To one side of the town stood the gaunt, grim walls of Bodmin Gaol. But above all there were people. Thousands and thousands of people!

The mine wagons trundled down a lane to a churned-up field, three-parts full of wagons, and the young men quickly moved off

159

in a rowdy bunch, eager to sample the delights of the town. The Reverend Wrightwick Roberts watched them go with a sad heart.

"Now, Josh, what are you going to do? Will you come with us?" Jesse Retallick asked.

"No." Josh was aware of the disapproving look his mother was giving to the barefooted Miriam. "I'll have a walk about the town and see what's going on."

"Well, you mind you behave yourself. Have you still got your shilling?"

He held it out towards her, grinning happily.

"Good, don't lose it. Off you go now, and be back here at six o'clock."

Soon Josh and Miriam found themselves among stalls and shops that displayed everything imaginable, from shoes to sweets and sweets to horses. Josh spent a farthing at the first stall on some sweets. They wandered along in bulge-cheeked silence until they found themselves before a great iron-studded gate, set into the high grey wall of the prison. Here the gallows had been erected on a raised platform and two oiled and pre-stretched ropes hung from the crossbeam. It was in this spot that the crowd was thickest, while the officer in charge of the military guard paced about on the platform, shouting to keep a clear passage between the prison gate and the gallows.

As nothing else seemed to be happening, Josh and Miriam took another walk about Bodmin and returned shortly before noon. The crowd had swelled to fill the whole vast space in front of the prison and overflowed halfway up the slope of the opposite hill.

At five minutes to twelve the prison gates swung open. Led by a single drummer, two columns of soldiers in bright red coats and white cross-belts marched slowly from the dusty courtyard within.

Shuffling between the lines of soldiers were the two wretched miners, heavily manacled and chained to each other. Their appearance was the signal for a murmur of anger from the crowd. The soldiers fingered their guns uneasily. The condemned men climbed onto the platform, aware for the first time of the vast size of the crowd. The hangman, his head hooded, then stepped forward.

160

"Brothers!" The voice of Wrightwick Roberts boomed out loudly. "Brothers! Join me in a prayer for these two sinners who are nearing the judgement of the Lord. Let us appeal for His mercy. Down on your knees and pray with me."

There was a rippling movement through the crowd as all of the women and most of the men dropped to their knees. The voice of Wrightwick Roberts continued, "Lord we thank Thee for this opportunity to ask Thy forgiveness. . . ."

"What's happening?" Miriam asked in a hoarse whisper. "Aren't they going to hang them after all?"

"Of course they are going to hang them."

"Why is Preacher Roberts thanking God then?"

"Shut up!"

Miriam fell silent. Preacher Roberts's prayer was a long one and when he had finished he ordered the crowd to stand and sing a hymn with him.

As the words rose from ten thousand throats the officer of the soldiers found it difficult to contain his impatience. He looked for the hangman and saw him standing beside the condemned men, his hands clasped in front of him, his chin thrust forward inside his hood as though he were in chapel.

When the third verse began, the officer spoke to the sergeant. The hangman was aroused from his religious fervour and persuaded to place the nooses about the necks of the two men. His action caused the singing of the crowd to falter.

The officer stepped forward. His voice was nerve-tight. "Silence!" he called. "Silence in the name of the Queen."

The noise from the crowd subsided quickly.

"It is my duty to see that the sentence of death passed upon Thomas Arthur Sleedon and William Joseph Darling is carried out in accordance with the laws of this realm. They have been found guilty of the murder of Henry Talbot, a militia man. Before the sentence is carried out they may speak their last words. May God rest their souls."

". . . And may He rot yours and the souls of all those who oppress the miners of this county."

An astonished Josh recognized the voice of his teacher, William

161

Thackeray. He stood in the midst of a group of miners who were stamping and shouting less than twenty yards from the gallows.

There was a murmur of agreement from the crowd, but William Thackeray had more to say. "The militia is supposed to uphold the law, not to carry out the orders of the adventurers who keep miners poor. The wrong men are on the scaffold," he shouted. "It should be the adventurers! The mine owners!"

"Yes! Take them down! Release them!" The crowd seemed to sway forwards towards the gallows platform.

The officer rapped out an order and the soldiers brought muskets to their shoulders. At the same time the hangman reached forward and gripped a large lever set into one of the uprights.

Above the shouting a woman's voice could be heard screaming, "Thomas! Oh God! Thomas!" One of the condemned men, a look of anguish on his face, took a step forward—and trod into eternity. The trap-door dropped down on oiled hinges and the men fell until the rope jerked them to a fatal halt.

There was a sudden hush. Then the woman who had screamed for Thomas Sleedon let out a long animal howl and Josh became aware that Miriam was clutching his arm painfully.

"It was horrible! Horrible!" she began sobbing.

Josh tried to comfort her, but too much was happening about them. The crowd was angry. As the soldiers cut down the two dead men a stone landed with a thud on the platform. It was followed by another—and another.

As the soldiers carrying the two bodies retreated towards the prison gate, the remaining soldiers formed a tight line facing the crowd and retreated step by step. As they neared the gate those on the extreme ends of the line came under attack from the bolder young miners. This provoked the officer into showing them the authority of the army. He snapped out an order. The line of soldiers stopped retreating and half of them dropped to one knee, muskets pointed at their tormentors. The officer raised his sword. It fell, a flash of silver in the sun, and the muskets spoke.

At the last moment the soldiers had raised their weapons and the musket balls sped harmlessly above the heads of the crowd. But the mob was thrown into panic and thousands fled. Holding

162

Miriam's hand, Josh ran with the crowd, not stopping until they reached the safety of the narrow thoroughfares.

His feeling of relief was almost immediately replaced by a sense of foolishness. No soldiers were pursuing them. There had been no second volley. But Miriam's tear-stained face was real enough.

"Oh, come on," said Josh, more harshly than he intended because of the discovery that he was still holding her hand. "It's all over now. Here, I'll buy you some more sweets—and we'll go to watch the dancing bear."

They saw the bear, an unhappy, degraded animal, and they bought more sweets. By late afternoon Miriam had succeeded in pushing thoughts of the hanging to the back of her mind.

As it was a special holiday the town's inns were open all day. There were many who took full advantage of the fact. Drunken men, and not a few women, became commonplace as the day wore on. Those unfortunate enough to fall in some inconspicuous alley were quickly relieved of everything of value by the gangs of young villains who followed them from the inns.

But it was trouble of a different kind that caught up with Miriam and Josh. When a fight erupted in the town's main street, Josh took Miriam down a narrow alleyway in an attempt to bypass the trouble-area. There they saw a thick-set man standing straddle-legged close to the wall of a house. Josh's instinct was to hurry past, but the man blocked their way. It was Herman Schmidt, the Sharptor mine captain.

"Well, well! And what have we here?" The accent was thick and guttural and in no way helped by the amount of alcohol he had drunk. He took a staggering step forward.

"What you want?" He was talking to Miriam. "You looking for a man? All right, Cornish whore. How much you charge, eh?"

Josh edged backwards and tried to pull Miriam with him but the German grabbed her arm. "You hear me? How much?"

"One guinea."

Josh looked at Miriam in amazement.

"A guinea? What you take me for?" Schmidt snorted derisively then stooped down to look more closely at her. "Um. You are young still. You have a room?"

She nodded.

"Then I give you half-a-guinea."

"A guinea."

"Half-a-guinea!" the German roared. "No woman is worth a whole guinea. Not even a German virgin."

"Miriam, what are you saying? Come away."

Without turning around she waved her free hand behind her back, signalling for Josh to go.

"What are you doing here, boy?" The mine captain peered at Josh, trying to focus his bloodshot eyes. "Don't I know you?" He shook his head. "I should know you, perhaps. But go away. Run off."

Josh stood his ground. The mine captain pulled a coin from his pocket and held it up. "Here. Is this a half-guinea?"

Miriam snatched it from him. "Yes."

Josh caught Miriam's hand, thoroughly alarmed, "Don't go with him, Miriam. He'll hurt you. Don't go . . . ."

Herman Schmidt said angrily, "When I give an order it is meant to be obeyed." The back of his heavy hand swung, knocking Josh off balance. He thought he heard Miriam scream as his head struck the wall. Then everything went black.

When he opened his eyes Miriam and Schmidt were gone. He felt sick. Whether it was from the blow to his head or the thought of what the German and the girl were doing together he did not want to know. He scoured the alleyways in the immediate vicinity but there was no sign of them. Soon the shadows began to grow long. Despondently he made his way back to the field where the wagons stood.

Gradually more Henwood villagers arrived. He saw his mother and father. Jesse looked for her son, saw he was safe and waved cheerily. Suddenly Miriam arrived. She was bubbling over with happiness, as though nothing untoward had taken place.

"Oh, Josh! You don't know how glad I am to see you. When you fell I thought Schmidt had killed you. As soon as I could I came back to look for you but you'd gone. Where have you been? I've looked everywhere."

There was no stopping her. The words poured out. "Look! I've been shopping. I bought a comb for my ma. Some tobacco for dad. A new cap for Morwen—he's always wanted one. There's some ribbon . . . ." She paused. ". . . And I've brought this for you."

She held something out to him. He tried not to, but he had to look. It was a pocket-knife. A bone-handled knife with two spring blades that folded into it. He was tempted. Very tempted.

"I don't want it."

Miriam's eyes opened wide. "You don't think . . . . ? You don't believe I went with that—that *animal?*"

A couple of women looked around at the vehemence of her words. Miriam lowered her voice. "I wasn't going to let him get away with the things he said to me. I took his money—and it was a whole guinea, not a half-guinea. When I found a house with the door open I took him inside and told him to go upstairs and wait for me in the bedroom. I expect he's still there."

She smiled, expecting Josh to smile in return. But Josh's thoughts were in a turmoil. "Taking his money was stealing. You should have come away with me when I wanted you to."

"It was *not* stealing. He deserved to pay for hitting you. Anyway, he had hold of my arm, remember? I couldn't have got away. If I'd struggled he would have hit me too."

The wagon had filled up fast and now the driver climbed up onto the seat. With many "Hups!" and "Heave ho's", the horses strained into their harness to begin the climb away from the town.

In the crowded, swaying wagon, Josh sat with his arms wrapped around his drawn-up knees. He was thoroughly miserable. The thing that bothered him most was that Miriam had been immediately aware of what the German was talking about. He looked at her again, but it was too dark to see her face now. "Miriam, I'm sorry."

There was no reply.

"I don't think you did anything wrong—and the knife is a lovely present."

She sniffed noisily and heavily. Then without a word the pocket-knife was placed in his hand.

He squeezed her hand awkwardly. "I wasn't much help, was I?"

165

"That wasn't your fault," she said indignantly. "He hit you."

There was silence between them for a few minutes and a song was started in the next wagon. Ahead of them a miner had jumped down and was leading the way with a lantern.

"Do you really like the knife?" she asked.

"Yes. It's the best present I've ever been given."

The singing gradually died away and only the soft clumping of the horses' hooves and the squeak and creak of the wagons broke the silence. Her head dropped to rest on his shoulder. He felt very grown-up and protective towards this disturbing girl who slumbered quietly beside him.

Chapter 3

William Thackeray rode back to St. Cleer in an excited mood. He knew his words had stirred the huge crowd. The thought that he had been partly responsible for the act which had sent the condemned men to the gallows never crossed his mind. He knew they had attended the meeting he had called at Kit Hill when their troubles first started. But Preacher Thackeray was to be found wherever the miners had trouble, urging them to join together to improve their lot in life.

Thackeray's preaching was not directed against the shareholders alone. He slated the government for their short-sighted agricultural policies which sent food prices soaring. The shortage of corn had been growing steadily worse throughout England. It had not been helped by laws which prevented corn from being imported, in a misguided attempt to protect the interests of the farmers. Thackeray also pointed a stern finger at farmers who took advantage of the laws to withhold corn from the markets, raising prices to a level that miners found impossible to afford.

The preacher was halfway to St. Cleer when he met a group of men travelling in the same direction as himself.

"Is that Preacher Thackeray?" one of them called to him.

"Unless I'm mistaken that's John Kittow of Caradon. What do you want with me?"

166

The small group of miners closed about him and John Kittow lowered his voice. "We'd like a word with you, Preacher. Somewhere quiet."

"I'll meet you any time, John. Won't it do here?"

"No, Preacher. Better if 'tis said where there's light to see who's listening and walls to stop them as shouldn't be."

"Then you'd better make it the chapel."

"Tomorrow night? After the late shift comes up?"

"That's all right with me, John. But won't you tell me something of what it's about?"

"Corn, Preacher. That's it in one word. Corn."

HERMAN SCHMIDT did not put in an appearance at the Sharptor mine the next day and word went around that the German had been arrested and kept in Bodmin's lock-up overnight. It seemed he would have been there still had he not got word to the Sharptor mine owner.

Theophilus Strike had gone to Bodmin and managed to smooth over what could have been a very serious situation. The German had been arrested on a charge of entering a dwelling-house with intent to commit a felony. There was also a charge of assaulting the constable called to arrest him.

For what remained of that summer, Herman Schmidt was a quieter, more reasonable man. Nevertheless, it was some weeks before Josh was able to see the mine captain without a sinking feeling in his stomach. He need not have worried. Herman Schmidt could remember nothing whatever of the events that had led to his arrest.

THE LIGHTS were burning until well into the night in the St. Cleer Methodist church for the meeting between Preacher William Thackeray and the miners of Caradon, led by John Kittow. It should have been one of the nights when Josh stayed late for his studies but he was ushered out early by the preacher.

Only selected miners were allowed into the hall that evening. Others who called were curtly told to conduct their business on another, more convenient occasion. Nobody questioned it. Far better to accept whatever the preacher was doing and then forget it.

Even so, there were many who wondered about the secret meeting, but they would not be kept in suspense for long.

CALLINGTON MARKET was smaller than many others in the county. But trade was usually brisk and lately it had become a collection centre for farm produce. From here it would be hauled to Cotehele quay and shipped down-river to the port of Plymouth.

This particular day began much like any other, although the observant onlooker might have noticed an unusually high proportion of miners. The corn market was at the very centre of the town, outside a stone-built granary. Here miner, countryman and town dweller crowded around the auctioneer as he called loudly for bids.

As the bidding began the calls came quickly. "Sixty-five shillings! Seventy, seventy-five shillings." At eighty shillings for a quarter all but the most determined dropped out, including the combines of ordinary people who had pooled their cash. When the price reached one-hundred-and-five shillings only the merchants remained—and none of them was from Cornwall.

Then a voice, deep and very Cornish, came from the back of the crowd. "Eighty shillings, and I'll take the lot."

The auctioneer smiled. "I'm sorry, sir, you're a little late. The bidding has reached one-hundred-and-five shillings."

"You heard eighty shillings and that's all you'll be getting. I'll take the lot." John Kittow pushed his way to the front.

"You can't do this! I've been bid more than one-hundred-and-five shillings. I am honour bound to sell at the best price."

"There's nothing honourable in keeping food from those who need it. Nor in robbing those who can pay more. Eighty shillings is a fair price for a quarter and that's what it will be sold for."

The auctioneer began to protest once more and John Kittow pushed him from his perch into the midst of the miners. Too terrified to struggle, he was passed over the heads of the cheering men to the rear of the crowd.

"Now!" John Kittow put up his hands for silence. "We're selling corn to whoever wants it. There will be no bidding. It's first come—first served. Is it agreed that eighty shillings a quarter is a fair price?"

There was a majority shout of assent but one man called out, "The farmers have made enough profit from corn. Sell it at sixty shillings. Forty, even!"

"None of that talk! There's been work put into the growing of it. A man is entitled to his living. Eighty shillings is what it will be sold for. Come on, now! What are you waiting for?"

Word went quickly through the whole market of what was happening and crowds thronged to the sale. Corn had been missing from their diet for so long that some young children had never known the taste of it. A few farmers protested at the unorthodox method of sale but when the crowd turned on them they withdrew, angry and sullen.

The whole affair was conducted in a most efficient manner, proving that the hours spent in discussion in the St. Cleer chapel had not been wasted. At one stage John Kittow saw an old woman, wrinkled face anxious beneath her widow's shawl, watching the proceedings but not pushing her way through to the front.

"Is it corn you're wanting, mother?" asked Kittow gently. "You come over here with me and we'll see that you get it without waiting."

"Ah, will I now?" the woman's voice was as old as her face. "And what d'you think I'll be paying you with?"

John Kittow noticed for the first time the frayed patches of her shawl. "You'll be a widow then, mother?"

"These twenty years," she replied. "And he went the same way that you'll go. With his lungs full of dust from the mine."

"We'll all go when the time comes," said John Kittow. "But there'll be no miner's widow leaving today without corn to fill her belly." He spoke to a miner who looked up from a half-empty sack. "Some corn for a miner's widow. As much as she can carry away."

He drew some coins from his pocket and threw them into the money bag. "If any more widows, or others in need, come for corn give it to them. Pay it from your own pockets. You'll get it back from the mine fund. But make sure the money goes into the bag. I'll have no one saying there has been any dishonesty here today."

Kittow proved himself a man of his word. When the last bushel of corn had been sold the money was brought to him and he passed it on to the farmers. They agreed reluctantly that it tallied with the amount of corn sold at the miners' price. Their business concluded, the miners of Caradon then withdrew from the town as peacefully as they had arrived.

The military was called out and a troop of soldiers rode into Callington the next day but there was very little that they could, or would, do. Though the price was not what the farmers had expected they still made a good profit from it. The regiment's colonel had no wish to blow up a minor rural incident into a people's uprising.

THE REMAINDER of that summer went quickly. For Josh it had been a season to cherish and he hoped it might never come to an end. But the long, happy evenings spent on the moor with Miriam grew shorter. Almost before they realized it, the winter wind was rattling leafless branches and the horses working the mine-pump capstans blew steam from wide nostrils as they trudged around in circles on their long road to nowhere.

"It's hard to believe that Christmas is only two weeks away." Jesse Retallick beat up the mixture for the pudding she was preparing. "It'll be baby Gwen's first Christmas. It's such a pity her father isn't alive to see her face when she opens her presents on Christmas morning."

"I believe Budge *will* see her face," said Jenny quietly. Tom Shovell had been a constant visitor to the house since the summer. He was a religious man and simple faith had restored a great deal of her peace of mind. The deep sense of loss was still there, but it was now possible to talk about Budge to her without having her dissolve into tears.

Jesse turned to Josh who was sitting reading in a corner close to the fire. "With Christmas over life will be very different for you, young man."

170

Her manner was jocular but there was sadness deep inside. The year 1839 would see great changes in the household. Josh was going away on an apprenticeship. Thanks to his education, Theophilus Strike had offered him the chance to become a mine engineer, and Josh would be away for close on three years at Harvey's foundry and engineering works at Hayle. There he would learn how to build and look after the engines Theophilus Strike planned to install in the Sharptor mine. Engines to drain the wet, deeper shafts.

Theophilus Strike had costed the whole operation very carefully. As the Hayle foundry was to build the engine, Josh would be involved with it from the beginning. His presence on the mine would avoid the necessity of calling an engineer from Hayle when something went wrong. Eventually, Josh's apprenticeship would save the mine owners a great deal of money.

He had not, of course, told Josh about this when he called him with his father for an interview. Instead, he had offered him the chance of three years at Hayle in return for an undertaking by Josh to work at the Sharptor mine for ten years. To his astonishment and Ben Retallick's dismay Josh had refused this offer. It was a desperate gamble. Josh now wanted to be an engineer more than anything else in the world. But ten years was a long time to be tied to one employer. Five years tied employment with a reasonable salary constituted his terms of acceptance.

Strike's astonishment had quickly turned to anger but it did not last. He knew there was not another boy at Sharptor with Josh's education and without an engineer he believed it would be foolish to buy an engine. And so he agreed to Josh's terms.

When Josh and Ben left the owner's office the miner had taken off his hat and regarded his son with incredulous respect.

"I never thought I'd live to see the day when a son of mine would call his own tune to a mine owner! Josh, if cheek is what matters you'll go far in this world."

"It wasn't cheek," Josh said, hiding his own elation. "I know what I will be worth to Theophilus Strike. He knows it too."

It was true. Josh and Preacher Thackeray had spent a whole

evening discussing the matter. Thus Josh had been able to attend the interview armed with the same facts as the mine-owner.

Now he looked affectionately at his mother as she busied herself with the pudding. "Don't let's talk about my going away until Christmas is over."

"And why not? It's something to be pleased about. Be thankful your father doesn't want his son to follow him down the mine. There's many who can't wait to get their children below ground. Moses Trago never wasted any time with his Morwen."

The mention of Moses reminded Jesse of something that had been on her mind for days. In a quiet, indirect way she had found out about the schooling Josh was giving to Miriam and she approved of it. If Miriam Trago could escape from the influence of the Trago family then she wished the girl luck.

"I haven't seen that Trago girl lately. What's she doing for Christmas?"

Josh looked surprised at the question. "I don't know. Probably nothing. They don't keep Christmas. Moses Trago says it's just another day. Except that he doesn't work."

"Then it's time she learned different. Tell her that she's welcome here for Christmas Day. That's if you'd like to have her?"

Astonishment and pleasure wrestled for supremacy on Josh's face. "Can I tell her now?" He slammed his book shut.

It was Jesse's turn to show surprise. "At this time of night? You're not going up to that Trago place?"

He shook his head. "No, she won't be there, but I know where to find her."

"All right. But be back before your father comes home from the chapel meeting."

It was dark on the hillside and a chill hung in the air, but Josh was too happy to notice. He crawled quietly along the tunnel to the hideout until he saw a soft glimmer of light ahead and he knew that she was there.

"Miriam! It's me," he called. He rose from the narrow gorse tunnel and advanced into the space between the rocks. A candle was tucked into a small recess so that it was well sheltered from

172

the wind. Beside it were jammed a couple of books, and behind them was a pile of paper filled with Miriam's crowded, untidy writing.

"Josh! What are you doing here? Is something wrong?"

"No, nothing's wrong." He held it back as long as he could. "I just wondered . . . how you would like to spend Christmas Day with us? Have dinner with us and everything."

Her expression made the journey in the dark worthwhile.

"Honest? Who said I could come? Your mother?"

He nodded.

Josh had become used to Miriam's impetuosity by now and after submitting to the first onslaught of violent hugging he broke free.

"Then that's all settled. I'll go back and tell Mother."

"Can't you stay for a while and help me? There's lots of long words in this book. I don't understand them."

"No. Dad will be home from the chapel meeting soon." He shivered. "It's freezing cold up here. I don't know how you can learn anything in this weather."

"Where else can I go?" She carefully placed her books in a tin box she had managed to acquire and tucked it well back into a crevice between the rocks. Then she snuffed out the candle and crawled through the tunnel behind Josh. Once out on the moor she took his hand in a perfectly natural gesture.

"I've always wanted to have a *real* Christmas. What's it like?"

He told her. Of the holly wreaths decorating the pictures and the mantelshelf. The small presents and the large meals. He tried to put into words the atmosphere of Christmas, of being part of a family. She listened in thoughtful silence until they arrived at the track that led to the Trago home.

"Are you sure I won't be in the way?" she frowned. "If it's a family thing, I mean."

"Of course you won't, you've been invited. Jenny and the baby will be there. Tom Shovell too, I expect. Besides, I want you to come."

"All right then." She was happy again.

"I've got to go now. I'll see you tomorrow—same time?"

"Yes." She leaned forward and kissed him on the lips. For all the clumsy inexperience of it, he walked home without feeling the cold, as tall as any man.

ON CHRISTMAS EVE, just before dusk, the Sharptor mine ceased working. The men came to the surface to be greeted by Theophilus Strike, who handed each man a large fat goose, freshly killed, and a half-guinea.

In the morning Josh rose before first light to begin building up the fire in readiness for the day. Usually this was the time when the presents would be opened but today they were waiting until Miriam arrived.

"I hope she won't be too late," said Jesse as she began frying breakfast. "I can't wait to see the baby's face when she gets her presents."

Josh walked to the window and caught a glimpse of colour in the mist. "Here's Miriam," he cried and stepped outside expecting to see her coming down the path. But he could see nothing. Puzzled he walked to the gate and again caught the glimpse of colour that he knew was her best dress.

"Miriam!" As he scrambled up the slope from the path she came out from behind the gorse thicket where she had been hiding.

"What are you doing? We've been waiting for you. We can't open any presents until you're there."

Miriam shrugged her shoulders. "I haven't seen you for a couple of days. I thought your mother might have forgotten she invited me. Or your dad might have said I couldn't come."

"What would he say that for? Hurry up! Everyone's waiting."

"Just a minute." Miriam bent down behind the bush and picked up a pile of badly wrapped parcels.

"What are they?"

Her chin went up. "They're presents. Everyone gives presents at Christmas." She did not add that it was a custom unknown in the Trago household. "What have you got for me?"

"Wait and see."

Now Miriam allowed some of her excitement to shake itself

loose. Only her mother knew that she would be spending the day with the Retallicks, and the secret was safe with her.

Jesse stood in the cottage doorway watching Miriam and Josh coming along the path. "Stop there!" she said suddenly, her words jolting them to an immediate halt.

"It's bad luck to enter the house with bare feet at Christmas," Jesse went on. She had been straight-faced until now, but seeing Miriam's dismay she smiled. "So we'll just have to do something about that. Here, child." She picked up a parcel from a chair just inside the doorway and handed it to Miriam. "A very happy Christmas to you. And don't stand there gawking," she said to Josh, "take her parcels while she looks at her present."

Speechless, Josh did as he was told while Miriam carefully opened the wrappings on her present. Inside was a pair of shiny black shoes, made in soft leather. Miriam's eyes said everything.

Hurriedly she placed the shoes on the ground and slipped her feet into them. They were a good fit and Jesse nodded her head in satisfaction, "I didn't think they would be far out," she said. "Now come on in and have some breakfast, child, before we let all the warm air out of the house."

Miriam smiled happily at Josh as she was ushered into the kitchen.

After breakfast they adjourned to the best room and it was time for the presents to be opened. Miriam had some anxious moments about the gifts she had brought, fearing that they might not be acceptable. But the remainder of Herman Schmidt's guinea had been well used. There was a leather purse for Mrs. Retallick and Jesse was clearly delighted with it. The gifts for Josh's father, Jenny, and the baby were equally well received. For Josh there was a neckerchief in bright colours.

Then Josh brought out his present for Miriam and she knew by the way the others lapsed into silence that it was something special. When she held it in her hands she thought it felt like a book—a thick book.

It was. When the wrappings were taken off she held a beautiful leather-bound Bible in her hands. Miriam opened the cover. Inside was written, "To Miriam Trago from Josh Retallick".

"Thank you, Josh," sounded totally inadequate, but it was all she was able to say.

"Talking about the good book, it's time to be thinking of chapel," said Ben Retallick, rising to his feet. There was general movement in the room and Miriam felt uncertain about what was expected of her but Jesse came to her rescue.

"We'll let them go off to chapel," she said. "You can help me with the dinner." To the others she said, "And don't you let Wrightwick Roberts ramble on until everyone in the chapel has a spoiled meal waiting at home."

Josh knew his mother had planned things this way. By the time he and the others returned from chapel she would have thoroughly assessed Miriam's character. The thought of it kept him fidgeting all through a service which seemed to go on for ever. But finally it was over.

"You're just in time," said Jesse as they filed into the house. She was smiling, and Josh knew that whatever she had been looking for in their guest she had found.

The meal Jesse served up, for the one day when the menu was not controlled by economy, was gigantic—she had saved up during the whole year for it—with Mr. Strike's stuffed goose as the centrepiece. Afterwards they sat around talking and playing word and guessing games—except for Ben Retallick who sat in his chair by the fire snoring gently for most of the afternoon and evening.

All too soon, however, Tom Shovell put on his coat and it was time for Miriam to go home too. At the door her reluctance to leave was so apparent that Jesse's heart went out to her and she hugged her close. "I'm sorry you have to go, my dear. It's been lovely having you. Mind you come here often to see us. I shall be very hurt if you don't."

Miriam kissed her impulsively and with everyone's "Good night" ringing in her ears she set off with Josh into the darkness.

Once out of the light of the cottage she took Josh's arm and hugged it to her.

"Oh Josh!" she said. "It's been such a wonderful day. The best in my whole life!"

176

MIRIAM'S CHRISTMAS with the Retallicks was supposed to have been a secret but she was not clever enough to keep it from the remainder of the Trago family for long and she suffered cruelly when Moses Trago found out.

It was Kate Trago who brought the news to the Retallicks. She knocked on their door on New Year's Eve at the height of a rainstorm. Jesse dragged her inside.

"I'm not standing out there to catch my death of cold for anyone," Jesse said. "Sit down by the fire and get warm. Now, tell me what's happened."

Josh was studying in the best room. Hearing voices, he came through to the kitchen.

"It was Moses," Kate was saying. "He found out Miriam had spent Christmas in this house and there was a terrible scene."

"Oh! And who told him she was here?"

"He found the shoes you gave her. I tried to stop her saying anything about them but she was too worked up to listen. All she kept doing was shouting for him to give them back to her. Then it came out. She said she'd spent Christmas Day here. It was the best day of her life, she told him. Oh! She said so many things. The more he laid into her the more she shouted defiance at him."

Josh's face had gone the colour of chalk. "Did he beat her bad?"

"I don't know!" Kate Trago was close to tears. "When I tried to pull him away he knocked me down. If it hadn't been for our Morwen I think Moses would have killed her."

"Morwen stopped his father?" Jesse knew the boy was big for his age. Even so, he was no match for Moses.

"Yes." Kate Trago began trembling violently. "While they fought Miriam was able to get out. I haven't seen her since."

"When did this happen?" Jesse asked.

Kate Trago looked shamefaced. "Night before last."

"*What?* And you haven't looked for her before this? The poor girl could be dying somewhere."

"I know—but I was so sure she would be here."

"Josh, have you seen Miriam?"

"No. But I think I know where to find her." He was already putting on his boots.

Kate Trago stood up. "I must go. I've left the younger ones alone up there. Take care of her—and tell her it's all right to come home. Moses won't touch her again. He's sorry for what he did. He wouldn't say it to anyone, but I know it."

"We won't argue about that now." Jesse's lips drew into a tight line.

Josh banged out of the house and into the bitterly cold night. Now that he had time to think he dreaded what he might find at the hideout.

At the entrance to the narrow gorse tunnel he paused and listened. He thought he could hear a sound from within and when he came into the clearing he recognized it for what it was, shallow, rasping breathing. He had heard it once before, when his grandfather was fighting a last losing battle with death.

Josh fumbled with cold useless fingers for the candle. Finally it lit and cast its flickering light across the clearing. Miriam was slumped in a corner, sheltered from the wind, with her back against the rock. Her left eye was puffed up like an apple and a bloody graze extended from the bridge of her nose across her forehead.

He dropped to one knee beside her and putting one hand gently beneath her chin he lifted her head. Weakly she tried to jerk it back away from him and the movement caused her to groan. He could see now that both her eyes were swollen and tight closed. She must have been lying here, completely blind, for two days and nights.

"Miriam! Can you hear? It's me. Josh. It's all right now. I'll get you out of here."

When he tried to lift her, however, he touched one of her ribs, and she cried out in pain as it grated beneath his fingers. The next few minutes were a nightmare. But by dragging, pushing and heaving he finally succeeded in getting her out onto the moor. Then during a swaying pause for breath he heard some people crashing through the undergrowth towards him. Thinking that one of them might be Moses Trago, Josh lowered Miriam quietly to the ground. Then whoever it was began to move away, up the slope.

"It must have been Josh," a man said. "It was too noisy for a pony."

Josh recognized his father's soft voice. "Dad! Over here."

Within seconds Ben and Tom Shovell loomed out of the darkness in front of him. "What are you playing at? Have you found the girl?"

"Yes, but she's hurt bad."

"All right, Ben. Gently now. I have her." And the big shift captain cradled Miriam in his arms as though she was a baby.

Miriam was laid up in the Retallick's bedroom for three weeks, while Josh slept in the kitchen downstairs. For the first four days the doctor from the Caradon mine was a daily visitor. He strapped her ribs—two of them were broken—and worked on her face. He feared her nose was also broken, but when the swelling around her eyes began to go down he was pleased to acknowledge that he had been wrong.

On the fifth day Miriam could see from one eye and progressed steadily thereafter. Kate Trago was a frequent visitor. She always came after dark and would sit next to her daughter's bed saying scarcely a word and wringing her hands nervously.

But when Miriam was able to sit out of bed upstairs for an hour each day she received a visitor who caused great consternation in the Retallick house. He too came after dark, but the fact that he knocked gently at the door and waited quietly for it to be opened was unusual.

Josh opened the door, and promptly slammed it shut. Turning to his father in alarm, he said, "It's Moses."

Ben Retallick leaped from his chair and Jesse reached for a heavy iron poker. Moses knocked again. Ben motioned for Josh to move farther into the room before going to open the door himself.

Moses stood before him, his hat held in his hands. "I've come to take Miriam home." It was a bald, matter-of-fact statement.

"Then you've had a wasted journey." Ben controlled his anger admirably.

Jesse was less reticent. "You take one step into this house, Moses Trago, and you'll feel this poker across your head. That girl has suffered enough at your hands."

"I haven't come here to quarrel, Mrs. Retallick. What has happened is done. It can't be forgotten. All the same, Miriam is my daughter and I want her home."

Moses Trago fought to maintain control of himself. Then a voice from the stairs made them all look in that direction. "Mrs. Retallick, please let him come in."

Miriam's face was still discoloured and she clung to the hand-rail unsteadily.

A look passed between Jesse and Ben, then Ben stood back from the door. "You can go up to see her. But father or not, she'll not leave this house until she's well."

Moses Trago stepped inside, his shoulders filling the doorway, and he went up the stairs into the room where Miriam slept.

Downstairs the only sound for a long time was the crackling of wood on the fire. Suddenly Josh said fiercely, "He's not taking her with him."

"Don't go climbing hedges until they are built," said Ben.

They heard the bedroom door opening and Moses Trago came clumping heavily down the stairs. He stopped in the centre of the room and looked from one to the other, finally settling his gaze on Jesse.

"She says she'll be coming home when she's well," he said. "Until then I'd be obliged if you'd have her here. I'll pay for her keep. And for the doctor. Here are two guineas."

"We'll take one guinea for the doctor," retorted Jesse. "Whatever else we do is because we're fond of the girl."

Moses Trago flushed angrily. "Then give this guinea to the boy," he said. "I hear he found her."

Josh's heart was pounding as he stood up. "I did that for Miriam. Not for your money. Buy her some new shoes with it to make up for those you burned."

He felt his mother's eyes on him. Kate Trago had not told her that during the fight in the Trago home Moses had thrown Miriam's shoes onto the fire. Miriam had told Josh and been more upset about it than she was for her injuries.

"You've got spirit but no money sense," said Moses looking at him from beneath shaggy brows. "I've already promised Miriam

180

some new shoes. I've also told her she can have schooling from that preacher at St. Cleer. When she's well enough her mother will come for her." He nodded, then turned and was gone.

"The cheek of the man!" Jesse all but exploded.

"Hush now," said Ben, "Moses Trago cannot change what he is. Keeping his temper tonight cost him much. At least give him credit for that."

MIRIAM RETURNED to the Trago home one week before Josh was due to begin his apprenticeship at Hayle. Both departures hit Jesse hard. She had become very fond of the girl. Her quick wit and an ever-ready willingness to listen and learn had endeared her to the whole household, even baby Gwen.

With Miriam out of the house, it was time to stitch and iron and generally prepare Josh for a stay in a town which, although hardly fifty miles distant, was as remote as the Highlands of Scotland to Jesse.

Josh himself put off thinking about it until the very last minute. He had finished his schooling with the Reverend Thackeray, and as a parting gift the preacher gave him an old wood and metal chest to carry his belongings. He also gave him some words of advice.

"While you're away you'll be learning new things and meeting new people," he said. "Never let them make you forget where you come from, or the men who remain here, working and dying in wretched conditions. If you hear of something that might make life easier for them, follow it up. And if you hear anyone at Hayle talking about a union of miners, listen to him. I'm convinced that's where the future of the miner lies."

He held out his hand. "Goodbye and good luck, Josh. May God be with you."

His next farewell was with Miriam. He had not been looking forward to it. "I'll write and tell you all about Hayle as soon as I arrive," he said, as they stood on the path between their homes.

"And I'll write straight back."

"Well, I'll say goodbye then." He held her briefly and kissed her cheek. "Take care of yourself, Miriam."

181

"And you, Josh. I shall miss you terribly."

He realized that he was going to miss her more than anyone else at Sharptor. He would have liked to tell her so but did not know how to begin. He turned and walked away. Looking back he saw her standing on the path, a teeth-chattering little figure waving bravely until he was out of sight.

That left only his family the following morning. Jesse fussed about him as he sat on the driving seat of the ore wagon beside Nehemeziah. "You be good, mind. No fighting—and write often."

"Yes, Mother."

The aged ostler flicked the reins and the wagon creaked away. Josh waved until the huddled group of his mother and father, Jenny, the baby, and Tom Shovell disappeared from view around a curve in the track.

Josh and Nehemeziah were on the first wagon of the day to leave the mine for Moorswater. This was the inland terminal of the canal linking the mining area with the sea port of Looe. From Looe Josh would travel on to his new home by sea.

Chapter 4

It was dawn when Josh's ship rode the tide into Hayle harbour. He stood on the deck, his packed trunk beside him, shivering in the cold mist which drifted across the Hayle river. It was a dull, unprepossessing scene. On the far bank were the ugly stone buildings of the works that were to be his home for the next three years. Smoke from the foundry and smelting chimneys belched forth thick and dirty, darkening the mist.

With the help of a longboat, the ship edged in towards the jetty and Josh hurried down the gangway. Then, struggling with his trunk, he set off along the busy quayside. Before he had gone twenty yards a boy of about his own age appeared alongside him.

"You Joshua Retallick?" he asked. Although Josh did not recognize the accent it was pure cockney.

"Yes."

"Tom Fiddler's the name. I've been sent to meet you."

The other boy grinned at Josh, his manner friendly. He took one of the handles of Josh's trunk and let it swing at arm's length between them. They walked off the quay, treading a muddy path between piles of rough ore, rusting girders and new-cast boiler parts, to a huge granite-block building. As they passed an opening as wide and tall as a miner's cottage, the heat and roar from within sent Josh staggering. "You'll soon get used to that," said his companion. "But at first you'll be gasping for breath whenever they open a furnace door near you."

They passed on into the single storey building that served as a dormitory and Tom pointed out the empty bed and locker allocated to Josh. He waited while Josh changed into working clothes, then took him to meet the works manager.

William Carlyon was a tall, hook-nosed, no-nonsense man. He dismissed Tom with a peremptory wave of his hand and leaned back in his chair. "So this is the young man we must turn into an engineer. All in three short years!" He sniffed derisively. "That is scarcely enough time to teach you to work an engine, let alone build or repair one."

He stood up abruptly and walked to the door, beckoning Josh to follow him. "But we'll make a start."

An hour later, Josh was helping a toothless old ex-miner shovel coal into the greedy furnaces and bring them up to a heat that would boil iron. For a week Josh carried out this task, returning to the dormitory at the end of each working day sweating and coal-grimy. The other apprentices were friendly enough, but they all worked a long day in different sections of the foundry, and there was little opportunity for him really to get to know them. In the evenings they spent a couple of hours writing notes or studying plans of engines.

It would be some time before he would get down to actual engineering. At the end of his week as a stoker he would be helping to load the ore into the furnaces. Then he would learn how to handle the molten metal that poured like a brew from hell into the waiting moulds. Boilers, pipes, beams and tramway lines, all were made at Harvey's Hayle foundry.

The apprentices worked a six-day week. The seventh day was

184

theirs, to do with as they wished, provided they did not miss the two-hour service held in Hayle Methodist chapel in the morning or tea at the works manager's house in the afternoon.

On Josh's first Sunday, he and the other apprentices, washed and wearing their best clothes, assembled outside the Carlyon house to escort the family to chapel. William and Molly Carlyon had two daughters, Sarah and Mary. Sarah was Josh's age but Mary was only six, spoiled by family and apprentices alike.

Josh took an immediate liking to Sarah and she to him. All the way to the chapel they chattered away. By the time they fell silent to pass in through the chapel door she had elicited details of his home, parents and a great deal more besides.

Inside the chapel Josh sat behind the Carlyon girls. He could not help noticing the whiteness of the backs of their necks and the golden hair drawn back in identical tiny plaits. Paradoxically it made him think of Miriam, of her brown skin and long, untidy black hair. A mood of homesickness rose in him and he wondered what she was doing at that very moment. He decided to write home after chapel and enclose a note for her.

Tea in the Carlyon house was one part of his new life Josh would gladly have foregone. It would have been less of an ordeal had he been seated with the other boys, but as he was the newest apprentice Mrs. Carlyon wanted to find out something of his background. So he was seated between herself and Sarah.

Mrs. Carlyon quickly established that his father was a miner in one of the smaller mines and Josh would be tied to the same mine for some years after his apprenticeship. After that she lost a certain amount of interest. Not so Sarah.

To the Cornish of the far west, Bodmin Moor was something vague and mysterious, shrouded in the mists of legend. Sarah was curious to know more about it.

When he began talking about the moor, Josh temporarily forgot his shyness. By the time he had finished he found that the whole company was listening.

"You know your moor well, Josh," said William Carlyon. "Take the same interest in engineering and Mr. Strike won't be sorry he sent you to Hayle." He stood up. "Now it is time to

185

send you all back to your dormitory to prepare for tomorrow. We look forward to your company next Sunday."

During the next weeks, Josh's life settled into a pattern that varied only in the work he was doing. Gradually he began to enjoy his Sundays with the Carlyons. If Mrs. Carlyon was not happy because Sarah spent most of the time talking only to Josh she never mentioned it.

That was a mild winter. When it gave way without a struggle to spring, Easter had arrived.

This was a weekend that Josh had been looking forward to for two very good reasons. One was that after the weekend he would at last begin to learn about the working of steam-engines. The second was that the boys were being given a four-day holiday, and he was going home, travelling with no less a personage than Francis Trevithick, son of the great Cornish engineer and inventor, Richard Trevithick.

Richard had married into the Harvey family and his son Francis had learned his skills with them. Josh had met him at the Carlyon house and it was there he made his offer to take the boy as far as Launceston in his own coach. From there Josh would have to walk the last miles to Sharptor.

At a minute past six o'clock in the Good Friday dawn, Francis Trevithick's carriage swung up to the works gate and Josh clambered inside. "Make yourself comfortable while you can," Trevithick told him. "There's little enough good road this side of Wadebridge. Now, tell me what you've learned at Harvey's."

Josh started to say that he had not been at the works for many months but Trevithick waved his excuses aside. "Nonsense! You'll have learned a lot, I'm sure. How do you bank a furnace to get the maximum heat from it? And what do you do to keep it at the highest possible temperature using the minimum of coal? Then what about moulding—you've done some of that haven't you?"

Josh gave Trevithick the answers he was looking for—briefly at first, but the engineer demanded more detail, probing the limits of Josh's knowledge. "And what are you going to do when you leave Hayle?" he asked finally.

Josh told him about Theophilus Strike and the Sharptor mine.

Trevithick questioned Josh sharply about conditions at the mine, then snorted, "This Strike ought to be horse-whipped for operating in such a primitive fashion. What provision is there for a man-hoist?"

Josh confessed that he had heard no mention of any—adding that he was determined to do something about it when he possessed more knowledge.

"Good for you. How long does it take a man to reach the surface from a deep shaft? Twenty minutes? Half an hour? By that time he's thoroughly exhausted. If his hand slips he doesn't have the strength left to save himself. If he survives the climb to crawl out of his hole the cold air is going to tear at his lungs as though it were a steel rasp. My God, boy! Our miners deserve better than that. Look here, I'll show you the way an ordinary pumping-engine can be used to bring men to the surface. My father designed it. It's the simplest principle imaginable. Persuade all mine owners to provide a lift for their miners and you are halfway towards forcing them to accept that they are employing human beings."

He produced paper and pencil and proceeded to illustrate his point. Josh took possession of each drawing as Trevithick discarded it. He thought of Budge Pearn. Had there been a man-hoist in Sharptor mine Jenny would not be a widow today.

"Preacher Thackeray is always saying the very same thing," said Josh.

"Preacher Thackeray?" frowned Trevithick. "I've heard talk of him. He's the man who wants all miners to unite. That's dangerous talk, young Retallick. Help to make the miners' lot an easier one by all means. That is Christian charity. But don't try to put ideas into a man's head that he is the equal of his employer. Now, do you understand the principle of the lift?"

Josh asked a few more questions. Trevithick answered him and drew quick diagrams, cursing as the coach lurched and jolted.

"It's far too bumpy now for drawing," he said finally. "Somewhere I have a detailed set of plans that my father once drew up. I will send them to you at Hayle. Tell me instead what you know of the principles of a steam-engine."

And so the hours and the miles sped by until they arrived at

Launceston. Josh left the coach and said goodbye to the engineer who patted him encouragingly on the shoulder. When the coach was well on its way, Josh turned off the road onto a track leading across the moor.

It was a bright clear day and he could see the ridge by Sharptor when he was three miles away. He was not the only one able to see for such a distance. Before he had gone another half-mile a laughing, panting Miriam was running to meet him.

"Josh! I knew it was you! I had been seeing cattle and ponies and all sorts of things that I thought were you. Let me look at you. You have grown taller! You have, don't laugh."

Josh hugged her, still laughing. He had not realized how much he had missed her. There were changes in her too.

"What's been going on while I've been away? Your hair! You've had it cut. And that's a new dress! I must have been gone much longer than I realized. You're not the same Miriam."

"Josh Retallick!" She looked at him for a moment, then laughed. "William said I must tidy myself if I wanted him to teach me."

It came as a shock to realize she was talking of Preacher Thackeray. She was going to his school in St. Cleer regularly now. All the same, Josh had been taught by Thackeray for years without ever referring to him by his Christian name. Miriam was prattling on, ". . . Jenny washed my hair and cut it for me. And my dad bought these shoes."

She saw his face and stopped. "What's the matter, Josh? Don't you like me as I am now?"

"I—I don't know. You have grown up so much while I have been away."

"I thought you wanted me to grow up," she said quietly.

"Yes." Josh felt awkward. "It's come as a bit of a surprise, that's all."

She took his hand and spoke, looking down at the ground, "It's a special sort of surprise, Josh—and only for you."

It was better then, walking home across the moor, linked hands swinging between them. By the time they reached the cottage it was as though he had never been away. Except that there was more to talk about. His mother fussed about him excessively, unwilling to believe he could possibly be fit after more than three months away from her care. Ben said very little after his initial handshake, but he looked well satisfied.

The weekend went all too quickly. Most of the time was spent around the house with his family, or on the moor, discovering the signs of spring with Miriam.

She walked as far as St. Cleer with him on his return. From St. Cleer he was travelling by coach service as far as Truro. The trip had been a surprise present from his father, though the money he had saved was only sufficient for Josh to travel on the outside of the coach, and he would have a seventeen-mile walk from Truro to the works.

They arrived at St. Cleer just as the coachman's horn called on travellers to board the coach. There were things Josh had wanted to say to Miriam. But now there was neither the time nor, of a sudden, the words. It was too late and he was miserable.

"Don't you want to go, Josh?" Miriam asked him.

"It's not that I don't want to go. It's . . ." he shrugged helplessly.

"Is it because of me?"

He nodded. "Yes."

"Then you've no need to worry, Josh. I will be counting the days until you are back. But quickly now, the coach is leaving."

He snatched a quick kiss and jumped up on the coach as the coachman cracked his whip.

"I'll write, Josh. I'll write." Miriam ran to the corner and Josh waved until the trot of the horses became a canter and St. Cleer and Miriam receded over the brow of the hill.

Chapter 5

There was little time for brooding in the weeks that lay ahead. William Carlyon was determined that the engineers trained at Harvey's should match the engines for which they would be responsible. Also, when he heard why Trevithick had sent the

189

plans for the man-hoists to Josh he not only saw that Josh received the fullest possible training as an engineer but that he was fully conversant with all the latest developments in man-hoist design.

Josh did not mind the extra work. He was a born engineer. His letters to Miriam and his family were full of his newly discovered skills and interests. Even on Sundays in the company of the Carlyon family he could speak of little else and this did not always please Sarah.

One Sunday, in midsummer, they were returning from chapel. He was in the middle of extolling the virtues of Harvey's latest engine when Sarah suddenly stopped and stamped her foot angrily. "I'm sick of engines! I'm surrounded by the smell of engines, bits of engines and men who work with engines. I *hate* engines!"

With that she lifted her chin and flounced off, leaving a stunned Josh staring after her.

It was with some trepidation that Josh went to tea that day with the Carlyons, but Sarah behaved as though nothing had happened. All the same, Josh was very careful not to talk about engines. Soon the conversation turned to horse-riding. The Carlyon girls had owned ponies for years, but for her recent birthday Sarah had been given a full-blooded hunter, Hector, a beautiful, spirited horse.

"Have you ever ridden?" she asked Josh.

"No. Except bareback on the cart-horses at the mine."

"Wouldn't you like to learn to ride properly?"

"Yes." It was an unthinking reply. "But I could never find the time."

"Of course you could." Sarah had him firmly on the hook. "Daddy, Josh says he would love to learn to ride but doesn't have time. He could ride Pedlar on Sundays, couldn't he?" Pedlar was the pony which had been succeeded by her new hunter.

"If Josh thinks he can fit it in with his engineering studies I have no objections."

"Now, then. Can we start at once?"

"I have no boots to wear for riding," protested Josh.

"Daddy, you never wear your riding boots now. Can Josh borrow them?"

William Carlyon grinned at Josh. "It's no use," he said. "Sarah has decided that you are to have a riding lesson. I would never hear the last of it if I spoiled her plans. Come along."

Josh followed him out of the room to return after a time wearing tall shiny riding boots. Sarah changed into a dark brown riding habit, and at the stables he saddled the horses under her instruction. Soon they were jogging across open country.

Drawing in beside him, Sarah said, "Why did you tell me you couldn't ride? You are doing splendidly."

"It's just like riding the mine horses," replied Josh. "In fact it's easier, there is something to hold on to and somewhere for your feet."

"Come on then!" cried Sarah. "I'll race you to the top of that hill." She dug her heel into the hunter's ribs.

Josh followed suit and it was now that he learned the difference between riding a slow-jogging pony and trying to sit one that is galloping. At one moment his face was buried in the coarse hairs of the horse's mane, the next, his head was jerked back and all he could see was sky. Fortunately the pony found it almost as uncomfortable to have such an uncontrolled weight upon its back. It slowed, so that Josh was able to bring it back under control and take it up the hill at a more leisurely pace.

Sarah had dismounted and was waiting for him, flushed from the gallop. Her golden hair had fallen loose and was hanging about her shoulders. "I won! Why didn't you give Pedlar his head? He enjoys a good run."

"He didn't enjoy it today," declared Josh, swinging gratefully to the ground. "I wasn't doing any of the things he is used to his riders doing."

Sarah laughed. "You'll learn. I'll show you on the way back. But look over there. Isn't that worth coming up here to see?"

She pointed to the north where the farmland sloped away to the edge of St. Ives Bay. A few red-sailed fishing boats leaned away from the wind in the sea beyond and closer to the horizon two packets crowded on full sails.

"It's beautiful, isn't it?" she said.

"Yes it is," agreed Josh. "But you have to see the moor to really know what beauty is."

"I've seen it," said Sarah. "We went to Barnstaple once and crossed over it. It's a bleak, dreary place."

"It isn't! Get away from the road and you'll find the rivers and the tors and the valleys. They're alive with more animal and plant-life than you will ever have seen in one place before."

"You really love the moor, don't you?"

Josh nodded, thinking of it as it would be at this time of the year. Sarah caught his expression. "And have you discovered all these birds and animals and plants by yourself?" she asked.

He cleared his throat before answering. "Sometimes by myself. Sometimes with Miriam."

Sarah crouched down and stroked Hector's nose as he pulled the grass. "Who's Miriam?"

He tried to describe the wild moorland girl but was aware that his word picture was a mere skeleton of the real girl. He did not know whether the fault lay in his telling, or because it was impossible to describe Miriam without having the moor near.

Sarah flicked the reins back over Hector's head. "I think we ought to go home now," she said, swinging up to the saddle before Josh could make a move to help her. On the return journey she told Josh how he should move with the pony, yet there was a reserve between them that had not been present before.

Back in the stable he thanked her for the lesson. "Will we be able to go again next Sunday?" he asked.

"Would you like to?"

"Yes. Very much."

Some of the sparkle returned to her. "All right. We'll make it a regular Sunday treat. We can go out early, before breakfast. That's the time I enjoy riding best."

And so riding became part of Josh's routine. He enjoyed both the ride and Sarah's company. The other apprentices grudgingly came to accept his good fortune. If they did not resent it it was because Josh never let up on his engineering studies. The more he learned, the more he found to learn.

192

WHEN HIS FIRST YEAR ended Josh spent a short Christmas interlude with his family and Miriam. He enjoyed being with them but even so his mind was constantly slipping away to tackle some engineering problem. He told Miriam about it when she commented on his preoccupied air. She accepted this proudly. She believed that Josh would one day be a brilliant mine engineer.

It was the summer of 1840 when something happened which might well have altered Josh's whole career. He was working in Harvey's foundry yard one day when a horseman came clattering through the gates. The rider was in almost as much of a lather as the horse he was riding. It was with a sense of foreboding that Josh recognized him as Nehemeziah Lancellis, Mr. Strike's gnarled little ostler.

"Josh! Josh, boy. I've brought bad news for 'ee. Best get home. Be quick 'bout it."

"What is it? What's happened?"

"'Tis Ben . . . he was working on a new tunnel off the main shaft. New man on the black powder set off a bad explosion . . . Roof's down with Ben and three more 'neath it. Schmidt won't have rescue work. He's back on the drink . . . no sense in 'im. Best get there 'n' sort it out, Josh."

"I'll go now Nehemeziah. I'll take your horse."

"No! He'm clapped, Josh! Wouldn't last half a mile."

"Josh!" It was Sarah. Running from the house she had heard most of what had been said. "Take Hector. He's the fastest horse you'll find."

"Can I?" Josh turned to William Carlyon.

"Of course! It's Sarah's horse to do with as she wishes."

Josh hurried away to throw off his working clothes and change. By the time he was back in the yard Sarah was leading the big horse fully saddled from the stable.

He mounted, a competent rider now with no fear of the stallion. Then, to a chorus of good wishes, he clattered out of the yard, soon allowing the big horse to stretch out into a mile-consuming gallop.

While Josh sped along the road between Hayle and Sharptor, Herman Schmidt, red-faced and angry, stood at the entrance to the collapsed tunnel of the mine, facing a sullen crowd of miners.

"Go back to work, all of you." His words were made harsher by the guttural German accent. "It is no good to stand around here. The roof has collapsed. The men inside are dead. There is nothing to be done, I say."

Tom Shovell stepped from the crowd. "With due respect, captain, that isn't our way. Ben and the others may well be dead, but we'll see that they have a decent burial. We owe them that."

"Them you owe nothing! Me you owe everything!" Schmidt shouted. "And I say you work—you hear? Work! If anyone tries to go into this tunnel he is no longer employed at the Sharptor mine."

Tom Shovell's face paled but he had no intention of retreating. "No, Captain Schmidt. We will dig out the tunnel until we find those men. Dead or alive."

There was a sudden commotion in the crowd as Wrightwick Roberts pushed to the front. "What's this? A meeting? Hold your meetings later. What we need now are men with picks and strong arms. Come on. Give me something to dig with."

"Nobody goes in there. I have said so," Schmidt repeated. "They must go back to work."

"They'll go back when they've brought out Ben Retallick and the others," said Roberts. "Come on, Tom. In we go."

With a nod the shift captain fell in behind the preacher. Schmidt moved to block their path and was sent reeling by Roberts. Before he had recovered his balance the entrance to the tunnel was crowded with miners, and candles were being lit and passed forward.

A hundred feet in, the preacher and Tom Shovell came to a tumbled barrier of rock that completely blocked the passage. "This doesn't look good," said Roberts. "What do you know about this tunnel, Tom? Is it loose rock right through?"

Tom Shovell looked crestfallen, "I don't know as much as I should, Wrightwick," he confessed. "I've been busy with a drainage problem in the main shaft. The man on the powder was a new man from the Kit Hill workings. He told me he was used to black powder blasting." He nodded, indicating the fallen rock, sending a shower of wax to the floor from the candle attached to his helmet. "But this isn't the work of an experienced man."

"We'd better get at it," said the preacher. Lighting other candles from the one he held, he placed them on rough ledges hacked into the walls. "There'll not be room for more than one man to work a way through here. I'll have first turn and you pass back the rocks I get out."

"We'll need a bit of shoring," Tom said. Then he called back over his shoulder, "Pass the word back along the tunnel."

Roberts strained at a huge block of granite. When it was reluctantly prised free a trickle of smaller rocks showered into the place it had occupied. These were soon cleared and the preacher climbed into the hole.

Gradually Roberts disappeared from view into the tunnel he was making. The shift captain moved candles forward with him. As the preacher advanced his progress slowed. With his great strength he was able to work loose large chunks of rock but since there was room for only one man inside the tunnel he had to man-handle them back to the beginning of the fall himself. But then, miraculously, the answer to this problem presented itself. Roberts had advanced only six yards when Moses Trago called to him.

"Come on out and give these weaklings here a hand, Preacher," he shouted. "I'll take a spell in there."

Wrightwick Roberts, his fingers torn and bleeding from the rough granite, submitted gratefully and backed out into the comparative spaciousness of the undamaged tunnel. Moses scrambled into the narrow space and continued the work as though his own life depended upon it.

By the time Josh finally slithered the frothing, sweat-darkened Hector to a halt at the entrance to the mine, the amount of rock being brought out was more than during a normal working day. He hurried down the ladder, and along the tunnel. When he reached the place where the fall began he stripped off his jacket and shirt and crawled into the hole, working his way forward to where Tom Shovell, Preacher Roberts and John Trago were backing up the man ahead.

The shift captain was scarcely recognizable beneath layers of

195

dust. "There's nothing hopeful to be said, I'm afraid, Josh. Things are looking bad."

"So they told me outside. I'd rather dig than think about it. I'm going up to take over ahead for a while."

"What are you doing back there?" Moses Trago shouted. "Having a bloody tea-party? Take this rock from me before I lose it."

"Josh Retallick has just arrived," called Tom, as he wrestled with a hundred pound rock. "He's coming up to take over for a while."

"Tell him to stay back there and save his breath for heaving stones. There's more than enough of them here."

The tunnel had progressed another ten yards when suddenly Moses stopped and called on the men to listen. The call went back until all was quiet. Then they heard the sound of metal upon rock, as though a pick-axe was being used—ahead of them!

Moses Trago began attacking the fallen rock with renewed vigour. "It's Ben Retallick!" he growled. Soon the clinking sound became clearer. Then there was a sudden cascade of shale and stones. When the dust cleared the excited rescuers saw the drawn face of a man peering at them from the underground tomb.

"Thank God! Thank God!" The face began to contort and it looked as though the man would burst into tears.

"Thank Him later, if you must." Moses Trago slithered into the open tunnel beside the man. "Where are the others?"

The rescued miner nodded behind him.

Ten yards on they came upon a second fall. Protruding from beneath this pile of rock a man lay, face downwards, the lower part of his body hidden by rocks. It was Ben Retallick.

He looked dead but as Josh dropped to his knees beside him, a flickering candle in his hand, he stirred with a groan.

"Aaah! Who's that?"

"It's all right, Dad. Don't try to move. We'll soon have you out."

"Josh! What are you doing here? Aaah!" The cry of pain came with a shifting of stones amidst the fall.

Wrightwick Roberts crouched alongside Josh. "Where does it hurt most, Ben?"

"It's the weight on my legs." Ben gritted his teeth. "I think my right leg is broken. But you get on with what you have to do. John Maddiver took the full force of the fall, with his brother. I think one of them is lying across my feet."

There was the sound of voices from the rescue tunnel and Tom Shovell stumbled forward, followed by Moses and a tall, thin man whom Josh recognized as the Wheal Phoenix mine doctor.

"We'll have him out in a few seconds," called Moses. "Preacher, give us some of your strength on this rock. You'd best call on your Lord to help us too. Josh, pull out your father as soon as he's free."

Moses and Tom Shovell stood shoulder to shoulder with Wrightwick Roberts. They strained together, muscles cracking, until slowly the thick slab of granite began to rise, inch by agonizing inch. At last, assisted by the doctor, Josh was able to pull his father clear.

As the slab of rock was lowered again Josh saw the fingers of a man protruding from beneath it at the place where his father's legs had been.

While the doctor examined Ben's swollen and discoloured leg, Josh began to thank Moses. "I don't need your thanks," said the big miner, churlishly. "I owed the Retallicks a debt for what you once did for my Miriam. That debt is now paid. The Trago family owes nothing to anybody."

After hearing the doctor's opinion that the fracture was a simple one, Josh left his father and made his way to the surface. Arriving there he was blinded by the sunlight and almost bowled over as his mother flung herself at him.

"Josh, what's going on in there? Have they found him?"

His eyes were more accustomed to the light now, and Josh saw Miriam and Jenny standing at his other side. Disentangling himself from his mother, he said, "The man they brought out. Didn't he tell you?"

"Tell me what? The man was a blubbering wreck. Not able to speak a single intelligent word."

"Dad's all right." His mother sagged with relief, "He's got a broken leg. But it's a simple break."

"How about the other two who were with your father?" asked one of the miners in the crowd.

"There's little chance of them being alive," replied Josh, remembering the fingers beneath the rock. "But Moses and the others are still digging."

A woman in the crowd began crying loudly.

"The price of being a miner's wife," said Miriam bitterly. "Her husband gone. A family to support and within the month she'll have to be out of her cottage. That's the system her husband gave his life for."

Josh looked at her in surprise. She was learning more than mathematics and English at the St. Cleer school. It could have been the Reverend Thackeray himself talking.

Twenty minutes later Ben Retallick was carried from the shaft and Moses came with him. He singled out Mary Crabbe, standing on the edge of the crowd.

"There's work for you, Mary."

"Both of them?" Her seamed old face was devoid of emotion.

"Both of them. Dead because Captain Schmidt employs second-rate men to do his blasting."

He said this deliberately loudly as Theophilus Strike came through the crowd. The mine owner heard, but chose to ignore the remark. He made his way to Ben.

"I'm pleased to see you safe, Ben. Herman Schmidt told me you were dead."

"And so he would have been had it been left to that German," put in Moses.

There were shouts of agreement from the crowd. Strike flushed and turned to Tom Shovell. "Captain Schmidt came to me with some story of a roof fall. Four men killed and you refusing to obey orders, he said. What is it all about?"

"There's one of his 'dead' men," said the shift captain, pointing to Ben. "Captain Schmidt wanted us to abandon any rescue attempt. He said it wasn't worthwhile."

"There seem to be a few matters here that need clearing up," said the mine owner. He turned back to Josh. "And what are you doing here? Why aren't you at Hayle?"

198

"I was brought word of what had happened and came straightaway."

Strike took in his scuffed riding boots. "Then you'd better get back there and not waste good learning time," he snapped.

"My horse will be ready to ride in the morning."

"*Your* horse, eh? I'm paying for you to become an engineer, Retallick. Not to learn how to be a gentleman and own horses."

"It's not my own horse and I've learned to ride on Sundays, when there are no lessons," said Josh defiantly. He did not like being spoken down to in front of Miriam.

Strike raised his eyebrows. "Young man, go home now and take your mother with you. I want to speak to your father. And to you too, Tom Shovell."

"Pig!" hissed Miriam as they went off. But Jesse's heart was light within her. Ben was alive, his injury far less serious than she had dared hope. And her son was home with her.

Ben came home carried by Tom Shovell and a crowd of off-duty miners. "Every one of them grinning like a sheep," commented the astonished Jesse.

It was with very good reason.

"Come along, Jesse," said Ben, his face all smiles despite his injury. "Don't be slow opening the door when your husband is carried home by the new Mine Captain."

"You, Tom?" His face betrayed the answer and Jesse hugged him. "Oh, I'm so glad for you! But what has happened to Captain Schmidt?"

"He won't be back. Seems he reeked of alcohol when he barged in on Theophilus Strike. He said a few things that one doesn't say to a mine owner. Josh, take note!"

"That's wonderful news, said Josh. "Sharptor will be a happier mine now."

"But that's not all the news, lad," said one of the men. "Ask your father who is to take Tom's place as shift captain, when his leg has mended."

"Ben! You've been made shift captain?" cried Jesse.

Ben nodded, then had to ward off his wife as she hugged him too. "Steady now, Jesse. Remember my leg."

"It's a pity it took Theophilus Strike so long to see sense," Miriam said, and went into the kitchen to stoke up the fire which had been allowed to burn low in the excitement of Josh's arrival.

"My God!" said Ben Retallick quietly. "Every time I look at that girl I see Jesse as she was when she was young. There's spirit there."

"Too much for my liking," said Tom. "I think a woman should be gentler altogether." His gaze followed Jenny Pearn as she too went into the kitchen.

Though Josh knew well that Miriam had more reason than most to feel bitter about the drunken Herman Schmidt, there were times later that evening when he too wished that Miriam was a more conventional girl with a less inquiring mind. The talk around the table over the meal moved to Josh's riding. He had to tell them about Sarah Carlyon and his riding lessons. Miriam asked a number of questions, but it was not until he was walking her home that she pursued the subject of Sarah.

"Why did she pick you for lessons?" she asked.

Josh shrugged. "I don't know. It just happened."

"Is Sarah very beautiful?" asked Miriam suddenly.

"No." Josh was aware he was lying. "Well . . . she's quite pretty, I suppose."

"More beautiful than me, Josh?"

"No." He was able to say it with complete honesty.

"Have you ever kissed her?"

"Of course not! She means nothing to me, Miriam."

"That's all right then." Suddenly Miriam turned and threw her arms about him. As Josh drew her into his arms she responded fiercely. Lips and bodies met in a passionate kiss that made Josh feel as though his whole being was on fire. The same heat was in Miriam until, as quickly as it had begun, she was pushing him away. "No, Josh. Please. Don't let it be like that with me."

He let his arms fall to his side. "I'm sorry."

Immediately she was back again. "No, don't feel sorry. I want you to need me like that. But please try to wait a while longer. It won't be too long, will it?"

"No, only until I come home and start earning."

She kissed him again. "I must go now, Josh."

"All right."

"Josh?"

"Yes?"

"I love you. I love you so much I could burst with it."

"I love you too, Miriam." It sounded strange now that he had finally put his thoughts into words.

"Honest?"

"Honest."

On his way home to the cottage Josh heard Moses and Morwen going up the path to the moorland cave-house, both of them singing drunkenly. He wished his apprenticeship was already over so that he could marry Miriam and take her away to be with him.

BACK AT HAYLE the weeks and months went by. Lost in sheer hard work winter merged with spring, and summer slipped into autumn. By November Josh was sufficiently well trained to go with a team of Harvey's engineers to install some machinery in a local tin mine. It was the best possible experience for him.

The work had only just been completed when the snows came. There was not a man or woman alive in Cornwall who could remember a winter like it. Hayle harbour lay still and silent, jammed with ships unable to move out because of the blinding snow. It hid the toll-roads and spread a thick blanket on the fields and tors. For Josh it meant that he was unable to make the journey to Sharptor for Christmas, a great disappointment.

Though there was no way of informing them at Sharptor that he would not be coming, both Ben and Jesse knew in their hearts that travel was impossible and they had voiced this opinion many times. Only Miriam nursed the hope that some miracle would allow Josh to come home.

"Perhaps it is only up here on the moor that the snow is so bad," she said on Christmas Eve. "It might be better farther west." She was wearing a new dress, pinched in at the waist in order to show off her slim, developing figure.

"No, it's the same all over the county," said Ben Retallick, reclining in the rocking-chair close to the roaring fire. "Not even a seagull could get home in weather like this."

"I wonder what sort of Christmas Josh will have at Hayle?" put in Jenny as she lifted a large steaming kettle from the fire.

"Oh, he'll do well enough," said Ben. "William Carlyon and his family will see to that. I think they've taken quite a fancy to our Josh. Theophilus Strike was talking to me about it the other day. He said that Josh was regarded as one of the most promising engineers they've ever had at Hayle."

Jenny came across the room and put a comforting arm about Miriam. "Never mind. I'm quite sure Josh will be home as soon as he can."

"It's all right for you," said Miriam, "Tom Shovell will be here for his Christmas meal." But the edge had gone from her voice and she managed a smile. Jenny was a very gentle, loving girl. Nobody was happier than Miriam at the romance that had sprung up between the mine captain and the young widow.

All the same, Miriam did not enjoy her Christmas. Not only was there the disappointment of not having Josh. There was also the misery of jealousy eating at her. For at Hayle, Josh was spending Christmas with a girl that Miriam knew instinctively was in love with him.

THE YEAR 1841 sped along as though it was in a hurry to get somewhere and the Wheal Sharptor's engine became an exciting reality for Josh. By late summer it was being assembled—the boiler, the massive beam and numerous pipes, gears and wheels. It was rare for a mine engineer to be involved in the manufacture of his own engine, and in this Josh was lucky.

Finally, all that could be done at Hayle was completed and the equipment loaded onto a ship to be carried around the coast to Looe and then by canal to Moorswater. There Josh would accompany the engine on the difficult overland journey to Sharptor.

Suddenly, all the months of studying were over. He was an engineer going out into the world of working men, his off-duty time was his own and he need not spend his evenings studying. It was a strange feeling. For almost three years Hayle had been

202

everything to him, home, work, and occasional recreation. Leaving it would be a wrench.

His parting with the Carlyons was difficult. He had become genuinely fond of the family. Especially, he had to admit, of Sarah. His feelings for her were not as tempestuous as those he had for Miriam, they were gentler, deeply affectionate.

When Mrs. Carlyon had hugged him and given him a motherly kiss, she said, "Surely you are not going without saying goodbye to the horses? Sarah, take Josh down to the stables. You have both had many happy hours riding together."

Josh walked with Sarah in silence to the stables. He opened the door and they went inside, into the warm and familiar smell.

"Goodbye, Hector, old chap," said Josh, patting the horse's neck as the big animal nuzzled his ear, "I'm going to miss you."

"Will you miss me too, Josh? Just a little?" It was a very unhappy little plea.

"I'll miss you a lot, Sarah. You've been very, very kind to me while I've been here."

She turned away from him and it was only when her shoulders started heaving that he knew she was crying.

"Sarah! Don't." He touched her shoulders and she turned into his arms, letting the sobs come noisily.

"Please don't cry." He held her close as she clung to him. Then he was kissing her and she was responding with a hunger that made his body react as it had once before. In another place. With Miriam.

He tried to move away but she clung to him in fierce desperation. "Don't go, Josh. Don't leave me."

"I must, Sarah. My apprenticeship is over. You know that."

She pulled away from him and looked down at the ground. "I'm making a fool of myself, aren't I?"

"No, of course you're not."

She nodded her head violently. "Yes. Yes, I am." She fumbled in her sleeve for a handkerchief and blew her nose violently. "I'm all right now," she said thickly.

"That's good." He put out a hand to take her arm. "We'd better go now. The men will be waiting for me."

"You go. I want to stay here for a while."

"Sarah, I can't leave you here like this."

"It's better, Josh. Really it is."

He hesitated. This was harder than he had ever imagined it would be. "All right. Goodbye, Sarah."

"Goodbye . . . . Josh?" He stopped and turned at the door. "Will you write to me? Tell me how you are getting on?"

"Of course I will."

"I'd like that. Goodbye, Josh. Think of me sometimes."

When he went outside the men were in the wagon. Harvey's were supplying a team of four men to install the engine, travelling with all the tools they would need. As soon as he climbed on board the driver whipped up the horses and they trundled off.

They arrived at Sharptor the following day. After a brief reunion with his family—Miriam was at work at the Wheal Phoenix—Josh hurried away to Looe, leaving his team to inspect the newly constructed engine house. He meant to ensure that sufficient care was taken with the engine on its way up the canal.

The boiler looked huge up on the jetty alongside the ship that had carried it. But it was the massive thirty-ton beam that was the most difficult item to handle. Josh expressed doubts about carrying it up the canal, but the canal company had a barge which had been built for this very purpose. The Wheal Caradon had used it two years before when they had expanded their workings.

Josh thought that if the Wheal Caradon had needed a special barge for their beam, they would probably have a wagon capable of handling the heavy equipment too. When the beam had been secured aboard the barge, Josh rode off to inquire.

THE PINCH-FACED Captain Frisby had responsibility for the largest copper-mining complex in east Cornwall. "The Wheal Sharptor, eh?" he said. "How much are you expanding? I'm not lending mine equipment to another mine that might put us out of business."

Josh looked around at the highly industrialized Caradon

complex, its numerous tall, black-smoked chimneys and general air of bustle and industry. Wheal Sharptor was not in the same class, and Josh said as much.

"That may be the way it is now," said the Caradon captain, "but who knows what may happen next year?"

Josh kept a tight grip on the anger boiling up within him. It was unheard of for one mine to refuse to help another when it would cost nothing.

"I don't think Sharptor will ever be a big mine," he repeated, "but one day you might need another engineer. You'll always be able to call on me."

"If ever I need another engineer I won't send for a boy," retorted the Caradon captain. All the same, he looked at Josh with a new interest. "Where did you pick up your engineering? Loafing in some boiler-house?"

"No, I learned it properly at Harvey's of Hayle," replied Josh. "The engine on its way up from Looe is one that I helped to build."

"Is that offer of yours a promise?" asked the captain. "If ever we have need we can call on you?"

"If you need help I'm sure Tom Shovell will be happy for me to come."

"Um! Well, I may hold you to your promise. You can take the wagon. But you'll have to provide your own horses. I'm not wearing out my horses for the Wheal Sharptor."

Josh was quite happy with that arrangement. The Sharptor mine had no shortage of good horses. Old Nehemeziah and his stable boys were able to muster seventeen pairs and as the horses jangled their brass-embellished harnesses the heavy wagon was hauled away from the mine with such ease that it might have been a pony cart.

At Moorswater the engine was transferred from barge to wagon and Josh began the slow return to Sharptor. It was midnight before he arrived, but the family had waited up with his supper. Only Miriam was not with them. He commented on that while he was eating.

"Miriam doesn't spend much time at Sharptor these days,"

explained his mother. "She puts in a full day's work at the Wheal Phoenix. Then she goes to St. Cleer to do her schooling. We've seen very little of her these past months."

"It isn't Miriam's fault, Josh," said Ben Retallick. "She's staying away in order to save us from any unpleasantness, that's all."

"I don't understand. What unpleasantness?"

Jenny Pearn rose from her seat in the corner. "It's my fault, Josh."

"Now Jenny . . ." Jesse Retallick began, but the young widow waved her into silence. "Yes it is, in a way. You've been away a long time, Josh. But d'you remember how Moses Trago used to be when he'd been drinking?"

Josh nodded.

"Now he's far worse. It's as though the drink has drowned the normal part of his mind." Jenny shuddered. "He came to the house when your mother was in the kitchen and must have thought I was here alone. He started mauling me. Your mother had to threaten him with the meat cleaver before he'd go."

"But that's not all of it," put in Jesse. "He began coming to the door to ask for Miriam. It meant nothing to him whether she was here or not. It was an excuse to leer at Jenny."

"And now Miriam's staying away so that he'll have no excuse for coming here?"

"Yes. I'm sorry, Josh."

But the following morning, when Josh let himself out of the cottage into the hill mist Miriam darted forward and the next moment he was embracing her.

"I'd almost given you up for lost," he said, holding her at arm's length in order to look at her. "Where have you been?"

"I expect your mother told you what happened, Josh. I'm not going to bring trouble on them again. Where are you going now? Can I walk with you?"

"I'm going to the Sharptor mine. We're going to begin putting the engine together. It's a fine engine, Miriam."

"I'm quite sure it is if you've helped to build it." She clung to his arm as they swung along the path and halted a short distance

206

from the mine entrance. "Will you see me tonight, Josh?"

"I'll do my best, but it'll be difficult for a couple of days. The men from Harvey's want to see the engine working by Saturday." He smiled at her. "But I'm home now, Miriam. We have a lifetime ahead of us."

"I know. I'm so happy I could burst. I won't wait around tonight. I'll go straight on to my lessons after work. You must go to talk with William, he is always asking about you."

It still sounded strange to hear her call the Reverend Thackeray "William". "Give him my regards," he said. "I must go now, I have a lot to do."

"'Bye Josh."

He kissed her quickly, then strode away to the mine. He could almost imagine they were married already and that Miriam would be waiting for him at the end of the day. But the bells that fate was planning to ring were not for a wedding.

Chapter 6

As Josh had anticipated, building the engine kept him working at a frenzied pace for the remainder of that week. The machine was scheduled for completion on Saturday afternoon. It would be another week before the long plungers would extend to the bottom of the shaft and link up with the water pump. But on Saturday the boiler would be filled, the fire started and the shiny piston rod would set the great beam rocking.

By four o'clock Theophilus Strike and some of his gentlemen friends were inside the boiler room watching the pressure gauge register for the first time. Peering in at the windows were the families of every miner who worked on the mine, together with those miners who were off duty.

Ben Retallick and Jesse were well to the front. Jenny Pearn should have been with them but she had stayed at home with young Gwen who was recovering from a bad bout of measles.

The steam pressure reached working level. Black smoke spewed forth from the tall stone chimney and chased the wind up the slope. The water began rattling in the pipes. Then, as the needle hovered halfway across the dial of the gauge, the Hayle engineer decided it was time. "All right, Josh. Open them now."

Josh twisted the steam valve and with oiled precision the piston rose slowly from its casing, pushing the beam with it. At the end of its stroke it returned equally slowly, with a faint sigh of escaping steam.

Theophilus Strike was impressed. "It's incredibly silent," he said. "I thought it would make a din you could hear for miles."

"You'll hear enough from it when it's driving the pumping-rods into the shaft," answered the Hayle engineer. "But she'll never be a noisy engine. You may thank your own engineer for that. He supervised the building of it well, Mr Strike."

From outside the engine house came shouts and cheers as the horse-operated water pump became a piece of history, and steam took over.

JENNY PEARN filled the kettle and set it on the fire in the kitchen. Behind her she thought she heard the latch on the outside door click shut.

"Is that you, Jesse? That was over quickly . . . . Oh my God!"

Standing swaying inside the room was Moses Trago, his face black with underground dirt and streaked with sweat.

Jenny put her left hand to her throat. The other felt behind her for the door frame. Slowly she moved along the wall. She had no coherent thoughts. She only knew she had to get away.

Moses' eyes followed her. He took two lurching steps into the room and made a drunken movement with his hand. "Come here!"

Jenny did not move.

Moses lumbered heavily towards her. Now he was close enough for her to know the strong animal smell that reached out from his body and the gin on his breath.

"Please, Moses, no." Jenny begged. "My babe. Don't . . . !"

He grabbed at her dress at the shoulder. She struggled to break free but his grip held and the fabric parted, baring half her upper body to the waist. Pulling her roughly towards him Moses closed a hand bruisingly around her flesh.

BEFORE LONG the heat in the engine room had become oppressive and almost everyone had left. Only Josh and Tom remained, chatting, when one of the village boys came panting up to the door.

"Captain Shovell! Captain Shovell! Ben Retallick says will you get down to his place. Quick as you can."

"Why, what's happened?"

"I don't know, but he looked terrible fierce. I could hear someone crying inside the house."

Josh and Tom Shovell set off at a run.

There were half a dozen or so men at the cottage, amongst them Wrightwick Roberts. They stopped talking when Tom and Josh entered the room. In the silence Josh heard a sound like the moaning of the wind. It came from the bedroom.

"Who's upstairs? What's happened?"

"It's Jenny," said Ben Retallick, his eyes on Tom. "Moses Trago was here while we were all up at the Wheal Sharptor."

The mine captain's hands closed into fists. "Evil!" he muttered. "Evil follows Moses like a shadow."

"Is Jenny hurt bad?" Josh's throat felt dry.

"That's something only your mother and Jenny will know," answered his father. "It looks bad. We found her lying unconscious on the floor with most of her clothes ripped from her."

Tom Shovell's fists twitched again. "We're wasting time. Let's get out and find him."

"Yes." It was a reluctant Ben who moved away from the stairs. "It's something that must be done."

"There can be no other way," said Wrightwick Roberts softly.

"I'll come with you," Josh cried.

"No. I want you to stay here, Josh," his father said. "Moses might come back."

He swung away and left the house, the other men following. Tom Shovell walked like a man in a bad dream.

"Ben!" Jesse was calling from the bedroom.

"He's gone out with the others."

"To find Moses? Oh my God!" She came down the stairs.

209

"Hasn't there been tragedy enough for one day? Josh, go and find them and stop them."

"Dad said I was to stay here." Josh looked at his mother. "And he's right."

"Right?! There will be no right done this day." She stood in front of him, pleading. "Josh. Don't think I'm worried for Moses Trago. He's forfeited all claim to human sympathy. But if your father and the others do what they have in mind they'll spill his evil onto all of us. Please go and stop them. I beg you!"

His mother's passionate outburst conjured up a series of confused pictures in his mind. But his father's words had left no room for argument. "I want you to stay here," he had said. If he left the house now and Moses did return, Josh could only blame himself.

He could not go.

BY DUSK there was no sign of Ben Retallick or the other men. Beyond the rocky heights of Sharptor a dark grey cloud was building and thunder rumbled. Jesse busied herself in the kitchen. Josh paced restlessly from window to door.

It had been dark an hour before there was the scraping of boots on stone outside. Josh hurriedly unlocked the door and the men entered the cottage grim-faced and silent. Except for one miner. "There'll be no need to lock the door against Moses Trago again," he said triumphantly.

"So you found him," Jesse said flatly. "You found him and you were judge and jury—and God himself."

"It wasn't like that." Wrightwick Roberts's big fingers tangled and untangled themselves jerkily. "He fell, Jesse. It was an accident. We had him cornered at the top of the old shaft and called on him to give himself up to us. He was throwing rocks to keep us back. As he stooped to pick up one he slipped and fell down the shaft."

"Did you actually see this with your own eyes, Wrightwick Roberts? Or did one of you who was closer to Moses say that's what happened and you all agreed it must be so?"

There was an uncomfortable silence during which Jesse

Retallick looked at each of the men in turn, hoping that one of them would meet her gaze.

"Tom, you'd better go upstairs to that poor girl. If she's awake she'll have need of your kindness. I only hope there were no witnesses to this night's work."

Again the men looked uncomfortable and Jesse gasped. "For God's sake! Someone did see you! Who was it?"

"There was no other to see what happened." This from Wrightwick Roberts. "Although the Trago girl was following us shortly before. But it really was an accident . . ."

Josh never waited to hear the last part of the sentence. He reached for his coat and bolted through the door. He could imagine Miriam following the men who were hunting her father. Hoping to find him first and warn him. Then witnessing his death.

The storm was almost overhead now. Between the rumbling thunder, the lightning picked out the bushes and rocks of the moor, enlarging them and giving them long trembling shadows. Uneven gusts of wind ripped through the undergrowth.

Finally Josh reached his destination. On hands and knees he crawled through the gorse tunnel into the rock hideout. It was silent inside and he thought he had guessed wrong. Perhaps Miriam no longer used her old hideaway. Then a sustained web of lightning broke up the sky and he saw her, crouching in a corner.

"Miriam!" He dropped down beside her. "I'm sorry. I really am."

He had hoped—expected—that she would fall into his arms and cling to him. But she showed no emotion. Her body was rigid. Only her lips moved.

"They killed him. They cornered him like a dog in a sheep pen. Then they killed him."

His hands went out to her shoulders, "They didn't mean to do it, Miriam. He slipped."

"No!" She spat the word out. "They killed him. I saw it."

"They wanted to take him back. He had to be caught after what he did." He tried to draw her to him but she remained stiff for another minute. Then suddenly, without any warning, she brought her mouth up to his. Fierce and demanding.

211

It took him by surprise but he responded immediately and eagerly. She slipped sideways to lie on the grass and he went down with her. Her hands slipped inside his jacket and began plucking his shirt loose from his trousers, clutching, clawing at his back. He rolled onto her then and she received him.

A LITTLE while later he stood up slowly, feeling rain pound against his near-naked body. She lay as he left her, unmoving.

Josh was uneasy. Self-consciously he pulled his clothes together. "Here, take my jacket. You're getting soaked."

He reached out a hand to her but she flinched back. "Don't touch me!"

"What's the matter? Did I hurt you? I'm sorry. But you wanted it to happen as much as I did. Didn't you?"

She ignored the jacket. "Did I, Josh? Are you quite sure? If I tell Morwen and Uncle John you forced me, held me down and took me, will they believe you—or will they believe me?"

"Miriam, you don't know what you're saying. We're going to be married. . . ."

"No!" The thunder rumbled away in the background. Wearily she shrugged herself back into her limp dress. "How can I marry you? Your father killed mine."

Josh attempted to deny it but her voice was a scream that cut him short. "He did! He did! He murdered him." Her voice broke. "It's over between us, Josh. Finished."

Josh took hold of her but she broke free, slipping from his arms. Before he could stop her she had gone, into the gorse tunnel.

"Miriam—come back!" He stumbled after her, but a flash of lightning ripped the sky, blinding him, and the wind only threw the words back in his teeth.

Chapter 7

Moses Trago was buried at St. Cleer with only his family present. The Reverend William Thackeray took the service. When it came to an end he put a comforting arm about Miriam's shoulders, and led her away from the graveside. Her mother and John Trago followed in their wake, but the scowling Morwen turned and walked off without a backward glance.

Josh had known about the funeral. But though he desperately wanted to speak to Miriam he knew better than to attend it.

He was still bewildered and unable to think straight about himself. For a couple of days after the night of the storm his unhappiness had been mingled with fear. But there had been no knock at the door. No crowd of angry miners eager to avenge the rape of a young girl. Now only the uncertainty remained.

Finally he tried to intercept Miriam up on the moor, on her way home from work at the Wheal Phoenix, but she never came. When he inquired he found she had not been to work since the death of her father. Then he changed his tactics and waited near the Tragos' rock home. Here he came into violent contact with another member of the Trago family.

Josh was watching the path from the cover of an ivy-covered rock when he heard a sound from the undergrowth to one side of him. He turned to see Morwen Trago.

"What are you spying on us for, Josh Retallick? Haven't you and your lot done enough?"

"I came up here to see Miriam," said Josh.

"Did you now?" Morwen Trago mocked. "Then you'll have a long wait because Miriam isn't here."

"What do you mean? Where is she? I must see her."

"Must? Who do you think you are? Just because you've been away to learn about engines, you needn't think everyone is going to jump to do your bidding. Go away and leave Miriam alone. She doesn't want to see you again."

"You're lying, Morwen. She'd never say that."

Morwen knocked Josh's hand from his sleeve. "No Retallick calls me a liar. I've told you to leave Miriam alone. This should help you remember it."

Morwen's booted foot lashed out, but Josh managed to twist his body away before closing and grappling with him. Wrestling and gouging, they rolled down the slope to land with a breath-taking thud on the hard-packed earth of the path. Few blows were struck on either side. It was a mauling, wrestling fight, until the hands of a man stronger than either of them reached in and prised them apart.

It was John Trago, the brother of Moses. "Hasn't there been enough fighting between our families? Is it going to be carried on by the sons now?"

Morwen began to struggle but John shook his nephew until his teeth rattled. "Stop it, I say!"

Morwen ceased his struggles and John Trago released them both. "Now. What's this all about?" The big man's voice was surprisingly soft.

"I caught him snooping around. Spying on us," said a surly Morwen.

"I was trying to see Miriam."

"You won't find her here any more," said John Trago. "She's at St. Cleer, at Preacher Thackeray's house."

"Thank you. That's all I wanted to know."

"Josh! You must leave her be." He had turned to go when the call stopped him. "She's getting married this coming week."

Shock and disbelief hit Josh with a near-physical blow. "Married? It isn't possible! Who. . . . ?"

"She's marrying Preacher Thackeray."

Josh's mouth hung open like an idiot's. William Thackeray had been his friend and tutor. He had taught Josh not only how to read and write, but even how to think. Furthermore, he knew of Josh's love for the girl. He could not be marrying Miriam. It would be a complete and utter betrayal.

"Don't try to see her, Josh," John Trago went on. "It would only distress her. This is a good marriage for Miriam. A chance to get away from the past and lead a normal life. If you think anything at all of her don't take that chance away."

But Josh hardly heard the rest of John Trago's words. He stumbled away along the path, his mind in a turmoil. He did not choose his direction and walked unknowingly. Aimlessly. When he did become aware of things around him he looked up to see the rock hideout just ahead.

He crawled gratefully into its shelter and sat looking at the spot

214

where he had lain with Miriam on that stormy night less than a week before.

Something metallic gleamed in a crevice between the rocks. It was a tin box. Lifting it down he prised off the lid and found a full record of the relationship between himself and Miriam. Not only were there all the letters he had sent to her while he was at Hayle but also the pages of arithmetic he had taught her. Finally, on a scrap of paper he saw a faded word. It was her name. "Miriam". She had been happy that day, delighted at seeing her name in writing for the first time. "I'll keep it for ever," she had said. It seemed that her "for ever" had come to an end.

Josh stood up, but not to go home. He set off in the opposite direction—to St. Cleer to see the Reverend William Thackeray.

At the gate to the preacher's small stone cottage behind the chapel, Josh hesitated. Coming across the moor he had rehearsed what he would say. He would tell him that for Miriam to marry anyone but himself would be a dreadful mistake. They, Miriam and Josh, loved each other and always had. He had thought of saying that they had already given themselves to each other but decided to keep that as a last, desperate bid to prevent the marriage.

While he hesitated William Thackeray came out of the cottage. Closing the door behind him he walked down the path towards his former pupil. "Josh! How wonderful to see you. How are you?"

Josh ignored the preacher's outstretched hand. Thackeray dropped it without changing his expression.

"I want to speak to you about Miriam," Josh blurted out, feeling awkward and adolescent.

"Yes, I know. But talking will not change anything, Josh. Miriam and I are to be married."

Josh couldn't understand how the preacher was able to maintain such composure. "She was going to marry me," he said, inadequately.

"I know that too. That is why I am glad you have come to see me, Josh. We have been friends for a very long time. I would have been unhappy in the knowledge that someone we both care for had come between us. Miriam feels the same way."

"Where is she now?"

"I'm sorry, Josh. That is something I am not willing to tell you. It would serve no useful purpose."

"I only want to hear her say the words."

"You will have to accept it from me, Josh. Miriam is going to be my wife."

The preacher's quiet, reasonable tone only made Josh angrier. "She can't marry you! She can't! Ask her about . . . ." He was going to tell Thackeray about the night of the storm but the words stuck in his throat.

"She has told me all I want to hear and we will be married on Sunday. I think—"

"I don't give a damn what you think!" Josh blurted.

"We really won't achieve anything pursuing this conversation." Thackeray moved off towards the chapel. "I'm sorry, Josh. I'll pray for your peace of mind."

Angry and ashamed at the tears that stung his eyes, Josh turned away. Thackeray had won, but he would not allow this man who had once been his friend to witness his humiliation.

But someone else witnessed his defeat. From her room upstairs in the preacher's home Miriam watched Josh walk away, hunched in his unhappiness. And it was his misery she shared, not William Thackeray's victory.

THERE WERE TWO weddings that month. In the chapel at St. Cleer, William Thackeray was married to Miriam Trago, while in the little whitewashed chapel at Henwood, Jenny Pearn became Mrs. Tom Shovell. Josh went to neither wedding. He made the excuse to Jenny that there were last-minute adjustments to be made to the pumps at the mine. He could not have sat through the service without torturing himself with thoughts of the other wedding.

Although his absence was for emotional reasons, there *was* something he was working on in the mine. And it was being done without the knowledge of Theophilus Strike.

The pumps were operated by a series of huge wooden rods, moved up and down by the rocking beam. They extended to the bottom of the shaft and rose and fell extremely slowly. Inspired by the plans given to him by Francis Trevithick, Josh was using this slow speed to provide a means of raising men to the surface.

The idea was simple. The length of the engine's stroke was some twelve feet and Josh had bolted blocks of wood to the rods at a distance of twelve feet apart. At the same intervals up the shaft he had built platforms into the wooden framework. It would be a simple matter for a man to step onto a block and ride up for twelve feet. Then he would step off and wait for the next stroke of the pump to ride up the next twelve feet.

Josh did not have to wait long for the mine owner's reaction. One afternoon Theophilus Strike arrived to inspect the pumping operation. "So, now we have become a modern mine," he said to Tom Shovell. "How is it looking down below?"

"Why not go down and see for yourself, Mr. Strike?"

Strike looked at Josh, who had made the suggestion, not certain whether it smacked of insolence.

"I've built a new idea into the pumping system," Josh went on. "It means that the men will be able to come up from the levels without using the ladders."

"What the devil do you mean?" Strike blazed. "Your job was to put in the engine and pumping system, not install some fool idea of your own."

"It's not exactly my idea," said Josh, realizing that Mr. Strike was capable of dismissing him on the spot. "It was Richard Trevithick's. His son gave me the drawings."

"Francis Trevithick?" There was an immediate change of attitude. The Cornish engineering family was highly respected. "When did he come to Sharptor?"

"He didn't. I met him at Hayle. Later, he sent me a complete set of plans his father had drawn up."

"And how much did this idea cost?"

"Virtually nothing. We made use of materials that were already to hand."

The mine owner looked searchingly at Josh. "All right," he said finally. "Take me down to the fifty fathom level and I'll see for myself how it works. Give me a hard hat, someone."

Josh led the way, stepping onto the block as it came up to its maximum height. The descent was easy. The platforms were sufficiently large and the low speed of the engine eliminated much of the danger. Certainly the primitive lift was totally lacking in safety measures, but it was better than a narrow, wet ladder for a tired man.

When his tour of inspection was over Theophilus Strike returned above ground. The minute he stepped onto grass once again it was obvious to everyone he had enjoyed the experience.

"I approve of your work, Josh. You have done well. Thanks, no doubt, to Trevithick's plans. I only hope your lift is not going to make my miners soft."

"At the end of a shift a man is already tired," said Josh, quietly but intensely. "Anyone who has ever seen them lying gasping for breath after climbing the ladders would never think it soft to find another way to get them up."

"Joshua Retallick, I like your initiative. But I do not need to be lectured on the lot of the miner. On the Wheal Sharptor a man is paid a fair wage for a fair day's work. No one is forcing him to stay. Do I make myself quite clear?"

"I think Josh was only trying to explain that we'll be able to use our older, more experienced men at the deeper levels now we have the man-lift," put in Tom Shovell hastily. "We haven't been able to use them before because the climb back up was too much."

"I am fully aware of what he was saying," replied the mine owner. "I hope he is equally certain of my meaning."

"You'll have to watch that tongue of yours," said Tom when the mine owner had gone beyond hearing.

"What did I say?" protested Josh. "I only spoke the truth."

"Strike doesn't want to know about that. While you've been away your friend the preacher at St. Cleer has been out and about complaining of the miners' conditions. Wherever he goes there's trouble. Strike knows you were schooled by him and it bothers him. Learn to choose your words when he's near. He may be a bit touchy but he's a good man to work for."

"He needn't worry about my association with Preacher Thackeray," said Josh bitterly. "He's no friend of mine."

218

Chapter 8

Close as the weddings of Miriam and Jenny had been, the births of their respective babies in the summer of 1842 were closer. Both children entered the world in the dark of the same night—hoping, some said, that the absence of light might hide their secrets.

Miriam's son was born after twelve hours of painful labour. She writhed on the bed in the cottage behind the chapel, fighting back the screams that each pain drew from her and the name of the child's father that was on her tongue. The pain had almost sapped the last of her strength when the baby finally made his way into the world, adding his cries to the gasps of his mother.

Jenny had an easier time, if such events are measured in terms of physical pain. By the time Mary Crabbe arrived to perform the duties of midwife, the birth was well under way. But there were no baby sounds heard in Tom Shovell's house. The baby, also a boy, was stillborn.

There was sympathy for Jenny, but little for the child. Those who saw it said it had the scowl of Moses Trago on its screwed-up face. As for Miriam, that her child was also conceived out of wedlock was unanimously agreed. Most of the gossips had it that William Thackeray was the child's father, but there were others who gave knowing looks in Josh's direction. For his part he gave no sign that he knew of their opinions. Or cared, if he did.

The engine at the mine was running well and word of his man-lift was spreading around the area. It was not long before Captain Frisby from the Wheal Caradon sent a messenger asking if Josh would call to see him.

Josh went that same day. Frisby came immediately to the point. "Tell me about this man-lift of yours," he said. "How much would it cost to put one into the Caradon?"

Josh grinned. "It would cost next to nothing. But since when has the Wheal Caradon been so concerned about its men?" It was well known that for all its great size and high production the Wheal Caradon miners were among the worst paid in the country.

"You sound like a union man," said Captain Frisby angrily.

"But I didn't bring you here to quarrel. I'm asking you to do this job for me. When can you start on it?"

"I can't," said Josh. "But send a couple of your carpenters across to the Sharptor tomorrow and I'll show them what to do."

"Will you inspect it when it's done? I don't want any mistakes."

"Yes, I'll do that," agreed Josh. "But what's wrong with your own engineer?"

"Caradon hasn't got a proper engineer at the moment," Frisby admitted. "You could have the job if you wanted it. I'll pay you half as much again as you are getting now. There would be no shortage of work. We have more engines here than you'll ever see at Sharptor."

Josh smiled. "Sorry, Captain. I appreciate your offer but I have a duty to my present mine owner. Pay half as much again to all your men and you wouldn't have to look for engineers. They'd be banging on your door."

"Yes, and so would the shareholders. Perhaps it is just as well you won't come to work for me. I have no shortage of men to preach about fair pay for the miners and about their union."

Captain Frisby was not the only one to become increasingly aware of union talk. It was something that had been discussed for years wherever miners gathered. Preacher Thackeray, for one, was dedicated to unionism. He was an eloquent speaker, and when he spoke men listened. Even Josh had attended one of his open-air meetings. The reason he did not attend any more was that Miriam now occasionally delivered a speech with her husband, and even though it had been more than a year since her marriage, Josh did not feel able to face her.

Time had brought changes for the whole Trago family. Soon after Miriam's wedding John Trago had come down the hill to the Retallick cottage. Although every inch a Trago he lacked the menace that had always travelled with his older brother.

"Well, come on in, man," said Jesse. "Though I can't think of a Trago who's crossed this doorstep without bringing trouble into the house."

"I hope all that is past, Jesse," said the big miner uneasily. "That's what I've come to speak to you and Ben about." He

220

cleared his throat. "I wanted to tell you that I hold no grudge against you or your family. No more does Kate. We neither of us believe the death of Moses was deliberate."

It was Ben's turn to look ill at ease.

John Trago cleared his throat once more. "I'm going to do my best to look after Kate and the children. I'll try to give them a bit more of life than they've been used to up to now."

"You have my good wishes, John," said Ben.

"There's something else. You see, I think the children should be brought up to feel they are just like everyone else. I want them to live without people pointing a finger at them. Whispering that they're the family of Moses Trago. The man who raped Jenny."

Ben nodded. "That makes good sense. How can I help?"

"You're a respected man in the village. If you put it about that you have no argument with us everyone else will do the same."

"We'll do that willingly," Jesse said firmly. "But what about Morwen?"

"Morwen's gone," John Trago said. "He thinks a soldier's life has more to offer him than being down a mine. I can't say that he's wrong." He edged his way to the door. "I'm very obliged to you. Kate will be too."

BY THE YEAR 1843 the copper mines were going through a boom such as they had never known. But the boom was not indicative of the country as a whole. Corn was again short, nobody knew why. And in Cornwall a slump in the market for tin had the tin miners wandering the county in search of work. A few mines, and the Caradon was one, saw the plight of the tinners as something from which to gain advantage. Captain Frisby took the tinners on at low wages and then cut back the pay of his own men. It aroused great anger among the established miners, but they dared do little. As Thackeray was quick to tell them, if there had been a union of miners such a situation would never have arisen.

Another result of the slump in tin mining was that the demand for mine engines dropped and the Cornish engine works had to search out new customers.

Josh was in the engine-house of the Sharptor mine when a

voice from the doorway said, "I'm pleased to see you haven't forgotten everything you learned at Harvey's, Josh."

Swinging around, he saw William Carlyon standing in the doorway. Then Sarah pushed past her father and flung her arms about Josh's neck. He was unable to ward her off because his hands were black with grease. There was nothing to do but enjoy her embrace until she finally released him.

"What are you doing here?" Josh spoke to Mr. Carlyon, but his eyes were on Sarah. She had grown taller since he last saw her. With her long blonde ringlets tied behind her neck she was a strikingly beautiful girl.

Carlyon smiled. "I have to go to Bristol on business. I thought it a good opportunity to give the family a holiday. Mary and Mrs. Carlyon are with your mother at the cottage."

As they talked Josh rubbed the grease from his hands.

"I rode all the way here on Hector," said Sarah. "And Mary rode part of the way on the pony you used to ride at Hayle. The rest of the time she rode in the coach with Mother. I changed into this new dress when we reached your cottage. Do you like it?" She struck a pose, holding the skirt out at her sides.

"It's beautiful," he said. "Far too good for an engine-house."

"That's what I told her, but she'd take no notice," said William Carlyon. "I would like to meet your father and Captain Shovell," he went on. "One of the men told me they were at the explosives store. Where will I find that?"

Josh started to lead the way but Carlyon stopped him. "No, just point me in the right direction. You see that Sarah gets back to the cottage. It's all right. We spent last evening with Theophilus Strike. I told him we should be robbing him of his engineer for as long as we were here."

Josh sent one of the miners to guide Mr. Carlyon to the explosives store. Then, after giving instructions to his engine-man, he set off with Sarah.

"Are you pleased to see me, Josh?" Sarah looked up at him provocatively.

"If you're fishing for compliments, then the answer is 'Yes'. You're even more beautiful than I remembered."

222

The Josh she had known at Hayle would not have been bold enough to pay her such a compliment and for a moment Sarah was taken aback. She looked again at Josh and saw the new confidence in him. He was a young man with the knowledge of his own ability.

"You've changed, Josh."

"Is that good or bad?" His smile was a challenge.

"I'm not sure. For you it is probably good. For me . . . ?" She shrugged and there was a moment of silence. Then she smiled, "Come on, Josh. If I don't get you home soon my sister will come looking for you. She's talked of nothing but seeing you for days."

When they arrived at the cottage Mary ran out and flung herself at him and Mrs. Carlyon made predictable remarks about Josh having "filled out". But she had a speculative look in her eyes when she watched Sarah and him together. It was a relief when Sarah asked if he would like to go for a ride. Soon he was riding Mary's pony along the path to the high moor, while Sarah followed on Hector.

Once above the ridge, they rode side by side through the bracken. Sarah gave Josh a warm smile. "This is just like old times. You don't know how I have missed you, Josh. Have you done much riding since you left Hayle?"

He looked at her sharply. Did she really understand so little about life in a mining community? "I'm a working man now, Sarah. I have little time to ride and no horse to use if I wanted to."

"I'm sure Mr. Strike would lend you one of his horses," replied Sarah. "He's a very nice man . . . ." She shrugged. "But it's far too lovely a day to have an argument. I'll race you to that circle of stones over there."

The circle of stones was a mile away and Sarah and Hector arrived a hundred yards ahead of Josh and the pony. "Phew! I'd forgotten a lot of things about riding," he said, laughing. "One of them is that unless you're in practice it leaves you as blown as the horse." He dismounted and helped Sarah to the ground.

She rested her hands on his shoulders and jumped down lightly. But when she landed she did not remove her hands immediately. Josh looked down at her and she came to him, arms meeting about his neck. As they kissed her ardour matched his own. Then she rested her head on his chest, still holding him tightly.

"Oh Josh! I have missed you terribly."

"I think you really mean it."

"You know very well I do . . . ." She stooped and thoughtfully picked up a raven's feather from the ground, black and glossy. "Are you really pleased to see me, Josh?"

"Very pleased." He was.

"What about that girl you told me about when you were at Hayle? Miriam? Do you still see her?"

"No. She married a preacher. Preacher Thackeray."

"Preacher Thackeray!" Sarah was happy again. "Mr. Strike was telling Daddy about him last night. He said that Preacher Thackeray is a troublemaker."

"Theophilus Strike is an employer. He's bound to oppose Thackeray who preaches for a union of all the miners."

"Don't tell me you agree with him?" Sarah was only half bantering.

"Of course I agree with him, Sarah. I'm bound to. He's trying to help men like me. I'm a miner."

"No. You aren't like those creatures we saw coming out of a shaft on our way here. They were filthy, horribly coarse men."

Josh was about to argue further, but he had no wish to spoil Sarah's day by explaining the facts of mining life to her. She was far too happy. She was also very lovely. He helped her back into her saddle and remounted himself.

"One day I'll take you down a mine," he promised, "then you'll see for yourself how difficult it is for a man to keep clean when he's working."

"I'll keep you to that, Josh Retallick."

At that moment a fox broke from a gorse thicket not twenty yards ahead of them. With a yell Josh kicked his heels into the ribs of his startled pony and gave chase. Sarah was slower off the mark but Hector quickly overtook Josh's mount. The chase ended when the fox scrambled up a bank where the horses could not follow.

Sarah thoroughly enjoyed the gallop. When, hot and pink, she arrived back at the cottage she gave the two families a dramatic version of the pursuit. Mary pouted with envy.

"If I had been there I'd have caught it," she said, determined to impress Josh. "I can ride as well as Sarah. You come and watch me when I go riding at home."

"I wish I could," replied Josh.

"You'll get that chance sooner than you expect," said William Carlyon. "That's the reason I wanted to see Captain Shovell today. I managed to pick up some business from Theophilus Strike last night. He said that, if Tom Shovell thought it a good idea, the Wheal Sharptor should have an engine for hoisting ore to the surface. He also said he wants you to come to Hayle to supervise the making of it, Josh."

While William Carlyon was talking, Jesse Retallick had been watching Sarah. She saw her face light up when her father said that Josh would be going to Hayle. Jesse was both pleased and saddened. Her son might not yet be aware of it, but she knew she was going to lose him to this girl one day.

JOSH TRAVELLED to Hayle early the following month. Harvey's foundry had not changed, but life was very different for him there. He was a guest in the works manager's home now. He discussed engines with Harvey's designers and although he lacked years his ideas were taken seriously.

But the time Josh spent at Hayle was not devoted entirely to work. He and Sarah had their favourite sandy beach which they would often visit, riding out along the cliffs above St. Ives Bay. On one evening, also, he accompanied Sarah and her sister to a concert, given in the chapel by a touring orchestra. It was a Beethoven programme and Josh found himself in a new land. He had discovered music.

"Isn't it beautiful?" Sarah whispered and he nodded in agreement, not daring to speak. When the music ended he applauded in numb amazement, returning to earth only when they left the chapel and went outside to the world of belching chimneys and clattering hooves.

The return was made harder because with it came the knowledge that he would probably never attend another concert. Such an event had nothing in common with his life at Sharptor.

"What is the matter, Josh?" Sarah asked. "Didn't you enjoy the concert? You're looking very unhappy."

"I enjoyed it very much. If I look sad it must be because I was thinking I might never attend another."

"Why not? We have a concert at Hayle a couple of times every year."

"But I'm not working at Hayle," he reminded her.

"You could be," Sarah declared pointedly.

"Yes, Josh. Come and work here," said Mary excitedly. "If you don't we will have to come all the way to Sharptor to see you and Sarah if you get . . . ."

"*Mary!*"

The young girl bit back her words and looked fearfully at Josh. To her relief—and Sarah's embarrassment—he laughed. The thought of marriage to Sarah had been with him as a vague, shapeless thought ever since her visit to Sharptor. He did not love her. Certainly not in the tempestuous way he had loved Miriam. But he was very fond of her. And he was lonely.

Looking back on it later, Josh knew that if it had not been for Mary's words he would never have made his decision. He would have been unable to summon up the courage had he not been aware that Sarah had herself discussed it—if only with her young sister.

"I want you to go home by yourself, Mary," he said gently. "I'm taking Sarah for a walk by the river."

"Mama said I was to come with you or people would talk."

"That was at the concert, silly! Go on home," Sarah said.

"It's all right, Mary. I'll explain to your mother."

Mary watched as Josh and Sarah turned off towards the river. Then she ran home as fast as she could go.

Josh avoided Sarah's eyes as they walked on, hand in hand. "We come from very different backgrounds, you and I," he began. "And there are things that must be made clear before I can say what's on my mind."

"Josh! You know yourself Papa is always talking of his mining background. He's very proud of it."

"Yes, but you've been brought up to expect things like a large house and nice furniture. A miner could never give you that."

"You keep talking of miners, Josh. You're an engineer."

"True. But I live and work in a mining community. There would be no horse, no concerts like tonight."

"Concerts are nice but they are not essential. I disagree about a horse. It would cost little to feed Hector if there was some grazing available."

"There are other things too. I spend hours at the mine and you would have no one to talk to. You would probably become bored and unhappy. I wouldn't like to see that."

They stopped at the water's edge and Sarah turned to him, the moon at her back hiding her face in shadow. "Josh, either you don't know me as well as I thought, or you are trying to argue yourself out of something. I am sorry if Mary made you feel that you had to say something. You don't. Now, shall we go?"

Her voice broke a little on the last word.

"No." He believed she must be able to hear his heart pounding. "I have made up my mind. What I am trying to say is . . . Sarah, will you marry me?"

"You mean it, Josh? You really mean it?"

"Yes, Sarah. I mean it."

"Oh yes, Josh! Yes! Yes! Yes!"

She clung to him and he could feel tears running warm and wet down her cheeks. "I thought you'd decided you didn't want to marry me, Josh. I was trying to be brave and sensible about it but I was so unhappy inside." She kissed him hungrily. "Josh, I love you so very, very much. And I'll make you a good wife. I can cook and sew and housekeep. *And* I'll get rid of Hector."

"No you won't. We'll find some way to keep him. I won't have anyone saying you lowered yourself to marry me."

Sarah laughed through her tears. "Oh Josh, you are funny!"

The Carlyon family were sitting in the parlour when Josh walked in with Sarah. There was an air of expectancy in the room. Sarah seated herself on the sofa beside her mother and looked

228

down at her clasped hands. Mrs. Carlyon gave both Josh and Sarah a questioning look.

"Sit down, Josh." William Carlyon pointed to the armchair that faced his own.

"I'd rather stand, if you don't mind. There's something I would like to say—I mean, to ask."

Instantly, Mrs. Carlyon was on her feet ushering Sarah and the vigorously protesting Mary from the room.

Josh continued to stand and cleared his throat twice before Carlyon said, "For goodness sake sit down, Josh. You want to marry Sarah. Now I've said it for you. It need choke you no more. Sit down and we'll talk about it."

Josh moved across the room and perched on the edge of the armchair.

"That's better. Now, you've already asked Sarah, of course?"

Josh nodded. "Yes."

"There's no need to ask what she said. I'm surprised she hasn't proposed to you, long before this. Do you have any idea where you might live?"

Josh said he had not.

"Good. That's what I was hoping you might say. Don't think I'm interfering, Josh. But Sarah is used to a little more material comfort than you are able to provide for her at the moment."

"I'm aware of that. I said so to Sarah."

"When I was at Sharptor I noticed a derelict house a couple of hundred yards up the hill. Had a couple of cleared fields behind it. Do you know where I mean?"

"Yes. We call it the idle farm. It's never been lived in during my lifetime. I think it belongs to Theophilus Strike."

"Couldn't be better. Josh, you and Sarah have my blessing. I'll buy that derelict farm for you as a wedding present, and give you a houseful of furniture. All I expect is that you get your miners together and put the house in order."

When Josh protested William Carlyon cut him short. "The house and land will be cheap, Josh. But it does mean that Sarah will be able to keep that horse of hers. And it will give me great pleasure to make you a gift of your first home." He beamed.

"Now that's settled. Call everyone back while I bring out the brandy. This calls for a celebration."

Josh returned home to Sharptor earlier than he had planned, to break the news to his family.

His parents were delighted. "She'll make you a good wife," Jesse said. "A daughter I'll be proud to welcome."

Theophilus Strike was happy to sell the old farm to William Carlyon at a fair price. For his own contribution to the wedding he undertook to supply all the building materials necessary for its renovation.

Later that weekend Josh inspected the farmhouse with his father. It was larger than Josh had expected, with four good rooms downstairs, and five up.

"It's going to be a major job," said Ben when the tour was over. "You've got little more than the shell of a house to work on. But the walls are as stout as you'll find anywhere and you'll live like a king when it's finished."

Josh smiled ruefully. "But there is so much to do and I'll be away for weeks yet supervising the finishing of the new engine. I can't see it ever being ready to live in."

"Nonsense! The first thing needed is a roof to keep the weather out. We'll have that done by the time you come home. Might have the floors down too."

Ben was better than his word. When Josh brought the new engine around the edge of the hill, he saw the once "idle" farmhouse standing proud and tall with new roof and doors, and windows that reflected the sun. The men from the mine had completed everything but the plastering inside. By working really hard at it Josh could have the house finished and be married to Sarah in little more than a month.

AT ABOUT this time an unforeseen incident occurred at the Wheal Caradon and Josh became involved in it. Captain Frisby had continued to take on destitute tin miners and now, even though the disgruntled copper miners were bearing the brunt of any tasks requiring special knowledge of copper mining, he cut their wages to correspond with those paid to the ex-tinners. The anger of the copper miners exploded. They downed tools and a noisy crowd assembled in front of Frisby's office, demanding that the decision be reversed.

Preacher Thackeray heard of the troubles and hurried to the mine. Standing on a rock so he could be seen by everyone, he applauded their actions and he praised their courage.

"What you do here today will be a yardstick for every mine in Cornwall," he said. "If justice prevails you'll have struck a blow that will be felt throughout the county. Remember it's your very livelihood you're fighting for—the future not only of yourselves but of your families."

"Tell that to the tinners!" called a voice from the crowd.

"While there are 'tinners' and 'copper-men' you'll never achieve anything," replied the preacher. "No stranger should come here and take away another man's livelihood by selling himself cheap, but you're all miners, and the day you accept that and unite you'll have won a great victory."

The roar of approval was interrupted by a question from one of the miners, John Kittow, the man who had master-minded the sale of corn in Callington market some years before. "That's all very well, Preacher. But all this talk of union is tomorrow talk. We've had our pay cut today. What do we do?"

"You do what you please," shouted one of the ex-tinners who had arrived for work. "We're going on shift."

The noise that went up from the men who had downed tools was an ugly one. "There'll be no work done tonight," called a Caradon man. "Not unless a tinner wants his head broken."

"Please, no fighting!" pleaded Preacher Thackeray. He turned his attention to the incoming shift. "This is your chance to show Frisby he can't set miner against miner. Show a united front. Call off your shift tonight."

"They can't do anything else," called one of the copper-men. "They won't get past us."

There was uncertainty amongst the tinners and Thackeray seized eagerly upon it. "I'm pleading with you not to try to work below ground tonight," he repeated. "Turn around and go home. I'll speak to Captain Frisby."

There was an earnest conversation among the night shift, a few lifted shoulders and general nodding of heads.

"All right," said their spokesman grudgingly. "But we'll be back for work tomorrow."

From his office Captain Frisby had watched them leave, and anger boiled up inside him, most of it directed against the preacher. When Thackeray came to his office to negotiate on the men's behalf, Frisby turned the key in the lock and refused to open the door.

"Captain Frisby," Thackeray called, "let me in and we'll talk this matter over sensibly—"

"There's nothing to be said. I've done talking—go away!"

For a few minutes William Thackeray tried to persuade the mine captain to change his mind, but Captain Frisby refused to acknowledge his presence and eventually the preacher went back to the miners.

"He's angry tonight," he said. "Give him time to cool off. If you can stop the morning shift from starting work he'll know you mean business."

"Preacher Thackeray!" John Kittow spat on the ground. "I don't like all this talk. All we want is to go back to work for the pay we were getting before today. If you have our interests at heart I suggest you warn the tinners not to try to come in to work until our pay is back to what it was. If they don't listen they'll be walking straight into big trouble."

"And that's your answer to Frisby? To cause trouble? Give him an excuse to call in the militia?"

"No, Preacher, I'm on my way now to ask someone to come and talk to Captain Frisby for us." He turned to the other miners, "You stay here. I'm going to find Josh Retallick and try to get him over here."

Thackeray's surprise at the mention of Josh's name was apparent but after a while he began nodding thoughtfully. "Yes. I'll concede that Captain Frisby might listen to Josh. But it's a lot to ask a young man to take upon his shoulders."

"You may be right. But I can't think of anyone else who can help us."

As Thackeray rode home he felt he had suffered a personal defeat. His was a great crusade, yet he had allowed the initiative to slip from his hands and pass to someone else. The thought was unusual, and bitter.

JOSH WAS in the kitchen of the Retallick cottage when John Kittow arrived. Josh had never spoken to the man and he was puzzled when Kittow said he would like to speak to him. "It's to ask a favour of you," the miner added.

"A favour? Something to do with engineering?"

"No. There's trouble at the Wheal Caradon. Bad trouble." John Kittow went on to tell him about the events that had followed Captain Frisby's wage cut.

"Why, the old skinflint!" Jesse Retallick was unable to contain her anger.

Ben waved his wife into silence. "Theophilus Strike won't like you getting mixed up in the Caradon's troubles, Josh."

"It isn't in Strike's time," retorted Josh. To John Kittow he said, "How do you think I can help? Preacher Thackeray is a more persuasive talker than I am."

"The preacher might be more used to talking," Kittow agreed, "but Captain Frisby knows you. You've been brought up in mining. You know our problems. You've done a deal of learning besides."

There was a long silence. At last Josh said, "All right, I'll come with you."

It was quite dark by the time they arrived at the Wheal Caradon, but few miners had gone home. They sat around bonfires near the main shaft. The earlier excitement had worn off and the shadowy faces in the firelight were those of worried men. Behind them the beam of the big pumping engine rocked slowly on its axle. Josh's engineer's mind noted that behind the steady thump of the engine there was another, less usual noise. The packing on the huge piston was disintegrating.

He smiled quietly to himself, then went on his own to the mine captain's office and knocked heavily on the door. "It's Josh Retallick," he called. "Can I speak to you?"

"If you come from that preacher you're wasting your time."

"Preacher Thackeray is capable of talking for himself," Josh said sharply. "Your miners asked me to speak to you. Out of regard for yourself and them I agreed."

There was no reply and Josh was about to turn away when a key grated in the lock and the door swung open. Two steps inside and Josh took a seat to face the weary Caradon mine captain across a large desk in the dim, lamp-lit room.

Captain Frisby's first words were defiant. "I am prepared to talk to you. But I'll not be dictated to by that rabble outside."

"Captain, that 'rabble' has built the Wheal Caradon into one of the largest copper mines in Cornwall. They can just as easily destroy it again."

"What do you mean, 'destroy it'? They won't get away with smashing equipment, not on this mine."

"Nobody will have to touch a thing," said Josh. "The piston packing is going on the pumping engine. I give it twenty-four hours before it breaks down completely. You haven't got an engineer at the mine, have you?"

"The engine-men can carry out simple repairs like that," said Frisby quickly.

"You've just cut the engine-men's wages," said Josh. "They're keeping the engines running at the moment, but I can't see them doing any repairs."

Captain Frisby licked his lips. A mere forty-eight hours without pumping would be sufficient to stop the new level from being worked for a very long time.

"All right. Tell the engine-men their pay stays the same."

"I'm sorry," said Josh, "But the engine-men must go along with the miners now."

"Then I hope the miners keep their families fed. They won't have a job to do it for them."

"I'm sure you're right," Josh changed his tactics. "And I don't suppose you'll find it easy to get another job after this."

The mine captain's head snapped up. "Me? The shareholders won't dismiss me for doing what I'm paid for."

"How do you see your job, Captain Frisby?"

"The same as every mine captain. To run my mine. Bring up the maximum ore and make a good profit."

"How much have your profits risen since last year?"

"They haven't," admitted Captain Frisby. "But a lot of man-hours have gone into opening up the new level."

"The Wheal Sharptor also has gone deeper to open a new level. Yet our profit for this year is running fifty per cent above last."

"The Sharptor's a small mine. You can't compare it with the Caradon."

"Then take the Wheal Phoenix. Their profit is up a hundred per cent."

"Luck!" argued Frisby, "They drove into a rich lode."

"No, Captain. There's never been such a boom in copper. Every mine in the county is riding high. When your shareholders see their dividends at the end of this year they're going to start asking questions."

Josh had put his finger on Frisby's real reason for cutting the miners' pay. It was his last desperate attempt to bring the mine profits up.

"It's the men," Captain Frisby mumbled. "They're lazy. If I paid them what they're worth their families would all go hungry."

"You're wrong." Josh stood up and paced back and forth across the office. "You had good men here, Captain. You must face the fact that your methods have failed. Pay low wages and you get second-rate work. You still have a few good miners left. Pay them well and let them set the standard."

Josh expected Frisby to argue but he stayed silent. Encouraged, Josh went on. "There are a few months to go before the dividend is called. Give your miners some encouragement. There's a good chance that your profit will be up enough to satisfy all but the greediest shareholder."

Josh could see the uncertainty on Captain Frisby's face. It was time to take his greatest gamble.

"Well, I've said all I have to say. I'll be going now."

"Wait!" The cry was one of sheer desperation. "If I agree to do the things you've mentioned, the men will think they've beaten me. I wouldn't be able to hold up my head on Wheal Caradon."

Josh shook his head. "That won't happen if you get the men working with you instead of against you." He had a sudden thought. "Who are your shift captains?"

Captain Frisby avoided Josh's gaze again. "I haven't any just at the moment. They've all left."

Josh shook his head incredulously. "Do you know John Kittow?"

"Yes. He's one of the men out there, isn't he?"

"He's the man who came to ask me to help," said Josh. "And he's a good sound miner. I've heard others say so. Make him your senior shift captain. Explain things to him. Tell him you've reconsidered the situation. He'll do the rest."

It took the captain a full minute to make up his mind. He nodded. "All right. I'll try things your way. Tell Kittow to come and see me now."

Chapter 9

As Josh's wedding date neared, the house on the hill occupied most of his spare time. There were still a hundred small improvements to be carried out and Josh was doing them all himself.

Sometimes he wondered what it would be like living there with Sarah. There were times when he had grave doubts about their future, but he had heard such fears were natural enough.

One evening early in March, he was upstairs painting one of the bedrooms when he heard the kitchen door open downstairs. It did not surprise him. His mother was a frequent visitor and always used that door. Then he heard a sound he could not place, a low gurgling noise. The stairs creaked and seconds later Miriam appeared on the landing, her young son in her arms. Josh's surprise was so complete he dropped the paint brush to the floor.

"Wh-what are you doing here?" he whispered.

"I'm sorry. I came to Henwood to visit my mother . . . . I'd heard about your house and I wanted to see it. But I didn't think you'd be here at this time of day."

The words came tumbling out, tripping over each other. In her arms the baby gurgled away completely unconcerned. Miriam turned quickly as though to run down the stairs.

"No, don't go! I mean . . . . You can look around if you like."

"I'd rather not, Josh. Not with you here."

"I'll go if it makes you feel any easier."

"Don't be silly!" Her laugh was softer, less uninhibited than he remembered. "It's your house."

"Yes."

She watched him move forward to the open bedroom doorway. "You're looking well," she said.

"Am I?" He felt awkward and tongue-tied.

She slowly walked down the stairs and he followed. Stopping in the kitchen she ran her finger over the dust on top of the new range. "This is a fine stove, Josh. Sarah will be able to cook some grand meals on it . . . . I always wondered whether you might marry her one day."

"That's funny." His expression belied the statement. "She always thought I would marry you. And so did I."

She turned to face him and he saw the anguish on her face. "Josh, don't talk about such things now. Please! Oh, I shouldn't have come. I'm sorry, Josh."

The baby tugged at the white woollen bonnet he was wearing, pulling it off and dropping it to the floor. Josh retrieved it and handed it over.

"What do you call him?" The baby had his finger in his grasp now. He was chubby, his eyes as blue as Josh's own.

"Daniel."

"Hello, Daniel." He jigged his finger up and down.

Miriam pulled the baby away.

"Don't, Josh. Don't!" she cried.

He beat her to the door and put his back against it. "Why not, Miriam? Why mustn't I play with him?"

"Don't make me say it, Josh. Please." The tears stood out from her eyes and she crumpled down onto a window-seat. "Oh God! Why did I come here?"

Josh moved away from the door and stood over her. He had

wanted some recognition of what had been between them, but seeing her cry like this threatened to tear him apart.

"I'm sorry. I shouldn't have pushed you into that."

She was shaking and it alarmed the baby.

"Here. Let me take him." Dropping to one knee he took Daniel from her and laid him on the floor on a pile of cloth that had been used to protect some newly-delivered furniture. Miriam fumbled in her sleeve for a handkerchief.

"William has been very good to me—to us, Josh. He's a kind man, who still speaks well of you. He has wanted to invite you to our meetings. But I dreaded seeing you again. I didn't know what I might do if we ever came face to face."

She raised her eyes to meet his and all the emotions he could see there were his own. Suddenly he was holding her. His mouth crushed hers and her arms were about him.

As abruptly as it had begun they drew apart, both shocked with the force of their feelings. "I'm sorry," he said lamely.

"It was as much my fault as yours." She picked up the baby and gave Josh a warm, gentle look. "Now I don't need to ask myself what I might do if I were to meet you," she said. "I have my answer."

"Don't go yet," he said. "Stay a while longer."

She shook her head, "No, Josh. I'm married now. You too have your future to think of."

"What future? I can't marry Sarah. Not now . . . !"

"Shhh!" She silenced him. "You felt sorry for me, that's all. Of course you'll marry Sarah and be very happy in this lovely house."

"You just can't walk out of my life, Miriam. Not again."

She smiled at him, in complete control of herself now. "You know I must. For everyone's sake. Be happy, Josh. I'll pray for that. Be happy." She opened the door and was gone.

JOSH'S WEDDING was proclaimed the event of the year in Hayle. The chapel, decorated with hundreds of flowers, was packed with guests and the ceremony was simple and moving. When it was over Josh and Sarah returned in a gaily-painted pony trap to the Carlyon house for a brief reception. Then they travelled to

Sharptor by coach. When the newly-weds arrived at their future home a fire was burning in the living room and there were fresh spring flowers everywhere. All provided by the wives of the Sharptor miners—it was their way of welcoming Sarah to their midst.

Much later that night Josh lay in bed, thinking about the future. Beside him Sarah was curled up, asleep. They had made love for the first time, but it was not a wildly passionate union. Josh realized then that love-making between them would never be an abandoned pouring out of love.

But this lack was the only fault Josh could possibly have found with Sarah. She was a promising cook, a good housekeeper. And she genuinely loved him.

"You've got a good wife there, Josh," said Ben Retallick one evening as he and Josh walked down the hill. "Mind you take good care of her."

Josh confirmed that he would.

"Have you seen anything of Miriam since you've been wed?"

Josh answered quite truthfully that he had not.

"Good! You were wise to break with her when you did. From all accounts she's leading her husband a merry dance."

"In what way?"

"By making him look a fool. Taking meetings of miners. Trying to tell grown men about the benefits of this 'union'."

Josh laughed. "I think Preacher Thackeray's well pleased with her. He believes not only in the equality of men—but women as well."

"Then he's more of a fool than I took him for."

"WHAT ARE YOU thinking about?" Sarah asked.

It was a sultry late summer night and the bedroom was filled with soft silver moonlight.

Josh pulled her towards him, "I can't sleep. That's all."

She snuggled closer. "Something's bothering you. Is it anything to do with that man who called this evening?"

"John Kittow? Not entirely. The miners over at Kit Hill are having some trouble. He wants me to go to a meeting they're holding tomorrow night."

240

She rose on one elbow. "You're not going?"

"I told John Kittow I would."

"Theophilus Strike won't like it."

"Sarah, this is none of Theophilus Strike's business."

"And the Kit Hill miners are none of *your* business."

Josh said nothing. It was their first serious argument. They lay side by side in silence for a long time before Josh heard a strangled sob.

"Sarah, please don't cry."

"Oh Josh! I'm so miserable!"

He turned and put his arms about her, soothing her until she stopped crying.

"I'm sorry, Josh. That was silly of me." She stopped him as he was about to protest. "No. You must do what you feel you should do. I have no right to object."

"You're my wife, Sarah. You have every right. All I wish is that you were interested enough to want to know what it's all about."

"But I don't want to know. I wouldn't understand it anyway. But you do, and I accept that. So please don't be angry with me."

THE KIT HILL men's grievance was with the mine store. Every mine owner ran his own store and it invariably gained a stranglehold on the miners and their families. It was the only place a man could obtain credit. His tools came from there, together with the essential items of furniture to set up a home. The cost was higher than elsewhere but few men had any choice.

Occasionally, if the owners thought some of the miners' money was escaping them, they became greedy and increased the store prices. This was the problem at Kit Hill.

The meeting got off to a slow start. When Josh and John Kittow arrived there must have been a hundred and fifty men standing in small uneasy groups.

John Kittow and Josh picked their way to a heap of mine waste that would serve as a platform.

"Unless someone starts talking to the men they'll all begin to leave," Josh said. "Who called the meeting?"

"A miner named Harry Reeve. I can't see him here."

241

"Well, if he can't bother to turn up for his own meeting I see no sense in staying."

"Give him a few minutes," pleaded Kittow. "Something must have happened to keep him away."

Suddenly a red-faced man, perspiration tracking down his face, pushed past them, up onto the heap of mine waste. There he turned to the crowd.

"Quiet, please. Listen! Listen to me!"

The noise died down slightly and the newcomer raised his voice. "Harry Reeve won't be coming here tonight. He's been arrested."

There was complete, stunned silence.

"Not only Harry Reeve. Four others also."

The crowd erupted into anger as the miners took up the cry of "Why? Why?"

"I'll tell you why," shouted the sweating man. "Because the adventurers thought they'd put a stop to this meeting by putting Harry and the others in the Callington lock-up. They are to be charged with incitement to riot!"

There was another roar from the assembly and a second man scrambled up onto the rubble. "We'll show them what a riot is," he shouted. "We'll go and get Harry out."

The crowd was for leaving on a rescue mission there and then. But the first man tried to bring some order to the meeting. "No! We mustn't do anything just yet. Someone went from Callington to fetch Preacher Thackeray. He'll know what to do."

"We already know what to do," shouted the second man.

Josh pushed his way roughly through the miners and climbed up to join the other two on the waste mound. "Wait!" he called. "If you go to Callington and break into the lock-up there's not a court in the county will find Harry Reeve and the others not guilty. You'll condemn them by your actions."

There were catcalls and shouts. But above the hubbub someone called, "It's Joshua Retallick. Let him speak."

"The worst thing you could possibly do is use violence. There are other ways of achieving your ends. But you must decide here and now what it is you want. Then make sure every last man in the Kit Hill mine is with you."

"That's the soundest advice I've heard at any meeting. You're absolutely right, Josh."

It was the Reverend William Thackeray. During the argument he had arrived unnoticed, his neat little gig making no sound on the soft grass. But it was not the preacher who caused Josh to become suddenly tongue-tied. It was Miriam, seated beside him.

Miriam was just as surprised to see Josh but she managed a faint smile. With her long, loose hair blown by the wind and her face flushed with excitement she still had all the wild beauty of the young girl Josh had explored the moor with. There was not a man at the meeting who was not stirred by her presence.

William Thackeray handed his wife from the gig and pushed his way to the front of the crowd with Miriam following. This type of gathering was his natural environment.

To the crowd he cried, "You've heard what Josh Retallick said. I endorse his every word. Is there any man who has other ideas? You! The bearded man at the front. What do you suggest?"

The bearded miner was unhappy at being singled out for attention. "I say we march on Callington and release Harry Reeve." But it was said hesitantly and without conviction.

William Thackeray turned to Miriam in a way that was familiar to any miner who had attended their previous meetings. "He suggests that this band of good men . . . this crowd of—let's say two hundred miners—march on Callington. What do you think would happen?"

Miriam looked over the crowd. "They are fine men. Each one capable of holding his own in a fist fight with any man."

Her clear voice rang out so that not one man missed her words. But some of the miners were looking puzzled. The preacher's wife seemed to be contradicting him. Then Miriam reached down inside the front of her dress and pulled out a small linen bag attached to a long drawstring looped about her neck.

"Yes, you are brave men," she said. "Any man who earns his living below ground has courage."

She held up the small linen bag for all to see and her next words rang out powerfully. "Yet this small bag holds enough musket shot to kill every one of you!"

243

The men were looking puzzled again but Miriam did not leave them in suspense for long.

"You wonder what this has to do with you? Then I'll tell you. At this very moment a full company of soldiers, regular disciplined troops, are riding post-haste from Bodmin barracks to Callington. *Every single one of those soldiers carries this much musket shot!*"

Pushing the bag back inside her dress, Miriam struck a pose with hands on hips. "Do you take the Callington magistrate for a fool? He knew what the rest of you would do when he arrested the leading Kit Hill unionists. There was a horseman on his way to Bodmin for soldiers before the ink was dry on the warrant for Harry Reeve's arrest!"

"Then what can we do?" called one of the miners. "We can't just stand back and do nothing."

This was a cue William Thackeray had been waiting for. "That must be for you to decide," he declared. "But first, how many of the Kit Hill miners are *not* at this meeting?"

"Not more than fifty," replied one miner.

"I suggest you make certain those fifty join with you to stop all work in the Kit Hill mine."

This provoked noisy mutterings among the miners. "What do you say, Retallick?" one of them called.

Josh had been standing at the rear of the group on the mound. Now he stepped forward, avoiding Miriam's gaze.

"I say do as Preacher Thackeray suggests. Get the others with you. Tell the captain you'll allow the engine-men to go in for one week only. By the end of that time the prices in the mine store must have been lowered and Harry Reeve and the others released. If they haven't been, tell him the engine-men will shut off the pumps and allow the mine to flood."

Josh's words received noisy approval. Then suddenly John Kittow was pushing his way to the front.

"I'd like to have a word with the men," he said, and Josh helped him up onto the pile of stones.

John Kittow came straight to the point. "We've been through troubles ourselves at the Wheal Caradon," his deep voice boomed out. "Because we know what it means to have support at a time

244

like this we held a meeting last night. It was agreed by our men that they would each give a shilling a week to help during the time you're not working."

The cheering and shouting showed what the men of the Kit Hill mine thought of the gesture.

"Not only that—listen now!" Kittow went on. "The Wheal Phoenix men have told me they'll each give sixpence a week too."

"We've done it! We've done it!" William Thackeray was pumping Kittow's hand and literally dancing up and down. "A union of miners has become a reality in Cornwall!"

His elation was almost matched by that of the miners. With the threat of starvation removed they knew they could win their fight. Josh, though still uncomfortable in Miriam's presence, found himself caught up in the infectious enthusiasm.

"Come, Josh!" Thackeray said. "We must celebrate our success with a glass of wine. The evening will turn sour if you don't come home with us."

And Miriam managed a "Please, Josh".

"Of course he'll come. He's been absent from our circle of friends for far too long."

At the preacher's house Thackeray put the gig away while Josh followed Miriam into the parlour. She lit a lamp and after a heavy silence, she said, "It's nice to see you here, Josh."

"Is it?"

"Yes. William has missed your friendship. We both have."

"Don't you think friendship might be difficult in the circumstances?"

"No, Josh. There are many things William doesn't know—and needn't know. But even if he did I feel sure he'd forgive us. As a preacher he's well aware of the weaknesses of men and women."

"What about Daniel?"

Miriam drew in a deep breath. "Daniel is part of William's family. He loves him very much." She looked at him and bit her lip. "Josh, let's not make tonight unhappy. I really am pleased to have you here."

William Thackeray had entered the room quietly. He saw the look on Miriam's face as she spoke to Josh but he said nothing.

Going straight to a cupboard he took out three glasses and filled them. Handing the glasses around he raised his in a salute.

"To the union. To the miners' fund and to a better understanding between all Christian men, whatever their lot in life. May they all be as God made them—equal!"

THAT VERY NIGHT the Kit Hill mine store was burned to the ground, the flames lighting the skyline atop the hill as though it were a midsummer night bonfire. It was difficult to say how the fire was started, but few men regretted the store's destruction.

The incident, however, sealed the fate of the five men held in custody. There had been hopes before that they would be brought before the magistrate on some trifling charge. But after the fire they were sent in custody to Bodmin Gaol to await trial, charged with conspiracy to destroy property. It was generally recognized that they had little chance of an acquittal now.

IT WAS A FEW DAYS after the Kit Hill fire that Theophilus Strike sent for Josh. When he entered the office Strike's voice fairly thundered out, "Joshua! What's this nonsense I've heard about you being involved with the criminals who burned down the Kit Hill mine shop?"

"I know nothing about the burning down of the Kit Hill store," Josh replied, meeting the mine owner's eyes.

"Don't lie to me, Joshua. I have it from a very reliable source that you were at the meeting that preceded the burning of the shop."

"Then your reliable source will have told you I warned the miners against taking any unlawful action."

"So you don't deny attending this meeting?"

"I don't deny it, Mr. Strike. I'm of the opinion the Kit Hill miners have a just grievance."

Theophilus Strike looked at him in amazement. "You have the brass to stand there and tell me quite blatantly that you support men who burn a building to the ground? I've a good mind to dismiss you here and now. Anyone who condones violence among miners is a dangerous man to have around."

246

Josh refused to be cowed. "I've never condoned violence or supported the destruction of any property. I'm in sympathy with the Kit Hill miners because they have a just grievance. Perhaps if I quote some prices charged at the Kit Hill store you'll understand." He began with the prices of foodstuffs. They were roughly twice the normal. Then he mentioned candles, and the tools a miner needed below ground. Some were almost four times the fair price.

Strike was shaken, but he was an owner, not a miner. "Even if the Kit Hill miners were being robbed, what business is it of yours? You're an engineer, not a miner."

Taking a deep breath Josh put into words what he had hardly been able to channel into conscious thought before.

"I'm an engineer now, Mr. Strike. I have you to thank for that. But long before I learned to be an engineer I was a miner's son. There were the evenings when I went to the top of the shaft to wait for my father to come up from shift and he wouldn't even see me. He'd crawl from the shaft and collapse on his belly, sucking in air with such a noise I feared his lungs might burst. No son should see his father in that condition, crawling like a wounded animal from a hole in the ground.

"I worked hard at Hayle, Mr. Strike. I was determined to master engineering. It was a way of making sure my sons would never see me lying on the ground at the top of a mine shaft. That's why I built the man-lift . . . . But it doesn't end there. I've seen what life is like outside a mine. I've ridden in a coach. I've been to a concert and heard music that I never knew existed. I'm realistic enough to know that every miner can't become a gentleman overnight. But there must be more for him than bed, drink and work.

"Maybe that's why I went to that meeting. Perhaps I wanted to tell them something of what I've just told you."

Strike was looking at him in a strange way. "It's well you didn't, Joshua. They'd probably have laughed at you. You're a humanitarian. I fear you'll find it an unrewarding field."

His anger had completely gone. "I'll be perfectly honest with you.. I sent for you with the express intention of dismissing you. I

247

had no thought of giving you a hearing. Now I have and though I must doubt your cause I can respect your sincerity."

Josh began to thank the mine owner but Strike cut him short with an impatient gesture. "Don't thank me, Joshua. In all probability I would be helping you more if I gave you an ultimatum: forget your ideas or lose your post here. But I believe you have to work out your own destiny—and God help you!"

THE KIT HILL miners kept the mine idle for a full week. Then, at an extraordinary meeting of the shareholders, it was reported that the engine-men were ready to join the miners.

The adventurers hurriedly arrived at a solution whereby the blame for the men's grievances was placed on Captain Frisby. It was grossly unfair, since he had only been carrying out their instructions. Nevertheless, with their scapegoat out of the way, a settlement was agreed and the miners resumed work immediately.

But there was to be no happy ending for Harry Reeve and those arrested with him. When the miners demanded their release they were told the matter was out of the adventurers' hands. The law must pursue its course.

Preacher Thackeray attended the miners' trial. Late on the second day Josh saw him coming across the moor direct from Bodmin. When he pulled his pony to a halt it was well lathered.

"The court found them guilty, Josh."

It came as no surprise. The whole countryside had been expecting it.

"And the sentence?" Josh asked.

"Fourteen years' transportation!"

Josh winced. Except in very rare cases such a punishment meant banishment for life. A man was shipped abroad, usually to Australia, to work as a convict for the duration of his sentence. Upon its expiration he was "free" to work for his fare home. If he could find someone to pay him more than a subsistence wage it would still take him years to save the fare.

The preacher shook his head sorrowfully.

"The men accepted the sentence," he said. "They had known all along what might happen to them because of their beliefs. But one day we'll win, Josh. We *must* win . . . . And each tiny victory, no matter how small, is a step closer to that goal."

Josh turned away. Must the price of each "victory" always be paid in imprisoned men and their starving children?

Sarah was in the kitchen when he got home and the exaggerated clatter told Josh that she was not in the best of moods. Nevertheless, he told her the outcome of the trial.

"Well? What did you expect?" she snapped. Her dislike of unionism had hardened since a visit to Hayle two weeks before. "You were a fool to get yourself involved. Mother thinks so too."

Josh paused. "What has your mother got to do with it?"

Sarah flushed. "Isn't it natural for a girl to talk over her problems with her mother?"

"I hadn't realized I was a problem."

"You know very well what I mean, Josh. It worries me to see you mixed up with something like this."

"It worried Theophilus Strike too. But at least he tried to understand why I feel so strongly about the union. That's more than you'll do."

"I have more important things to occupy my mind."

"What sort of things? Whether to wear the blue dress rather than the pink one to Launceston market?" It was spiteful and he knew it, but it was out before he could bite it back.

Sarah placed the pan she was holding carefully in the cupboard and dried her hands before answering him.

"No. The sort of thing that is occupying my mind at the moment is whether I will bear you a son or a daughter."

"You—you're pregnant?"

"Yes."

"But why didn't you say something before?"

"You've been so involved with this silly union business that I was scarcely able to gain your attention long enough to tell you anything. Anyway, I wasn't absolutely certain. That's why I went home. Doctor Scott examined me and told me for sure."

"Why did you see the doctor? Is something wrong?"

His concern brought a smile from Sarah and she was no longer angry.

"Of course not. It's usual for a woman who is having a baby to see a doctor."

"But Mary Crabbe delivers just about every baby in the district. Jenny didn't see a doctor when she was expecting."

"Well, I'm not Jenny," said Sarah sharply. She looked suddenly unhappy. "You haven't even said you are pleased!"

"Of course I'm pleased." He took her into his arms and kissed her very gently, "And I think you're very clever . . . ."

Chapter 10

In December of that year of 1844, Josh should have been leaving with Sarah to spend Christmas at Hayle, but an abnormally wet winter was causing concern in the Wheal Sharptor. The great engine was pumping at twice its normal speed yet barely managing to hold its own against the water. In these conditions, Josh felt he could not leave the mine. The baby wasn't expected for nearly five months so, in spite of Sarah's sulking he decided to stay on for a while longer.

A carriage sent by Mr. Strike was taking Sarah to Hayle. Josh settled her into her seat. "Now, you take care," he said, "and keep well wrapped. I'll be with you on Christmas Eve."

"I wish you were coming with me now," declared Sarah.

"So do I," said Josh honestly. "But it won't be long. In the meantime you'll be surrounded by your family. They'll make you feel like the Queen."

But for the second time in his life the weather spoiled his Christmas plans. The day after Sarah left the temperature dropped rapidly. Snow began to fall at dusk and gradually put a covering on the sodden ground. Then the wind increased and snow and wind vied in their efforts to outdo each other.

The battle raged for five days before a brief truce was called on Christmas Eve. From the bedroom window of the house Josh looked down on a pure, white, featureless world, with neither track nor hedge showing through the snow. He had never known such weather. There would be no Christmas at Hayle for him.

THE CHRISTMAS he shared with his parents was happy, like so many others, except that he could not help feeling guilty about not being with his wife. It was not until the new year that a gentle thaw set in and Josh was even able to send a letter off to Sarah with the coach from St. Cleer. He hoped she would come home soon, for the house felt big and empty without her.

But the snow thawed and a strong drying wind blew in from the east and still she did not return. He was beginning to get anxious when a letter arrived at last from Hayle.

It was a lengthy tale of woe. Sarah's Christmas had been spoiled because Josh was not there, and she went on to chide him for not having come with her before the snows came. Finally, she stated that worrying about Josh had brought her so low her mother had refused to allow her to travel until she was fully recovered in health and spirits. The tone of the letter so alarmed Josh that he set off on Hector to ride to Hayle that weekend.

It came as an anti-climax to arrive at the Carlyon home and find nobody there. The shift foreman let him into the house and told him the family had gone out to visit friends.

It was dusk before the Carlyons' small coach rumbled in through the works gate and Sarah alighted, laughing gaily with her sister. She did not look ill. When she saw Josh there was a confused silence before she flung herself at him.

"Josh! What are you doing here?"

"I came because I received your letter telling me how ill you were."

Sarah looked embarrassed, but her mother came to her rescue. "And so she has been ill. Today is the first day she has been anything like her old self."

Sarah squeezed his arm affectionately. "It's lovely to see you, Josh."

"I'm very relieved to see you looking well," he replied. "I've been imagining all sorts of things as I rode here."

William Carlyon came into the house and shook Josh's hand warmly. "It's good to see you again, my boy. I've been surrounded by these women since before Christmas. Let me get you a drink. What'll you have?"

Josh said he would have a brandy and William Carlyon poured the drink. Eagerly Mary handed it to him.

"Will you be able to stay with us for long?" she asked.

Josh shook his head. "Until Sunday only."

There was an immediate outcry from Sarah. "Why, Josh? Surely the mine can spare you for a few days?"

Josh put down his brandy. "I thought you would want to come back with me. If you are feeling well enough."

Mrs. Carlyon threw up her hands in horror. "It would be madness. The poor girl has been so ill."

Since his arrival Josh had been nursing a suspicion that Sarah's mother was trying to arrange things so Sarah should have the baby at Hayle. "The journey would be worse for her next week," he said. "Even more so the week after."

"Why not let her have the baby here, Josh?"

He had been right. Now it was out in the open.

"It would be much, much better from Sarah's point of view." Mrs. Carlyon waxed enthusiastic. "Doctor Scott would be on hand. He's known Sarah since she was a child, and he's very good at delivering babies."

"We have doctors at Sharptor too."

"Mine doctors," Mrs. Carlyon snorted. "I wouldn't trust one of them to deliver a litter of pigs."

William Carlyon stood up. "Josh is right. Sarah's place is with her husband. We shouldn't interfere." He held up a hand to silence his wife. "I know she hasn't been too well, but there's nothing wrong with her now."

"Well! I'm only trying to do my best for Sarah. If that's going to be considered interference there's nothing more to be said! Come along, Mary. Upstairs and change your dress before you get it filthy playing about."

She swept out of the room followed by her younger daughter. "I think that could be termed a 'royal exit'," commented William Carlyon. "Now, if you'll excuse me, I need to check with the foreman that everything is well in the foundry."

Sarah and Josh were silent for a few minutes after he left. "Don't you want to come home, Sarah?" Josh said at last.

"Oh, Josh, of course I do!"

"Then what is it?"

She looked down at her hands and tears filled her eyes. "I'm scared, Josh."

"Scared! Of what?"

She shrugged helplessly. "Of everything. Of spending so much time on my own. Of the moor. Most of all of having the baby."

"Don't you want the baby?"

"Yes! Yes, of course I do. It's just . . . Oh, I don't know, Josh. I don't seem to have got to know anyone at Sharptor. I feel a complete stranger."

"But Sarah, you've only lived there for a short while. And the folk are concerned about you. There isn't one of them who hasn't asked after you since news got around about the baby. Why, they've even asked as far off as St. Cleer."

Sarah looked at him quickly. "You mean Miriam?"

"Yes."

"Do you wish you had married her instead of me?" Her bluntness took him by surprise.

"Is that what you believe?"

"I don't know what to believe. I only know that I get knotted up inside when you are off somewhere with that preacher because I think you might be talking to her. I imagine you comparing us and wishing you had her instead of me."

He was relieved when she dropped her gaze. "Sarah, I married you because I wanted to. Nobody forced me to do it. I was—and am, very proud to have you for my wife. I've known Miriam all my life. I couldn't forget her if I wanted to. But you are my wife and Miriam is married to my friend. Need I say more?"

"No. I'm sorry, Josh." She rose from her chair, more relaxed now. "Poor Josh, I've given you a bad time, haven't I? Never mind, we'll go back to Sharptor and I'll be a dutiful wife." She managed a pale but happy smile. "And I do love you. Husband."

THEY WENT HOME to Sharptor as planned on Sunday and the next months were very happy ones for both of them. It snowed sporadically until the end of February but the snow rarely lasted longer than two days. And it was pleasant to sit indoors in front of a crackling log fire with snow floating down outside. During these months the house on Sharptor became a home.

There was no shortage of work at the mine. The main pump needed an overhaul and Josh worked hard with his assistants to complete it in record time. Then there was his latest man-lift innovation, a proper cage lift with improved gearing. It was a sophisticated system which meant that the men could be taken down to the working levels and brought up to grass in record time. In an emergency it could prove invaluable.

Josh showed the plans to Theophilus Strike one afternoon and the mine owner was enthusiastic. "It's a great piece of design," he said. "I can see it having uses in mines far beyond the Cornish border. You must patent it."

Josh protested that it would have to be proved first. But Strike was not to be put off. "It will work. Anyone can see that. If you won't patent it I'll do it for you."

He was as good as his word. Later, when the system was installed he frequently brought fellow mine owners to watch it at work. Within one month of its trial run a mine-engineering company in the north of England was negotiating with Josh to install a similar system with Josh to receive a fair percentage of the profits they made on it.

Then, early in March, his brief period of contentment came to an end when he arrived home from the mine one night to find Sarah lying back in the rocking-chair in the kitchen, her face pale and frightened.

"Thank God you are here, Josh!" She rolled her head from side to side, a spasm of pain gripping her. "The baby. I think it's coming. Oh, Josh, help me. Help me! Please!"

Josh gripped her forearms until the pain passed. "Don't move, Sarah. I'll go and find the doctor."

"No!" she screamed. "Don't leave me!"

"I must get help, Sarah."

"No, stay with me, Josh . . . ." Her voice rose in a cry of animal anguish as the pain came back again.

He was in a terrible quandary. The baby was not due for

254

another seven weeks. Something was seriously wrong. Yet if he left Sarah alone even for a short while she might become hysterical.

Then he heard a sound from the track that went past the house. He opened the door and in the gloom made out the shape of a cart.

"Hey! Stop!" He ran from the house waving his arms and the cart creaked to a halt. It was being driven by a farm lad.

"I need your help," said Josh. "My wife is in the house and our baby is coming." He dug into his pocket. "Look! Here's a shilling. Go down to the mine and tell them that Sarah Retallick up at Idle Farm needs help quickly. Have you got that?"

"I've got it." The boy snatched the coin and whipped up his horse as Josh rushed back into the house.

He found Sarah struggling to her feet. "I thought you had gone. Oh God, Josh, I'm scared! Help me."

He held her tight until the latest spasm passed. Then he guided her gently upstairs to their bedroom and helped her into the special nightdress she had set aside for this occasion.

"I'm just going down to put water on the stove. That's what they did when young Gwen was born."

"Don't be long, Josh. Don't leave me alone."

He hurried downstairs, threw logs onto the fire and put all the pots and kettles he could find on the stove. Then an agonized scream from Sarah sent him rushing upstairs again.

"It's coming! It's coming! I can feel it."

Sarah was not exaggerating. Her frenzied thrashing had caused her nightdress to work up, and there, just emerging from her body, was the dark head of a baby. There was no time for nervousness now. Josh took hold of the baby's head as Sarah screamed in agony. He was never sure whether it was his doing or whether nature supplied the twist that turned its shoulders. But suddenly the baby was there, a tiny, damp, bloody object.

Sarah lay back on the bed, sucking in great noisy gulps of air and Josh was left wondering what to do with the motionless baby when he heard the door open downstairs. "Josh! Sarah!" his mother called. "Are you up there?"

"Come quickly. The baby's here."

Jesse Retallick ran up the stairs and saw Josh crouched holding the baby. "Has it cried yet?" she asked.

"No." Josh shook his head.

Throwing off her cloak, Jesse took the baby and, hanging it head downwards by its ankles, slapped it on the backside. Once. Twice. Three times.

With a frown she put a finger inside its mouth checking that the throat was clear. Then she smacked it again. The fourth slap brought forth a cry like the feeble mewing of a kitten.

Jesse Retallick was worried. "Tom's trying to find Mary Crabbe," she said. "And your father's gone for the mine doctor at the Phoenix."

Poor Sarah, exhausted by the pain and effort, opened her eyes. "Josh. What is it? Is it a boy? Have I given you a son?"

"It's a boy," said Jesse.

"I'm glad," Sarah murmured wearily. "Can I hold him?"

"Not yet, my love." Jesse turned to Josh. "Get me some of that hot water I saw on the stove. And some towels."

Josh was only too pleased to have someone else give the orders. He ran up and down the stairs, carrying hot water and towels up, and empty pots down to be refilled. After one such trip he returned to discover Jesse tucking blankets round the tiny baby in the still not completed cot.

"I want a hot-water bottle filled for the baby. You hear me?"

Josh's father came into the kitchen as he was filling an earthenware bottle from the kettle.

"It's a boy," said Josh. "I delivered it." He noticed the frown on his father's face. "Where's the doctor?"

"He was too drunk to get any sense out of. Are Sarah and the baby all right?"

"I don't think Mother is very happy with either of them. You'd better go up and see her." Taking the bottle he went up the stairs ahead of his father. In the bedroom Jesse was kneading Sarah's stomach as though it was a pile of dough and, without pausing, she looked questioningly at Ben. "The doctor wasn't available," he said, going to the cot. "Is this our grandson? Is he all right?"

256

Jesse took the hot-water bottle from Josh, wrapped it up well and pushed it down beside the still infant.

"There's no sense in trying to hide it," she whispered. "The baby has come much too soon. It's a weakling. But I'm more worried about Sarah. The afterbirth has got to come away but I'm getting no help from the poor girl. She's desperately tired. Oh, if only Mary Crabbe was here!"

IN SPITE OF ALL Jesse's efforts, the baby died soon after. Nor had she much success with Sarah.

"Josh," she called, "come up and sit with Sarah. Keep her forehead cool. She's in a fever."

Sarah's appearance shocked him. She was gaunt and haggard, her cheekbones unhealthily prominent. As he bathed her forehead he tried not to let his gaze wander to the sheet-draped cot in which lay the body of their child. He was aware that having the baby had been very important to her. Now it was dead.

It was nearly dawn before he heard Mary Crabbe's wheezing approach up the stairs. She stood in the doorway, her hair uncombed, gazing about her and waiting for her breathing to become less laboured.

"Get out!" she snapped at Josh. "And take that with you." She pointed to the draped cot, "It's ill-luck to have death in the room with a sick mother. Hurry up!"

When Josh went down to the kitchen, Ben told him he had sent a rider to Hayle. The Carlyons needed to be told of the night's happenings.

He and Josh were talking quietly when Jesse hurried in for another pot of water. "It's all right!" she announced, "Mary Crabbe's done it. The afterbirth has come away."

The relief in the room was enormous.

"I've known Mary all my life," Ben said. "A woman like that is worth her weight in gold." He looked sympathetically across at Josh. "I'm sorry about the baby. Seems the little chap came into the world too soon, that's all."

"Or too late!"

Nobody had heard Mary Crabbe come down the stairs. She

stood in the doorway, hair awry, as solid as a toad. "There are few eldest sons in these parts who weren't begotten in the fern of the moor." She cackled. "There's more love to be found there."

The men looked at each other but Mary Crabbe had not finished. "And there will be precious little love to be found in this house. Shame, yes. And more. But you'll find out. Oh yes! You'll find out soon enough!"

Pulling her dirty shawl about her shoulders, she shuffled out of the house. In the silence that followed they could hear her talking to herself as she walked away down the track to the village.

"I think her mind has finally gone," said Ben sadly. "She's so old she doesn't know what she is saying half the time. Forget her words Josh, and remember only her deeds."

"Yes." Josh nodded his head. He looked pale and shaken. Then, turning abruptly, he said, "I'm going up to Sarah."

Sarah was lying quite still, her eyes closed. Josh felt her forehead. It was cool now.

"Josh?" Her lips hardly moved.

"Yes. I'm here, Sarah."

"I'm sorry, Josh."

"Shhh! You've done nothing to be sorry about."

A tear crept from her eye and tracked rapidly down her face. "No. It wasn't meant to be, Josh. It should have been Miriam here bearing your child. I've always known that. She belongs to the moor as you do. I have no place here."

"Now what kind of talk is this?" Jesse had been gathering soiled bedding. She brushed back a wisp of fair hair from Sarah's face, then took Josh's arm. "Leave her, Josh. She's had a bad time. Go off somewhere and rest yourself."

IT WAS DARK when the coach carrying Sarah's mother rolled into the yard of the old farmhouse. Seconds later she swept up the stairs to the bedroom where Sarah still lay in an exhausted sleep. With only the briefest of nods to Jesse, she went directly to the bedside. Tight-lipped, she shook her head in a gesture of displeasure at what she saw, and walked from the room.

Josh was downstairs making tea when the two women came in.

"A fine mess you've made of looking after my daughter . . ." Mrs. Carlyon launched straight into the attack. "'We have doctors at Sharptor too', you said. What of your doctors now?"

"Mrs. Carlyon, the baby was so early that nobody was ready. I did my best. It wasn't enough. But I don't think I could have done more."

"And what about Sarah? She is a very sick girl."

"Sarah is an exhausted woman. But she'll be all right if you don't upset her."

"Upset my own daughter!" Mrs. Carlyon bristled. "I came here with a reckless coachman, bounced about until I'm covered in bruises, and now I'm told I mustn't upset my own daughter!"

"Sarah is your daughter. But she's also my wife. My father sent to tell you what was happening because he thought you had a right to know. But if I thought you were going to add to Sarah's distress, I'd put you back in your carriage this minute."

Mrs. Carlyon appeared to be actually swelling with rage as Jesse moved in to smooth things down.

"That's enough, Josh. Go and fetch some logs for the fire while I pour Mrs. Carlyon a cup of tea. Go on now!"

He went, reluctantly. Later Jesse made him promise to hold his tongue and not quarrel with Sarah's mother. But that night, as Josh made himself up a bed in a small bedroom, he had the uncomfortable feeling that he was an interloper in his own home.

WAKING IN THE morning light, Josh heard the murmur of voices from the bedroom along the corridor. Flinging back the bedclothes he hurried along to Sarah's room. She was lying propped up against pillows, her eyes dark hollows. Mrs. Carlyon sat beside her.

"Hello, love." He kissed her and took her hand. "How are you feeling this morning?"

"Much better, thank you."

"I'll go and freshen myself up." Mrs. Carlyon had not thawed from the previous evening.

"No. Don't go!" Sarah cried. Without warning she burst into tears. Josh's arms went about her, but he could not stop her sobbing. Determinedly, Mrs. Carlyon eased her from his arms and laid her back against the pillows. "Leave us now," she said. "She's too upset to reason with."

Bewildered, Josh left and readied himself for work. He could still hear her crying as he went out.

He worried about her all day. That evening he rushed straight home and up to the bedroom where he was greatly relieved to see Sarah sitting up. But as soon as he spoke to her she began weeping uncontrollably once more.

This state of affairs continued for days. Nothing he said could prevent Sarah from crying whenever he entered the room. He tried talking to her, telling her that losing the baby was not her fault. But she would not listen.

He tried kissing her, but she flung her head violently to one side. "No, Josh. No—I don't want to have another dead baby. Please, no more . . . ."

He tried holding her and saying nothing but the crying sounded even louder in the silence. Always in the background was the tight-lipped presence of Mrs. Carlyon.

After a week he despaired of life ever returning to normal. He had a guilty feeling of relief when Mrs. Carlyon announced she was taking Sarah home to Hayle for a long period of convalescence.

"What do you mean a 'long period'?" he asked.

"I mean for just as long as it takes her to become a healthy, happy young woman again. I'm worried about her state of mind."

"Yes. All right. Sarah will be better with someone to talk to. Up here there is nobody but Jenny of her own age. And having me around doesn't seem to be helping."

But Josh was deeply unhappy. During their brief time together he had learned to love Sarah. It was a quieter, less devouring love than the one he had shared with Miriam, but he accepted that there were degrees of love. Now the girl who had come to his house as a bride was leaving it, with only a tiny tombstone in the village graveyard to record her stay.

WITH SARAH GONE, Josh lost all purpose in life. For the first few weeks he leaned heavily on his family and friends. He visited Jenny and Tom Shovell and spent hours playing with young

260

Gwen. Also he called on Preacher Thackeray, Miriam and Daniel.

"Josh! How good to see you." Thackeray grasped Josh's hand in both his own. "I can't tell you how sorry I am about the baby and poor Sarah. I heard she was very ill."

"Yes." Josh sighed. "She's with her parents at Hayle."

"An unhappy time for you, I fear." He gave Josh a calculating look. Then, "Come into the parlour, Josh—we've a lot to talk about. Have you heard about the miners' benefit scheme? Sixpence a week collected from each miner guarantees him ten shillings a week if he's home because of an injury received in the mine. Think of the peace of mind that will give to an injured miner . . . ."

He and Josh discussed the miners' union until Miriam called them into the kitchen. The discussion halted for a while as little Daniel was to eat with them. He provided the topic for conversation until the meal was over.

Daniel was a bright, attractive child, now in his third year. In his presence Josh became unusually tongue-tied, wanting the boy to talk to him, yet not sure of his ability to reply. At last the meal was over and Miriam led Daniel away to bed, ignoring his vigorous protests.

"That young man has a strong will," commented Josh.

"I suspect it's an inheritance from his mother," replied Thackeray. "She's one in a million. She teaches in my school now, corrects my sermons, and can hold her own in a union meeting. She's the perfect wife for a minister."

Josh did his best to agree with him.

Thackeray rubbed his hands. "Now, we've been discussing the benefit scheme," he went on. "What do you *really* think of it?"

"I can't see anyone raising objections," Josh replied. "Theophilus Strike is anti-union, but even he will see that this is for the good of every miner. And the fact that it won't cost him a penny will help."

But Theophilus Strike did not see it that way when Josh put it to him a few days later. "We don't need such a scheme in the Wheal Sharptor!" he declared. "Our accident rate is lower than any mine in the county."

"One roof fall at the wrong time would alter that," replied Josh. "I thought you'd welcome the scheme."

"I welcome nothing that has the smell of unionism behind it. Who thought of it? That St. Cleer preacher?"

"As a matter of fact he did."

"I thought as much. No doubt he will administer it and call the tune. Don't let yourself be fooled by high ideals, Joshua. That preacher wants to become a power in this part of the county. This is his way of doing it. To me it's no more than a personal annoyance. Others will stop at nothing to stamp it out. When they're ready to make a move, someone will suffer. This preacher is far too slippery for it to be him. Make sure it isn't you."

"Then you agree to the men contributing to a benefit fund?"

"Would it make any difference if I didn't? No, Joshua. I won't stop them. But I do have a word of warning. A Sharptor miner serves only one master—me. I'll not have any preacher coming here to tell me how to run my mine."

"I don't think it will come to that, Mr. Strike."

"Think! Boy, you stop thinking when you walk away from an engine. Now, be damned to your unionism. Find your father and tell him I want to inspect the new deep level."

Theophilus Strike walked out of the office, leaving Josh looking after him. Josh had argued for the preacher, but he knew how dangerous William Thackeray could be if he chose. Soon after Harry Reeve and the other Kit Hill miners' leaders were transported there had been an ugly rumour that the preacher had arranged their arrests. It was said he was jealous of the stature they were gaining in the eyes of the Kit Hill men.

But as quickly as he remembered, Josh shrugged it off. Preacher Thackeray had done a great deal for the miners' union. To doubt him now would be totally unworthy.

Then, as the weeks passed after Sarah's departure, Josh's mood changed. He began spending his evenings at the Cheesewring Inn in Henwood village, where he could forget the lonely house on the tor and the girl who was no longer there.

One night in early summer Josh roared his goodbyes from the inn doorway and lurched out into the village street. For a long swaying moment he allowed his eyes to become accustomed to the gloom. Then a soft voice at his elbow said, "Hello, Josh."

Startled, he turned towards the voice. "Who's that? Miriam? What are you doing here?"

"I've come to see you. But I'm not going to talk to you outside this place. Let's walk."

He shook her hand from his arm. "Leave me alone. I can get home on my own."

"That's not what I've heard. Come on, now. Don't cause a scene and embarrass me."

"I wouldn't want to embarrass the Reverend's lady." He straightened his shoulders and stepped forward deliberately, making almost twenty yards before hooking his toe into the mud-scraper beside a door and dropping to one knee.

"Damn!" he muttered as Miriam grabbed his arm and got him back onto his feet. "What are you doing here?" he demanded. "Where's William?"

"He's at home, looking after Daniel. My mother isn't well. I'm staying with her till tomorrow. No—don't pull away."

Josh allowed himself to be guided along the track. He was all right, he told himself, except that his legs seemed to be in more of a hurry than his body. "Why aren't you with your mother now, instead of fussing with me?"

"I'm 'fussing' with you because I've brought a letter from St. Cleer for you."

"A letter? Where is it? What are you doing with it?"

"It arrived on today's coach from Hayle. I said I would bring it with me. I thought it might be one you were waiting for."

"I am, Miriam." He was thinking clearly now, the slur gone from his words. "It's the first one since—since Sarah went away."

"Yes. I thought that might be the case."

Not until they were inside the house, though, did Miriam hand him the letter. Tearing it open, he began to read excitedly. Gradually his expression changed from delight to surprise, then to dismay.

Miriam was watching him closely. "Is it bad news, Josh?"

Instead of speaking, he handed the letter to her.

My dear Josh—it began—Forgive me for what I have to say.
It upsets me to write so, but I feel it is the only honest thing to do.
You know I was never really happy at Sharptor. Mother has said
many times it would have been better had we never married and I
now realize it is true. I have brought only unhappiness to you, dear
Josh. I was not even capable of giving you a child. My tears threaten
to wash away every word that I write, but it must be said. I do not
want to see you ever again. Whatever you may decide to do with
your life, I wish you the happiness and success I know you can
achieve. God bless you. Sarah.

"You can't take any notice of this letter, Josh," Miriam said.
"The poor girl is sick. She must have worked herself up into a
terrible state to have written this."

Josh looked at her with unseeing eyes. "I knew she wasn't
happy at Sharptor. But that would have changed. Now . . . ."

Miriam stood up and smoothed the waist of her dress. "You
have your problems, Josh. I might be partly to blame for them.
But I hate to see a good man destroying himself. And you won't
find any answers inside an inn."

"Where do you suggest I start looking for the answers—Hayle?"

"That's up to you, Josh. Sarah's being looked after—but what
about you? Will you cease being Josh the engineer now and
become Josh, the Sharptor drunk?"

"No, Miriam." He was serious. "From now on I'll manage
without the aid of the Cheesewring Inn . . . ." Punching a fist into
the palm of his hand, he spun on his heel.

"Where are you going?"

"To Hayle."

JOSH'S UNHERALDED appearance at Harvey's foundry brought a
variety of reactions from the Carlyon family, ranging from Mary's
unreserved pleasure to open hostility from Mrs. Carlyon. Sarah
was not downstairs and her mother made it clear she had no
intention of allowing Josh to go up to her.

"I knew I should never have allowed her to send that foolish
letter!" she exclaimed angrily.

"It was a letter from your daughter to her husband," Josh said, equally angrily. "She had every right to send it."

"What's all this?" William Carlyon came into the room and shook his son-in-law's hand warmly. "What sort of greeting is this for a man who looks as though he's ridden through the night?"

"I don't care if he's ridden for a week. Sarah is not well enough to see him," Mrs. Carlyon persisted.

At that moment the door from the hall opened and Sarah came in. She looked quite normal and healthy until she saw Josh. Then she froze, her hand flying to her mouth. And although at first glance she had appeared to be the same Sarah he had known, there was something in her eyes that disturbed him greatly. It was a lost, unreal look.

"Sarah!" As he moved towards her she shrank back. "Sarah, I won't hurt you. I've just come to see you. . . ."

She looked around, seeking some way of escape, her face twitching as though she was in physical pain.

"There, you see? You're terrifying the girl." Mrs. Carlyon could hardly keep the triumph from her voice.

"Sarah, it's me. Josh."

Sarah cringed back until she was touching the wall. Then she edged along it sideways, moving towards the door.

"Sarah, Josh wouldn't hurt you," Mr. Carlyon told her.

"Leave her alone. Go away!" cried her mother.

"Sarah! Sarah!"

Her hand touched the door handle. She turned it—and was gone. Josh rushed to follow her but Mrs. Carlyon barred his way.

"Leave her! Haven't you done enough?"

"All right! All right," said Josh wearily. "You've proved your point. But when's she going to be better? When am I going to be able to talk to her?"

"When I, and the doctor, say so," replied Mrs. Carlyon. "Not one minute before."

Josh felt tired and sick. Whatever anyone said, there could be no arguing with the look on Sarah's face when she saw him.

"You'll let me know when that time comes?"

"When she's quite well again, I will."

"Very well. If you'll make sure she's all right now, I'll return to Sharptor immediately."

"Nonsense," said his father-in-law. "You must stay for a meal."

Josh shook his head. "Thank you, but no. I . . ."

"Sarah isn't in her room. Mama! Papa! Sarah isn't here."

The cry came from Mary, who had followed her sister out of the parlour. Mrs. Carlyon ran from the room and Josh heard doors being opened and slammed shut as she searched upstairs. Then she returned, sheer hatred on her face as she looked at Josh. "Sarah isn't up there anywhere," she said. "If anything has happened to that girl it will be your fault."

"That's enough, Molly," said her husband. "I'm sure Sarah's quite safe. Probably in the garden."

It was Josh who noticed that Hector was not where he had left him, near the front gate to the Carlyon house. And in the street outside Harvey's they spoke to an old man who had seen a girl with flowing golden hair galloping a horse out of Hayle along the St. Ives road.

Josh and William were quickly mounted on horses belonging to Harvey's.

"Have you any idea where she might be heading?" William flung over his shoulder as they sped along the open road. "Was there a place you were both fond of?"

"Only one along this road," Josh shouted back, "and I pray to God she hasn't gone there."

But his fears were soon realized. They found Hector with trailing reins and heaving sides at the top of a narrow track that clung to the jagged cliffs above St. Ives Bay. Below was a familiar tiny patch of shingle.

Twice on the way down Josh slipped. He prevented himself from falling only by clinging to the coarse grass growing in the crevices of the rock.

There was nothing to be seen at the bottom of the cliff. Only the water of the high tide lapping at the ragged black teeth of the rocks. Josh was to remember those rocks.

As more men arrived from Hayle the search extended for miles along the coast. But it was not until after midday, when the tide had ebbed away, that a man standing on the cliffs above cried out that he could see something caught in the rocks.

A fishing boat from St. Ives, one of half a dozen called to join the search, went close in while Josh and Mr. Carlyon watched helplessly from shore. They saw the boat swing broadside onto the rocks, the men at the oars straining to hold it off. Then one of the young men left his oar and plunged over the side. Twice he dived down into the water. And when he surfaced the second time he was dragging something behind him.

Sarah Retallick had been found.

JOSH WAS MOUNTED on Hector and ready to return to Sharptor. He was desperately weary but he could not bear to stay at Hayle for a moment longer. Sarah would be buried in the little Hayle cemetery and Josh did not want to be there. He wanted to keep his own memories of Sarah. A beautiful girl with long fair hair who had shared a brief part of his life.

"You mustn't blame yourself, Josh. She didn't know what she was doing. It wasn't your fault." In spite of his own deep grief William Carlyon was far kinder than his wife had been. There would be nights when Josh would wake in a cold sweat hearing her screaming "Murderer!" at him.

"Goodbye, Mr. Carlyon," he said. "I'm sorry to have brought such unhappiness to your family. Whether it was my fault today or sometime in the past I'll never know. . . ."

Josh would not trust his voice further. He reined the horse around and rode away from Harvey's, taking the road to the east.

Chapter 11

After Sarah's death Josh threw himself into his work with a vigour that awed those who were obliged to work alongside him. He constructed a pump to force clean air into the newest working shaft in the Sharptor deep level, and set about making modifications on his man-lift. The royalties from it were beginning to come in regularly now.

There were other problems that summer. A reversion to the corn policy of a few short years before meant that the bulk of the coming harvest would be sent from Cornwall to the towns of the southeast and the new industrial centres of the Midlands. Again the miners raised their voices against the corn laws. Because he had nothing to stay home for in the evenings, Josh threw himself wholeheartedly into their cause.

All through that hot summer of 1845, Josh, William Thackeray and Miriam travelled around Cornwall addressing meetings. The Miners' Union was now an accomplished fact. At one evening meeting on the sands at Par, three thousand miners turned up to hear Josh and Thackeray spell out what the corn policy would mean to the mining community.

"Well, Josh," said Preacher Thackeray as they set their horses towards home after the meeting, "I think Parliament has done our task for us. The Cornish miners are united as never before. If we can keep them together we'll be able to improve their lot a hundredfold."

"That's if the militia doesn't interfere," said Josh.

"What if they do?" declared Thackeray. "The militia won't be able to keep the mines running."

"The adventurers won't starve if the mines are closed a while. The men will. And with tempers running hot someone will get hurt."

Preacher Thackeray looked at Josh in exasperation. "Don't be so parochial," he said. "Think of the cause as a whole. If the militia are called in and miners are hurt—or killed—public sympathy will swing to our side."

"Tell that to the families of those who die," retorted Josh.

"An admirable sentiment, Josh," said William Thackeray. "But extremely limiting to real progress."

Josh smiled. "Had anyone told you a few years ago that three thousand miners would attend one of your meetings, you'd have been delirious with joy. Today you've witnessed it. And you talk of 'limited' progress."

The preacher shrugged. "When you have three hundred you dream of three thousand. When that's achieved you look for thirty thousand. That's ambition, Josh." He kicked his horse into a canter. "Miriam has a rabbit pie waiting for us tonight. Tomorrow will take care of itself."

The subject came up again during the meal. Miriam was well aware of her husband's ambitions and it was to him she spoke.

"What happens on the day you have your thirty thousand miners gathered together? How long do you think you would be allowed to lead them?"

"I'm sorry, Miriam. I don't understand."

"Calling meetings and discussing ways of improving the living standards of the miner is all right. It's part of a minister's work. But march at the head of thirty thousand men and I think there will be a very different reaction."

"I have no plans to march anywhere. My plan is for the miners to blockade the ports peaceably. To prevent grain from being taken away before every Cornish miner is provided for."

"And do you think you're going to appear at the ports of Cornwall and take everyone by surprise? It's too late for that. There's been so much talk of the miners uniting, the adventurers have become alarmed. Rumour has it in Bristol that the Somerset militia is being mustered for service in Cornwall."

"Then I hope they have the sense not to interfere with any peaceable action taken by the miners," said her husband. "That would certainly precipitate violence."

"It would never come to that," said Miriam. "The army will arrive first and arrest the men who lead the miners. Your fight is with Parliament. They hang men for that."

"I fail to understand you, Miriam!" He got up from the table angrily. "What do you want me to do? Drop out of the movement because there might be trouble?"

"No." Miriam was as calm as he was angry. "I am merely saying that you should restrict what you say in public to matters affecting miners' welfare. Anything else should be discussed with a few of the leaders. In private."

For a moment Thackeray looked as though he had been struck dumb. Then he banged his fist on the table. "She's right, Josh! She has more brains than I. If we carry on the way we are there can only be one end. On the other hand, if I am heard to preach moderation what grounds could they possibly have for arresting me? From now on we're going to do some very clever and serious planning."

But changing the image of the Union was not easy. When public meetings were called, the men expected to hear scathing attacks on the iniquitous corn policy. Instead, they were told of the safety measures provided in mines as a result of Union representation.

Questions about the corn laws were carefully sidestepped. But on most nights of the week the chapel at St. Cleer was occupied by groups of leaders, and messengers galloped the roads of Cornwall with news and instructions for the master-plan that was being formulated.

What that plan was soon became clear. One farmer, more eager than his fellows, brought the first creaking wagonload of corn down the steep lane to Boscastle harbour. He found the way blocked by two hundred grim-faced miners. There was no violence and little argument. But so impressed was the farmer with their determination that he promptly turned around and sold the whole of his wagonload in Camelford market, contrary to the orders of Parliament. The same thing happened to the next farmer. And the next.

The news was hailed throughout the county as a miners' victory. The more naive among them awaited the changes in the law they were sure it would bring about.

Parliament had other ideas. The rumours from Bristol had not been false. The militia arrived, and was garrisoned in towns throughout the county. But by far the most ominous threat came when the 32nd Foot—Cornwall's own regular regiment—returned from overseas duty and moved into garrison at Bodmin.

One of the soldiers with the 32nd was Morwen Trago. And he soon arrived at Preacher Thackeray's gate in St. Cleer.

Miriam was overjoyed to see him. Army life suited him: he looked very smart in his red coat with the white cross-belts. William Thackeray stayed in the background while they reminisced, intruding only to keep Morwen's tankard filled. But when the conversation showed signs of flagging the preacher joined in.

"You've led an interesting life since you left the mine, Morwen. You'll find things much quieter in Cornwall."

"Don't you believe it!" The ale had caused his cheeks to glow fiery red. "They don't pay soldiers to sit on their backsides, Preacher. They've got us down here for a reason."

"A reason for the army here in Cornwall?"

"Ah! You'd be surprised. We've been told this outcry against the corn laws is just an excuse to start a revolution. But they'll have a surprise when they start."

"I'm quite sure they will." Preacher Thackeray leaned back in his chair and looked at the half-drunken soldier. "But I doubt whether your regiment would be sufficient to defeat the whole of the county should they choose to rise."

"It isn't only our regiment." Morwen waved his tankard unsteadily before his face. "There's militia coming from Wales and Devon. Then there's the navy."

"The navy?"

"Yes. The miners are trying to stop corn from leaving the ports, aren't they? Well, the navy has its men-of-war just outside the ports. At the first sign of trouble they'll come in."

"Men-of-war, eh?" Preacher Thackeray mused. Morwen, he saw, was now staring and glassy-eyed. "I think I'd better help our guest up to the spare bedroom," he said to his wife.

When William returned downstairs, he began pacing the floor. "So Parliament is expecting trouble? Sending marines, militia and a regular regiment against us." He looked at Miriam speculatively. "One thing is clear though. Morwen's not aware of my involvement or he wouldn't have said as much as he did."

"What does that mean?"

"It means that it must already be accepted my interest is purely in the welfare of the miner."

NOW THE MILITARY authorities brought a plan of their own into operation. The farmers were ordered to inform the nearest magistrate when corn was ready for delivery. A small party of militiamen would then accompany the corn-laden wagons to one of many large barns hired specially for the purpose throughout the county. A guard was placed on the barn until all the corn for that area was gathered in. Then, under full escort, it was taken to the nearest port. The idea worked so effectively that the county authorities told Parliament the matter was fully under control.

The miners saw themselves defeated. Where two weeks before they had boasted of their victories, they now condemned the Union for not staying one step ahead of the soldiers and they began preparing for a more violent form of protest.

Josh was appalled. At a meeting he stood up and told the miners why. "There is absolutely no excuse for the use of force now," he told the miners' representatives. "Most families have corn. Properly husbanded it will last the winter. If we remain patient, we will win."

Had Preacher Thackeray sided with Josh they might have turned the tide. But recently the two men had failed to agree on many Union principles. There were times when Preacher Thackeray felt jealous at the respect the engineer commanded. He voted against Josh's moderate policy.

Perhaps there were other reasons too for the cooling-off in their friendship.

Before Morwen Trago had left the preacher's house after his visit he had walked with Thackeray in the garden. They spoke of many things, of the troubles in the county and the changes that had occurred in the mining industry since Morwen left it. When Thackeray mentioned Josh's inventions, Morwen expressed misgivings about the preacher becoming too friendly with the Sharptor engineer. It was not wise he said, in view of Miriam and Josh's attachment in the past. Then he dropped his bombshell. He had heard some of his officers talking, he said. Josh's name had been mentioned in connection with leadership of the Union.

William said nothing then, but both reasons for Morwen's concern nourished seeds that were already planted in the preacher's mind.

LATE IN AUGUST of that year Jenny Shovell gave birth to a son. News that she was in labour came to the Retallick house shortly after dusk. Jesse threw a shawl about her shoulders and Josh went along to the Shovells' house with her.

Inside, it looked for all the world as though Jenny was having a party instead of a baby. Some of the women from the village were already there, as were a number of Sharptor miners.

They were all talking in the kitchen when old Mary Crabbe came in. Respectfully the men stepped back to allow her through. She had almost reached the door that led to the stairs when she stopped. It was as though someone had called her. Turning, her wild dark eyes came to rest on Josh.

"Out of this house, Josh Retallick," she shrieked. "I'll deliver no baby beneath the same roof as you. Or the curse on you will be laid on the child."

There was a horrified silence. Tom Shovell looked apprehensively from the woman to Josh and back again, utterly bewildered.

"It's all right, Tom. I'm going," said Josh.

"Ignore the old fool, Josh." This from one of the younger miners. "It's the full moon. You know what she's like at such times."

"Yes, there's a grown moon," cackled Mary. "But before there's another you'll have reason to know how crazy Mary Crabbe is."

"Oh, come on, Mary!" said one of the shift captains. "Josh has had his troubles. Give the boy some luck now."

"If I thought it would do any good I would," said the old crone. "But if you mind the business of others you must expect to inherit their troubles. That's all I have to say."

With that she shuffled from the room. Josh left the house at once. He was superstitious enough to believe Mary a true witch. And he could not recall one forecast she had made that had not come true.

THE FOLLOWING day a worried Jesse Retallick spoke to Josh about Mary Crabbe's words.

"It's this stupid Union business." She made a gesture of

resignation. "I don't know what will become of you, Josh. You're a young man. Why don't you find yourself a nice girl and marry her? You could have the choice of any girl in the county. You've got a good job and that fine house on the tor."

"I don't want the house. And the last thing I want is to marry another girl and take her there."

While they were talking Ben had appeared to be sleeping in his chair. Now suddenly he stood up and crossed to the window. "I thought I could hear something while you two were arguing. It seems the soldiers aren't content to stay in their barracks waiting for trouble. They've come looking for it."

Josh hurried to join his father at the window. He saw about sixty soldiers marching up the road from Henwood village. Keeping time to the steady, monotonous beat of a lone drummer, they headed south towards the Phoenix and Caradon mines. Along the way they had collected a motley following of miners' sons and farm boys who ran alongside, jeering and catcalling.

"Let's take a walk up to Sharptor," Ben said to Josh. "I won't rest easy until I see the soldiers clear of the mine."

But the soldiers appeared to have no designs on the Sharptor mine. As Josh and his father climbed the hill they saw the men turn down the track to the Phoenix mine, the drummer silent as the men broke step on the uneven ground.

"The fools!" exclaimed Josh. "What do they think they're doing? If some of the Phoenix militants are still above ground there'll be trouble."

"Then we'd best go down and see what we can do to stop it."

"No. You stay up here and make sure none of the Sharptor miners interfere. I'll see what's happening at the Phoenix."

Josh set off at a run. It was a couple of hundred yards to the mine and the soldiers reached it before Josh.

The officer allowed the men to break ranks and they stood around, arrogant in their smart uniforms. One of the young boys working on sorting ore hurried to fetch the mine captain. When he arrived he left the officer in no doubt as to who was in charge of the Wheal Phoenix.

"What do you want here? And tell your men to stay clear of

the machinery. Apart from the danger to them, the crusher they're leaning against cost a lot of money."

"I came here for water for my men and a place where they could rest and eat a meal," said the officer.

"Water they're welcome to." The mine captain turned to one of the boys. "Jimmy, go and fetch two buckets of water." He turned back to the officer. "As for a rest and meal, this is a working mine. I'll not have my boys distracted while your soldiers lounge around eating. There's a whole empty moor around us."

"That's hardly a sociable attitude," said the officer. "We're your county's own regiment. We even have a man from your own mine in our ranks."

"I've already seen Morwen Trago. He's welcome to come visiting any time. But not when he's wearing a soldier's uniform."

"Then I think we'll go to the mine on the hill." He nodded up at Sharptor. "Perhaps we'll receive more civility there."

"Don't waste your time," said Josh as he came up. "Soldiers would be as much in the way at Wheal Sharptor as here."

"Oh?" The officer's eyes glittered angrily. "Are the men of the Phoenix spokesmen for every mine in Cornwall?"

"I'm not from the Wheal Phoenix. My name is Retallick. I'm the engineer at Sharptor."

"Retallick? I've heard that name before."

"It's likely. Retallick's a common enough Cornish name."

"Well, I've no wish to put a strain on the hospitality of such generous hosts," said the officer. "Fall the men in, Sergeant." He half-bowed towards them. "Goodbye, gentlemen." Looking directly at Josh, he said, "I feel quite sure we'll meet again, Mr. Retallick. I look forward to it."

Placing himself at the head of his soldiers he rapped out a command and they marched away down the hill from the mine.

"I think we convinced them they aren't needed hereabouts," said the mine captain.

"No doubt," replied Josh, "But they didn't tell us their reason for the visit. I'm sure they had one. Furthermore, I think they might have achieved it."

He did not explain further but turned and made his way up

the hill to Sharptor. Inevitably, it seemed to him, the scene was being set for violence.

It came on a beautiful hot day in late September. Josh was cleaning his hands in the tub outside the engine-house when a convoy of laden coal wagons creaked into the mine.

"Them from Wheal Caradon has got themselves a parcel of trouble," called old Nehemeziah Lancellis as he climbed stiffly down from the lead wagon.

"Oh!" Josh was instantly interested. "What's happened?"

Nehemeziah spat into the dust. "'Tis this damned corn business. Whole lot of 'em downed shovels. Gone to Looe to stop a corn boat leaving. Damn fools."

"That's ridiculous!" Josh was alarmed. "They know the soldiers are at Looe. They'd as soon shoot a miner as a rabbit."

"Don't know about such things," said old Nehemeziah. "But I was to tell you where they'm heading. Spoiling for a fight, I was told."

"Is Preacher Thackeray with them?"

"Him?" Nehemeziah laughed derisively. "He's the spoon that does the stirring, not the pot that sits on the fire."

Josh's mind was racing. The men were on foot. It might be possible to take a horse and head them off. "Have you any idea what time they left?"

"Don't know. I got news of it an hour ago. They'd be well on the way now."

The chances of preventing the miners from reaching the port were very slim indeed, but Josh would try.

He was not the only one worried about the Caradon miners. A mile from Looe, he caught up with John Kittow. The Caradon miner's leader was bounding along on a pack-horse that had seen better days. When Josh reined in beside him all he seemed able to say was, "Fools! The bloody fools!"

"What are their plans?" asked Josh.

"Plans. They've no plans. They're going to keep the corn from being loaded onto a ship. I doubt if they've thought beyond that."

"Weren't you able to stop them? They usually listen to you."

"They might have listened to me, had I been at the mine."

The shift captain swore. "I was over to Callington to hire a couple of blacksmiths. When I got back it was to a mine without miners. How did you find out about it?"

Josh explained. "And I hope we'll be in time to avoid bloodshed."

Rounding a bend down the hill into Looe town, the roar of a large crowd of angry men greeted them, coming from the wharf just beyond the arched bridge. On the bridge itself were farmers' wagons, tailed back to the western bank of the river. The soldiers who had been acting as escorts were forming up close to them. But these were not foot-soldiers. They were mounted, wearing the blue jackets and plumed helmets of Dragoon Guards.

Josh kneed Hector forward. The scene at the dockside was even worse than he had feared. There must have been six or seven hundred miners, the Caradon men having gathered support along the way, packed in a tight swaying mob on the open jetty.

Between the wagons and the angry miners a line of soldiers, red-coated here, stood with guns held ready. An officer was arguing with a small group of miners, the same one who had led his men into the Wheal Phoenix. Josh spurred his horse down into the crowd.

A magistrate was proclaiming the Riot Act to the miners, declaring them officially a "riotous assembly". This was sufficient in a court to justify any violence that might be used against them. Even so, it might still have been possible to avert bloodshed.

Then, in the middle of a heated argument, the officer grabbed the shirt-front of one of the miners. The miner struggled and struck out wildly. At the same time, two of the men with him began raining blows upon the officer.

This was sufficient for the sergeant with the platoon. At a hoarse command every second man in the line dropped to one knee, rifles aimed at the seething mass of miners. Before a horrified Josh could do or say anything, a volley of shots rang out. When the drifting, acrid smoke cleared, half-a-dozen miners lay sprawled on the ground. There were shouts and screams as the crowd began to push away from the red-coated soldiers, only to find their retreat barred by the mounted dragoons who had advanced from the bridge with drawn sabres and now bore down upon the defenceless miners, hacking about them.

Josh rode at the foot-soldiers, calling on them not to fire again. He was too late. Another volley was ordered and more miners slumped to the ground. Josh found himself caught in the charge of the dragoons. Frightened by the noise, Hector reared, crashing down against the horse ridden by one of the dragoons. The soldier's mount slipped on the smooth cobblestones and crashed to the ground, carrying its rider with it.

Then Josh was in the middle of the hacking sabres. A steel blade slashed across his back and a burning pain seared through the muscles of his shoulder. Hector stumbled and Josh was thrown to the ground. He clambered to his feet and there in front of him, not fifteen feet away, was the officer in charge of the foot-soldiers. Bloodied and bruised, he pointed in Josh's direction and called upon his men to shoot.

"Get him! Get that man! I want him!"

All was utter confusion now, foot-soldiers, horse-soldiers and miners running or fighting all over the wide jetty. Josh saw an opening and ran for it. From somewhere close behind a gun roared and it felt as though someone had struck him a hard blow in the left arm. He spun about and clutched it just above the elbow. Hot blood oozed between his fingers. Then, miraculously, John Kittow appeared, still mounted and with Hector's reins in his hand. "Quick, Josh!" he called. "Get up. Hurry!"

Josh swung into the saddle and clattered after the Caradon miner, through a narrow passageway. Then they were on a street lined with shuttered shops, galloping past the bridge and out of the town.

They rode hard for another mile before John Kittow pulled his horse in alongside Josh. By now the fire in Josh's back was burning and his arm throbbed alarmingly.

"My God, Josh! You're a bloody mess. Let me have a look at those wounds."

Josh swung from Hector's back, staggering as his feet touched the ground. The miner stripped Josh's shirt from him and began swabbing Josh's wounds with his neckerchief. His arm was quickly cleaned. The musket ball had gone straight through, without touching the bone. Josh's back was a different matter, laid open from the left shoulder to the right side of his waist.

"I don't like the looks of this, Josh. You must see a doctor as quick as we can reach one."

"It better be a doctor well away from here," said Josh, gritting his teeth against the pain. "That officer brought his men around the mines. I told him my name and he said he'd heard of me. I doubt very much if my wound was the result of a chance shot."

"No. I'd swear it was Morwen Trago who fired. And if they know your name they'll come for you at Sharptor." Kittow stripped off his shirt and began tearing it into strips. "I'll do what I can with this. But it won't last long, Josh."

He laid strips of cloth along the sabre cut, then bound the remainder of the shirt around Josh's body to hold it in place. "That will have to do for now. Can you get back on your horse?"

Josh nodded, with more assurance than he felt, and they set off again, following the line of the canal towards Moorswater.

By the time they reached the head of the canal, Josh was reeling in the saddle.

"You're in no fit state to ride any further, Josh."

"I'll be all right in a few minutes." It came out as a mumble. Josh rested both hands on the horse's neck, trying to ignore the pain that burned his arm and back.

Another three miles put them onto the moor west of St. Cleer. "We'll make those rocks up ahead," said John Kittow. "I'll leave you there and find a doctor."

"Go into St. Cleer," gasped Josh. "Speak to Preacher Thackeray. Tell him what's happened."

At the rocks John lowered him to the ground only half-conscious, and left him with Hector's reins twisted about his wrist. "I'll be back in half an hour," promised the miner.

It was a clear night with a full moon balancing on the horizon when John Kittow rode off. Sometime later Josh was wakened from an exhausted sleep. Looking up he saw the moon high in the sky above him. It must have been well after midnight. John had been gone far too long. Something was wrong.

Then he heard the sound which had disturbed him. It was the jingle of harness. Painfully he rose to his feet and held Hector's head still, relying on the rocks to hide him as horsemen passed along the track not twenty yards away. They were troopers. He felt sure they were searching for him.

When they disappeared from view Josh mounted Hector. The effort caused the blood to flow once more from the wound in his back. He kneed the horse forward, away from the track, heading for Sharptor and the cottage of his parents.

It was fortunate he stayed clear of the paths. As he picked his way down the last hillside close to the cottage Hector slipped, dislodging a stone. Josh heard an exclamation from someone standing in the shadows to one side of the cottage.

"Who's there?" The soldiers had been expecting him.

Josh pulled Hector about in a tight turn. Behind him he heard the dragoons mount hurriedly. Then horses were crashing through the bracken after him. He coaxed Hector into a canter, the movement jarring his wounds unmercifully. He would be unable to keep going like this for long. His only chance lay in outwitting them.

Crouching low, he coaxed Hector into a gallop in an effort to gain some distance, then risked a quick glance behind him. He could not see the dragoons but he could hear them shouting. He had to act now.

Pulling the horse to a halt he jumped awkwardly from the saddle. Slapping its haunches, he called, "Go, Hector! Give them a run, boy."

It was as though the big horse understood. With head high it set off at a gallop into the night, leaving Josh to sink down into the tall ferns a few feet from the path.

The dragoons were well spread out as one by one they passed the place where Josh was hiding. When the last of them had pounded into the distance Josh stood up. He knew where he must go. He had not been there for some years but he had no trouble finding the tunnel through the gorse. It was slightly overgrown, but he got to the rock hideout safely and collapsed on his face. The soldiers would not find him here.

JOSH WAS RIGHT in assuming something had gone seriously wrong with John Kittow.

The miner was a reliable shift captain, but sadly he did not have a quick, inquiring mind. If he had, he might have wondered about the number of horses tethered near the preacher's house. As it was he simply hurried to the door, banged upon it and, when it was opened by a pale, wide-eyed Miriam, he blurted out, "Where's Preacher Thackeray? I must see him, Josh is badly hurt."

When the uniformed figure of Miriam's brother, Morwen Trago, stepped into the light behind her, John Kittow was stunned. By the time he recovered it was too late. Two dragoons rushed from the shadows and John Kittow was a prisoner.

They dragged him into the kitchen and pushed him into a chair. Miriam was bundled into the passageway outside. Triumphantly, Morwen said, "So my shot didn't go astray. Where is Josh now?"

John Kittow glared at him and said nothing.

"Don't be stupid, Kittow," said Morwen Trago. "It won't be well received at your trial if it comes out that you protected him."

"My trial for what? All Josh and I did was try to stop the miners causing trouble."

"That's a likely story," grinned Morwen Trago. "You and Retallick were leading them. Inciting them to violence."

"You're a liar, Morwen Trago. A true son of your father. Where's Preacher Thackeray? He'll know I'm telling the truth."

"I doubt whether my brother-in-law will know anything of the sort," replied Morwen Trago smugly. "He was here when everything was happening. Now he's gone to do what he can to comfort the miners you and Retallick misled into such a stupid venture."

He signalled to the dragoons. "Take him away."

JOSH SLEPT fitfully through the night. Twice he heard horses passing along the path beyond the gorse passage. But the soldiers would find nothing in the darkness.

When next he woke the sun was high in the sky. It took him a few minutes to place where he was, to be aware of the sounds about him, the distant steady thump-thump of the Sharptor mine engine, and farther away, the mixed noises of the Wheal Phoenix. Out there it was a normal moorland day. But Josh was aware his life would never be the same again. He felt stiff and during his exhausted sleep he had moved, causing his back to bleed extensively. He was much weaker than he wanted to believe.

He tried to get to his feet. Using the rocks as support, he shuffled the few steps necessary to see out through a small aperture that gave a view over the needle-spined gorse. There he saw soldiers, red-coated ones, beating through the undergrowth. But they were beating up the slope, working away from his position. That was hopeful. They might even have already searched the area where he now was. But it did mean he could not risk leaving the hideout yet.

He looked up at the sun. It was still early afternoon. There was no hope of contacting anyone during daylight. It would be risky enough in the dark. He sank back on the dry earth, tired and with a strong feeling of hopelessness.

He was still there when Miriam found him soon after sunset. Word had come back to St. Cleer that he had been chased into the darkness above the Retallick cottage, that the soldiers had taken his horse only a mile away. Immediately, Miriam had known where Josh was hiding.

When she saw him lying so still her first thought was that he was dead. But when she dropped to her knees and touched his face his eyelids flickered open and he tried to speak.

"Shhh!" Miriam whispered. "Keep your voice very low. I've got food and some bandages. Are you badly hurt?"

"I don't know. I think my back's on fire although my arm throbs more. But how. . . ?"

"John Kittow said you were hurt last night before they took him away."

"Took him away. . . ? Why? He did nothing wrong. We went to Looe to try to stop the miners."

"They're saying you led the rioting. That John Kittow was with you. He's to appear before the magistrate tomorrow."

"But William knows the truth of it. He knows I've always been against violence. John felt the same way."

Miriam's expression changed. "You mustn't expect William to say anything, Josh. For or against you."

"But he must! He knows John and I are innocent. He knows the arguments I put forward at meetings. He can tell them."

"And admit that he's one of the Union leaders, Josh? No, expect nothing from William and you're not likely to be disappointed." There was a bitterness in her voice. "Besides, I don't think he'll be in Cornwall very much longer. He's been called to London. The Church authorities want to know about his activities here."

"Will he go?"

"He must. But he intends leaving as the leader of a successful campaign. There's already news that Parliament has stopped the export of corn from Cornwall and other country districts."

Josh sagged visibly. "Then the miners were right. Their way was the only way to get results."

"No!" Miriam was having difficulty in separating the strips of cloth from his wound where the blood had dried through them. "There wouldn't have been time for news of the fight at Looe to have got to London. Parliament made their decision before the miners marched on Looe. If the men had been a little more patient there wouldn't be seven of them lying dead."

Miriam had water with her and some herbal balm. She dressed his wounds as best she could, then gave him the food she had brought. He ate it greedily. When he had finished she said, "What are we going to do with you now, Josh?"

"There's no need for you to do anything, Miriam. You mustn't become any more involved. Think of yourself and young Daniel. How were you able to get away to come to me today?"

"My mother isn't well these days. I don't need an excuse to come to Henwood to visit her."

"All the same, I'd rather you weren't mixed up in this. . . ."

"I'm already involved." She looked down at him. "William has always known how close we were as children. But in recent months he seems to have become strangely jealous. Then again, he resented the way the miners looked to you. He's a very ambitious man—I believe he saw you as a threat to his ambitions. And since Morwen first came to see us they've talked together. Once Morwen even came to the house with his officer."

She watched him unhappily. "I believe William has a lot to do with you being hunted now, Josh. Do you see why I'm sure he'll do nothing to help you?"

"But how could he have known I'd go to Looe? He couldn't have arranged that."

"I don't know. Unless he sent someone to tell you about the miners. Anyone who knows you could guess what your actions would be. Once there Morwen and his officer could pick you out."

"No, Miriam. I don't believe anyone would do that."

"You wouldn't do it, Josh. It isn't your way. But William would." She stood up and brushed down her dress. "I'm going now, Josh. You'll be safe here tonight. I'll return tomorrow with more food. No, don't argue. I want to."

Josh spent a thoroughly miserable night. Around midnight the wind rose and within an hour it began to rain, a chilling skin-soaking drizzle. When Miriam came early next morning, she found him cold and shivering, crouching like some sick animal. She had set out from her mother's house with some hot broth in a covered bowl. It was no more than lukewarm when she fed it between his chattering teeth, but it was sufficient to stop his shivering.

"Uncle John is going to get word to your father at the mine this morning, telling him not to worry about you. But we must get you beneath a roof somewhere so I can have a doctor look at your wounds."

"Yes, but what roof? I'm a fugitive."

"I know one place where you'll be safe. In your own house. The soldiers have already searched it and found it empty, and they're not guarding it. They're expecting that you will make for your parents' cottage. Isn't there a hay-loft above the stables?"

Josh nodded.

"Then that's the place. It isn't far if we go straight across the moor. You've got to make the effort, Josh."

"All right. Let's start now."

The crawl through the tunnel was not too difficult. Once outside he got to his feet with Miriam's help. They staggered drunkenly for about twenty yards before he fell, dragging her down with him.

"I'm sorry," he gasped. "I don't think I can make it."

"Of course you can. You've *got* to do it now we've started. The soldiers will find you here if you stay."

Painfully he regained his feet. This time he covered twice the distance before tripping. Once more she helped him to his feet. And so it went on. Fifty yards. Twenty yards. Once a mere fifteen. After what seemed an eternity they arrived at the wall behind the old farmyard. Miriam helped Josh over and pushed him up the ladder to the loft. With a groan he dropped gratefully into the sweet hay.

"We've done it, Josh. I told you we would." Suddenly there was a sound in the yard outside. They froze. Footsteps approached the door of the stable below them.

"We know you're up there, Josh Retallick." It was Morwen Trago. "Come down or I'll take great delight in coming up and shooting you again."

Miriam's eyes showed a disbelief that was quickly replaced by terror. "He must have been watching for us!" she whispered.

Josh nodded.

She looked at him tearfully. "Let me speak to him. . . ."

"No! I don't want you involved." Holding her arm to prevent her from getting up, he called, "Morwen! You know I'm here alone?"

There was silence as the implication of Josh's words sunk in.

"If you say so," Morwen answered.

"I do say so. Because I'm alone and have no wish to see my property torn apart I'll give myself up."

"Then come down."

"There must be some other way, Josh," Miriam whispered.

"No. You've risked too much already. I'm going now. Stay until we're well clear." He kissed her quickly then staggered to the ladder. "I'm coming now."

Soldiers are not renowned for their gentleness and Josh's captors were no exception. They handled him roughly as they tied his hands behind his back and pushed him out of the stable. Luckily, he managed to keep most of their blows from his back.

For all that, he was a sorry sight as they marched him past the Retallick cottage. Seeing him from the window, Jesse screamed and ran outside. The soldiers pushed her back roughly, but Ben came out behind her and his booming voice stopped them.

"That's our son you have there. If you hope to get out of mining country with your lives you'll let his mother speak to him."

Tom Shovell and some off-duty miners had come, drawn by the commotion. They formed up behind the shift captain and the soldiers realized the truth in Ben Retallick's words.

"She'll have to be brief," said Morwen, giving in surlily.

"Josh, what have they done to you?"

"My arm is bleeding a little, that's all. It looks far worse than it really is. Everything is going to be all right. I'm not guilty of anything. As anyone who was at Looe knows."

"That's what John Kittow told the magistrate," replied Jesse. "But he was sent to Bodmin Gaol to await trial."

"Then the truth must wait to come out at the trial," said Josh. "Don't upset yourself. I must go now. Please don't worry."

Chapter 12

Bodmin Gaol was comparatively modern, the stones having not yet acquired the smell of decay and dirt found in most other prisons of the realm. Here was only the smell of imprisoned man—his sweat, his filth, and his fear.

In a large communal cell Josh was reunited with John Kittow and the nine other miners who had been arrested on that violent, late-summer day. All the others were strangers to him.

"I'm not going to say I'm pleased to see you," said John Kittow, leading Josh into a comparatively clean corner of the huge cage. "As the day went by my hopes rose that you'd made good your escape. How are your wounds? And what's been happening to you?"

Josh told the Caradon shift captain of his adventures since the Looe battle. And he told him he had heard that William Thackeray might be responsible for the misfortune that had befallen them.

"Now you mention it," mused John Kittow, "the miner who told me the men were on their way to Looe said something about having sent Nehemeziah on to tell you. He could well have been acting on Preacher Thackeray's orders. I wondered at the time why he should be bothering. But why would Thackeray do such a thing?"

Josh shrugged and said nothing.

"Well, don't worry, Josh," John Kittow went on. "Our own miners won't allow us to rot away in here. They'll force Thackeray to take some action to get us out."

"You're fooling yourself if you believe that, John. The judge must make an example of us. It wouldn't do for miners to believe they can take the law into their own hands. No, John. Preacher Thackeray has won."

That night an evil-smelling, greasy meal was distributed. The food was every bit as unpalatable as it looked, but all that Josh spurned was grabbed and gobbled up by other inmates of the common cell.

Then, the following day, Josh was brought a meal of beef and vegetables. When he expressed his surprise he was informed by the gaoler that Theophilus Strike had arranged for him to have meals brought in from outside. There was enough good food for Josh to share with John Kittow. A doctor also arrived, who examined Josh's wounds and pronounced himself satisfied with them. Furthermore, that same day a roly-poly little man was escorted into the cell who introduced himself as Reuben Button, the solicitor engaged by Strike to examine the question of Josh's defence.

Button oozed confidence from every pore. "Now," he said, seating himself on a stool the warder had brought for him. "Tell me exactly what happened. From the very beginning."

Josh told him. At the end of his story the solicitor frowned, looking quizzically at his client. "You're quite sure you're leaving nothing out?"

"I've told you everything," replied Josh. "Apart from knocking the dragoon from his horse—and that was hardly a premeditated act—I did nothing. My sole object in going to Looe was to stop the miners from doing something stupid."

"Why then were the soldiers so anxious to apprehend you?"

"There are two possible explanations. The first is Morwen Trago. We were boys together and he has no reason to be fond of me or my family. He was one of the soldiers at Looe, the one who put a bullet through my arm."

"I see." The solicitor was busily writing. "And the other reason?"

"The officer in charge of the soldiers brought them around the mines recently. He took them to the Wheal Phoenix. While he was there I warned him to keep away from the Wheal Sharptor. He asked for my name and I told him."

"Well! Well! Previous bad blood between yourself and the officer in charge of the soldiers."

There were many more questions before Mr. Button finally folded his papers and tucked them away.

"I think we have a very strong case," he said. "But of course this *was* a riotous assembly. That is most serious. However, we have an interesting defence. Very interesting. Now, I have another little matter to attend to."

He waved a scented handkerchief in front of his nose as a door leading to the main section of the prison was opened and the odour from within escaped. "Mr. Strike—whom I must say I have found to be a very generous man—wishes that you be made as comfortable as is possible prior to your trial. He has authorized me to obtain a private cell."

"I'm much obliged to him," said Josh. "Would it be asking too much for John Kittow to enjoy the privilege with me?"

289

"Provided little extra expense is involved I see no problem," said Mr. Button.

He was as good as his word. Before nightfall Josh and John were lodged in a cell on the first floor of the gaol.

The days passed with very little to disturb the monotony, apart from the visits of either Mr. Button, or the solicitor engaged by the Union to defend John Kittow and the other miners. Josh's wounds healed satisfactorily. They had one bad day when they were told that an additional charge was to be brought against them, that of being party to a conspiracy, contrary to the Treasonable and Seditious Practices Act. It was on such a charge that the Kit Hill miners had been convicted and transported when the mine store was burned down.

Then, the day before the trial was to commence at Bodmin Assizes, Josh had two very special visitors. Miriam came, and she brought Daniel with her.

Josh was appalled. "You should never have come. It's not right for Daniel to be in such surroundings."

"I feel the same about you," she replied with a forced smile.

For a long time they spoke of nothing in particular. Then John Kittow asked to be taken out for exercise. Such was Theophilus Strike's influence that the two men were able to take exercise periods whenever they wished.

When the Caradon mine leader had gone, Josh asked, "Does William know you're here?"

Miriam shook her head. "No, but it would make little difference if he did. He and I have been going separate ways since your arrest."

"You mean you've left him?"

"No, we're still living under the same roof, but that's all."

"Miriam, I won't have you ruining your life on my account."

"You're not the sole reason for things being the way they are, Josh. William knew I wasn't in love with him when we married. But I liked him, and I respected him. That respect has gone now and without it I find our relationship impossible."

"I'm sorry." It was totally inadequate.

"You needn't be. I've accepted it and William has many other things to occupy his mind." She lifted her eyes to his. "What do you think will happen at the trial?"

He shrugged. "My solicitor says we have a strong case. I hope he's right. I understand the prosecution will be asking for the death penalty if we're found guilty of all charges."

He saw the look of horror on her face and hurriedly added, "But he's quite sure we needn't fear that."

"I should hope not! You're innocent. Neither you nor John had anything to do with what happened!"

She clung to him then and Josh kissed her hungrily. The fire was still there between them, but a cell was no place for romance. "Miriam, please go now. And whatever happens, take care of yourself and Daniel."

Tears were commonplace in Bodmin Gaol and the gaoler avoided looking at Miriam as he let her and Daniel out of the cell.

IT WAS A DULL, sullen November day when Josh, John Kittow and the other miners were taken to the Assize Court for trial. They were all squeezed into a long prisoners' dock with steel spikes adorning the rail around it. Before them was the raised bench and the deep red padded chair reserved for the judge.

To one side of them the jurors formed a double line, uncomfortable on their hard benches. In the well of the court, between the judge's bench and the prisoners, were the tables reserved for barristers. And behind the dock where the light was dimmest, the public benches were packed to overflowing with miners and the families of the accused men.

A door at the rear of the judge's bench opened and a court usher appeared. "Silence for His Lordship Judge Denman."

The occupants of the courtroom rose to their feet with a scraping of chairs. A short, bulbous-nosed man with flowing grey wig and red robes swept in and took his seat. "Be seated!" he called.

The scraping was repeated and everyone sat down again. The prisoners sat down with them but were prodded to their feet as the clerk began calling out the names of the accused men.

Then he read out the charges, his dull voice droning out, in legal jargon, statute and section against which they were alleged to have offended. When he had finished he called upon each of them to state whether he was "guilty" or "not guilty".

One after another the men declared their innocence. On the first occasion the reply brought a small cheer from the gallery. The judge in a stern voice informed the court that unless the public refrained from voicing their feelings he would have the court cleared. Then the prisoners were allowed to be seated and the case against them began to unwind.

"It is," the prosecuting barrister declared, "quite simple and straightforward. Prior to this unhappily eventful day the miners had been stirred up by men like the defendants Retallick and Kittow, and misled into forming unconstitutional alliances, such as the Miners' Union. They disagreed with Parliament's policy on the sale of corn, and they deliberately set out to use force in order to change it. This disgraceful day at Looe was not a thing decided upon a few hours before the event, it was part of a well thought-out plan. Gathered together were men from mines throughout east and central Cornwall. They knew exactly where to go, proof beyond any reasonable doubt of a treasonable conspiracy to achieve their selfish and dangerous aims.

"Although undeniably guilty the men standing before you in this court were—with two exceptions—simple miners. The two exceptions are Joshua Retallick and John Kittow, who were important members of the mining community. And, mounted and in clear view of the others, these two led that cowardly, unlawful mob. That is briefly the case for the prosecution. Now I will proceed to call witnesses who will prove it beyond any shadow of a doubt."

First came the magistrate, pompous and eager, to tell how, disregarding the insults hurled at him by "hundreds of miners bent upon mischief" he completed the reading of the Riot Act.

Mr. Button, seated beside the barrister defending Josh, leaned over and whispered something. The barrister stood up.

"Magistrate Phipps, I am quite sure you behaved with commendable courage. Indeed, would I not be right in saying that you behaved with composure? That you assessed the situation in a calm and brave manner?"

292

The surprised magistrate beamed. "I did my best, sir."

"Then no doubt you were aware of the composition of the crowd. Were they afoot or mounted?"

"Why, they were afoot, of course."

"All of them?"

"Yes."

"And yet the prosecution has informed the court that my client Mr. Retallick, and Mr. Kittow, were both mounted. Am I correct in assuming that neither man was present when you read out the Riot Act? They were not members of this riotous assembly?"

The magistrate opened his mouth and closed it again. "We-ell . . . . They might have been at the back. There were a lot of people there."

"But you did not see them?"

The magistrate was forced to agree that he had not.

The counsel employed by the Miners' Union used his questioning time trying to make the magistrate say that the miners were in fact behaving in a quiet and orderly manner. His argument was remarkably lacking in conviction.

Next came the evidence of the soldiers. It followed closely the story told by the prosecuting counsel. They spoke of being ordered to fire into the crowd to save their officer, and to defend themselves. Their evidence was well rehearsed. Nobody, unless he had been at the scene, would have doubted them.

The dragoons' evidence was far more damning. They told the truth as they had seen it. When they arrived on the scene, Josh and John Kittow were part of the crowd. One dragoon told of being attacked by Josh and falling beneath the feet of the horses. It was, he insisted, a deliberate attack.

"Surely not," argued the barrister representing Josh. "Was my client armed?"

The dragoon grudgingly admitted he did not believe so.

"Yet you had a sabre drawn and were prepared to use it upon my client?" The eyebrows of the barrister were a statement in themselves. "And you are telling us that Joshua Retallick—unarmed—*attacked* you? Attacked a soldier with a sabre clear of its sheath, raised and ready for use?"

"Yes, sir. He had his arm raised to strike me."

"I submit it was far more likely his arm was raised to protect himself from the blow of an upraised sabre."

"No, sir. It was a deliberate attack on me."

The barrister shook his head, "If that was true it would make my client a fool. I'll be proving later that he is far from that."

Then it was the turn of Morwen Trago. He swore that Josh had been with the miners at the time they entered Looe, urging them to attack the soldiers. He had seen him strike down one dragoon and when Josh had been about to attack another, he, Morwen Trago, had fired at him, wounding him in the arm.

"Is it true," asked Josh's barrister in cross-examination, "that you knew Joshua Retallick as a boy?"

"Yes. We lived close to each other on the moor."

"And did you like him?"

A shrug again. "I neither liked nor disliked him."

"No? You must be someone with a remarkable talent for forgiveness, Corporal Trago. Is it not true you believe Joshua Retallick's father to be responsible for the death of your own father?"

"He *was* responsible."

"Surely not. Didn't your father rape a girl who lived with the Retallicks? When pursued I believe he slipped and fell into a disused mine shaft and was killed?"

"No! He didn't fall. He was pushed."

"That may be what you choose to believe. It is certainly not corroborated by the known facts. But, be that as it may, do you still claim that you have no hatred for anyone who bears the name Retallick?" The court was hushed as the jury waited for Morwen Trago to reply. He said nothing.

"Never mind," said the barrister. "There are certain silences that shout louder than words. But I put it to you that you did *not* see my client arrive with the miners. That you have concocted your own version of the day's events. What is more, if you told the truth about what you saw on this fateful day not only would Joshua Retallick be acquitted but he would leave this court with the praises of the learned Judge ringing in his ears. For attempting to prevent the bloodshed that took place on that day."

"No! That's not true!"

But Morwen Trago's cries were drowned by the noise from the public gallery. This time there was no silencing the crowd. It was at this stage that the judge adjourned the proceedings for the day.

On the return journey to the gaol the accused miners were in an optimistic mood, convinced that the mood of those in the public gallery represented the view of the jury. But the next day, when it was the time for the defence to present its case, it soon became apparent to Josh that there were few sympathetic witnesses, and their case was held together by a very frail thread.

Of those in the dock only Josh was called to tell his story. He told how he and John Kittow had ridden into Looe in a vain attempt to head off the miners. Yes, he admitted, he had knocked a dragoon from his horse. But the fault lay with the horses rather than with their riders. His manner was quiet and straightforward enough to impress the jury. But then the prosecuting barrister began to cross-examine him.

"Joshua Retallick, you have told the court you rode to Looe in great haste when you were told of the miners' action?"

"Yes."

"Is it not true you set off knowing when you caught up with them you would be able to influence them?"

"I hoped they might listen to me."

"You 'hoped they might listen'. No doubt they had listened to you in the past when you addressed their meetings?"

"I addressed very few meetings."

"You agree there were some?"

"Yes."

"So you are not denying that the miners regard you as a leader of this union movement?"

"It is a Miners' Union and I have spoken to them."

"Thank you, I think we are in agreement. You are a leader of this so-called 'union'. Now, let us pass on to some of the things you have told the court. They do not seem to agree with what has been said by the witnesses who came before you. You say you went to Looe in a vain attempt to prevent the miners from doing something which you now agree was 'stupid'."

"Yes."

"But when you discovered they intended carrying out their plan of seizing the corn you decided you would join them."

"No."

"Further, when you saw the dragoons moving in to quell this riot you personally led an assault on them."

"No, I have said what happened."

"You have told us what you would dearly like this court to believe, Mr. Retallick. If the jury and I choose not to believe your version of the day's happenings I trust you will forgive us."

With this the prosecuting counsel sat down. His questioning over, Josh was returned to the prisoners' dock.

Then came the character witnesses to speak on behalf of the miners, shift captains in the main. But there were two adventurers from the Caradon mine to speak for John Kittow. They praised his diligence and spoke of him as a man of integrity.

When it was the turn of the character witnesses to speak on Josh's behalf it was the beginning of a series of surprises for him. The first was Theophilus Strike. In his usual forthright manner the mine owner called the charges against Josh "preposterous!"

"Joshua Retallick," he said, "is a brilliant engineer. His contribution to mine safety is recognized far beyond the borders of his own county. He has patented a mine lift that will revolutionize current safety standards."

Theophilus Strike went on to say that he had never heard Josh either preach or practice violence. His interest in the Miners' Union was a humanitarian one. The mine owner had in fact discussed it with him. He was perfectly satisfied that Josh was concerned with the well-being of the miner and nothing more.

The next witness was William Carlyon.

The Harvey's works manager smiled sympathetically in Josh's direction as he took the stand. He too spoke of Josh as a brilliant engineer with a great future.

"I believe your relationship with the prisoner is closer than that of two men who are both engineers?"

"Yes." William Carlyon's voice was pitched low. "He was my daughter's husband."

296

"Was?"

"My daughter died as a result of childbirth. The baby died also."

The statement brought Josh sympathetic glances from the jury.

"So, Joshua Retallick had recently lost both his wife and his child. It left him a lonely man, I would imagine?"

"Yes."

"In order to overcome such desolation most intelligent men would probably devote themselves to something that would occupy both their time and thoughts. A cause, perhaps. Something like a Miners' Union?"

"I would say that was highly probable."

"Do you think he would become involved to such an extent that he would advocate violence, Mr. Carlyon?"

"No. Josh is not a violent man."

"That is what I too believe. Thank you, Mr. Carlyon."

The prosecuting counsel questioned William Carlyon closely, but failed to shake him.

It was time now for the prosecution to conclude its case. The prosecuting barrister stood up to address the court.

"My Lord. Gentlemen of the jury. You have listened to the evidence in a case of the utmost seriousness. A case involving a section of the community placing themselves above the law, attempting to impose their will upon others. This is a crime aimed at the very structure upon which our way of life depends, the upholding of law. You have heard the evidence of honest men. They have told you how these men in the dock, with others, marched upon Looe. They knew soldiers would be there. They knew they would have to fight to have their way.

"From his own lips you heard Joshua Retallick admit he was in the habit of addressing meetings of these miners. 'Union' meetings. Retallick did not admit he was responsible for conspiring that the miners march to Looe. We could not expect him to do that. But I am sure that you, the members of the jury, will recognize the truth. John Kittow is perhaps more misguided than evil. But he is as guilty as Retallick. You will—you must—find him and the other prisoners guilty as charged."

In a heavy silence the counsel for the prosecution sat down.

The miners' defence barrister made a long repetitious speech that had the jurors fidgeting on the hard benches and said nothing new. Then it was the turn of Josh's counsel.

"My Lord. Gentlemen of the jury. I have no intention of taking up much of your time. Allow me to remind you of the facts that have emerged.

"There was a disorder at Looe on the twenty-fourth of September of this year. That is beyond dispute. But the magistrate who read the Riot Act, a cool, calm citizen, did not see Joshua Retallick. Of course he didn't. Joshua Retallick was not there!

"Ah! You might say, but the soldiers saw him. Of course they did. All I dispute is *when* they saw him. I am not suggesting they are lying. Simply confused. They were excited, perhaps fearful—and who can blame them? They were greatly out-numbered. But what a pity they did not allow Joshua Retallick to talk to the crowd.

"He had gone to Looe in a vain attempt to prevent the miners from behaving foolishly. It was an action in keeping with his character. His concern for the miner was well known. His employer knew of it, and came here to inform this court that Joshua Retallick was no criminal but a man and an engineer held in high esteem. William Carlyon also confirmed Joshua Retallick's standing in the world of engineering. This is the man you are asked to judge now. A brilliant engineer. A man who cares for the miner. No stranger to personal tragedy. Is it feasible that he would act in a manner so completely out of character, as the prosecution would have you believe? No, gentlemen of the jury. I ask that justice be done this day. That you allow Joshua Retallick to leave this court a free man."

The deep silence that followed his speech was broken by the judge. "Thank you, gentlemen. If you've finished I will sum up the case for the jury."

He went through the case in a somewhat haphazard manner, leaving out portions he felt disinclined to emphasize. When he finished the prisoners were prodded to their feet, the judge rose and bowed and the jury filed off to their room.

The jury stayed out for an hour, during which time the prisoners were kept in the cells. Then, with a flurry of excitement, they were hustled back into the courtroom as the jury returned.

"Gentlemen of the jury. Have you reached a verdict?"

"We have," replied the foreman.

"And how do you find the prisoners?"

"On the charge of riotously assembling, we find the prisoners Retallick and Kittow not guilty. All the others guilty."

There were some gasps from the public gallery. The judge frowned. Whether it was due to the verdict or the noise in his court was difficult to tell.

"And on the charge of being parties to a treasonable and seditious conspiracy?"

"We find all the prisoners guilty."

This time there was no denying the shouts of "No!" "No!" from the public gallery.

"Silence!" This from the judge. He looked at the men standing in the dock.

"I shall deal first of all with those of you found guilty of being part of a riotous assembly." He read out the names of the miners. "This is a most serious crime. One which cannot be tolerated in any civilized country. You are all grown men and fully responsible for your own acts. In light of this I sentence you to transportation for a period of seven years."

There were groans and cries from their relatives.

"Now I come to the other charge on which you have been found guilty. Conspiring to commit treason. I can think of no more serious crime. This is something which is aimed at the very foundations of the land. Allowed to go unchecked such actions can have only one outcome. In France we have seen it happen. Those men I have just named will serve a further fourteen years' sentence of transportation, to run concurrently with their previous sentence."

This provoked more cries from the public gallery. When the court ushers and some of the soldiers moved in to stop it there was some scuffling at the rear of the courtroom. "Take the men I have already sentenced down," ordered the judge.

When all was quiet again he looked at Josh Retallick and John Kittow and his lips drew to a tight, thin line.

"Kittow. You are, I feel, a man who has allowed himself to be led by his companion. Nevertheless, I cannot overlook your part in this grave offence. I therefore sentence you to be transported for a period of fourteen years."

John Kittow swayed in the dock and Josh gripped his arm in sympathy. He had no illusions now as to his own fate.

"Joshua Retallick, I can find little to say in your favour. You have been found guilty of a crime which a man of your intelligence could conceivably have carried through to its logical conclusion—overthrow of organized government. Such an offence carries with it the death penalty. I will tell you quite openly that it was my intention to pass such a sentence upon you. That I do not do so may be a mistake on my part. But the evidence of William Carlyon moved me, for even judges have emotions. He suggested that personal tragedies may have impaired your judgement. For these reasons alone I will exercise mercy. Joshua Retallick, I sentence you to be transported for life."

"That's not justice! He's an innocent man! You're sentencing an innocent man!"

Josh recognized Miriam's voice before pandemonium broke loose in the court. He turned to see her but was hustled down to the cells as soldiers, ushers and constables moved in upon the shouting, stamping crowd in the public gallery.

OUTSIDE THE COURT building Theophilus Strike, himself angry at what he considered to be a gross miscarriage of justice, watched the more vociferous objectors to the verdict being hurled into the street. When two soldiers appeared carrying Miriam between them Strike stepped forward to her rescue. Not stopping to argue, the soldiers released Miriam and hurried back inside.

"Young lady! Aren't you the Trago girl who married Preacher Thackeray?" Strike asked.

Miriam's anger had boiled away, leaving her cold and dispirited. She managed a simple "Yes."

"I thought I recognized you in the court room." He took her

arm and led her away along the street. Any resentment she might have had towards him was dispelled by his first words. "I refuse to believe I see defeat in your face. No child of Moses Trago could possibly have heard of the word. Do you have a horse or carriage to take you home?" Miriam shook her head. "Good! I have a carriage at the inn along here. I'll give you a ride home and on the way you can tell me why you are so sure of Josh Retallick's innocence."

WILLIAM THACKERAY was writing a letter in his study when the carriage drew up outside the chapel cottage. He watched in amazement as Theophilus Strike stepped from it and handed Miriam out. The mine owner chatted seriously to her for a few minutes before climbing back inside the coach.

When Miriam entered the house her husband demanded to know why she had been travelling in a carriage with the mine owner.

"He brought me back from Bodmin Assizes. That's where all Josh's friends have been today—together with those of his enemies with the courage to so declare themselves."

"And who won the day? Josh—or his 'enemies'?"

"He was sentenced to transportation for life."

"How tragic." At that moment Miriam hated him for his hypocrisy. "Poor Josh did much for the miners."

"Then why weren't you in court to tell that to the judge? You could have helped him."

"I would have been pleased to help had it been possible. But who would have taken my word against all those witnesses who actually *saw* what went on?"

"You would never have gone into that courtroom. You would have been far too worried that your part in the matter might come out. The conspiracy to involve Josh that you, Morwen and his officer were part of."

"What an incredible suggestion, my dear. But in view of your distraught state I'll ignore it."

"You ignore it if you wish. I doubt if Mr. Strike will."

"Strike? You told him of your wild imaginings?"

It was the first time she had ever seen genuine fear on his face. It told her much. William had indeed deliberately involved Josh in the Looe riot. "Far more than that, William. I gave him facts. I told him of the meetings between you and Morwen. Gave him the date the officer came here with him to meet you."

Now she called on a calculated bluff. "And I told him of the conversation I overheard between you and the officer."

Miriam watched the battle between fear and anger being fought on William's face. The victory went to anger. Without warning the preacher's arm swung and he struck her across the face.

"You Judas harlot! This is the thanks I get for taking you into my home and giving you my name. Don't you think I knew what had gone on between you and Josh before? Oh yes, I knew—but I forgave you. Now you would give up all you have here—all that's decent—for someone who would be best forgotten."

"I gave up all that was decent years ago, William Thackeray." She fingered the side of her face where he had struck. "I'll be leaving your house in the morning. Daniel will go with me."

BUT MIRIAM still had one last distressing meeting with her husband before the break became final.

It was after he returned from London and his long-awaited appearance before the Church authorities. It had been a stormy and unsatisfactory meeting for Thackeray and it showed in the way he slouched in the saddle riding into Henwood village.

Miriam opened her mother's door to him herself. Thackeray had not anticipated a doorstep confrontation but he did his best to project some of his old authority.

"I've come for you and Daniel, Miriam."

"Then you've had a wasted journey, William."

"You're my wife, Miriam—and Daniel is my son. If necessary I'll seek recourse to the courts."

"No, you wouldn't. You fear what I might say in a courtroom."

"I fear nothing that might be said here in Cornwall. It would not follow us to London and that's where I've been ordered."

"What I have to say would follow you to the grave, William. So don't make me say it."

302

"Miriam, please, forget what's gone. Let's try to start again. I have to return to London but we can work together for others there just as we did here."

"Did we? No, William. I *thought* that was what we were doing but it was all to build your reputation. The price of it was far too high. I don't want to see you again—ever."

"But what will you do? And Daniel—you must consider him."

"I have. I'll work on the mine for him. And he'll get a better education from me than most other boys about here."

"I beg you, Miriam. Don't let it end like this. For Daniel's sake if not mine. Where is he? Let me see him. Just once. . . ."

"No!" The cry was torn from her as her husband's composure disintegrated before her eyes. She despised him, but she was sorry for him also. Turning, she fled into the house.

THE PRISONERS sentenced for the Looe riots were taken in chains from the court to the prison hulk, *Captivity*, lying off the naval dockyard at Devonport. This battered shell of an old man-of-war was a nightmare. When the prisoners were still fifty yards from the dark shape the stench was enough to make a man puke.

The sentenced miners made their way precariously up a slippery gangway in the darkness and Josh was parted from John Kittow. It happened so quickly that he had no time to say "Goodbye". One minute they were being pushed around by swearing gaolers checking chains. The next, they were being thrust into separate holds.

He never saw John Kittow again. Three months after he climbed aboard the *Captivity*, the ex-shift captain died, the victim of a typhoid outbreak on the foul hulk.

Josh and the men with him were pushed down a steep wooden ladder into a dark and indescribably stinking hold. All around were the sounds of men, moaning, snoring and coughing. The hatch cover was slammed shut and the miners left to grope their way forward in the blackness. They finally found a small space and by easing out other prisoners they made room to sit down.

Sleep was out of the question. They were part of a waking nightmare. Only when the grey dawn filtered reluctantly through cracks between the rotting boards did the miners realize the darkness had been kind to them. There was filth everywhere. Convicts lay chained together like wild beasts. Red-eyed and unshaven they put gruff questions to the newcomers, resentful of their recent freedom. They asked about the world of which they were no longer part, a world that belonged to another lifetime.

For five ghastly weeks Josh was on the *Captivity*. He knew nothing of the things going on outside. Many times he feared for his sanity. He learned to fight like the worst of his fellow prisoners for the food that was lowered to them twice daily. Once he gloated for a whole day when he was able to steal two handfuls of tasteless porridge instead of the usual one.

Then one day the hatch cover was removed at an unusual hour and one of the gaolers called his name. The warder made Josh climb halfway up the ladder before he would come down to loose the chain attaching him to the others. Then, with only the chains about his ankles, Josh awkwardly climbed the rest of the way and shuffled after the gaoler to the hulk overseer's office.

The overseer looked at Josh in distaste. "Your name Joshua Retallick?"

"Yes."

The overseer sniffed. "You're not my idea of a brilliant engineer."

Josh's hopes took a sudden, unreasonable climb. "I was an engineer once," he said.

"There'd better be no 'was' about it," said the overseer. "I've a letter here from a Mr. Carlyon which says you're to be sent to Australia. Going on a regular immigrant ship with a warder on his way to Botany Bay with his family. Seems they've found copper in Australia and need someone out there to install some engines. It's all here, together with a release order signed by a minister of the Queen. There's another letter from a Mr. Strike, promising to pay all expenses incurred in your transfer. Why he needs to bother himself with a convict I don't know." He sniffed his disapproval. "Your ship is lying at Falmouth. You'll get out of those stinking rags and be taken there under escort. But remember, Retallick, you'll still be a prisoner."

It was unbelievable. Josh was unable to accept the truth of it—

not even when he stood on a cold jetty, shivering in a chill east wind, the hulk a dark smudge on the river behind him.

The two escorts travelling with him said very little. They set off by coach and arrived at Falmouth in the early afternoon of the next day. There they boarded a sailing vessel larger than any Josh had seen. He was escorted to a cabin in the bowels of the ship and handed over to his gaoler for the long journey to Australia.

Samuel Evans was a very different man to the gaolers on the hulk. He was a family man and spoke to Josh as a man would speak to another man.

"Hello, Joshua. I've heard a great deal about you. I can do nothing about the fact that you're a convicted prisoner. While we're in harbour you'll be locked in this cabin. Once we put to sea you'll be free to wander about the ship. However, the captain has reminded me that I'm responsible for your good behaviour. Do I have your word you'll not attempt to escape?"

"You have it—and my deep gratitude," said Josh.

"Good, then it's settled. We should sail on the morning tide. You're fortunate to have good and wealthy friends, Joshua."

When the warder left, Josh sat down on the narrow bunk. He felt like weeping. There were still many problems ahead of him but the nightmare, the dreadful nightmare of the hulk was over.

The next day a strong northeasterly blew from the land. In no time at all the vessel was well out into the Channel.

After the evening meal Evans took Josh on a tour of the ship. Then, aware that Josh would want to savour his freedom, the warder left him alone on the deck. From now until they arrived at their destination, Josh would be treated as a free man.

It was dark and deserted on the deck. Josh made his way to the stern. Along the coast of the scarcely discernible land that was Cornwall he could see the lights of cottages. Josh felt loneliness well up inside him. He thought of his parents in the cottage on the slopes of Sharp Tor and the miners whose companionship he had taken for granted. And Miriam. . . .

He shivered. It was cold.

A figure came up to stand close to him. Josh half-turned but could make out only a pale shadow that was a face.

"Josh, is that you?"

He could not believe it. "Miriam?"

"Oh, Josh!" She was in his arms, holding him as though the wind might tear him away from her.

Now he was certain the whole thing was a dream.

"What are you doing here?" he asked at last. Suddenly he stiffened. "William! Is he here with you?"

"No, Josh. And don't let's mention him after tonight."

"And Daniel . . . ?"

"He's here on the ship with me—with us. Come down to my cabin and see him. I have a lovely cabin, Josh. Theophilus Strike got it for me."

"Strike? What has he to do with you being here? Miriam, will you please tell me what's happening?"

She laughed happily. "I'll tell you the whole story when we get below."

Her cabin, though not large, was very comfortable. It had two bunks, on the smaller of which Daniel lay sleeping. Miriam took off her cloak and began to explain her presence on the ship.

"I was at your trial," she began.

"I know. I heard you," Josh smiled.

"Mr. Strike heard me too. I was thrown out onto the street by the soldiers and he came outside to find me. He'd recognized me as Morwen's sister, he said, and had heard I was Preacher Thackeray's wife. In view of this he couldn't understand why I should be standing up in court shouting your innocence. I told him what I believed had happened, that William and Morwen had arranged for you to become involved in whatever happened at Looe. He was very interested. He said he would cause inquiries to be made. Then he took me home to St. Cleer in his coach.

"William saw me alighting from the coach and demanded to know what I was doing with Theophilus Strike. I told him exactly what I had told Mr. Strike."

"Wasn't that a foolish thing to do?"

Miriam shrugged. "I was so angry it didn't matter. But William was so frightened he struck me. It was the first and last time. The next morning I took Daniel to Henwood to my mother's."

"But that doesn't explain how you came to be here. . . ."

"Patience, Josh. Theophilus Strike wasn't able to obtain any further evidence and asked your father to tell me this. Incidentally, both your father and mother know I'm here with you."

"And they approve?"

"I think they were deeply shocked at first, but the day before I left Henwood your mother came to see me. She asked me to give you the love and blessing of both of them. She said she'd be happy knowing you would have me to look after you."

"Poor Mother. But. . . ."

"I know—the story of why I'm here. . . . Two weeks ago Mr. Strike came down to the village to speak to me again. He wanted to know what I intended doing with my future. He asked me a great many very personal questions. Then he told me the great news. He said William Carlyon had received an order for mine engines from a man who had discovered copper ore in Australia. And the man not only wanted the engines but also a good engineer.

"At once Mr. Strike journeyed to London. When he returned he had a letter which said you could go to Australia and work the engines, providing your fare was paid in advance, which he did immediately. I think he must have some very important friends."

"Thank you. That explains why I am here! But I'm still no wiser about you being here too."

"Well," said Miriam, "among the questions that Mr. Strike asked me was why I was so concerned about you. I told him."

"You told him what?"

"I told him I loved you. That I'd always loved you and that I only married William because in some horribly confused way it seemed that I was being loyal to my father.

"He asked me whether I believed it possible for you and me to make a new life together if we had the opportunity. I told him 'Yes'. That was all. He arranged for me to come as a passenger on this ship."

"If I live to be a thousand I'll never be able to repay Theophilus Strike for all he's done for me," said Josh.

Miriam's answer was to cling to him fiercely. "We can start our new lives from now, can't we, Josh? I have a lot of money here for you. Mr. Strike said it's royalties on the patent of one of your inventions."

"He's a good man," said Josh. He suddenly held Miriam away from him. "But what about Daniel?"

"What about him, Josh? He's still little more than a baby. *You* are his father. You've known that all along."

She looked at him with tears of happiness on her face. "My passage was booked on this ship in the name of Mrs. Retallick. We have our son Daniel Retallick with us and are heading for a new life together."

"You mustn't forget I'm still a convict, Miriam."

She waved his words aside. "Only in name. When we get there you'll find that Theophilus Strike has sorted everything out for you. You'll start work as an engineer. In a short time everybody will have forgotten you were ever a convict."

Slipping away from him she took down a small tin box from a shelf by her bunk. Opening it she took out a piece of crumpled paper which she smoothed out and gave to him.

"Do you remember the day you wrote this for me?"

Written on the paper in a childish handwriting was a single word, "Miriam".

He nodded. "I remember. You made me write it so you could copy it. Then you persuaded me to teach you to read and write."

Miriam took the paper from him and looked at it with as much pleasure as she had shown on that moorland day when they were children.

"But now," she said, "you have something far more important to teach me. You have to teach me how to live, to be a complete person again. Will you do that, Josh?"

"I can only teach you the things I know myself, Miriam." He trembled a little as he drew her, soft and yielding, to him.

"We'll both have to learn about them together."

E V Thompson

If a wide experience of life is essential raw material for a novelist, then Ernest Thompson is unusually well equipped for what promises to be a brilliant future.

He left school at the age of fifteen to join the Royal Navy and saw action in the Korean War. After nine years he joined the Bristol police force, where he was a founder member of that city's "vice squad", and later experience included security service for BOAC in Hongkong and in Rhodesia's Department of Civil Aviation.

When he returned to England he bought an ancient motor-cycle and set off for Cornwall to be a full-time writer. A year later, broke but still writing, he swept the floors at a clayworks, then went to London to be a hotel detective.

But he missed the Cornish countryside, so he bought a derelict copper-miner's cottage in the village he describes in *Chase the Wind* and found a job not far away in Plymouth Dockyard. His cottage is shared by his wife—and also by four dogs, two cats, ducks, chickens and goldfish. Evenings and weekends are spent writing, roaming Bodmin Moor, discovering old mine shafts and deserted engine-houses and tracing the history of the Moor.

Chase the Wind is E. V. Thompson's first novel, and it won first prize, out of over two hundred entries, in a competition sponsored by British and American publishers for the best historical novel of the year.

The Badgers
of Summercombe

A condensation of the book by
EWAN CLARKSON

Illustrated by Edward Mortelmans
Published by Hutchinson, London

The badgers are a proud and ancient race. Mysterious, stubborn, fearless, for centuries they have withstood every assault on their underground sets and the territory surrounding them. Badgers are surely the supreme survivors— or at least they were until man became impatient for more land, and posed yet another threat to them.

Ewan Clarkson, whose books on seals and falcons have delighted us in the past, traces here the story of one such badger, Borun, heir to the fortress of Summercombe. With a wealth of fascinating nature lore, Clarkson describes Borun's adventures—his battles, his strange wanderings, his even stranger friendships in the wild—and how his fate becomes intimately involved with that of Polly Shaw, the solitary owner of the cottage in the wood. Their interests—and their enemies —are the same. Their story is a dramatic, deeply moving plea for a quieter, simpler way of life.

TOBAR

It was raining again. Tobar lay just inside the entrance of the hole beneath the tree, listening to the drip of moisture from the leafless branches, sniffing the warm, damp wind that swept in from the Atlantic Ocean. Somewhere a blackbird sang a throaty serenade to this, the false promise of spring, for although the February days were lengthening, and the sun held a soft warmth, winter could still return, locking the land in frost and blanketing the fields with drifting snow.

Two days previously his mate, Mela, had retired to a small isolated corner of the badgers' underground home. Here, on a bed of dried fern and shrivelled oak leaves, she had given birth to her cubs. As yet Tobar had not been permitted to share the joys of parenthood with her, but this was a familiar pattern in Tobar's life, for he was old and had seen many litters raised by his mate.

He was old and he was lean, for the long months of winter had taken their toll. But he still weighed over thirty pounds, and his yard-long body, built for strength rather than speed, was in no way weakened by the ordeal of winter.

Now, as daylight faded and the blackbird settled to roost, he emerged into the open, his nose still questing the air and his ears alert for any hint of danger. Once satisfied that all was well, he set off at a brisk trot, down through the wood towards the valley.

Halfway down the hillside the woodland ended abruptly, to give way to a network of small fields, each bounded by a thick hedgerow and a ditch. These ditches were a favourite hunting ground for Tobar. He shuffled slowly along, his questing snout finding earthworms, an odd acorn overlooked by the pigeons the previous autumn, and now and again the sweet bulbs of bluebells, already putting forth green shoots. These Tobar dug from the moist earth with his powerful forelegs, and crunched with noisy gusto before moving on towards his main objective which lay in a field some distance away.

The previous year the farmer had planted potatoes in this field, and Tobar had developed a liking for the sweet white tubers. Now, although the crop had been lifted and the field prepared for resowing, many potatoes still remained, either on the surface or buried only a few inches deep.

Unfortunately the field lay on the other side of a road. Once this road had carried little traffic other than that belonging to the local people. Then a new motorway was built a few miles to the north, and what had once been a quiet country lane became an access road on which traffic flowed in an almost unceasing stream.

Tobar hesitated a long while before he crossed the road. The roar of the traffic bewildered him, and the glare of headlights, to eyes little accustomed to anything brighter than the dimness of the woodlands, was painful in the extreme. Nevertheless he persisted, loitering on the verge of the road and waiting for a lull in the traffic. Even when it came, Tobar could still hear the deep roar of a heavy lorry climbing the hill in the distance, but it seemed a long way away. He did not know, as he set off across the road, that a fast sports car was coming down the hill.

It accelerated round the bend as he reached the centre of the road, seeming to pin him to the ground with the twin beams of its headlights. Instinctively he turned away from the glare and began running down the road, straight into the path of the oncoming lorry. For a brief moment the world was ablaze with blinding light and filled with the thunderous clamour of the diesel engine. Then he felt a heavy blow across his back, and there was nothing but a dark, empty void.

314

THE HEIR TO SUMMERCOMBE

Five hundred years before the birth of Christ, a band of savage and warlike people from the marshlands of Somerset had come north to the valley of Summercombe, carrying weapons and implements of iron and driving before them flocks of sheep, goats and scrawny cattle. Here they found well-drained, fertile land on which they could graze their herds and grow their meagre crops. Above this gentle, sun-warmed valley towered a weather-worn outcrop of limestone rock, and here, close by a spring, they built their fort, a sturdy structure of timber and stone surrounded by a wall and ditch.

Below, on the wooded slopes of the hill, where the rocks lay so close to the surface that their craggy heads were exposed, was another stronghold, old before the coming of men, so old that its origins are lost in the unwritten annals of prehistoric time—a labyrinth of tunnels dug deep into the hollow of the hillside by the badgers of Summercombe.

The iron men are gone now and their passing was so long ago that of their existence there is now barely a trace. Yet in the stronghold under the earth, life remains the same. The badgers have kept to the old ways, the ways that have served them well, that serve them still.

Here, deep in the darkness of the hill, Mela the sow badger groomed her solitary cub. Originally she had given birth to three cubs, but one had failed to draw breath and another had a heart deformity and had slipped into a coma from which there was no awakening. As soon as their bodies had grown cold, Mela had eaten them, clearing away their remains in the same fastidious manner she had disposed of the afterbirths. Without their soft, squirming embrace to invoke mother love they were of no interest to her. Instead, she concentrated on the living.

This third cub, Borun, was about four and a half inches long when he was born and weighed three ounces. His short fur was a dirty white and as yet the prominent black stripes of his face were but faintly etched. Blind and toothless, he was totally dependent

315

on his mother, but since he was now assured of a more than ample supply of nourishment he showed promise of becoming an exceptionally robust boar.

As Mela washed his plump, wriggling body with long strokes of her smooth, pink tongue, she began to grow increasingly uneasy. The day was well advanced and she felt sure that her mate had not returned. She should have heard his purring call of greeting as he passed by the nesting chamber on his way to his own quarters. She was at a loss to understand his absence. Shortly before dusk fell, she slipped out of the nursery, leaving Borun lost to the world in a warm milky slumber.

The evening was fine, but a cold wind from the north sent ragged black clouds racing over the crest of the hill, and the upper branches of the trees sighed and groaned. Mela stood in an amphitheatre of bare, trodden earth. Above her were the dark openings of her citadel. The badgers made no attempt to disguise the whereabouts of their set, as it was called. Seven holes were visible, some so small that it did not seem possible that a badger could squeeze down them, others so large that it would be quite possible for a grown man to crawl inside. At the entrance to each a great mound of earth bore testimony to the mining activities that had taken place inside the hill. Over the years the badgers had excavated hundreds of tons of earth and small stones, and indeed the arena in which Mela stood was paved with yellow sandy subsoil, some of it dug out centuries ago.

Mela went straight to an entrance beneath a great oak tree where she and Tobar had last shared quarters before the birth of her cubs. Passing between the oak's roots, she followed the tunnel with the assurance of long familiarity, now dipping down, now squeezing flat to pass beneath a mighty rock whose base formed the roof of the tunnel. Thus she came to the sleeping chamber, but the bedding was cold, and the scent of her mate was stale on the crushed bracken.

She moved on exploring the whole set. It took her a long time, and at the end of her search she remained disquieted.

Meantime she was aware of other needs. She was both hungry and thirsty and it was now quite dark. First, however, she visited

316

the latrine, a series of small open pits screened by elder thickets in a part of the woodland the badgers had set aside for this purpose. Then she moved off through the wood, following a wide, well-worn track that led to where a small spring bubbled out from beneath a limestone outcrop. Here she drank deep.

The wind was rising now and stray gusts tugged at the trees, ruffling the hair on Mela's back as she moved out of the woods and into the fields. The wind, and the light of the moon as it shone fitfully through the scudding clouds, had a curious effect on the badger's appearance. One moment she looked dark, almost black, and the next she appeared to be as white as her newborn cub.

The explanation lay in the colouring of her hair. Each long hair on her back and flanks was white at the tip, the middle was dark brown, almost black, and the lower third, to the root, was again white. So, as the wind disarranged the even lay of her hair, she seemed to change colour.

Almost at once she was lucky in her foraging. A mole, burrowing among the grass roots in search of earthworms, came so close to the surface that it made the ground heave. Instantly Mela pounced, tearing at the turf to expose the tunnel and thrusting her long snout into the cold, damp earth.

She devoured her victim completely, skin, fur and bones, even the tough, spadelike forefeet. Then she moved on, not daring to linger lest she should leave her cub unprotected for too long, although there was little danger from other predators. Stoats and weasels had too much respect for their cousin the badger, and even a fox was unlikely to venture into the set as long as her scent was fresh around the entrance. The chief danger to Borun was that of chilling, for he was not yet old enough or active enough to keep himself warm.

She snatched a few mouthfuls of grass, and behind the bark of a rotting tree stump she discovered a colony of hibernating snails. Her hunger satisfied, she hurried back to the set. The cloud had thickened, and flurries of snow were beginning to fall.

Borun woke as she entered the chamber and burrowed blindly to her side, thrusting his nose at her flank and kneading her with eager paws. Relaxing, she fell into a half doze, while outside the snow continued to fall, drifting in the strong northerly wind.

It snowed all night and for most of the following day, but by nightfall the blizzard had passed. The wind died, and the moon shone over a white and silent world. Mela emerged briefly, but finding she was still alone, returned to the warmth of the nursery. At times like these there was nothing to do but sleep and conserve energy. Although the reserves of fat she had accumulated the previous autumn were now dwindling, she could readily draw upon them for a few days without suffering any inconvenience.

For three days and nights the frost held. In the bright moonlight the rabbits emerged from their burrows, to flounder through the snow and gnaw the bark of young hazel shoots. Some died, caught in the jaws of the lean red foxes that lay in ambush among the snowdrifts. Beneath the snow, through the maze of passageways between the stems and roots of the rough herbage, weasels harried the mice and voles, while the white owl floated in vain over the fields and was eventually forced to compete with the farmyard cats around the rickyards, where rats and mice robbed the farmer of his grain.

Then the wind rose again, this time from the south, blowing wet and warm and bringing rain to wash the snow away. For two days life was a shivering, sodden misery to the small creatures of the grasslands, who woke to find their homes and highways flooded with icy water. Then the sun shone, the blackbird sang and the tide of spring flowed once more.

Snug in the confines of the set, Borun continued to thrive. His eyes opened on the eleventh day, and at a month old he was exploring the confines of the nursery. His mother left him on most evenings now, but never for long periods. As he grew older and stronger he spent hours playing with her, tugging at her hair and trying to nip her with his baby teeth. Mela bore the torment with good humour, seeming to realize that the exercise was vital for his development.

He got his first glimpse of the outside world on a fine warm evening in the middle of April. On several occasions already he had left the nursery and crept hesitantly along the tunnel, but each time his nerve had then failed him and he had scuttled back

318

to the safety of the nest. On this night, however, his mother nosed him gently out of the chamber and along the tunnel. So he emerged, to sniff the sweet-scented air of spring and to sit trembling with mingled fear and excitement, secure between the stout forelegs of his mother. Mela was equally nervous and after about ten minutes she drove him underground. But the next night he stayed out longer and made several short exploratory dashes around the mouth of the set, while Mela growled a warning only if in her opinion he strayed too far.

She had now long since ceased to look for her mate. But once, as she was crossing the dew-drenched valley in the grey light of an April dawn, she heard the distinctive pad of feet that heralded the approach of another badger, and she stopped still, whickering a call of greeting, for she was sure that it was Tobar. Then she realized her error. The badger was a stranger, and he stood aloof, respecting her sex and her right to be present, but offering no friendship. After a moment she moved on, and the young boar, a bachelor, returned to his own set, which he had dug in an old rabbit warren on the other side of the valley.

IN THE WEEKS that followed, as spring matured into full-leafed summer, Borun grew in strength, stature and wisdom. Each evening as the sun set and the last light of day lingered beneath the trees, he emerged from the stuffy confines of the set, a small, snub-nosed replica of his mother, to breathe air fragrant with the perfume of green growth. The sharp smells intoxicated him, and his pent-up energy exploded in a wild capering romp, a headlong gallop around the area, up and down the worn paths, in and out of the bushes, until at last he collapsed at his mother's side.

During this outburst Mela was content to relax, lying stretched out in the cool evening air. Then, when the first wave of exuberance had passed and Borun had sobered down a little, the serious business of his education could begin.

She led him along the ancient badger highways that criss-crossed the wooded hillside, taught him to use the latrine, and showed him the spring. She encouraged him to rip bark from rotten tree stumps in search of beetles and woodlice, and showed him where the bank voles built their nests. He learned to dig for bluebell bulbs, to locate the fat white cockchafer grubs among the grass roots, to stalk earthworms as they glinted in the starlight on the short, sheep-bitten turf of the pastures, snapping them up before they had time to withdraw into their burrows. Best of all, she taught him how to find young rabbits.

Rabbits swarmed everywhere in the valley, honeycombing the banks with their burrows and robbing the farmer of his grass, five rabbits consuming enough to feed a sheep. Some years previously they had been virtually wiped out by myxomatosis, a virus disease artificially introduced into Britain, but a few individuals remained immune, and from these survivors the rabbits began once again to populate the land. Since in favourable conditions a rabbit doe could produce a litter of five or six young every month from January to June, their numbers were soon restored.

Before the arrival of her litter, each doe rabbit dug a short, blind burrow on the edge of the warren, scooping out a nest and lining it with fur plucked from her own breast. If she left the burrow for any reason, she would block the entrance against marauders. Many of these nest chambers lay close to the surface of the soil, and Mela taught Borun to listen for the muffled squeaking of the young. Whenever they located such a nest, Mela dug down, tearing away the turf with her powerful claws and scratching away the soil until she broke through into the nest chamber. Intensely excited, Borun tried hard to help with the digging. He was as yet more of a hindrance than a help, but his small forelegs grew stronger as the weeks passed.

The badgers were true opportunity feeders, ready to sample anything that came within reach of their questing snouts. From time to time they came upon birds' nests containing eggs or young, and these they ate, as they did snakes and frogs when they were to be found. This caused Borun to make a tactical error when one night he caught a toad between his jaws. The secretions from the toad's warty skin burned his gums and tongue and caused him to shake his head in anger. The toad crawled safely away and thereafter Borun was careful to avoid his like.

On another occasion Borun made a more serious mistake when

he happened on a nest of leverets. Borun did not know that while a mother rabbit might flee in terror, an angry mother hare was made of sterner stuff. As Borun ran at the leverets, he was knocked sideways by a resounding blow across the ear. Even as he tried to recover he was kicked again and again, and if his mother had not come to his rescue by distracting the hare he might have suffered serious injury.

By preying on the rabbits and the voracious cockchafer grubs that ate the grass roots and sometimes swarmed in such numbers as to destroy whole fields, the badgers were unwittingly helping the farmers. Yet because they went about their affairs in secret and at night, their efforts went largely unnoticed. More evident was the occasional damage they inflicted, as when they wrecked a hedge bank in pursuit of rabbits, or flattened cereal crops. Both Mela and Borun savoured the sweet milky grains of young wheat and oats, and Borun could never resist romping and rolling through the stalks. His high spirits sometimes infected Mela, so that she played with him. Between them they could flatten quite a large area in a very short time. The loss to the farmer was not serious, but it was irritating and gave the badgers a bad name.

For much of the time, however, the badgers limited their foraging to the wood. From a distance the wood looked like a cloak, flung carelessly across the shoulder of the hill, extending for about a mile. In places it was perhaps a quarter mile deep, a tiny remnant of the vast deciduous forests that had spread across southern England following the retreat of the last ice age. It had survived because the slopes of the hill were too precipitous and rock-strewn to make it worth while attempting to clear the land for pasture, and until comparatively recent times woodland was an important asset to any estate. Wood was needed for a multitude of purposes, from faggots for kitchen stoves to charcoal for blast furnaces, from floorboards to farm wagons, from tool handles to chairs, tables and beds. Oak and ash were highly prized for their straight-grained, strong timber and good burning properties and the smooth, straight rods of hazelwood were made into hurdles to give shelter to the sheep at lambing time. So dead wood was cleared away and scrub cut down to give light and air to the more valuable trees. In the autumn herds of pigs were allowed to graze through the woodlands, to grow fat on the acorns and to fertilize the ground with their droppings.

Then came a period when the woods were allowed to fall into disuse. The trees grew all awry, so close together that in competing for light they outgrew their roots and fell one against the other. Beneath them flourished thickets of nettle and elder and a jungle of twisted brambles, from which sprang the climbing tendrils of honeysuckle and ivy.

The rich moist leafmould of the woodland floor supported a host of flowering plants. First to flower were the tiny wood anemones, spilled like drops of congealed moonlight around the trunks of the trees. Then came massed banks of purple violets, and primroses like pale yellow stars. In May, as the cuckoo called and the swifts flew screaming over the meadows, the sunlit glades glowed with the blue haze of the bluebells, their bell-shaped blossoms giving off a perfume so strong as to mask all others. In high summer the tangle of bracken and briar was so tall that only the rosebay willow herb could tower above it, but the woods were sweet with the scent of the climbing honeysuckle and dog rose.

Unwanted and ignored by man, the damp leafmould, the yeasts and fungi, the flowers and plants, the bees, wasps and other insects, the mice and voles, the squirrels and birds and bats, all were so conjoined and interwoven as to become as one. And in the warm, heady stillness of a summer night their energy could be felt as a soft, low vibration that was the pulse of the living earth.

The badgers were part of the pattern of woodland life. If at times it seemed that they were dedicated to a lifetime of demolition, as when they tore open a vole's nest, or wrecked a rotting tree stump in search of grubs, this was illusion. Such behaviour, wanton and wasteful though it might seem, assisted in the recycling of the elements of nature, so that life, in all its bewildering complexity, could be reborn, fresh and new, over and over again.

One day in June, when the badgers ventured farther afield, Borun was startled to see his mother attacking the top of an earth bank in a high state of excitement. The coarse hair on her back stood out at right angles, making her appear twice as large as normal, and as she dug she gave vent to a series of high-pitched grunts and squeals. A small flock of sheep stood bunched together watching as she sent showers of earth and large stones thudding down into their field. Borun clambered up to join her, but she ignored him, and since he could see nothing that could justify the expenditure of such energy he grew bored and wandered away.

The bank had been built almost a century ago, of stones loosely piled together, packed with soil, and thatched with turf. Thus secured, it had withstood the ravages of wind and rain for season after season, but it could not long withstand an assault by a badger. When Borun returned the bank was down, the lane partly blocked by rocks and soil, and Mela had uncovered her prize.

It was a large ball made from some papery brown substance, and several black and yellow insects buzzed around it in a sleepy, stupefied fashion. Mela broke open the ball, to reveal row after row of fat white grubs, and once Borun had tasted them, he understood why Mela had gone to so much trouble to unearth them, for to a badger there is no greater delicacy on earth than a wasps' nest.

The badgers finished their feast, and after rooting about for any grub they might have overlooked, they moved off into the night. An hour later the sheep, led by an old ewe, filed out of the field through the gap dug by Mela, and made off down the lane.

FOR MR. FLETCHER of Bidewell Farm, that day started as on any other morning. Quite unaware that he had suffered any loss, he went about his routine tasks, tending to his pigs and milking his small herd of Friesian cows. So it was not until after breakfast that he took his stick and walked up the lane that led to the valley.

Two miles away, old Miss Ponsonby paused in the act of dressing to glance out of her bedroom window. With a shriek of dismay she hurried downstairs to the kitchen, seized a broom and charged out the back door and into the vegetable garden, where a small flock of sheep were browsing contentedly on her lettuces. She was an energetic old lady, and the sheep, panicking under the fury of her onslaught, scurried bleating out onto the road. Miss

Ponsonby firmly latched the gate, and then, since she was not yet properly attired to appear in public, she hastened back indoors.

At that moment the owner of the sheep was staring with horror at their empty field. The flock which was missing was a very special one. They were Ryelands, very hardy and resistant to disease, producing high-quality meat and yielding heavy fleeces of soft fine wool. With them the farmer hoped not only to make a handsome profit, but to gain prestige by exhibiting them at the various agricultural shows. Now he had lost them.

At first he thought he had been the victim of sheep rustlers, but then he found the gap in the hedge. For a moment his feeling was one of relief that the sheep had only strayed, but then he found the remains of the wasps' nest and his anger grew as he recognized the identity of the culprit. Hurrying back to the farm, he flung open the door. "The Ryelands have gone," he shouted. "Broken out of the field—heaven knows where they are now."

Mrs. Fletcher appeared from the kitchen, drying her hands on her apron. She had never approved of her husband's obsession with Ryelands. "If you want to keep your fancy sheep, you need to spend more time with your fences," she remarked tartly. "They're a disgrace."

Fletcher's eyes bulged and his neck reddened. He was a big man, normally placid and easygoing, but at times like this rage made him inarticulate. He found his tongue at last. "It was a badger, you stupid woman. A badger broke the bank. I'll have him directly. In fact, I'll kill every badger in the county."

Just then the telephone rang. Mrs. Fletcher picked up the receiver, and then called to her husband. "It's for you. Seems Miss Ponsonby has found your sheep."

In two strides Fletcher was at the telephone. "Where are they?" he snapped.

"Why, down in the village by now," replied Miss Ponsonby. "I was . . ." She was left talking to herself. Fletcher was racing for his Land-Rover.

He ran his sheep to ground in the churchyard, grazing placidly among the tombstones and stubbornly resisting the somewhat half-hearted efforts of the verger to drive them out.

On his way back to the farm with them Fletcher had a painful interview with Miss Ponsonby, who had been lying in wait. It was a depressed and weary man who finally penned his sheep securely in a field close by the farmhouse.

It took him the greater part of a day to repair the damage done by Mela to the earth bank, a day of hard labour under the hot sun. He then took time off to visit the ironmongers in town.

THE WEATHER continued hot and dry, with little or no dew at night. The pastures became arid and brown, and the earthworms lay deep in their burrows, tightly coiled to conserve moisture.

These days Borun and Mela emerged from the set in full daylight to forage through the wood. In spite of the drought, the badgers continued to feed well. Nests of young rabbits were still plentiful. There were fat brown cockchafers that droned through the air in clumsy, laborious flight and pitched on the ground with an audible thump that never failed to attract the badgers' attention. And always there were mice and voles. Left to themselves the voles alone would destroy the world. There could be as many as five hundred of them to the acre in neglected grassland, and if such a heavy population grew unchecked it would have consumed more than ten tons of vegetable matter per year, more than the most fertile acre could produce.

The vole population was now at its peak. Every female was pregnant, each was raising a litter of five or six young. In three weeks' time she would have weaned that litter and be giving birth again, while the survivors of her first brood, if any, would be fast approaching maturity. Fortunately, few voles lived longer than six months, and not one in a thousand survived for more than a year. The remainder got eaten by foxes, cats, stoats, weasels, hawks, crows, owls, herons, jays and badgers. Grass snakes and adders took them from their nests, and even the fat old toad took an occasional infant if it ventured too close. It was as though some supreme intelligence had processed the vole as a prepackaged survival ration, not too big or too small, containing all the essential ingredients, blood, bone, fur, and meat, in an easily available form. As a final touch of genius, it was ordained that the supply would be available for twenty-four hours a day, for the vole divided each day into two-hour periods of activity, with short rests in between.

With such a surfeit of food, Borun developed rapidly. He was now almost half grown and quite able to forage for himself, but badgers are sociable animals, so mother and son continued to keep each other company. Gradually, however, a change was coming over Mela. She felt irritable and frustrated, frequently impatient of Borun's demands to share whatever food she found. Quarrels were frequent, and on occasions Borun got sharply nipped for importuning too persistently. In short, Mela needed a mate, for now was the honeymoon season of the badgers.

The fine spell ended at last, with low cloud obscuring the moon and a thin drizzle soaking gently into the dry earth. The earthworms, sensing the presence of moisture, climbed up their burrows to emerge into the night, and Borun and Mela fed well, for once without quarrelling over the spoils.

Maybe it was her pleasure over the feast of earthworms, or maybe it was the pent-up desires smouldering within her that made Mela careless. She ran down the hill, pushed through a gap in the hedge and started to slide down the bank. Next moment she was held tight by the constricting wire of a snare, set none too expertly by Fletcher a week ago, which gripped her around the waist. She hung head down, screaming with rage and pain, while Borun whimpered anxiously behind her.

The noose had been set too wide, or it would have caught her around the neck, strangling her as she fell. As it was, she was still alive, but trapped. She managed to claw herself around and pull herself back onto the hedge bank, where she began to bite and tug at the roots and branches around her. She dug and fought and tore until her pads were broken and her claws torn, her gums bleeding and raw, but to no avail. The farmer had fastened the snare to the root of a gnarled old hawthorn, thicker than a man's arm, and so tough and strong that it would have held a bear.

Towards dawn she ceased to struggle and lay exhausted, her coat matted with sticky earth and blood. Borun had tried to help by attempting to bite through the wire, but it had foiled every attempt to cut it. Now as he approached her she screamed and snapped at him, half mad with fear, and so at last he went and crouched down some distance away, afraid of her in her rage. Still he lingered, long into the grey daylight, while Mela lay amid the wreckage of the hedge she had demolished in her struggles.

Footsteps alerted Borun. They drew nearer. His frayed nerves failed him and he bolted. As he reached the sanctuary of the woods he was deafened by the blast of a shotgun.

Borun remained in the set throughout the day and for most of the following night, emerging just before dawn and creeping fearfully, almost unwillingly, to the site where he had left his mother. The bank had been repaired and the gap plugged with a bush of thorn, but Mela's body still lay in the ditch where Fletcher had thrown it. Borun approached cautiously, the hairs on his spine erect. He called, a low, hesitant greeting, but there was no response. Then he drew nearer, and sniffed around her corpse. Recognizing the smell of death, he turned away and finally made his way slowly back into the woods. Ever after, he avoided going near the place.

Gradually, in the days that followed, he began to forget about her, but often in the evenings he would wander disconsolately about the set, pausing at each entrance in turn, listening, but hearing nothing but the silence of the hollow hill. At length he would turn away, padding down the worn trail to start another lonely night's foraging.

STRANGE COMPANY

Over the years Summercombe Cottage seemed to have settled cosily into the side of the hill at the very verge of Summercombe Wood, so that now the thatch, green with moss, merged with the canopy of the trees, and the weather-worn stone of the walls exactly matched the hue of the yellow sandy soil. Tendrils of ivy, which had sent their suckerlike roots deep into the crevices between the stones, further obscured its outline, so that from across the valley the cottage was barely visible, except when a thin grey column of smoke rose from the chimney.

All day the sun had shone down on the garden, warming the rich, moist soil so that the ranks of vegetables, the peas and carrots and cabbages, the green-leaved lettuces, and the golden bulbs of the onions, seemed to swell visibly by the hour. Now the sun was westering. As it passed behind the cottage, just before it slid beneath the crest of the hill, its rays penetrated a small casement window and a beam of soft rosy light fell upon the sleeping form of a white cat, curled at the foot of the bed in the spare bedroom.

In response to the sun's caress, an ear twitched, the cat raised his head, opened his eyes, and yawned. Then he lay still as his senses alerted him to the pattern of his surroundings.

Almost at once he realized that something was wrong. There should have been the rich smell of cooking, but only the stale smells of yesterday lingered on the air. There should have been a scattering of tiny sounds, all significant, all related to the time of day. There was nothing, only the ticking of the clock in the living room, the faint creaking of timbers as the house cooled after the heat of the day, and an intermittent rustling in the roof as the bats beneath the thatch began to wake from their daytime sleep.

For a short while the cat, whose name was Vandal, remained on the bed, hoping at least to hear his favourite sounds, the rattle of a saucer and the rhythmic scrape of a tin-opener, sure signs that a meal was ready. Vandal waited in vain and eventually he slid off the bed, stretched, and made his cautious way downstairs.

The living room and the kitchen were deserted. The ashes of the fire were cold in the hearth, and the breakfast table lay uncleared. Vandal turned, and went back upstairs, to pause and scratch at the closed door on the landing. In the past this act had always evoked a response. This evening it brought nothing.

Vandal returned to the kitchen. The situation was not entirely novel to him. In the past he had been left alone on several occasions, but each time there had been food left out for him, and milk in a saucer under the table. This time there were only the stale remains of his breakfast, which after sniffing tentatively for a while he rejected, performing a ritual burial act with his paw on the tiled floor surrounding the plate.

Then he left the house through the cat-flap. Outside the air was cool and fresh, and heavy with the scent of elder flower and honeysuckle. Vandal sat for a while watching the chickens, which, having heard the rattle of the cat-flap, had crowded in eager anticipation around the door of the hen run. All day they had scratched without reward at the bare earth of the run, seeking for some overlooked scrap of food. Now with empty crops they crooned hopefully, gazing with bright eyes towards the house.

Vandal lingered, enjoying the familiarity of their presence. He was just over half grown, and at an age when he still desired company, had not yet fully acquired the self-sufficiency that marked his kind. In his memory lurked images of an ample lap clad in rough tweed, a billowing satin bosom, and an endearing voice that used to croon to him as he lay, full fed and half asleep, in front of the flickering light and warmth of the fire.

Without the reassurance of such a presence, he felt insecure. So he sat on, in the company of the fowls, until darkness fell and one by one the hens went to roost in the fusty darkness of their coop. Then, reluctantly, he moved away in search of supper.

He leapt onto the loose stone wall and dropped down into a clearing in the fern, and at once the mystery of the night surrounded and captivated him, so that he forgot his earlier unease. The air was filled with soft, furtive sounds, a rustle in the dry leaves, a flurry of movement in the honeysuckle vines, a crashing far off. He moved cautiously but confidently along the badger track, a predator alone in a world in which he was superbly equipped to survive.

He killed quickly and fed, his prey a short-tailed vole, not bulky enough to induce in him the lethargy that followed gorging to capacity. So he moved on and surprised yet another vole as she scurried towards her nest of dried grass. This time he played with his victim, tossing her in the air and allowing her to crawl a few feet towards sanctuary before clawing her back and patting her, soft-footed until at last she died of fear. When at last he was convinced that she would run no more, Vandal ate her. Then, aroused by the squeaking that emanated from the nearby nest, he clawed out and ate her young.

So the night passed, but with the coming of the dawn Vandal was once more drawn towards the comfort and safety of the cottage. He retraced his steps in the direction of the house and had almost reached the wall when, rounding a bend in the path, he came face to face with Borun the badger cub.

The cat froze, and so did the badger. They stood in the moonlight, immobile, each waiting for the other to move first. For perhaps half a minute neither animal flinched, and then Borun sank down on one haunch, and scratched himself vigorously with his hindclaws. Even to Vandal it was clear that this gesture could in no way appear aggressive. In token of acknowledgment he licked the inside of his forepaw, and then groomed his chest. Then he sat down and waited for the badger's next move.

Borun nodded his head several times, peering at the cat with myopic eyes, and then advanced. As he drew nearer Vandal's nerve slowly began to crack, until at last he stood up, ready to flee or attack. Then Borun moved to one side, and, as Vandal circled to keep facing him, the cub passed him by, and rejoining the track trundled slowly out of view.

Five minutes later the cat was back in the spare bedroom where, after a prolonged and vigorous grooming session, he fell asleep. From time to time his body twitched as he dreamed about badgers and the voles that scurried and squeaked in the silver-splashed shadows of the moonlit wood.

He woke suddenly to the sound of vehicles being driven slowly up the track that led to the cottage. He heard the slamming of car doors, footsteps, and a hubbub of alien voices, and then he fled, out of the cottage and into the sanctuary of the woodshed where he crouched behind a pile of logs. He waited a long while, and although he was tempted to creep out and make acquaintance with these humans, fear held him back.

Outside the front door of the cottage, the village policeman stood talking to the doctor, as attendants bore a white-shrouded burden to the waiting ambulance. "It was the postman who reported it. He noticed that a package he'd delivered yesterday was still wedged in the letter box. Seems the old girl got up as usual, fed the cat and had breakfast, and then felt unwell and went back to bed."

The doctor nodded absently. He was late for his surgery and anxious to be away. "There's a brother, I believe?"

"That's right," nodded the policeman. "He lives down in the village. I'll call round and see him directly. Someone will have to see to the hens and so forth. I expect the cat's about somewhere too."

"Probably he's taken to the woods by now," said the doctor. "At least there's plenty of food about for him. The rabbits seem to have come back thicker than ever since the myxomatosis."

One by one the vehicles departed, and once again the silence of the summer day hung heavily over the deserted cottage. Gradually the stuffy heat of the woodshed grew unbearable, and at last Vandal crept out. This time, however, he did not return to the bedroom, but sought the leafy green shade of the woods. So he did not hear the arrival of the old man who fed the hens and the rabbit. Nor did he know that on the tiled floor of the kitchen were a saucer of fresh milk and a plate of cat food.

THE LONG SUMMER DAY was well advanced when Vandal next woke. For a while he lay still, couched on a bed of dried leaves that filled the hollow of an old ash stump, listening as the sounds of the day gave way to those of the night. Somewhere the distant drone of a tractor coughed and died, and a dog barked briefly in the silence. The thin, dry bleat of a half-grown lamb scraped across the evening air, and as if in answer a crow called, once, twice, as he winged his solitary way across the wood.

In response the woodland came alive with movement. Bats began to flicker black-winged between the tree trunks, and from the undergrowth came a brief patter of feet, a scuffle and a muffled squeak as two mice fought a lilliputian duel, their tiny tempers white hot with rage. The nightjar detached himself from his roost on the bare branch of an oak and flew off to circle the cattle that grazed in the meadow, hawking for the flies that swarmed around the beasts. The woodcock in the fern opened her eyes and flopped away, ghost-like among the trees, to probe for worms in the marshland at the bottom of the valley.

Vandal slipped from his perch and padded off through the shadows. A dormouse shredding bark from the honeysuckle vine for her nest saw him as he passed beneath her, and whisked her tail as she fled upward into the high branches. A bank vole caught his scent and froze in the shelter of a fallen branch. A young rabbit feeding among the ferns was not so alert. Vandal sprang, and there was a brief flurry of movement, a flash of white fur, and the next moment Vandal was dragging his limp prey into the shelter of the bushes.

Half an hour later the cat lay sprawled, rather more than comfortably full and disinclined to action of any kind until his supper had settled somewhat. Then he got up, to prowl aimlessly through the wood. Thoughts of the comfortable bed in the cottage lured him to return. Yet he could not forget his unease at the empty silence of the house, and the sudden invasion by so many strangers. Nor could he expect any companionship on his return, for somehow he knew that his mistress had left the cottage. So he wandered on, and eventually emerged onto the badger track at the exact moment that Borun joined it, fifty yards away.

So the two animals met again. For a long while each stood stock still, waiting for the other to make the first move. Both were certain that they had nothing to fear from each other, both were young and immature, and each nursed in his heart a feeling of loss, of loneliness, and a desire for companionship. Slowly, infinitely slowly, Vandal crept nearer and nearer to Borun, who remained rooted to the spot until at last they touched noses.

There followed a tentative inquiry into each other's person, the pair sniffing each other carefully. Borun had little scent, for like all badgers he was scrupulously clean. Vandal, for his part, smelled strongly of rabbit, which puzzled Borun. Finally satisfied, however, Borun set off down the track, with Vandal dancing along behind him.

During that first night Vandal watched, intrigued, as Borun wrecked a rotten tree stump, scooping up the beetles and other insects that tumbled in all directions. He grew bored when Borun dug for roots among the bracken, but brightened up when the badger found a vole's nest, pouncing on the fleeing mother while Borun demolished the young ones. But he was not interested in food, and willingly allowed Borun to take possession of his prize.

By dawn, they had invented a curious game of tag, in which Borun first rushed at Vandal, who sat still as a statue until the very last moment and then sprang high into the air, so that Borun shot headlong under him. Then Vandal chased Borun, cuffing him with his paws, but making sure his claws were never unsheathed. Borun, long used to far heavier blows, nevertheless squealed in pretended terror and turned somersaults in his efforts to avoid them.

The game ended with the coming of daylight. The two made their way to the spring and quenched their thirst, and then as of habit Borun returned to the set. Vandal hesitated outside the entrance for a moment, and then, as Borun's rather portly rump disappeared into the darkness, he followed. The bed of fern and leaves was comfortable, and Borun's warm flank soft and reassuring. As the tractor in the valley grumbled into life for yet another day, as the nightjar returned to his roost on the oak branch, and the sun climbed high in the sky, the strange companions slept.

Gradually, in the days that followed, the pair worked out a scheme of coexistence. Although Vandal was content to accompany Borun on his nocturnal foraging and lend assistance when necessary, he preferred to hunt and kill alone, early in the evening before the countryside had become soaked with dew.

Often, when Borun emerged from the set, there would be a portion of rabbit waiting for him, and this was most acceptable to the badger cub, who was still at times inexpert and bungling in his attempts to find food.

For much of the time too, Vandal preferred to sleep alone. Catlike, he chose to change his sleeping quarters regularly, to bask in the sun of early morning and late evening, but to seek shade during the noonday heat. So he had a succession of sleeping places near the set, each chosen in relation to the direction of the sun and wind. Only when it rained did he join Borun in the set, and as the summer wore on this happened less and less.

Early on an August morning, as the sun shone from a cloudless sky, and the wind rustled through the acres of ripe wheat, Vandal was roused from slumber by a distant high-pitched bark. The yapping was persistent, rising and falling on the breeze, but drawing nearer. Fully awake now, Vandal listened, poised for instant action.

A terrier had escaped just after dawn from the farm where it was kept to control the rats that swarmed around the rickyards. It had one idea in mind, and that was to run wild among the hordes of rabbits that swarmed amid the hedgerows, and as he hunted and killed, and missed, and chased again, he slowly went silly with excitement, barking hysterically the while, and running from warren to warren, until at last he entered the wood by the badger trail.

Vandal lingered a second too long. The terrier spotted him, and with a joyous yelp, dived after him as Vandal made for the shelter of the set. Vandal reached the entrance with the terrier in close pursuit.

The badger woke to hear the scrabble of claws and the snuffling bark of the dog. Next moment Vandal burst into the main chamber a split second before the terrier, and as the cat turned to face his adversary the dog leapt at him, aiming for the throat, but seizing him at the side of the neck. As Vandal screamed Borun leapt to attack, and with a sudden lurch of fear the terrier felt the badger's teeth sink into his foreleg.

In the darkness the noise and confusion were bewildering to all three contestants. The terrier yelled as Borun's teeth grated on bone, and Borun released his hold, leaping for the terrier's throat. He caught the dog instead behind the ears, holding it by the scruff of the neck and effectively preventing it from biting any more. The dog struggled frantically, shaking Borun around the chamber, and forgetting about Vandal, who had broken free when the terrier opened its jaws to yell.

Enraged, Vandal sprang at the dog, biting and slashing with razor-sharp teeth, all the while clinging to the dog's back with claws that gored deep. Finally he brought the powerful muscles of his hindlegs into action, ripping the soft flanks of the terrier with a terrible back-raking kick.

Between them, the companions might well have succeeded in killing the terrier, had it not, with one last effort, managed to reach the tunnel and brush the pair off. It crawled painfully back to the farm, where Fletcher, who had been prepared to give it a beating for straying away, could only look at it in wonder and dismay. He told his friends about it in the pub that evening. "Little old dog looked as though he'd been through a threshing machine. He's cut and tore and scratched . . . One drink of milk he's had, and laid like a dead thing ever since. What manner of beast could do that to him I can't imagine."

Nor, for that matter, could anyone else. The two assailants were little the worse for wear after their adventure. Borun had a few scratches, dealt him in error by Vandal in the height of the mêlée, and Vandal had a nasty tear in his neck. Carefully, they administered first aid to each other, licking those injuries the other couldn't reach, and their wounds healed without complication. The terrier recovered in time, but he never went near the wood again.

AS SOON AS Polly saw the cottage she knew she had found the place she had been looking for. It was September, and the garden was derelict and weed strewn, but in her mind's eye she saw it well tended and trim, with rows of vegetables flourishing again in the plump soil. There was a lawn, with a gnarled old damson tree. In the spring bulbs would force their green spears above the grass, first snowdrops, then crocuses, purple and yellow and white, and then daffodils, nodding in the wind and flaunting their golden trumpets in the thin March sun. There were apple trees, a peach tree, and a neglected raspberry patch, and behind the cottage a range of stone outbuildings, including a woodshed still stacked with dry logs.

Inside, she pottered around, visualizing the firelight winking on her few pieces of silver and the furniture she had garnered so carefully over the years. Up in the best bedroom she admired the white walls and the sagging oak-beamed ceiling, and peered out of the tiny casement window below the thatch, gazing into the shadowy woods. "Chintz," she said. "I can go chintz mad."

"I beg your pardon," said the agent, an apprehensive young man in his early twenties.

Polly flushed. She had not realized that she had spoken aloud. There and then she made up her mind. She would buy Summercombe Cottage, and as she came to her decision the years fell away, years of dusty, chalk-impregnated classrooms, with their hordes of unruly, shrieking children, years of marking papers, and endless academic argument in the smoke-laden atmosphere of shabby staff rooms. At last she was free; there was no one in the world to dictate to her.

The agent was delighted, for none knew better than he the defects of Summercombe Cottage, isolated, draughty, damp and riddled with woodworm. Her solicitor thought her quite mad, and said so in no uncertain terms. But Polly was adamant. A plump, defiant little figure, her dark hair gathered in a bun at the nape of her neck, and her chin quivering with determination, she resisted all efforts to dissuade her. So it came about that in a remarkably short space of time, at dusk one late autumn day, she struck a match and lit the first fire in her new home. As the yellow flames licked hungrily at the dry sticks, the scent of wood smoke evoked memories of October evenings long ago. She poured herself a drink and sat down amid the packing cases that littered the floor, while outside the last light faded from the hills. There was no hurry to unpack. She had only herself to please, and there was all winter ahead. Then she went out into the garden.

The stars shone white in the cold air above the sheltering shoulders of the hills. Alone in the darkness, she sensed the presence of the earth and felt strangely at one with the valley and the hills and the silent trees. It was a feeling that was to grow in the weeks that followed, as by day she laboured in the garden, and by night sat at her sewing machine, or wielded a paintbrush in the darker, more cobwebby corners of the cottage.

One of her first acts was to fix a bird table in the boughs of the damson tree. From the table she hung hoppers for peanuts and sunflower seeds, lumps of fat and suet, a large marrow bone, and pieces of bacon rind. Her first task each morning was to replenish the table, and then she could sit and enjoy her own breakfast as the birds arrived to take theirs.

She was astonished at the variety of the visitors. Blackbirds and thrushes hopped about on the grass beneath the tree. Chaffinches and greenfinches, hedge sparrows and linnets jostled and pushed each other on the table, and were themselves chivvied by a solitary robin. Tits came, blue tits, great tits, a coal tit, and a pair of willow tits, in such a confusion of colour and design that Polly had to buy a bird book in order to identify them all. Nuthatches were regular visitors, and occasionally a woodpecker arrived, his vermilion cap nodding as he surveyed what was on offer.

Late one evening Polly sat beside the window. The curtains remained undrawn, and the window was open, for the weather had remained dry, and the nights unseasonably warm. A book lay on her lap. Suddenly a muffled squeaking in the garden roused her from her reveries, and she peered cautiously out of the window, hardly daring to breathe lest she frightened whatever it was away. Out of the shadows came a family of hedgehogs, looking like animated pincushions as they waddled across the turf on short bandy legs. They fell upon the remains of the bird food on the lawn under the damson tree with squeals of delight, and foraged busily around, moving surprisingly fast for such ungainly-looking creatures.

Polly watched entranced, until finally they trundled off into the night. Later she lay in bed wondering what she could do to encourage them to stay. Hedgehogs, she had read somewhere, were most beneficial to gardeners, eating all manner of insect pests. Even if they weren't, she thought, they were worth fostering for their entertainment value. She had to go into town the following day, so she would see what she could find.

The town was hot and noisy and smelly after the peace of Summercombe. Polly was glad when she could load her week's provisions into the back of her old Morris and drive back up into the valley. At the farm she stopped to collect her milk, and to ask if, for the next few days at least, she could have an extra pint.

"Expecting company then, Miss Shaw?" Mrs. Fletcher's curiosity about her nearest neighbour did not get enough nourishment to satisfy it.

"Why no," began Polly, and then hesitated. She had been about to explain, and then decided not to. She was considered eccentric enough in the village without giving cause for further gossip. "I—I get very thirsty working in the garden," she said instead. Then she took her extra pint and hastened away before the farmer's wife could question her further.

Her sense of relief when she reached the sanctuary of her cottage was almost overwhelming. She dumped the box of groceries onto the kitchen floor, and rummaged around until she found the cat food she had bought for the family of hedgehogs. It was in a garishly-coloured package with a picture of a fat, complacent cat licking its lips. Polly opened it: the contents looked revolting. She emptied the food into two bowls, poured the extra pint of milk over them, and then carried them out into the garden, setting them down under the damson tree. Then she returned to the house to prepare something a little more appetizing for herself before assuming her vigil beside the window.

They came soon after dark, having remembered from the previous night that there were some very interesting titbits to be found beneath the tree. It occurred to Polly that she had been overgenerous with the cat food, but she was astounded at the amount the hedgehogs were able to consume. It was not mere gluttony that drove them to excess. Soon the frosts would come, and then the hedgehogs would seek some refuge that was sheltered and dry. There, buried beneath dried grass and leaves, they would hibernate. Their body temperature would fall, their heartbeats slow, and their breathing almost cease, as they sank deeper and deeper into a coma that would last until the warm days of spring. In readiness for that time the hedgehogs were now accumulating a thick layer of fat, enough fuel to keep their metabolic processes just ticking through the long winter months. So through the autumn they ate and ate.

Even so, they did not quite manage to empty the bowls before they moved off, and Polly left the remains of the food on the lawn, in case the hedgehogs returned later in the night. She went to bed feeling very pleased with the success of her experiment, and fell asleep wondering if the manufacturers of FIT KIT ever imagined that their product would be used for feeding hedgehogs.

At that moment, Borun and Vandal entered the garden.

For both animals, the task of finding food had of late grown more difficult. Those young rabbits that had survived the first few weeks of existence had grown lean and fast and wary. The prolonged drought had not helped, for the earthworms had hidden themselves away until the coming of the rains. Worse, for Borun, was the fact that the acorn crop had failed. Like the hedgehogs, Borun needed at this time to accumulate a layer of fat against the time of the hard weather, when instead of foraging he would pass the long nights drowsing in the warmth and security of the set. For Vandal the problem was not so serious, although normally he would have put on some weight at this time of year. Both he and Borun, moreover, were still growing, and the demands of muscle and bone had to be met. Though far from starving, their appetites were keen, and so they had taken to roving farther afield. On this night, greatly daring, they had come to explore the garden of the cottage.

Almost immediately they found the food the hedgehogs had left, and Vandal, who had not tasted cat food or milk for a long while, soon cleared one bowl. Borun, slightly more suspicious, sniffed the food carefully, but after a few tentative licks he found it to his liking. He polished the bowl, then turned it over hoping to find more. Disappointed, he began scavenging under the damson tree for the scraps that had fallen from the bird table.

The taste of the cat food revived old memories for Vandal, and Borun looked up from his foraging to see the cat sneaking away round the corner of the house. Borun followed, to find Vandal sniffing at the back door.

The cat-flap was still there. Vandal pushed cautiously and it opened. He stood for a moment, his head just inside the kitchen, listening and waiting in case anything stirred. All was still, and he slid through into the house, the flap closing behind him. After a second's hesitation, Borun followed him, and for a long time the pair stood motionless, eager to explore yet poised for instant flight.

Polly had never been a tidy housekeeper, and since she had come to live alone she had grown more and more heedless of convention. The groceries she had bought that day still stood in their box on the kitchen floor. Borun, ever curious, was eager to discover what treasure this strange square tree stump might contain, and his strong claws were soon ripping through cardboard and paper and plastic. A flour bag broke first, but after a few licks Borun turned his attention elsewhere. Cornflakes were much nicer. Borun crunched happily for a while, until he found the sugar. This was better than all the wasps' nests in Somerset, and Borun licked and scrunched, all the time burrowing deeper into the box.

Vandal watched uninterestedly. What Vandal craved was a long cool drink of milk. He remembered that in the past all he had had to do was to rub himself against the door of the refrigerator and mew. Then his mistress would open the door, take out the milk, and pour it into a bowl. Automatically, Vandal went through the routine, not once, but several times.

Nothing happened. No one came, and Borun was still head and shoulders inside the carton, oblivious to everything but the sugar. Indeed, he might have stayed there all night, had he not broken into a packet of detergent. He came out backwards as if he had been shot from a gun, snorting and sneezing. When he had recovered somewhat he saw Vandal scratching and rubbing against the refrigerator door.

Unfortunately for Polly, the door of the refrigerator was of the

kind that is held by a magnetic catch and it presented no problem to Borun. Three rashers of bacon, some cheese and an egg disappeared inside the badger, while Vandal pushed and mewed, still impatient for his milk. It stood on a shelf in a jug. As Borun stood up on his hindlegs and thrust his greedy little snout further into the refrigerator he dislodged the shelf. The jug slid forward, and Vandal got his milk, rather more than he required, all over his head and shoulders.

The crash of the falling jug woke Polly. She lay for a moment, cold fear clutching her heart. Then she pulled herself together and got out of bed. If there were intruders in the house, it was better she faced them standing, than abed at their mercy. With any luck, they would not realize she was alone in the house, and if she gave them plenty of warning, they might flee.

Noisily she opened the bedroom door, stood for a moment on the landing, and then began to clump heavily downstairs. Outside the kitchen door she stopped and listened; but only the sound of the ticking of the clock came to her ears, so at last, screwing up all her courage, she stepped inside and turned on the light.

Her first reaction was one of horror and disgust. The shambles that had once been a cardboard box held a revolting mixture of flour, sugar and cornflakes, all mixed with detergent. The floor was strewn with torn scraps of paper and cardboard, and covered with floury footprints. The refrigerator door was open, its few remaining contents spilled in a pool of milk.

Then Polly spotted the milky paw marks leading to the cat-flap, and she realized what must have happened, although she was unsure about the exact identity of her nocturnal visitors. It certainly wasn't hedgehogs, and while some of the prints looked like those of a cat, others were larger. Certainly no cat could wreak such havoc as this. Suddenly a mental image of Mrs. Fletcher came to her. "Expecting company then, Miss Shaw?" Standing there in the ruins of her kitchen, she began to laugh.

She went back upstairs and dressed, then set to work to clean up the kitchen. Ruefully she reflected that she would have to make another journey to town to replace those provisions that had been ruined. Her last act before retiring was to nail a stout batten of wood across the cat-flap and so prevent any further visitations.

It was close on noon when next she woke, and consequently bedtime found her wide awake. Once again she had put out food for the hedgehogs, and they had been and gone. Still she sat on, hoping to discover the identity of the invaders of the previous night. The moon rose and journeyed across the sky, the fire died in the hearth and the room fell chill. Then, at last, the rattling of the bowls alerted her, and she peeped cautiously out of the window. She saw the cat at once and at first thought he must have come up the track from the farm. Then she remembered Mrs. Fletcher telling her about a white kitten called Vandal that was missing after the previous owner of the cottage had died, and wondered if it could be the same cat that was now feeding on the lawn.

Borun had his back to the window and at first she did not notice his grey form. Then suddenly he turned, and Polly caught her breath in surprise and delight. As she watched, Vandal disappeared around the side of the house and she heard the rattle of the cat-flap. Suddenly, all was explained.

Vandal's attempts to gain entry to the kitchen failed and he rejoined Borun on the lawn. Only when they were quite certain that not a single crumb of food remained uneaten did the pair move off into the night, leaving Polly alone at the window.

They came every night after that and Polly made sure that there were adequate supplies of food available. On the third night she put the food out as usual, and then, dressed in warm dark clothing, she sat down at the foot of the damson tree.

Half an hour passed, and then she saw the white figure of the cat materialize out of the darkness. Close behind him came the young badger, and both animals made straight for the feeding bowls on the grass. Then Vandal noticed her and froze, one paw raised, ready to flee at the slightest sign of danger, but reluctant to forgo his supper unless it was absolutely necessary.

Polly sat motionless, hardly daring to breathe, and at long last Vandal relaxed, crept forward, and began to feed. Reassured, Borun did likewise, and found that as well as the usual cat food and milk there was a slice of bread and honey in his bowl. This find went a long way towards easing his nervousness and he cleared his plate before helping Vandal to finish his meal.

Each night Polly positioned the bowls a little closer to her, and within a week the pair were feeding beside her feet. Soon they were taking scraps from her hand, though both shied away if she tried to touch them. As darkness came earlier each evening, Polly no longer sat under the tree to await her guests, but simply took the bowls out to them when they arrived.

Then, one night, Borun disgraced himself. Sooner or later the hedgehogs were bound still to be feeding when Borun and Vandal appeared. Polly had thought about this, but knowing the hedgehogs' trick of rolling into a tight prickly ball when molested, she felt quite sure that they would be safe. She did not know that badgers have a way of dealing with hedgehogs.

So, when the encounter finally did occur, Polly watched unconcerned, and with a certain amount of detached amusement. Three of the hedgehogs scattered and ran, but the fourth, which had delayed flight a little too long, curled into a ball. Borun strolled over to it. Gingerly, he rolled it onto its back, and then, before Polly could do anything to stop him, he plunged his claws deep into the place where the head of the hedgehog met its tail, and prised the unfortunate beast open. He gave one quick bite, the hedgehog squealed and died, and Borun was already crunching its skull when Polly attacked him with a broom.

Borun gave a gruff bark of fear and fled, closely followed by Vandal, leaving Polly to reflect rather shakily on the strength of the dark forces she had been impertinent enough to try to tame.

The next night nobody came for supper. The hedgehogs were

too afraid of meeting the badger again, and Borun was understandably reluctant to face an angry woman armed with a broom. Next morning, however, Vandal surprised Polly by appearing in broad daylight and sitting on the garden wall. She brought him a bowl of milk and he lapped it up before disappearing back into the woods.

He appeared more frequently after that, often hanging around the garden for hours at a time, and then, one night, as a gale roared through the trees and howled in the chimney, he scratched at the door. When Polly opened it he came in to sit on the rug in front of the fire, as if he had never been away.

The explanation was quite simple. Borun was spending more and more time asleep in the set, and as winter wore on life in the woods was growing ever more uncomfortable for Vandal. No longer could he pass the long day snoozing in the sun, and the dark, stuffy confines of the set were not particularly agreeable to him. So he had returned from the wild, and though he still saw Borun from time to time, they were no longer such close companions. The partnership, such as it was, had served its purpose; now it was ended.

So Vandal stayed, readily accepting a bowl of milk when it was offered and occasionally a dish of cat food, though on the whole he preferred to catch his own food. And Polly, who at first was inclined to accept her adoption by Vandal with amused indignation, came to look forward to his company during the long winter evenings, and the soothing sound of his deep-throated purr as he relaxed by the fire.

COUNTRY TRAVELS

One Eye the vixen came to Summercombe early in the new year, when the January moon shone white over a valley locked in the grip of a hard black frost. Here she was courted and won by the old dog fox that lived at the top of the wood, and for a fortnight the woods and hillsides echoed to the sound of their love calls.

The courtship was brief, and afterwards the pair went their separate ways, the dog fox back to his old haunts, and the vixen to the shelter of a gorse thicket on the slopes of the hill. Here she slept by day, basking in the pale winter sunlight, or lying curled in a ball, impervious to the cold, with her pads tucked close to her body and her face and nose covered by the dense brush of her tail. By night she hunted, quicker and more light-footed than a cat, possessed of a cunning and patience that more than compensated for the loss of her eye.

It was now almost a year since the injury had occurred. Late one afternoon she had stalked a heron as it stood in the shallow waters of a stream that flowed sluggishly between ice-rimmed banks. As she sprang, the vixen's hind foot slipped on the ice, and although she seized her prey, it was by the wing rather than the throat. In the struggle that followed, in a flurry of icy spray, the dagger-like beak of the heron caught her across the eye. A moment later the heron died as the vixen's teeth closed on her throat. In her savage joy the killer barely noticed her own injury, but gradually the scratched cornea turned opaque and white, leaving her blind on one side. In the weeks that followed One Eye fared badly, as she learned to adjust to her impediment. Consequently she did not breed that year, and the unborn cubs she now carried were to be her first litter. So the days passed, and as the icy bonds of winter melted before the warm breath of spring, One Eye's flanks grew rounder. If she was perhaps a little slower on her feet, it still meant no reprieve for the rabbits of Summercombe.

On a bright day in late March, as the daffodils in the churchyard shone yellow amid the grey of the headstones, and the sable rooks in the elms above solemnly discussed the mechanics of repairing their nests, the North Somerset Foxhounds gathered on Summercombe green. Riders on horseback clattered in from all directions, several resplendent in hunting pink. Ruddy-faced farmers in weather-worn tweeds sat astride heavy hunters and children nervously straddled fat ponies. The master sat a little to one side, raising his hunting crop in salute to each newcomer, and talking quietly to his groom. The landlord of the village inn bustled about, chivvying his wife and daughters, who handed round trays laden with the traditional stirrup cup. The rest of the villagers looked on.

The church clock struck eleven, and the hounds moved off, flowing in a liver and white stream up the lane to Bidewell Farm. With a creaking of leather and jingling of harness the horses followed, while those who were to follow the hunt on foot or by car also moved away, each to seek the best vantage point for watching the chase.

One Eye, asleep in the gorse thicket, heard the clamour of the hounds as they poured through the valley, and watched as they spread out over the hillside opposite to converge on a small clump of hawthorn bushes that stood leafless amid a sea of rust-red bracken. After a few minutes they moved on, threading in and out of hedges and checking every bramble patch and weed-strewn ruin, gradually working their way along the hillside until they reached the head of the valley. Here they turned about, to cover the hill where One Eye lay.

Only then did she slip away, climbing towards the rocky ramparts of the hill. Here the russet gleam of her coat was spotted by a watcher standing on the site of the old fort. The man waved his hat and yelled to the hunt, who toiled behind the hounds on mud-spattered horses, spurs dug into flanks as the riders urged their mounts forward. Hounds fanned out, foaming through the rocks and withered fern, and then came a burst of their song as they converged upon One Eye's scent. She led them downhill now, back into the valley and up towards its head. Twice she lost them and managed to snatch a few moments of much needed rest: once by zig-zagging between the terrified members of a flock of sheep, and again when she dived into a drain which led through a hedge mound and through which hounds could not follow. The hounds bayed in frustration at the entrance to the drain, until an older, wiser hound mounted the bank and picked up her scent on the other side.

She had gained some time, but she was slower now. Her tongue lolled and her one good eye was glazed as she gained the shelter of the wood. The panting of her laboured breath was clearly audible as she stood beneath the trees, listening again for the sounds of pursuit. Still the hounds came on. She circled around, keeping just inside the wood, and as she reached the highest point of the woodlands, she passed within a few feet of the old dog fox.

Now her strength was failing fast. She staggered as she ran, and once she fell, to lie on her side for a brief moment before turning downhill, following the worn badger track that wound through the undergrowth. At the entrance to the badger set she paused, and in that instant she realized that the hounds were no longer following her, that the hideous belling cry that had haunted her throughout the afternoon was gradually growing fainter. Gratefully, she slipped into the tunnel, and when she found a chamber lined with old and musty bedding, she collapsed.

Ten minutes later and a mile away, after a screaming run that led hounds in a dead straight line across country, that left the horses far behind and unseated two riders, the old dog fox was torn to pieces. It mattered nothing to him. His old heart had burst, and he was dead before the first hound closed on him. He won fame, of a kind, in the annals of the hunt, as an old warrior who had provided one of the longest runs of the century. Only the master guessed the truth, but he was too wise to spoil the beginnings of a legend.

BORUN was not immediately aware of the presence of his uninvited guest. The refuge One Eye had chosen was the old nursery, a part of the set Borun rarely visited, and it was not until dusk that the badger, emerging, found the atmosphere around the set redolent with the musky odour of fox. He tracked the scent to its source and, having confirmed his suspicions, he departed on the night's forage, grumbling to himself as he trotted down the track. There was nothing he could do about the situation. To the badger, foxes, like frost and snow, were an inevitable fact of life.

For sixteen hours One Eye lay exhausted. Then, as the grey dawn turned to silver over the misty landscape, she crawled from the set and made her way stiffly through the wood in search of water. She found it at the limestone spring, and having drunk her fill, limped painfully back to the set. Here she met Borun, and the two animals stared in hostility at each other before disappearing to their separate quarters. Time had caught up with One Eye. Now she could not leave the set even if she had wanted to.

In the next few hours she gave birth to four cubs. In spite of her physical ordeal, the cubs were strong and lusty, and they thrived. Within three weeks they made their first stumbling appearance at the mouth of the set, small, sooty, furred imps with bright eyes, short pointed noses, and big ears, wobbling about on rubbery legs and waving ridiculous little wisps of tails.

For a week or so the cubs played at the mouth of the set, romping like kittens under their mother's watchful eye, but when Borun passed they sat very still, affording him the respect a child might give a crotchety old uncle. Then, as the cubs grew older, their mother began to wean them.

The woods and fields of the valley were alive with young birds and animals too silly and inexperienced to survive for long, and One Eye brought back to the set young rabbits and pheasant chicks, voles, mice and leverets, lapwings, partridge, and moorhens. Occasionally she even brought lizards and slow worms, and once a luckless green woodpecker, caught napping as he probed the turf of the woodland floor for grubs late one evening. Mice and voles she brought by the mouthful, appearing at the set with the tiny corpses packed sideways between her jaws, the tails hanging down on either side of her muzzle like a drooping walrus moustache.

After a while she began to bring back her victims alive, and these she released for the cubs to chase and kill. As she brought back more, far more, than either she or the cubs could eat, the area around the set became littered with the remains of small corpses, many of which the cubs continued to use as playthings, the pelt of a rabbit, the wing of a moorhen, the leg and foot of a pheasant.

Now the sweet sickly scent of rotting flesh was added to the

aroma of fox, and during the warm sunny days the air was loud
with the buzzing of blowflies, come to lay their eggs on the
rotting meat. Some of the flies even found their way into Borun's
sleeping quarters and roused him from his slumber. It was
getting to be too much for him to bear.

The climax came one night in June. For some days One Eye
had realized that conditions in the nursery set were growing too
cramped for herself and four lumping great cubs. The air was
stuffy, the bedding foul and verminous. Taking advantage of
Borun's absence, One Eye went on an exploration of the main
set. She found Borun's sleeping chamber, freshly lined with grass
and dry leaves, and knew at once that nothing could suit her
needs better. Just before dawn she led her cubs down there, the
smallest bringing up the rear and dragging his favourite
plaything, the rabbit pelt. This he abandoned three feet inside
the tunnel.

Borun returned to find his entrance putrid with the stench of
fox, and he did not need the evidence of the rabbit skin to tell
him what had happened. The entire set was now contaminated
by the presence of the foxes.

It was too much. He could not endure the discomfort and the
mess any longer. Abruptly he turned away from the set and
padded off into the wood. For a moment his humped grey back
was visible among the undergrowth, and then he was lost in the
shadows of the trees.

He took the path uphill, and as the sun crested the horizon he
entered the tangle of rock and twisted thorn that clung to the
hillside below the Iron Age fort. Here he spent the day, curled
in a tight ball at the foot of a gnarled old hawthorn tree, until
the sun sank below the shoulder of the hill. Then he got up,
scratched, shook himself and set off into what was for him
unexplored territory.

He crossed the windswept plateau of the old fort, picking up an
occasional beetle from the short, sheep-bitten turf, but all the
while heading purposefully southeast, away from the valley of his
birth. Soon he was in farmland again, wide fields planted with
barley and root crops, surrounded by carefully tended hedges

351

and banks. A barn owl, drifting white and ghostlike over the land, swerved in startled surprise as Borun raised his black and white snout skyward, and a hunting stoat chattered angrily from the safety of the tangled hedge roots as he passed by.

Then he came to woodland again, a well-fenced plantation of young spruce trees growing tall above the rotting stumps of what had once been giant oaks, trees that had been felled so that the swifter-growing conifers could provide a cash crop for the farmer. Borun skirted the plantation until he came to a narrow rutted track, twisting between high banks, still littered with the leaves of the previous autumn. On top of the banks tall beech trees grew, their trunks silver in the moon that now shone down out of a starlit sky. Their tough old roots twisted and twined like great grey serpents over the eroded banks, while overhead the branches met in a graceful arc to form a canopy of leaves, black and metallic in the lunar light.

Some two hundred years ago a landowner had divided his land into fields, surrounding each one with a beech hedge and a ditch. The beech saplings had formed a stockproof barrier, and since the dead leaves hung on through the winter, they also provided shelter from wind and rain. At the same time, by allowing sections of hedge to sprout up, the farmer assured himself of a constant supply of firewood.

Then came the industrial revolution and a cheap and seemingly inexhaustible supply of coal. Following that came a world war, a shortage of manpower and the invention of barbed wire. The beech hedgerow became an anachronism. Now all that remained of the hedge was an avenue of tall trees and a tangled trelliswork of roots.

Here, Borun came to a hole. It was little more than an over-grown burrow, scratched and dug and tunnelled by generations of rabbits, but there was ample room for Borun, and he clambered inside. After a short distance underground, the tunnel widened out into a sizeable chamber beneath a beech bole, where Borun surprised a startled doe rabbit, who was too witless to flee. Borun grabbed her, and twenty minutes later, feeling uncomfortably full, settled to sleep.

Some hours later he awoke to instant alertness, roused by the deep-throated barking of a dog. He lay still, listening. Then came a scratching at the mouth of the tunnel, not three feet away. There came another bark, and then an excited, high-pitched whining, followed by a soft snuffling sound. Suddenly the chamber was filled with the scent of dog, and Borun backed against the far wall, head down, hair bristling, and white teeth bared, ready to fight to the death. Next moment he relaxed, as the dog suddenly moved away in obedience to a whistle.

Outside in the lane the gamekeeper growled at his Labrador affectionately, "Who gave you leave to go off rabbiting, I'd like to know? Come in to heel."

The dog fell in behind the man, who walked on, his gun crooked comfortably over his arm. Again he spoke, more to himself than to the dog. "I see the pheasants have been feeding well. There's fresh leaves upturned that weren't disturbed yesterday."

BORUN PASSED an uneasy day in the hole under the beech tree. Long before sunset he was waiting at the mouth of the hole, anxious to be away from this place with its threat of danger from man and dog. In fact, Borun had unwittingly strayed onto a game preserve, and was doubly fortunate in that the retriever had warned him of his peril so soon after his arrival on the estate and that the gamekeeper had so far failed to notice his presence.

The old deciduous woodland had been allowed to remain merely to act as cover for the pheasants that swarmed in the undergrowth. In the autumn many of these birds would die, shot by syndicates of businessmen who were prepared to pay high fees for the privilege of hunting them, and so the pheasants represented as valuable a crop to the farmer as the cereals he grew. Borun's presence would not have gone unnoticed for long, and it would not have been tolerated, even though it posed little threat to the pheasant population.

The pheasants were flying to roost as Borun left his hideout, exploding out of the undergrowth with a clatter of wings and perching in the branches of the trees, their plump forms dark silhouettes against the night sky. Borun passed beneath them, following the course of a grassy ride that traversed the woodland. Soon he was out in open country again, crossing wide flat fertile fields which ended abruptly in an escarpment of low limestone cliffs. Below the cliffs a belt of thick woodland fell away to more open parkland, with tall trees casting deep pools of shadow in the bright moonlight. Beyond the park, shimmering like a silver snake, lay the broad sweep of a river.

The river was old and wide, meandering through meadows, loitering on the last stage of its journey to the sea. It was fed by scores of tributaries, pouring their waters down out of the hills that lay to the east and south. These waters contained one priceless asset, for they welled up out of the chalk, and were rich in dissolved calcium from the skeletons of creatures, long extinct, which once had swarmed in the sunlit shallow waters of a tropical sea. Slowed down and sun-warmed, the river maintained an immeasurable quantity and diversity of life, as the calcium provided a rich, alkaline medium in which vegetable and animal plankton flourished. This supported vast armies of freshwater shrimps and insects, which in turn contributed to the great size of the river fish, the chub and trout, the perch and pike and roach. So a legacy laid down millions of years ago was returned once more to the living.

Borun fed well that night and the next, hiding by day in the dark recesses of a huge old hollow oak tree that had fallen one night in a winter gale ten years previously and now lay in a corner of a field, conveniently out of the farmer's way, overgrown with a thick tangle of bramble and briar rose. Late on the evening of the second day, however, he woke to a strange hubbub and disturbance. Footsteps reverberated along the riverbank. Men called to each other on the still evening air. Somewhere in the distance, car doors were slamming. A transistor radio played tinny music, and a paraffin stove hissed as its flames blossomed like a blue rose around the base of a kettle.

Nervously Borun peered out from the curtain of foliage that sheltered the entrance to his hideaway, unable to comprehend the sight that met his eyes. As far as he could see in the rapidly gathering dusk, men lined the river on both banks. Others were still arriving, each laden with a mountain of gear, and carrying a bundle of fishing rods, latecomers in search of a vacant space. Meantime, those who had earlier staked their claims were busy assembling their rods, and setting up large umbrellas, collapsible chairs, and beds. Here and there, some were even erecting tents.

Borun was witnessing what had now become an annual event in modern England, the opening night of the coarse fishing season. Nobody quite knew how many anglers there were, but the association that leased the fishing rights of this river had a membership of over ten thousand. These so-called coarse fishermen fished for freshwater species other than salmon and trout, and angled purely for sport, returning their catch to the river at the end of each outing. Some fish died as a result of handling, but most survived and lived to grow larger and be caught another day.

Not every member turned out on the opening night, and many would return to the city in the morning, to sleep, or to yawn their way through a weary day at office or factory. Others would come to take their place, and so it would continue throughout the summer, with numbers dwindling as the earlier novelty wore off, but always with someone in attendance by day or night.

The anglers had a profound effect on the country scene. The sheer weight of their numbers eroded the banks and wore the grass bare, killing it so that when the winter floods came the grass no longer held the banks in place, and the floodwaters washed them away.

Many anglers too used bread in large quantities as ground bait, throwing it into the stream to attract shoals of fish to the area around their hooks. Often surplus bread was left lying on the bank, or was thrown into the rushes bordering the stream. While much of it was eaten by birds, the remainder attracted rats, who took up permanent residence by the stream. Others left litter, always unsightly and often dangerous. Small rodents squeezed their way into discarded bottles, only to starve when they found themselves unable to climb out up the slippery sides. Birds were trapped, snared by lengths of nylon line, which cut into their legs so tightly that even if they did not die the victims escaped only at the cost of losing a limb. The majority of anglers were quick to condemn such practices, and most were agreed that much as they enjoyed the camaraderie of the riverbank, they would be only too happy to exchange it for solitude, and a stretch of the river to themselves. As things were, however, the very popularity of their sport was going a long way to destroying it.

When the fishermen showed no signs of moving, Borun slipped out of the hollow tree and made his way upstream, giving the riverbank a wide berth. For the remainder of the night he foraged successfully and in peace, and at dawn crept quietly into a wayside thicket, grunted contentedly and slept.

The thicket in which Borun had taken refuge comprised a few tall ash trees, protected by an undergrowth of blackthorn. It stood in a patch of wasteland that lay beside a wood, at the meeting of two roads. A rough track led across the wasteland, following the boundary of the wood, and screened from the road by the thicket.

The long day dragged on in silence under the sun. Once a magpie flew into the thicket, and his raucous cry, as he spotted Borun asleep in the shade, ripped the air like rifle fire. Then he flew away and was lost to sight beyond the wood. The wasteland was still again, save for the drone of countless busy insects. No one came near, for the roads were dusty and forgotten.

The afternoon was almost over when a motley cavalcade of swarthy travellers arrived at the wasteland. One by one they pulled onto the track, parking their vehicles behind the screen of the thorn thicket. First came an expensive saloon car, towing a large black and white caravan that sported lace curtains at the windows, and shone with chromium plate. Next came an open lorry, half loaded with a collection of scrap metal, rags, and wooden crates, and also towing a caravan. Finally came a closed van, towing a third caravan, older than the others, but still shining with bright green paint.

The travellers were Romanies, whose ancestors had migrated out of India centuries ago, to travel west and spread out across the whole of Europe. This family, the older man and his wife, the two sons and their wives, together with four children, a goat, a crate of hens, and a pack of lean, hungry mongrel dogs, had been strawberry picking in the south and were now moving slowly north to

356

Gloucester, where soon there would be plums, apples, and hops to pick. They lived by casual labour, and on their travels they bought (and sometimes stole) scrap metal, collected rags, and sold clothes-pegs and artificial flowers. This wasteland had been from time immemorial one of their "atchin tans", or stopping places. Being isolated, it posed little danger to them from police or angry landowners.

The silence of the wasteland was shattered as the travellers set about preparing for their stay. The children were dispatched to collect firewood. The women began to make ready the evening meal, and the men unhitched the caravans and checked that they stood level. In a very short space of time a big black cooking pot hung over a crackling fire, the goat was tethered and grazing contentedly, and the hens were pecking busily among the caravans. The family gathered around the fire, the men with gaudy neckerchiefs knotted about their throats, the women with their auburn hair coiled in plaited ropes around their heads, the children ragged and dirty, but happy and well fed. They joked and gossiped among themselves for a while, and then one of the sons remembered the dogs, still cooped up in the back of the van.

He strolled over and opened the door, and they poured out, a joyous, yelping ill-assorted crew, each chosen and kept for his particular qualities. There was a great grey brute, half collie and half greyhound, which could run down a hare in fifty yards. There was a retriever, which could bring back a partridge chick to the hand alive, so soft was his mouth. There were two whippets, which working together kept the family supplied with as many rabbits as they could eat and sell, and a tiny rough brown terrier which had earned his owner many a pound by killing rats. Free at last from the stuffy confines of the van they raced around for a while, chasing each other's tails and engaging in mock combat, until at last, as their first euphoria waned, they settled down to explore their surroundings.

All this time Borun lay in the thicket, awake and anxious, listening to the tumult of sound. Although tempted to flee, he nevertheless remained where he was, waiting for darkness, for he was in strange country, and he had no idea which direction to take.

The terrier found him first, and his hysterical yapping brought the others to the scene. Borun set his back to the base of an ash tree and waited, his white teeth bared in a snarl of defiance, confident that he could deal with both the terrier and the whippets, should they attempt to close with him. When the bigger dogs arrived, however, he knew that he was outnumbered, and taking a desperate chance, he screamed with anger and charged at the terrier.

The little dog yelped in fear and leapt aside, leaving Borun free to bolt. As the larger dogs floundered around, hampered by the undergrowth, Borun burst through the thicket and shot out into the clearing like a hairy cannonball, only to stop short at the sight of the Romany family, sitting in a half-circle around the fire and staring in amazement at his sudden appearance.

Borun hesitated only briefly. Then, as one of the men leapt to his feet and snatched up a heavy stick, he swerved and ran for the woods. Yet even before he had covered a few yards he knew that he would never reach his goal, for the grey dog had broken free of the thicket and raced around to cut off his escape. There

was only one way for him to go. In a last desperate attempt to find sanctuary, he jumped through the open door of one of the caravans, while the dog, knowing the terrible penalty that awaited him from his master if he followed, stood and howled outside.

The man with the stick moved forward, confident now that Borun was at his mercy. He was halfway through the door of the caravan when the older man cried out, "Wait!"

The son turned, scowling, but obedient to the command. "What's to wait for, father, when there's a badger pelt worth five pounds for the taking, and badger hams to smoke over our fire?"

The father made a gesture of impatience. "You'd make a poor bargain if you did not wait. I know a man not far from here who would give not one, but *four* five pound notes for this badger, but it must be delivered alive, and in good condition."

The son thought about this for a few moments, then he carefully closed the caravan door. "All right then. Who's this fool who would part with so much money for an old badger? And how do you propose to take the brute alive? It'll tear you to pieces if you go near."

"Patience, patience," said the old man. "He runs a kind of zoo, not far from here, a wildlife park he calls it. I sold him fox cubs in the spring and he told me then that if ever I found a live badger he would buy it. As to taking it alive, watch, and you will learn."

He moved over to the lorry, and from out of the pile of scrap

359

metal he pulled a length of iron piping about five feet long. Then from the driver's seat he took a length of strong, thin cord. One end of the cord he knotted tightly to the end of the piping, and then threaded the cord back down the tube, so forming a noose. Next he went to the wood and cut a long hazel wand, trimming the twigs and leaves from it with his pocketknife.

"Get me that wooden crate off the back of the wagon," he commanded his son, "and a hammer and some nails to fasten down the lid."

When all was ready he took the hazel wand in his left hand and the pipe in his right, the noose hanging in a wide loop. Then he stepped inside the caravan.

Borun was crouched in a tiny space between the stove and a bunk bed. The old Romany advanced towards him very slowly, the hazel wand pointing towards Borun, the loop of cord hung over the wand. Borun watched the wand, for this seemed to offer him the greater threat. He did not notice the noose. When the wand was within six inches of his snout he snapped, seizing the hazel between his jaws. Being green and pliant, it did not sheer off, but merely splintered, and Borun hung on grimly as the old man pulled firmly on the wand. The noose slid down the wand and settled softly over his head. Next moment the man had pulled it tight.

Borun's scream died in his throat as he felt himself swung into the air. Choking, clawing at his neck, twisting, squirming, he was carried out of the caravan door and lowered into the box. As his feet touched the wooden floor the lid was clapped on and darkness descended, but mercifully the cord around his neck suddenly slackened, and once more he was able to breathe. For a few seconds he was deafened by the banging of the hammer as the lid was nailed down, and then he was left in peace.

With the badger successfully captured, the travellers settled down to their evening meal, and when it was over they loaded the crate into the back of the van and set off back down the road. The journey was short, but to Borun it was a nightmare of noise, made even worse by petrol fumes and the hateful smell of dog. At first he tried to claw and bite his way out of the crate, but it was new and strongly made, and he could make no impression on the wood. Exhausted and half suffocated, he lay down, his claws torn and bleeding.

At last the van stopped and the engine was cut. Alert again, Borun waited and listened, but all he could hear were voices which went on for what seemed an interminable while, now raised, now low and pleading. Then the van door was opened, the crate was lifted out and carried away, Borun inside standing straddle-legged to keep his balance. The box was set down, the nails in the lid were drawn, and Borun fell in a heap as the box was turned suddenly on its side. Then the lid was pulled to one side and light flooded in, light and sweet fresh air.

Borun crouched motionless in a corner of the crate. He was in no hurry to leave, for he could smell the men outside and hear their heavy breathing. He was not left in peace for long. A broom was pushed into the crate and Borun was prodded with it. Borun snapped and tore at the bristles, but they pricked his lips and gums, and at last he bolted from the crate.

Dazed and bewildered, he could see only that he was in a small enclosure, with smooth walls and a concrete floor. Then he spotted a pile of straw in a corner and dived into it, burrowing down until he was lost to view. The owner of the park, satisfied that he had a live badger in good condition, paid over the twenty pounds he had promised, and the Romany folk departed, well content with their evening's work.

The arrival of Borun, however, had taken the owner of the park by surprise, and since there was no suitable accommodation, he had housed Borun temporarily in one of a new range of pigsties, from which there seemed no possibility of escape. Here he left Borun to recover from his ordeal, with a bowl of water and a dish of meat, together with two slices of bread plastered with honey.

Darkness fell, but Borun remained hidden in the straw pile. For a long time he stayed awake, trembling with fear, but slowly his heart stopped hammering, his limbs ceased twitching, and he ventured out, feeling stiff and sore. The water revived him, and he licked the honey from the bread before beginning to explore his surroundings.

361

The sty was divided into two parts, a sleeping compartment with a raised concrete platform, windowless and roofed over, and an outer yard, with walls four feet high and a steel gate. There seemed to be no possible avenue of escape, but Borun persisted in his explorations, covering every inch of the enclosure, from time to time standing on his hind legs and reaching high up the walls in the hope of finding some foothold. There was none.

Yet unknown to the owner, the labourer who had built the pig-sty had skimped the job. The specifications had called for two inches of concrete laid over hardcore, but in one corner of the sleeping compartment the covering was of less than half an inch. The labourer had seen that he was about to run out of concrete. It was almost time for him to finish work, and he was too lazy to mix any more, so he had filled the corner with loose earth and spread thinly over it what mixture he had left. The concrete cracked, but in the darkness no one had detected the flaw. Borun found it, and began to scratch.

Gradually he raised the slab until at last he could get his strong snout underneath it. Three quick jerks and the slab broke in two halves which Borun dragged away, exposing the soft loose earth beneath. Now he began to dig in earnest, loosening the earth still further and dragging it back by the armful. Before long he was lost to sight, and the floor of the pigsty was covered with fresh soil.

He came to the foundations of the walls and dug down until he had passed under them. Then he began to dig upward. From time to time he rested, and once he took time off to return to the enclosure to drink. There was still an hour of darkness left when he emerged into the open.

The night was warm and windy, the stars hidden by a veil of cloud. Borun wandered around, seeking some way out of the walled garden, but each path he followed ended against a brick wall, a fence of chicken wire, or a cage whose startled occupant peered at him through the darkness. A porcupine rattled its quills. A great horned owl snapped its beak and crouched low on its perch. A roosting peacock awoke to screaming, flapping flight, and an elderly lynx ceased his endless prowling to growl a throaty warning. Borun's nerves were almost at breaking point when at last, quite by chance, he found the main entrance and walked out under the turnstile.

A long winding drive stretched away across parkland studded with ancient elms. Borun hurried across the tussocky grass, anxious to get as far away as possible before dawn. Yet he knew that he could not travel far. A great weariness was on him, and a ravenous hunger.

The parkland ended abruptly beside a main road, and here Borun was in luck, for the corpse of a rabbit lay still warm on the verge where it had crawled after being struck by a passing car. Borun picked it up and hurried across the road, settling down to a late supper as soon as he was safely hidden in the bushes.

It was light by the time he had finished, and the clouds of night were dispersing before a chill breeze that heralded the rising of the sun. Below him the hillside fell away in rolling heathland, a thick carpet of dark heather interspersed by clumps of gorse, spindly birch trees, and here and there a stand of pine. Beyond the heathland lay a river, and beyond that a ridge of hills ending in a steep limestone escarpment. Something about the hills struck a chord in Borun's memory, but he paid no heed. He set off across the heathland, along a twisting narrow track that wound between the white stems of the heather. Then he stopped and sniffed the ground carefully.

There was no doubt about it. Another of his kind had passed this way, and only a short while ago. The knowledge filled Borun with a strange excitement. He moved off down the trail, quickening his pace as the scent grew stronger, until he came to a hollow in the side of the hill where the ground was bare of vegetation. At the foot of a twisted old gorse bush a hole had been dug, and the sweet musky aroma that had so excited and disturbed Borun hung all around it. He moved closer and called, the greeting emerging as a soft purr.

He waited, but no response came, so he called again, louder, and this time he heard a muffled padding deep in the earth. Respectfully, he drew back a little, standing very still as cautiously, inch by inch, the other badger emerged. She was smaller than he, trim and slender, and she stood blinking in the strong morning sunlight, one paw raised and her nose questing the air.

Borun moved slightly, and for a moment she made as if to dive back into the hole, but then she came forward until the two animals touched noses. Then they sniffed each other over face, ears and neck. Both badgers were trembling, he with anticipation, she with nervousness.

Then she turned, and made her way back into the set. Borun stood outside, irresolute, wanting to follow but unsure of his welcome. He turned away, half determined to depart, but then he heard her call, and saw that she was back at the mouth of the set, watching him. He walked towards her and she backed slowly away from him, leading him down out of sight into the cool darkness of the set.

There was only one tunnel, quite short, but it led under a great slab of sandstone and then widened out into a sleeping chamber lined with a deep litter of fern. Borun was vaguely conscious of her snuffling near him and rustling the fern, then a great wave of exhaustion swept over him and he fell into a deep sleep.

HANDA

Handa had been born in the same year as Borun. She and her brother had left their parents' set the previous autumn, and for a while they had shared a home on this heathland. Then one night a month ago her brother had wandered away alone and failed to return. Since then she had led a solitary and none too happy existence. Now Borun had come into her life.

It was late in the evening when Borun woke to find himself alone in the sleeping chamber. Handa was waiting for him outside the set, and she trotted over to greet him as he emerged. The sun was setting, illuminating the sky in the northwest and shedding a soft rosy lustre over the shaggy cloak of the hillside.

Together the two badgers lay on the bare baked earth, still warm from the sun's rays, listening and waiting as the first pale stars appeared and dusk stole out of the valley below. A few rooks flew

364

lazily overhead, winging back to roost after a long day's toil in the fields, and an owl wafted low over the heather, dropping out of sight and then rising with a small burden clutched in one of its talons.

As if by tacit assent the pair rose and moved off downhill, Handa leading the way. Gradually the heather gave way to rough grassland, sour and ill-drained, invaded by bracken and coarse rushes. Glow worms shone like fallen stars amid the grass stems, and white moths fluttered over the fern, to fade and vanish among the dark alders that lined the riverbank. Slugs were feeding on the damp vegetation. The two badgers sought them out, selecting the fattest and rolling them carefully on the grass until they had removed the slime. It was a slow business, but the badgers were in no hurry as they worked their way across the marshy pasture.

They came at last to the river, where they paused to drink. There they disturbed a moorhen roosting in the reeds with her half-grown chick, sole survivor of a brood of seven. The mother flew out of the water, calling to her youngster to follow, but the witless chick panicked and ran away from the river. Handa gave chase and Borun followed, driving it farther into the field. Yet try as they might, they could not catch the chick, for no matter how hysterical it might be, it could easily outrun them. The chase became more of a sport than a serious hunt for the badgers, so when at last the wretched bird dodged past Borun and plunged into the river, the pair watched it go without any great show of regret. They trotted along the riverbank together, side by side, jostling and pushing each other and pulling each other's ears. Gradually their play grew more boisterous and frenzied. Then, quite suddenly, they paused, and in that moment Borun made Handa his mate.

Their honeymoon lasted until all the wheat and barley had been harvested and the fields lay tawny and sere under the maturing sun. They began to grow fat, gleaning the grain that had fallen on the stubble and feasting on the blackberries that shone in juicy clusters in the hedgerows. All around them the earth burgeoned with wealth as the full-blown beauty of the summer mellowed into misty autumn.

Then came the acorn crop. The hard fruit spattered down from the high branches of the oaks, while from the chestnut trees fell spiky green purses, out of which burst succulent, shiny brown nuts. This year too, the beechmast ripened, an uncommon event, and the squirrels went quite silly burying far more of the seed than they could ever eat, even if they were able to find their stores again.

Although she was putting on weight, and three months had passed since she and Borun had mated, there was still no sign that Handa was about to bear young. Yet the alchemy that had brought them together was still at work within her, and all was well. Three fertilized ova lay at rest in Handa's womb. They would remain dormant until the longest night of the year, when her body would then accept and nourish them. Why all this should be so is a question to which there is as yet no answer. It is a mystery perhaps understood by the silent oaks beneath whose roots the badgers have so long survived, but it may forever elude the inquiry of man.

The purple of the heather darkened to deepest brown and the western gorse, which had worn a coronet of gold flowers, resumed its sombre green. Gales came stripping the birch of its brassy leaves, and rain lashed the earth, turning the waters of the river to muddy beige, in which dark drowned alder leaves danced a slow and stately dance. Then the sun shone again, but on a changed world in which the nuances of colour were soft and indistinct, a muted landscape of faded browns and greens, against which the purple of the bare birch twigs glowed with a rare beauty. At night a hunter's moon hung in the sky, and in the mornings frost silvered the skeletons of the flowers of summer.

Then, late one afternoon on a grey autumn day when mist hung over the river and moisture clung to every twig, men armed with mattocks and spades came to the badgers' set. A fox hunt was due to be held next day, and the master was anxious that it should be a success. There had been complaints from the farmers that foxes were getting too numerous, and that too many escaped the hunt by going to ground. So the hunt committee had agreed to pay two labourers to stop as many holes as they could find.

Borun and Handa heard the muffled thumping and banging as the earth-stoppers did their work, and they waited for a long time after the men had left before they dared venture out of the bedchamber. It was only then they discovered that across the entrance was a large block of sandstone, which had once formed part of the roof of the tunnel.

The block was too firmly embedded to be pushed aside. It took many hours of patient scraping and burrowing, dragging soil a pawful at a time into the sleeping chamber, before Handa was at last able to squeeze past the rock. Then she was able to dig from outside, and it was not long before Borun too could crawl free.

Outside, in the fresh damp air, the badgers shook themselves vigorously, to free their coats of the loose particles of soil. Then, although they were weary, hungry and thirsty, they began a slow, meticulous inspection of their home. The set was ruined beyond repair. The tunnel had caved in and the sleeping chamber now was draughty and exposed. Everywhere, too, the ground was redolent of humans. With a gruff bark of anger Handa bolted away downhill, and Borun followed at a gallop, anxious not to lose track of her.

Once clear of the vicinity of the set, Handa quieted somewhat. When Borun unearthed a cache of acorns, buried by a squirrel in leaf mould under the parent oak, she ate heartily. Neither animal had any intention of returning to the ruined set, but they were not unduly concerned about finding shelter. Each could call to mind half a dozen refuges in the countryside around: holes dug by foxes, abandoned badger sets, and passages under the sandstone rocks that littered the hills. So it was not until an hour before dawn that Handa led the way up the side of the hill to where, she knew, a fault in the rock face allowed access to a dry and roomy cavern.

It was no good. The entrance had been blocked with a massive slab of stone. Handa turned away, heading downhill to an old quarry, in the corner of which a vixen had raised her young. The earth had long since been abandoned and no taint of fox remained, but here again, the earth-stoppers had done their work well. A tree stump had been thrust into the mouth of the hole.

Given time, the badgers might well have cleared the blockage, but daylight was fast approaching and both animals were weary.

Now Borun led the way to an earth mound in the middle of a small beech wood. The mound was an ancient grave, the tomb of a Bronze Age chieftain. There was a way in, Borun knew, at the base of the oldest beech tree. The hole was still there, and it had been overlooked by the earth-stoppers, but now it was inhabited by an old and irascible badger, half mad with toothache and pains in his joints. He stood just inside the entrance, growling and snarling, and Borun, who was quite big enough to master the old warrior, turned away. He could not ignore those instincts that taught him to respect the territorial rights of others. They left the tomb, and its testy old custodian backed off, muttering, into the dark recesses. Soon, his bones would join those of the Bronze Age warrior, and their spirits would become as one.

It was full daylight when the pair finally found refuge in a small cave at the foot of a low sandstone cliff. A dense mat of ivy screened the entrance to the cave and so the earth-stoppers had missed it. Yet it was a poor sort of refuge, draughty and damp and cold, and the badgers lay huddled together on a bed of loose stones in the driest corner they could find. For a while they forgot their discomfort in sleep, but nightfall found Borun wakeful and restless, padding to and fro at the entrance to the cave.

Across the valley a limestone escarpment was stark against the winter sky. Something about his surroundings pulled at Borun's mind, evoking memories of a valley and a wood, where voles were fat and plentiful, where rabbits ran among the fern and no man came near. As darkness fell he set off towards the river, moving purposefully without pausing to search for food. Handa followed, not knowing where she was going or why, but content merely to go with her mate.

Borun himself had no clear intention, no positive plan. He knew only that as long as he travelled in this direction he felt satisfied and content. The moment he stopped, or turned aside, his restlessness returned. So he journeyed on, until at last he was brought up short by the broad expanse of the river, now brown and turbulent with winter rain. Here he checked. Then, on impulse, he turned left and followed the river downstream. Handa plodded behind, as patient and trusting as ever.

Borun's instinct led him true. After his capture by the Romanies, he had without knowing it been carried across the river in the van. Now that river lay before him, sprawled like a great snake across the valley floor, swinging in wide curves as it meandered to the sea. But it lay aslant his path rather than across it, and by heading downstream Borun was drawing nearer to his goal. How he was going to cross the river was a problem which had not even occurred to him.

The going was easy, along a wide track worn bare by the boots of countless fishermen, and the pair made good progress until Handa rebelled. A tree trunk lay beside the path, its bark crumbling and rotten. The thought of all the food hidden under the bark was too much for Handa and she called a halt in order to feed.

Borun, once his interest was aroused, was happy to join her, for his earlier restlessness had now much abated. Together they ripped the log apart, licking up the grey woodlice that scattered in all directions, and crunching the colonies of hibernating snails. Beneath the bark, in the spongy timber, lay the fat white grubs of boring beetles, and best of all, in the soft ground under the log, they found a congregation of frogs, deep in their winter sleep.

His hunger appeased, Borun was once more ready to move, but Handa felt certain that yet a further treat lay in store beneath the log. Borun chivvied her, anxious to be off, and she gave in, grumbling to herself a little, but obedient to his will.

Ahead of them now the river was spanned by a bridge on a high earthern rampart. Together the pair clambered up the bank, and found themselves on a wide level track, with steel rails shining dully in the starlight. Borun approached them nervously, with Handa close behind. He was halfway across the first rail when he realized that it was singing, and the song, a high-pitched whine, grew steadily louder, accompanied by a rhythmic clicking sound.

Borun started back, almost bowling Handa over in his fright, and the pair of them retreated, crouching in the grass as the whine grew to a hurricane of sound, a deafening roar, a mighty pounding that made the earth shake. As they watched, too terrified to move, lights from the carriage windows flicked over their faces. Then the train was gone. The noise faded into the distance and died.

It was more than half an hour before Borun and Handa dared venture once more onto the track, and this time they approached with even more caution than before. The rails were silent, however, and Borun led the way across the bridge and over the river.

The two badgers followed the railway for about half a mile until it joined another track running east to west. Borun hesitated briefly before crossing. They slid down the embankment and crossed a field, only to be caught up short by another obstacle, a broad stretch of water extending interminably in either direction.

Years ago the canal had carried a heavy volume of traffic. Barges ferried coal, timber, iron ore, hides, and fragile articles, such as pottery, which would not stand a jolting journey over the rough roads of that time. Then came the railway. Slowly the canal fell into disuse and nature came to reclaim her own. In summer, water lilies carpeted the water and flag bloomed along the banks. Each autumn the weeds died down, to decay into thick black mud. Very slowly, the canal was being filled up, and there would come a day when it would once more be dry land.

Borun paused. Then he turned left along the overgrown towpath. A moorhen swam away from the shore as they approached, a swan raised his long white neck to hiss at them, and a water vole dived into the water with a musical plop.

Shortly they came to a narrow bridge which led across the canal and into a small copse. Here they found a rich harvest of bluebell bulbs, and they dug the crisp juicy roots from the soft mould, feeding until dawn forced them to seek refuge in a hollow log.

With the coming of the night Borun was again anxious to be on the move, but Handa insisted on feeding first. For a while Borun joined her, but as soon as his appetite was appeased he nagged at his mate until at last she followed him out of the wood.

The direction he had to take was now clear in Borun's mind, but the way was not easy. After crossing several fields they found themselves in a narrow lane. High banks topped with sheep fencing kept them from the fields on either side, and once a passing car braked and swerved to avoid them as they darted in panic across the road.

The lane led them through a village, where dogs barked from behind closed doors, then uphill, until they came to a rough tangle of fern and stone. Here Borun stopped to sniff the air appreciatively before leading Handa into Summercombe wood.

A few minutes later they arrived at the set. One Eye had long since departed, and time had obliterated the traces of her tenancy. After a thorough exploration, Handa set about clearing out the set. Beneath the trees there was dried fern in plenty and deep drifts of crisp, fragrant leaves which Handa dragged in until the sleeping chamber was full. Long before dawn the set was habitable again.

The badgers had returned to Summercombe wood.

AT THE TIME of the winter solstice, as the north star blazed over a land chilled with frost, Handa's body accepted the dormant eggs within her and began to nourish them with her blood.

January passed, with icy east winds holding the land in thrall. In February the wind blew from the west, turning the snow to a grey blanket of slush that vanished in a night. A thrush shouted from the topmost branch of an ash, and the plump catkins on the willow shone silver in the sun.

One evening, as the sun blazed blood-red beneath massed banks of cloud, Handa emerged alone from the set and disappeared into a thicket of holly close by. A rabbit had once dug a burrow there, and Handa began to enlarge the hole so that it was just big enough for her.

She was already well underground when Borun sleepily emerged, to sit scratching himself at the mouth of the set. He could hear Handa at work in the holly thicket, but he paid little heed.

Digging was second nature to the badgers, and they were both frequently at work clearing debris out of a tunnel or enlarging a sleeping chamber. For the moment Borun was content

to lie at the mouth of the set, waiting for Handa to join him on the night's forage.

After two hours, however, he began to grow impatient and padded over to the thicket. Deep underground he could hear a muffled thumping, but when he tried to enter the tunnel he was pushed aside by Handa as she emerged backward, dragging a large stone in her arms.

He called to her, but she ignored him, bustling away down the tunnel to reappear almost at once with an armful of sand, most of which went over Borun. He settled down to wait once more, but it was late in the night before she condescended to join him in a search for food. She was hard at work again the following night and this time Borun did not wait for her, but went off foraging alone, returning from time to time to call for her, until at last she was ready to join him.

By midnight on the third night she was taking in fern for bedding. The nursery she had dug was a model of its kind. The entrance was small and discreet. Just inside, it took a right-angled turn, sloping upward to pass between two rocks. Again it turned through ninety degrees, this time to the left, leading deep into the earth. A step up over a slab of stone, and then down into a nursery chamber from which no cub could stray, and to which no harm could come. The slab of sandstone rock was a vantage point from which she could drop on any intruder.

Not until the nest chamber was lined to her satisfaction did Handa consent to join Borun in foraging, and even then she would not stray far. Long before dawn she led the way back to the set and vanished into the nursery. Borun waited a while, but she did not reappear, so he retired to sleep alone. The following evening he called to her at the mouth of the nursery set, but there was no response so he padded off alone. He was not to know it, but he was the father of three lusty cubs, two female and one male.

From the moment of their birth, the cubs flourished. Handa was able to feed them well, for she was young and healthy. On the first night a little before dawn she went alone to the spring to drink. On the second night she met Borun and the pair exchanged a brief greeting before she returned to her young. On the third night she joined him for a short foray, and ever after that she would leave her cubs for a brief spell while she foraged with her mate.

There was no shortage of rabbits and voles, and although the spring was cold there was a good yield of fresh green grass. During the drought of the previous summer every tree and shrub had thrust its roots deep into the earth, searching for water, tapping rich new sources of minerals in their quest. Now they were reaping the benefit. Every tree, as it blossomed, showed promise of a heavy fruit crop to follow. The yellow hazel catkins were thicker than ever before, the blackthorn bloom spread like snow, and the flowers of the oaks, which normally passed unnoticed, flourished until the trees looked as if they had been sprayed with liquid gold.

By the middle of March Handa had decided that the nursery was no longer big enough, and she took over part of the main set, refurbishing an old chamber. In digging, she turned out an old skull, yellow and crumbling with age, its teeth long fallen from the sockets. Borun sniffed at it curiously as it lay on the sand outside the set. It was the skull of his great-grandfather, who had died in that very bedchamber.

Once the new nursery had been furnished to her satisfaction, Handa brought her cubs across, one by one. So Borun met his family for the first time, and though at first Handa snarled a warning when he tried to enter the nursery, she gradually relaxed her rules.

By now the cubs were snub-nosed miniatures of their

parents, tottering about the nursery on rubbery little legs, and Borun was able to play nursemaid, allowing the youngsters to tug at his ears and hair, while Handa took a much needed respite above ground.

WOODLAND ENCOUNTER

On a bright April morning, with a blustery wind sending white clouds scudding across a sky as blue as a thrush's egg, Polly Shaw discovered the badgers' set.

She was walking that day through the sun-dappled shade of the woodland, the leaves of the previous autumn crisp and dry underfoot, when she came to the badger track. She followed it as it twisted and wound under the trees to open out at length into the wide arena beneath the trees. Immediately she recognized the set for what it was. She did not go near it, but instead circled around seeking about her for a vantage point to which she could return that evening. She hoped to see a badger emerge, perhaps the very one she had fed two autumns before. She found a place in an old ash stump, shaped for all the world like a large armchair. All it needed to make it comfortable was a cushion.

She devoted the rest of the day to her garden, finishing off the last of the spring planting and staking the peas newly emerging from the soil. The afternoon was well spent when the sudden appearance of Vandal reminded Polly that she had forgotten to collect the milk. She was tempted to go without, but she knew that if Vandal did not get his daily ration he would spend the evening rubbing against the refrigerator and miaowing at the top of his voice. With a sigh, Polly put away her gardening tools and set off to the farm.

Mrs. Fletcher greeted her with that subdued air of triumph that befits the bearer of important news. "Have you seen the papers, Miss Shaw?" she trumpeted as Polly crossed the farmyard. She was confident that Polly had not. That was why she had waited impatiently all day for this moment.

In the farm kitchen the front page of the *Advertiser* lay

displayed for Polly to see. Glaring banner headlines leapt out of the page: NEW BY-PASS PROPOSED. SUMMERCOMBE WOOD THREATENED.

Swiftly Polly ran her eyes down the column of print. "If a proposal by the County Council meets with approval from the Department of the Environment, a new by-pass will divert access to the motorway from the existing road, which passes through the village of Summercombe. For some time now residents have complained that the ever increasing volume of traffic has brought noise and atmospheric pollution to the village, and lately fears have been expressed that there could be danger to life and property.

"The proposed route will carry the by-pass along the side of the hill, across land which is mostly unproductive and infertile."

There was a map indicating the path of the proposed new road. Polly could see that Summercombe wood was in danger of being bisected along its whole length, and worse, the by-pass would skirt the front of her garden. She took a deep breath, determined that she would not give Mrs. Fletcher the satisfaction of seeing that she was distressed.

So she was smiling as she turned to face Mrs. Fletcher. "I'm afraid the *Advertiser* is a little premature with its news. After all, this is, as yet, only a proposal."

Mrs. Fletcher was nettled. "Everyone I've spoken to so far thinks it's a fine idea. I've no doubt myself that it will go through."

Polly took her milk and fled. In spite of her apparent lack of concern, her heart was heavy as she made her way back to the cottage. Already in her imagination she could hear the sullen roar of diesel engines, an unending procession of heavy lorries thundering past by day and by night. As she turned in at the gate, a blackbird flew to the hedge with a worm in his bill. For a few moments he perched on a dead branch, to warble a snatch of song.

Polly wondered how many people knew that a blackbird could sing with a beakful of worms. How many ever got a chance to find out? Suddenly she was aware of the privilege of her position, in enjoying the best of both worlds. She accepted without question the gifts of progress. She had electric light, television, her record player, a greater store of possessions than any previous resident of the cottage ever had. Without these benefits, would she still retain a sense of wonder for the natural world, or would she become just another drudge, ill-nourished and in poor health, cursing an alien environment?

She did not know, but she was honest enough to admit that if she herself expected a high standard of living, then she had no right to deny it to anyone else. The new by-pass was intended as part of that system by which living standards were maintained. The motorways carried potatoes to the cities and fertilizers to the fields. They brought everything from sugar to cigarettes, from new books to nylon underwear, and if the system was not ideal, at least it worked.

The by-pass, while reducing the quality of her life, would greatly improve that of the residents of Summercombe, and when it was built perhaps they, instead of her, would be able to stand in their gardens and hear a blackbird sing. She herself was the sacrifice, and not much of one at that. She was well past middle age, and she might well be dead before the by-pass opened, or unfit to manage alone. Already she could feel twinges of rheumatism after a day in the garden. One thing was certain. She could not appeal against the plan. It meant too much to everyone else. She would just have to wait and watch events. After all, no dream lasted for ever.

She thought of herself and her garden. She liked to think it was a haven for wildlife, yet each week she ruthlessly destroyed slugs and snails, caterpillars and greenfly, ants' nests and earwigs. It was no good denying it, she was as guilty as the next person in waging war on the wild, and the by-pass, when it came, would be no more than a logical extension of her activities in the garden.

She was still brooding as she set off through the woods. The blackthorn had shed its bloom and the white petals lay like snowdrifts among the purple haze of bluebells. Rooks were calling to each other as they drifted lazily overhead, and a thrush sang in a rich contralto. The aroma of the woods rose strong and sensual on the warm evening air, and everywhere the beauty of the new green leaf was bewildering in its rippling diversity of shade and texture.

She reached the ash stump and settled herself comfortably on the cushion she had brought. Below her the clearing lay silent and empty as the green-dappled light of day slowly turned to yellow in the setting sun. There was no breeze, and as Polly sat watching and listening her senses slowly became attuned to the tiny sounds that dropped into the pool of silence, the buzz of a beetle, the soft clap of a bird's wings, a slow, smooth rustle that marked the passage of a snake. Stealthily, secretly, the magic of the woodlands wooed and possessed her, so that she became as one with the ancient oaks and the fragrant fertile earth. The affairs of mankind grew small and far away.

Suddenly, a loud sniffing noise alerted her and peering down into the clearing she saw to her delight that a badger had emerged from one of the openings and was standing in the arena, its back to her and its head nodding as it stared into the trees. As she watched, it flopped over onto one haunch and proceeded to scratch its flank vigorously, its claws making a loud rasping noise against its hide.

Polly's mouth was dry and her heart beat furiously. She was terrified that she would cough or make some movement that would alert the animal to her presence. Then, to Polly's joy, a second badger emerged, and a few seconds later the clearing was alive with bustle and noise as three cubs poured out of the set. Spellbound, Polly watched them begin a wild and joyous romp, racing in and out of the bushes, yelping and bickering and chasing each other's tails. For some twenty minutes the cubs played, lying in ambush and pouncing on each other, until the games ended in a prolonged and strenuous wrestling match, with all three rolling in the dust. Handa and Borun kept watch, making sure that no cub strayed too far, but otherwise interfering little with the cubs' boisterous play.

A vigorous grooming session followed. Handa inspected each protesting cub in turn, holding it down with a firm forepaw, releasing it only when she was satisfied that the required standards

378

of cleanliness had been met. It was late now, and the moon had risen, filling the arena with silver light and plunging the bushes into deep shadow. The badgers faded into the night. Polly was alone.

She waited a while, half hoping they would return, but also giving them time to get well clear, so that she would not alarm them. Then as she made her way back to the cottage, suddenly she remembered the by-pass, and realized that she was not the only sacrifice to progress. The badgers too would be dispossessed. She tried to dismiss the problem from her mind, but she slept badly and it kept returning all the following day in spite of everything she could do to keep herself occupied.

She was relieved when at last the day was far enough advanced to allow her to escape to the woods. There at least she would find solace. The evening was sultry and humid, and the mutter of thunder heralded the coming of a storm. Nevertheless, she set off, her cushion under her arm, moving slowly through the trees.

Practice had taught her to pick her way through the woods without sound. Thus she was rewarded by small cameos: a stoat poised in a clearing, one paw raised as its nose quested the air; a hen pheasant nervously leading her chicks across a path; a grass snake lying coiled beneath the fern. She was alert to sounds too, and could distinguish between the short, sharp rustle that told of a bank vole diving for its nest, and the scratching of a lizard as it scurried for cover over the dried leaves, a sound exactly like a pen nib scratching over parchment.

So when she heard a rustle in the undergrowth, a few yards to her right, she stopped and listened. It came again, and then she heard what sounded like an exasperated groan. She moved forward cautiously, not knowing quite what manner of beast might be hiding in the woods.

A bearded face stared out from a clump of elder, a face with gimlet dark eyes and black curly hair. The face spoke. "I wonder if you would care to render a little assistance here?"

Striving not to laugh, so great was her relief, Polly climbed up the slope. The voice was so precise that in this setting it sounded incongruous.

379

A man, well past middle age, lay half reclining in the thicket, attired in a neat jacket of Norfolk green. He made no attempt to rise as she approached, but contented himself with a wave of his hand.

"I'm afraid I've got myself into rather a predicament. Your arrival is most timely, ma'am."

"What happened?" queried Polly.

The man pointed in the direction of his foot. "I slipped, and my foot has somehow got trapped under a root."

Polly looked, and sure enough the man's leg was gripped tight, just above the ankle, between a tough elder root and a rock. "Perhaps if I could get your boot off . . ." she began.

"I fancy my foot is now too swollen, but if you could loosen the laces, it might be more comfortable."

He sighed in relief as Polly did as he asked, but it was clear to her that she could not remove the boot without cutting it. Suddenly it occurred to her that the solution was to saw through the root.

"If you could just be patient for a little while longer," she said, "my cottage is not far away. I'll go back and get a saw, and then you'll soon be free."

"I would be most grateful," said the man. "I promise you I won't go anywhere."

Polly laughed. Then she remembered her cushion. "If you put this behind your head," she offered, "it might be more comfortable."

"Such luxury," sighed the man, settling back. "I'm so glad you came along. If I might make one more small request? My haversack is lying just up the hill where I dropped it. In it are my cigarettes and matches. With them I can wait content."

Polly scrambled farther up the hill and retrieved the haversack. It was surprisingly heavy, as though it was full of rocks, and the handle of a geologist's hammer stuck out of the flap. It was not until she was halfway back to the cottage that its significance struck her. Even then there was no time for speculation, for the impending storm was now much nearer. The skies were darkening, and an ominous breeze ruffled the leaves of the trees. Still, she

380

voiced her question in the form of a comment, as she sawed through the elder root. "You're a geologist, Mr. . . . ."

"Firth, ma'am, Rupert Firth. Yes, I am. That is why I find myself here, and all because a group of megalomaniac bureaucrats think they can build a by-pass here."

Just then the root parted, and the geologist was free. Gingerly he stood up, testing his leg with his weight. "Not broken. Sprained, I think," he grunted, "and swollen with the constriction."

"I brought a broom back with me," said Polly. "If you put the head under your armpit, you can use it as a crutch."

"A splendid idea," murmured Firth, and they set off through the woods, he leaning on his makeshift crutch and she following, burdened with cushion, saw and haversack.

TWENTY MINUTES later Rupert Firth sat sipping a large whisky as Polly applied cold compresses to his ankle, while outside the full fury of the storm unleashed itself. Rupert glanced out of the window and shuddered. "Miss Shaw," he began, "I can't think how I can ever repay you for your resourcefulness and kindness."

Polly could, but for the moment she held her peace.

"It's none of my business, I know," continued Firth, "but could you satisfy my vulgar curiosity by telling me why a lady of your mature years was walking through the woods at that hour, carrying, of all things, a cushion?"

"Simple," said Polly. "I was going to watch badgers."

"Ah yes," nodded Firth. "I saw the sets earlier today."

"They won't be there much longer if the by-pass is built," said Polly quietly.

There was a long silence, as Firth sipped at his glass. Finally, he spoke.

"What do you know about geology?" he asked.

"Nothing," admitted Polly.

"You ought to know something," said Firth sternly. "You can't begin to understand the hills and valleys unless you know something about their anatomy. Have you a few slices of bread?"

Polly got to her feet. "I'm so sorry. You must be starving."

Firth laughed. "Please. I want the bread for quite a different purpose. Fetch it, and you'll see."

Polly brought four slices of bread on a plate, and Firth stacked them one on top of the other. "The rocks that form the backbone of this hill may be anything up to two hundred million years old," he began. "They are sedimentary rocks, formed of sand washed down by extinct rivers, and then compressed by further layers of sediment until they become limestone. So these layers were built up, like these slices of bread, with perhaps a smear of something in between. Now the earth lies in chains, but from time to time she stirs, she moves, and strives to break her bonds."

He took the slices of bread by the four corners, pressed them down and pushed inward, so that the centre of the top slice rose in a hump, forced upward by the slices underneath. "Sometimes this happens and then, as you can see, the layers of rock that form the hill slope down and out, so that if one was to cut into the side, the slabs would slide away downhill."

"And this hill happened like that?" queried Polly.

"Right," said Firth. "And if anyone was to interfere with it, then, on such a night as this, as water seeped between the layers of rock, lubricating their surfaces, parts of the hill could well slide away."

"Could the hillside not be buttressed, to keep it from sliding?"

Firth nodded. "Indeed. But whoever undertook the work would have to be prepared to write a blank cheque, for no accurate estimate of the cost could be made. Even then the work could not be guaranteed."

Polly felt a surge of relief. "So the by-pass will never be built?"

"It will be built somewhere, no doubt. Probably along the floor of the opposite side of the valley. You'll see it from here, but it will be at least a mile away at its nearest point."

Suddenly Polly felt ten years younger. "Well, Mr. Firth, you've amply repaid me for rescuing you."

"Call me Rupert," begged Firth. "And now I must, somehow, relieve you of the burden of my presence."

"On a night like this? You'll do no such thing. You can occupy the spare bed. I'm sure that at our age we can dispense with the proprieties. In the morning I'll drive you to the doctor to get that leg examined." A sudden thought struck her. "Oh, I didn't think. Someone might be wondering where you were. . . ."

Firth shook his head.

"There's no one. I'm a widower, have been for a long time. I had planned to find a hotel for the night."

"That's settled then," said Polly. "Help yourself to the whisky while I scramble some eggs."

She was abashed to discover she was blushing, and scurried away into the kitchen, scolding herself for being a stupid old maid. All the same, she could not suppress a lilting happiness at the thought that whatever else this night's work had begun, it had laid the foundations of what she hoped would be a long friendship.

EPILOGUE

Work began in earnest on the new by-pass along the other side of the valley one late December morning. At the end of the first day, as the excavators ground to a standstill and the mechanics slouched wearily back to their waiting cars, Borun stood in a thorn thicket, his striped head nodding slightly as he surveyed the scene. Polly, too, gazed at the raw yellow scar in the valley, now mercifully veiled in twilight.

Borun glanced skywards and a star shone in his eye, the same star that had shone thousands of years ago on badgers watching the building of the Iron Age fort at Summercombe. How many more changes might the star witness before the sun burnt itself out, leaving the world locked in a pall of ice? For the badgers of Summercombe, and for western civilization, perhaps time was running out. But for the moment the badgers at least had won a short reprieve.

Ewan Clarkson

"This is the world of Borun's breed".

Ewan Clarkson had taken me to the valley of Lustleigh Cleave on Dartmoor, just a few miles from his home. Through the rain that pelted down from a leaden sky, I peered into the shimmering mist-covered depths where thousand upon thousand of silver birches, close packed like a myriad of armoured soldiers, swayed rhythmically to the command of the biting March wind. It was an awesome sight: a glimpse of southern England as it must have been two thousand years ago before the Romans came and began to clear the trees to bring us civilization. . . .

There are not only badgers here (if you can see them) but also countless birds and other creatures, including wild mink. Not surprisingly, it is one of Ewan's favourite spots in Devon. "I could spend a lifetime up here just observing and contemplating," Ewan told me. "Mind you, I might take time off to do some fishing. Better than slogging away at writing."

Ewan has had many jobs, from bus driving to zoo keeping, but has made his living mainly by writing about animals, angling and the country scene. He was born in 1929 in Cumberland, spent his childhood in Cheshire, and at one time lived in Bath (where the coming of the M4 and the fate of a nearby badger community first gave him the idea for his latest book).

He now lives with his wife Jenny and their two children in Moss Rose Cottage, a delightful two up two down white thatched Devon house that they have handsomely enlarged, mainly by their own hard work and building skills, to accommodate seven other members of the family, four generations in all including a year-old grandchild. Two miles from the estuary of the Teign, it is an almost self-reliant community. Jenny, a keen seamstress, can tailor a suit for her husband, and with her mother is becoming expert at making the local and famous Honiton lace. Ewan is an enthusiastic fisherman, bringing back a regular haul of fresh bass and mackerel from the sea or, after a night on the shore, a bucket full of prawns. In addition, he coaxes the half acre strip of garden beside the cottage to yield its maximum of fruit and vegetables, while the family comb the fields and hedgerows for delicacies such as mushrooms and blackberries.

Preservation of our natural resources is a subject of vital concern to Ewan Clarkson. He is very much aware of being himself part of the cosmic cycle. He enjoys every day, always finding something fresh to wonder at and perhaps to write about. It was while he was actually writing *The Badgers of Summercombe* that, out of his study window, he first saw a blackbird actually singing with its

beak full of worms. He based the behaviour of Vandal on one of the family's three cats. As for the other animals in the book, an old dog fox lives in the next door field and the garden itself has all manner of visitors.

The names, Tobar, Borun and Handa, incidentally, are Scandinavian—a reminder that badgers first came to this country by walking across land now submerged beneath the North Sea. Mela is derived from *mel* the Latin word for that favourite treat of badgers, honey, which is also the basis of their scientific name, *Meles Meles.*

Ewan, the author, is clearly looked on with great respect by the locals. When their village was threatened by a road scheme, it was to him that they came to write their letters of protest and to mount what turned out to be a thoroughly successful campaign. On the other hand, it seems that Ewan, the naturalist, is regarded with affectionate tolerance. His neighbours have grown used to such strange ways ever since a few years ago when, on the strength of a successful book about peregrine falcons, he commissioned a skilled thatcher to model a large version of that predatory bird to mount on the top of his cottage. Apart from decoration, he hoped it would provide a deterrent to smaller birds nesting in the thatch. The falcon was duly delivered and mounted on the roof. Soon onlookers had assembled in the lane outside.

"What do you call it?" one of them wanted to know.

"The sun god Horus," he was told.

"Ever since," Ewan assured me, "I have been known around here as *him wi' that damn bird Horace.*"   N.D.B.

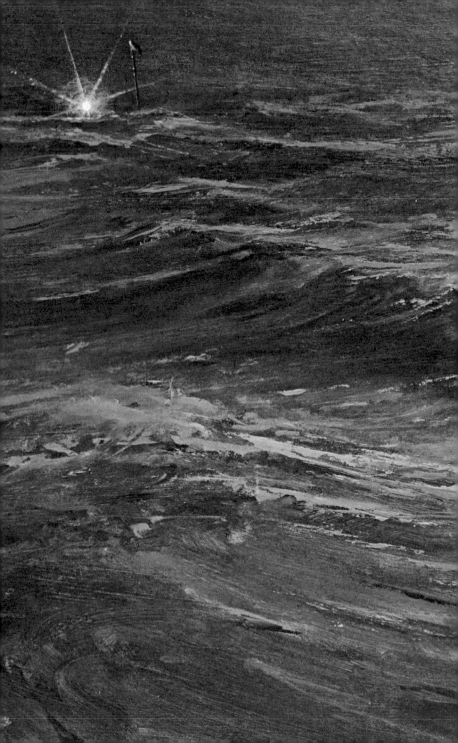

OVERBOARD

a condensation of the book by
HANK SEARLS

Illustrated by George Jones
Published by Raven Books in association with
Macdonald and Jane's Publishers, London

The boat was far out to sea, seventy miles from Tahiti, when Mitch Gordon, yachtsman and one-time lawyer, awoke in the small hours of the morning to find himself alone. The ship's cockpit was deserted, his wife Lindy gone, disappeared overboard, the safety line trailing uselessly from the stern.

For thirty-six desperate hours he searched for her in the mountainous Pacific swells, and for thirty-six hours, kept afloat by her life-jacket, she fought a solitary battle against the sea, against the bitter cold of the night and the scorching heat of the day. If they were ever to find each other again it would be through the strength their shared memories gave them, their life together, the good times and the bad. . . .

This is a novel of extraordinary power and understanding, taking the reader from the relentless commercial jungle of life in the big city to a thrilling climax far away on the high seas. It is a story packed with the drama of man's fight against the elements, and against the darkness in his own soul.

PART ONE: DAY

Chapter One

She had vanished while he slept, sometime before dawn, one infinitesimal speck detaching itself from another under unseeing stars. And now as the sun rose astern, the southeast trades began to die so that his speed slackened and his search slowed.

He sagged at the helm, shivering in panic, alone with a cat, forty miles from the nearest island. In early apricot light, he was still backtracking. He forced himself to look at his watch. It was 5:15 a.m. Papeete time.

The ketch had been pounding southeast, steered automatically by a wind vane, bound from Bora Bora to Tahiti, now seventy miles away. In darkness, at 3:12 a.m., he had discovered that she was gone.

When the first instant of paralysis had passed and he found that he could function, he had dropped the man-overboard flag, tied by a twenty-foot line to a life buoy and a floating strobe light. He had acted instinctively, but perhaps prematurely. There was no reason to think that she was anywhere near.

He had found himself whimpering in fear but capable of elementary calculations. He had reversed course instantly and set the wind vane to steer the new heading. By force of will, he had plotted his estimated position. And he had searched for their logbook, hoping her last entry would help pinpoint the time she had gone. He could not find the book. He had tried to call Papeete Radio. There was no reply.

He climbed to the spreader halfway up the mast and clung to the ratlines there for two hours, scanning by starlight the path they had sailed. The lopsided moon sinking to the west was useless. It was not darkness, anyway, that would hide her; it was the unceasing swells. Even from twenty-five feet up the mast, the blinking strobe light had been lost within minutes, astern among mountainous seas.

It was three days before Christmas, high summer in the Society Islands. He faced a day of simmering heat and squalls. Eyeballs wind-dried and stinging, he clung to the shrouds as the sun rose. His hands and feet were already raw from the teak ratline rungs. His skin smelled sourly of terror.

He hung on past sunrise as the wind vane steered him back over the track they had come. A few minutes after dawn the breeze fell off till the boat began to wander, groping for the wind. So he swung down, released the steering vane, and took the wheel himself. At deck level he was too low to see well, but he had no choice.

To fend off despair, he considered once more a hope that had helped him through the hours aloft. If she had been wearing her flotation jacket, there was a police whistle tied to the zipper just for this, very loud and shrill.

He moved toward the hatch, intending to duck below to check the foul-weather locker. Hand on the hatch top, he stopped. He was afraid to face her bright orange jacket hanging there. It was better to assume she was in it.

He glanced back at the rising sun shafting through a squall line. She could be watching it too. "Now look," he muttered to no one, "I haven't asked for a goddam thing until now. . . ."

He found his eyes filling with tears. Astonished, he massaged them with his fingers until his vision cleared. Then, to raise his eye level, he grabbed a shroud near the wheel, balanced with one bare foot on the cockpit coaming and steered with the other. He glanced at a squall line to windward, and saw one of her cloud people, a perfect matador wearing a scarlet-fringed hat. He almost called her topside to see it, realized that she was gone, pulled back just in time from the edge of tears that would blind him. He regarded instead the threat of a squall.

The usual morning revival of the trade winds would bring the squall down on him. She could be hidden under it if rain moved across his path. Meanwhile, without the trades, the boat was simply marking time, while she struggled somewhere ahead.

He was impelled to move faster. He started the engine and jammed it full ahead, but its sound frightened him. His main chance was to hear her, not to see her. When he was down in the troughs, all he could see were dark blue hills heaving around him. With the engine drumming, he could miss her if she were fifty yards away.

But her chance of spotting him was very much greater. The mainmast towered above the wave peaks forty feet. It would be she who discovered him. He had better be ready to hear her when she did.

He cut the engine. Now, in the silence, the boat's crawling pace chilled him. He envisioned for the first time her body somewhere ahead, trailing strands of bronze hair, spiraling downward into water turning midnight blue. The vision overcame his fear of the unanswered question of her jacket. He took a final sweep of the horizon, stumbled down the companionway ladder, and opened the locker.

Her jacket was gone. He sagged with relief. Incredibly, he found himself on his knees, head bowed in thanks. Feeling suddenly foolish, he got up and went topside.

The breeze freshened, speeding the squall. From below he heard the ship's clock strike three bells: 5:30. His euphoria trickled away. Now he became convinced that he had passed her soon after his panicky turn, in the black hours before dawn. Everything suddenly pulled at him to reverse course.

He fought the impulse to play the hunch. She could just as easily be bobbing in the next five miles as in the last ten.

SHE WAS SWEPT to the crest of a swell. It broke in her face. Her eyes stung with the foam. She squeezed them shut, lying back in her flotation jacket, clinging to the plastic jerrycan she had torn from the trailing line.

The morning sun was hot on her forehead. She felt feverish and let her head sink to cool it. If he didn't find her soon, she'd boil like a lobster.

Her guaranteed waterproof watch had stopped at dawn, but she guessed that it was six or seven in the morning. She had been in the water for three or four hours.

Until daybreak she had been freezing. She still shivered, but now she could not tell if she suffered more from heat or cold. Maybe by noon she would be warm. But of course he would find her before then.

The jacket that was saving her life was the worst of her discomforts. It kept slithering up her body and chafing her armpits. The nylon safety belt was rubbing her belly raw too. She kept it on anyway. It might help him drag her aboard. Besides, it was proof that she had semi-followed their rules, even if she had obviously not clipped it to a lifeline.

She gripped the plastic container firmly. She valued it for its buoyancy, afraid that her jacket might eventually turn soggy. And it was a link with the boat. When water would trickle in through its broken handle, she would drain it and plug it for a while with her finger. Then she would forget and it would fill again.

The whole nightmare was past belief. Safe in her bunk at 3:00 a.m., she had been deeply engrossed in a paperback. Fifteen minutes later she was thrashing idiotically in the boat's wake.

She let her mind drift back, looking for some excuse. She had been snug with the cat in the forward cabin. The kitchen timer had croaked from its niche, telling her that it was time for her half-hour survey of the horizon. She spilled M. le Chat from her belly, snapped off her bunk light, and groped with her feet for the varnished cabin flooring.

The cabin, when the boat was beating into the wind, sloped at 30 degrees. She swung herself aft, making no move without a hold on something, feeling alternately light and heavy as the boat pitched wildly in its battle with the seas.

She sidled past the trunk of the mast, feeling a trickle of water down its face: the canvas mast boot was leaking, as usual, and Mitch kept forgetting to tape it down.

That was her current complaint. That and the squeaking of the steering cable. Tomorrow she would get him to squirt it with oil.

In the main cabin, by the moonglow through the skylight she

could make out Mitch's form on the leeward bunk. His massive shoulders and the line of his body, after more than twenty years of marriage, were still sexy to her.

Maybe it would all work out once they got back.

She groped for her jacket in the foul-weather locker and put it on. She picked up her safety belt and cinched it on too, then she took the logbook and the flashlight from their niches above the chart table and climbed to the cockpit.

The night was warm but the wind whipped her hair. She snapped her safety belt to a fitting on the mizzenmast, with slack enough to move around the cockpit but not much farther. Clinging to a shroud for balance and carefully keeping her eyes just above the dark horizon, she scanned the whole 360 degrees, stooping to see to starboard under the drumming sail. She checked the port and starboard running lights; both okay. The stern light had been out since the last island, another job for Mitch.

She shone her flashlight on the dial by the wheel and logged the speed—5.1 knots—and the mileage. She checked the compass course. South-southeast, right on. She checked her watch: 0304. She logged that too, as 0300, then shone her light on the steering vane. It was working tirelessly, but behind it she noticed that the mizzen sheet was caught up on the stern light.

She was supposed to awaken Mitch if she had to leave the cockpit for any reason, but for so trivial a problem it seemed silly. She tried first to reach the line with her foot, straining at the length of her tether. She could not quite touch it, so she stuffed the logbook under the cockpit seat to protect it from spray and unclipped her safety belt hook. She should have snapped it to a lifeline before she stretched to kick the mizzen line loose, but it seemed so close that she did not.

She was balanced on one leg, clinging to a shroud, and reaching out her toes for the line, when a wave smacked the port bow. The boat lurched under the impact, throwing her off-balance.

She lost her grip on the shroud and pirouetted wildly. She grabbed at another shroud, only tipping the wire cable with her finger. Her bottom hit the stern rail and for an instant she balanced there, flailing for a handhold. She screamed Mitch's name, once.

Then she was in the rushing sea, fighting instantly to find the safety line they trailed behind the boat. She grabbed the slimy rope and lost it. At the last moment she glimpsed the crazy plastic container bounding at its tail.

She caught the container, but it snapped off in her hands. The rope whipped away, streaming phosphorescence. She found her breath and shrieked as the dark hull pulled away. She remembered her whistle, jammed it into her mouth, and began wetly to shrill.

She continued to blow long after the boat was lost in the swells. The moon, tipping precariously, was blotted out by a wave, no worse than the one that had spilled her overboard, but monstrous from her angle. She rode up its face like a cork, glimpsed the top of the mainsail. She whistled again, and listened.

Nothing. She screamed his name once more.

Then she lay whimpering, while the enormity of it all soaked in. Once she thought she saw a flash. If he had dropped the strobe light, he had heard her go and was looking for her.

She didn't see it again. After a while she decided that she had imagined it.

When dawn came and she saw no sail, she was shaken and scared, as much for him as herself. *She* knew that she was okay; *he* knew nothing.

THE SUN EDGED higher. He clutched the wheel, unable to shake the compulsion to retrace his track. His guilt was enormous. He had brought her here and never really told her why.

Three weeks ago they had sailed into Bora Bora, isolating themselves in a lagoon away from the village. They were exhausted, licking their wounds from a hurricane. Licking other wounds as well. That night she asked him idly when their cruise had really begun.

"When we spotted the boat," he said too quickly.

"You're not leveling," she said. "And we promised."

He had caught a quick image of himself at fourteen, reading in his bedroom in a San Francisco penthouse. It was a year after Pearl Harbor. His dad had just signed on for another suicidal tour of duty as a front-line doctor with the Second Marines.

Mitch's gut still twisted at the thought. Homework had become impossible, and Mitch anesthetized himself with the South Seas fiction of Melville, Conrad, and Jack London. Rationally, he knew that the islands he was adventuring among were dead or would be ruined by the war, but he saw himself among them anyway, skippering a trading schooner, with a slim Polynesian mistress, outwitting pearl traders and rescuing heiresses.

That was when their cruise had really started. He had held to his South Sea fantasy through his own war in Korea and during two years of medicine at college. But Lindy already blamed herself because he had quit medicine for law. To lay the postponement of his adolescent dream on her too would be cruel.

"I *am* leveling," he said flatly. "The cruise started when we saw the boat."

THE SOUTH SEAS might have rested forever between the covers of Melville if it had not been for an unemployed house painter with a paralyzed wife, and a sturdy two-masted ketch, painted red. The house painter had shambled into his law office four years ago, and the ketch had crossed his path two years later.

For the house painter's wife, Mitch had filed the largest medical malpractice suit in the history of California law, for one and a half million dollars. If he had not been awarded the judgment—thirty percent of which was his, as filing attorney—he could not have retired at forty-three.

He had filed, reluctantly, against a well-trained young surgeon and the University of California Hospital. The patient's tragedy was real enough: she had gone in for a hysterectomy and come out paralyzed. The trouble was that no one knew for sure what had happened. Mitch had hesitated. He had never taken a malpractice case. The ghost of his father, who after all the wartime heroics had died years later of a tumor in bed, still hovered, sardonic in his view of lawyers who sued doctors.

But the woman's plight was awful. She was in a leased iron lung, a cheerful schoolteacher with a little-girl smile who had been supporting an alcoholic husband and two children.

He agonized for weeks. Lindy begged him to drop the whole

thing if it bothered him. His partner, Bernie, smelling blood, grew restless. Finally, Mitch filed. The hospital and insurance company lawyer wanted to settle: the doctor, only half covered, refused. This made Mitch feel better. The surgeon was asking for it. In two years, when he came to trial, he would probably learn to trust his lawyer.

In the meantime, the law firm of Gordon, Bertelli continued to prosper, as it had for twenty years, and life in San Francisco stumbled along. Mitch's son graduated from high school, oozed into Berkeley, flunked out, was sent to Humboldt College, up the coast.

When the trial date was a month off, Mitch began to awaken earlier every morning. He would lie staring at the ceiling, attacked by nameless apprehensions.

Then, on Saturday, with the trial scheduled to start on Monday, the red ketch had sailed into his life. He and Lindy had been crewing for a race on her father's sloop in San Francisco Bay. Puffy clouds scampered above the bridge, and burgees and pennants snapped as the racing fleet drove toward the starting line.

The red ketch was a double-ender, an Atkins design of functional grace and beauty. His father-in-law very nearly rammed her amidships.

The ketch had been cutting scornfully through the mob of competitors, bound on business of her own, secure in her right-of-way on a starboard tack. Lindy's father, cutting toward the start, was driving obstinately onward.

Lindy saw the threat and groaned. Mitch spoke up. "Collision course, Shawn," he warned. "He's got the right-of-way."

"He's not racing," muttered Shawn. White hair whipping, face pink, he looked like a demented gnome.

Mitch toyed with the thought of doing nothing. A little bump might wake up Shawn's tired blood. But Lindy might get shaken, and it would be criminal to let the pretty red ketch get hurt.

He yanked the wheel from Shawn and headed the sloop into the wind. In a drumroll of fluttering sails they slowed, clearing the ketch's stern by three feet. A tall, spare figure at the ketch's wheel regarded them sourly.

"Dammit, we lost the start," Shawn growled.

Mitch hardly heard him. He had the binoculars on the ketch, trying to focus on the name. He had seen the hull shape before. Plans for her prototype lay in a crate in their basement, with an article he had cut from *Yachting* twenty years ago. It was a smaller version of the formidable pilot boats built by the Norwegians in the 1880s. You still saw the originals, ninety years old, plowing on forever. No one could afford to build them anymore.

Lindy was watching him. Bundled in his ancient navy jacket, peering from the fur-lined olive hood, she looked as young as she had at eighteen, a brown squirrel peeping from foliage. She nodded after the ketch. "You look as if you'd just seen paradise."

He grinned. He felt suddenly lighter. A solid cruising boat could do that to him, sparking the dream. "I liked the boat."

SUNDAY MORNING Mitch dug out the boat plans from the basement. Instead of polishing the malpractice case for Bernie, who would argue the brief on Monday, he wasted half the morning in his den overlooking Raccoon Strait, calling yacht brokers about the red ketch. Nobody knew her.

When he gave up on the boat to concentrate on the brief, his back began to ache. He blamed it on an old football injury and jammed a pillow behind it. He was working when his son tapped on the door and walked in.

Tony was twenty—a very young twenty—almost as tall as he, with grey eyes like his own and black wavy hair as thick as his own had been. He had been hanging around the house for weeks. It seemed an eternity. Now he exuded charm, alerting Mitch. "I finished the cars, Dad, so I'll take off, okay? Nancy and I—"

"Yeah," Mitch murmured, "Nancy . . ." She was the neighbors' daughter, a shy girl of impeccable manners. Tony was in love with her and everyone knew it: her father, her mother, the postman. The two could disappear into thin air when you were talking to them. "Did you *wax* the cars," Mitch asked, "or just wash them?"

"I thought I'd wax them tomorrow."

"Today, okay?"

"Nancy—"

"Get her to help you." He swiveled back to his desk. Something bothered him. "Hey, wait."

Tony froze. "Yeah?"

"*Tomorrow?* Tomorrow you're heading back to college."

"Look, you're busy. Talk to you later, okay?"

There was nothing he would rather have done than to have talked to his son later. But Tony had already dropped pre-law for forestry. He couldn't let him drop out altogether.

He arched his spine, which quickly went into some sort of spasm. Heavily, he prepared his soul for battle. To attack was lately repugnant to him, which was the reason that he was letting Bernie plead their biggest case in court. "You packed?"

"Not exactly. Look, I better wax the cars. . . ."

"*Pack*. Then wax. First things first."

His son regarded him miserably. "Nancy—"

"The *hell* with Nancy!" growled Mitch. He was instantly sorry. Wordlessly, Tony started out the door. Mitch half rose to follow him, then sat down again. The kid should realize that at twenty he was too old to be drifting like an empty beer can in the surf. And be grateful that his father cared. But he was damned if he was going to chase him around the house groveling and wreck his back for good.

AFTER DINNER Mitch lay on the bed, so that Lindy could knead his spine. She was only five years younger than he but somehow, effortlessly, kept herself looking like a daughter instead of a wife. Her hair was thick and vibrant, her skin tanned and young, her hazel, gold-flecked eyes clear as the day they had met. He thought of her as bronze and amber, lighted somehow from within.

Justice Holmes, their Alsatian, licked his arm soothingly. None of it was fair. The dog stayed in shape, chewing on newsboys. Tony stayed in shape, chasing Nancy. Lindy stayed in shape, playing tennis and vacuuming the house. While *he* got fat, supporting the whole ménage, and his back grew feeble.

"You know why your back hurts?" Lindy murmured.

He sensed her diagnosis and didn't care to hear.

"It's the surgeon. You're not like Bernie, it bothers you."

398

"*What*, for cripe's sake?"

"Knowing he saved her life."

"He paralyzed her first!" Her fingers found the knot in his spine. "Hey, you've done it!"

"*We* think he paralyzed her," she murmured, getting up.

He felt a flash of pain and his back clenched again. "The case," he said softly, "is solid."

His back began to throb, but he stood up without wincing. He was damned if he'd let her know, after all her work, that her treatment had failed.

NOW THAT she had wrecked his Sunday, she felt awful. She should not question his work. She had been annoyed because he was sending Tony back to college against his will. Her pique was silly. Mitch was right. Tony had to finish.

He should know it too.

She found him in his room stuffing socks, shirts, and jeans into an orange backpack.

"You'd think Dad went through college as a Trappist monk," he growled. "Didn't *he* ever flunk anything?"

"No." Her son looked so disappointed she handed him some ammunition. "He did quit medicine for law. And I quit as a sophomore."

"Well, but that was *me*. Right?"

Her face flamed. "What do you mean?"

He poked a finger through a hole in a ski sock, then tossed it into a wastebasket. She retrieved it silently, and looked up at him.

He muttered: "Well, you quit because you were pregnant, okay?"

She started to protest, but changed her mind. It was time he knew. "Yes," she admitted. "Did *Mitch* tell you?"

"No, your wedding picture in an old *Examiner* I saw at Grandad's apartment before he moved to the Club. The date was wrong."

Her father had moved to the Bohemian Club ten years ago, so for at least that long Tony had known about this one. "That was pretty sharp, for a ten-year-old," she suggested.

"To know my own birthday?" He smiled. "Thanks." He wanted to know if they'd lived together before getting married, and she told him no.

"He was back from Korea, with this drink and be merry for tomorrow we die aura, and, well, I was only eighteen." Now she was apologizing to her own son.

"So you got married to be polite," he reflected.

"*Polite?* No! We were in love. *You* happening didn't change a thing." Not strictly accurate, maybe, but about *that* she didn't really know, herself. Her throat was tight. "Polite!"

He studied her. His eyes were as gray and soft as his father's. And as inscrutable. "I'm sorry," he said. "Okay?"

"I guess." She went down to darn his sock.

Chapter Two

He was suddenly in the sail's shade. He had drifted 10 degrees off course. He spun the wheel quickly, still tempted to turn around. But he simply could not unless he knew when she had gone, and the only documentary evidence, the logbook, seemed nowhere.

He had awakened her at midnight to stand her watch. He had shaken her shoulders, not even bothering to kiss her awake, as he used to do before Jean-Paul. But he must not think of that now.

He had told her to check topside for squalls every half an hour: the boat was far enough from land and steamship lanes so that she could sleep in the intervals. She should set her kitchen timer to wake her up. Then he had crawled into his bunk. The last words to the woman he loved were par for the recent course: "Every time you go topside, log the speed."

His eyes went blind again with tears. "Oh, God," he mumbled, half strangled. He had to quit sniveling if he was going to see at all. He tried to focus his mind on the facts that would help to find her, to estimate her drift and his, but his brain was unable to compute unless it knew *when* it had happened.

He searched for a clue in his memory, a scream or a whistle half heard in his sleep. He had come awake suddenly, an hour and a half before dawn, and had glimpsed the Southern Cross racing across the skylight. The illuminated compass at the foot of his bunk cast a glow on varnished cabin beams and tinted the clock and barometer to a brassy rose. All very shippy, and once one of the delights of awakening at sea. But, like everything else, dimmed with a year aboard, and too familiar.

The starboard steering cable had chirped in the lazaret, their storage space aft. The sound drove the cat crazy and bothered Lindy too. He'd kept promising to oil it. From forward, where he assumed Lindy lay half asleep, came the moan of a plank strained a year ago. He had intended to have it replaced, but there was no use doing it now if they were selling the boat.

He knew he couldn't go back to sleep so he decided to go topside. He rolled from the bunk, handed himself along overhead grab rails like a commuter on a lurching subway, and climbed the companionway ladder. He ignored a tug of guilt as he brushed past his safety belt. He had made her promise him, and had promised her, always to wear one topside at night, but since Jean-Paul, such promises did not seem to matter.

He was troubled vaguely by something wrong. He inspected the self-steering vane aft. Irwin, as Lindy had christened it, was steering with his customary precision. Mitch was still uneasy. Aft of Irwin, a mizzen sheet was fouled on the stern light. Hanging tightly to a mizzen shroud, he kicked it loose. For a moment he gazed astern at the green track they laid.

The thick yellow safety line writhed in their wake. You were supposed to grab it if you fell overboard. It should have been dragging an empty plastic container as a buoy astern. But he could not see it.

He began to haul the line in. When its end was twenty feet astern, he could see that the container was gone. He hauled the rest quickly aboard. The loop he had spliced to the handle of the missing jerrycan was still intact. The cap must have loosened. The container must have filled with water and become so heavy that its handle had broken off.

He tossed the line back and was turning away when he felt rippling fur at his ankles. It was M. le Chat. The cat was a gift from a waitress in Tahiti, intended as rat insurance. It usually slept at the foot of Lindy's bunk. Mitch looked at it uneasily. He was suddenly impatient to return below. He picked up the cat and spilled him roughly down the companionway steps. Turning, he noticed that Lindy's safety belt was not swinging on its hook next to his. That was strange. A year at sea had taught them to keep safety gear in place.

The cat scooted back up the ladder. He caught it, carried it below, tossed it into the head compartment, and slammed the door.

He was apprehensive now, inexplicably nervous. He ducked forward and brushed aside the curtain to the forward compartment. Her bunk light was not on. Shaken and frightened, he groped for the light, missed, felt in the bunk itself. "Lindy?" Tight with terror, he found the light at last and flicked it on.

The leeward bunk was empty. So was the other.

"Lindy?" he shouted. "*Lindy!*"

A bolt of panic tore through him, paralyzing him. He began to tremble uncontrollably.

When he could move again, he moved swiftly. Sometimes, when it was stuffy below, she slept topside on the dinghy's plywood sea top, her safety belt clipped to a line. He scrambled topside.

He could see by moonlight that the dinghy was bare. He went aft, where the strobe lamp, horseshoe buoy, its sea anchor, and the man-overboard pole were all connected by a line, ready for action. He hurled the lot into the wake. He found himself sobbing quietly, not sure why he was dropping it all here when she could be hours away.

The floating strobe, weighted to stay in place and bob erect, began to flash: one lightning blink, visible for miles, every five seconds, so long as its battery lived. Its first flash caught the pole's orange flag in midflutter. The second flash silhouetted the flag just peeping over the crest of the next swell. By the third flash the thirteen-foot pole had dropped out of sight astern in a trough.

He still could not believe that she was gone. He flicked on the spreader lights, illuminating everything on deck and halfway up the mast. She was nowhere topside. Okay, she might have washed over and be dragging half drowned from her safety line. He would pull her aboard and revive her, and they would laugh about it tomorrow.

Feet on the rail, hands clinging to shrouds, he swung far out to port, then scrambled to starboard, peering fore and aft. Nothing.

He switched off the spreader lights, which had already wrecked his night vision, and turned to disengage Irwin. He reversed course in a flapping panic of sails, so shaken that he found difficulty in adding 180 degrees to their heading of 160 to find the reciprocal bearing. Finally, he simply began a turn toward the winking light. When it was dead ahead, he tried the sum again.

He squinted at the compass. It tossed and twisted. He managed to steady it at last on 340, almost NNW. In three minutes he was close to the strobe. The search was starting now.

He tightened a knob on Irwin, giving the vane control and freeing himself to act. He ducked below to check the time on the chronometer above his chart table. 0320 local time.

He leaned on the chart table, chewing a pencil. Say he had discovered her gone eight minutes ago, at 0312. He reached for their logbook above the chart table. Strangely, it was not where they kept it. He searched the cabin wildly, throwing clothes and pillows everywhere. The log, with its half-hour entries, would give him a clue as to when she had last been aboard.

The log was nowhere, and there was no more time to waste. So he penciled in a shaky estimated position on the chart, labeled it 0312, and picked off his latitude and longitude. His hands trembled so badly that he had to do it twice. Then he hurtled through the cabin and clicked on the radio-telephone. He switched to the international emergency frequency and called Mahina Radio in Papeete, over and over.

Papeete was only seventy miles southeast, but he got no response. He began to broadcast anyway: *Mayday*, then his latitude, longitude, and present course. When he still raised no reply, he decided that his signal was being blanked by the mountainous crags of the island of Moorea fifty miles to windward. It was then that he had lunged back topside, swung up the ratlines, and begun his useless predawn vigil halfway up the mast. He had stayed until the failing wind forced him to take over the helm.

Now, still not knowing when she had gone, he forced his attention back to the skies. Eyes taut with fatigue, he tried to estimate how much time he had before the first squall hit him.

The sun had broken from behind mushroom clouds and turned the water to windward into a lane of hammered brass. It was impossible to search it with the naked eye. He dashed below for his Polaroid sunglasses. When he could not find them, he tore into his drawer and flung clothes, handkerchiefs, and socks around the cabin. He discovered them finally where he always kept them, in a net above his bunk. He barged back topside, took the wheel.

The squall hit in a blinding sheet of rain and spray. For five minutes he could not see upwind at all, and to leeward not more than a hundred feet. Somehow *Linda Lee* slogged through it. The wind shifted, and when he thought they were safe, another squall blustered through, with thirty-knot gusts.

When the wind shifted and the trades began again, he placed the vane in charge. He slung binoculars round his neck and climbed the ratlines to the spreader. He pulled himself to a sitting position on its flat upper surface, clinging to the mast for balance.

He tried to study the water up-sun with his binoculars, but he was dazzled by dancing gold. He let them swing from his neck and searched with the Polaroid glasses alone. Two white terns were flashing off his quarter, spiraling upward together. They were delicate, ethereal creatures with translucent wings, always in pairs. The Tahitians called them love terns, and the fishermen steered for them to find *mahimahi*—dolphin. Lindy had wondered what happened to one when the other was lost in a storm. Her sensitive lawyer, man of words and infinite feeling, had had an answer for her, of course: "They find somebody else, honey. One good tern deserves another."

He winced. He stared at the area of ocean beneath the birds, looking for whatever kept them over that particular spot.

There was nothing, anywhere.

THE DAY the trial began, the back spasm seemed to have shortened Mitch's left leg by half an inch. He limped into court feeling more like a personal-injury plaintiff than a lawyer. He

was tired of the classroom smell of courtrooms, but he had scheduled himself to remain next to Bernie, in case he was needed.

Bernie wore his poverty-lawyer suit, a blue double-breasted that he seemed to keep better shined than his shoes. When he regarded the jury, his dark eyes pleaded with it to sympathize with a night-school lawyer who had come up the hard way.

Mitch felt a quiver of panic. A million and a half! They had gone too far. He discovered suddenly that he really didn't want Bernie to succeed, and felt a jab of pity for the white-faced surgeon, with his future in the hands of a dozen jurors.

Court adjourned late. Mitch fought his way onto a crowded Sutter Street bus to get back to his office. Three blocks in advance of his own stop he began to inch his way to the door, but he was two blocks past his office building by the time he was expelled to the sidewalk like a pip from a squeezed grapefruit.

It took him fifteen minutes to gentle his car up the ramps out of the office garage, trailing the whole stenographic population of their building, only to join another crawl up Sutter Street. If the city got any more crowded, traffic would someday freeze forever, glacierlike, on the hills.

When he got home he found that Tony had left, as instructed, for Humboldt. After dinner he went to his study, to call Tony's dormitory. The phone rang first, cutting off his good intention. It was Lindy's brother, Bobby, a real estate broker.

"Mitch, that stretch of beach you have up near Bragg?"

He felt a jab of irritation. It was more than a stretch of beach; it was private cove sheltered by towering rocks. They had a vague idea of building a home on it when he retired.

He felt a sudden thrill. If they won the case, in any reasonable amount, he could probably quit *now*: get shot of the traffic, the depositions, conferences, office coffee. . . .

Ridiculous. Quit to do what? He was only forty-three. "I can't sell it, Bobby. It's the only place in the world with fresh air."

Bobby told him that an owner a half-mile north had won permission for a mobile-home park. Mitch felt sick. "He's out of his mind."

"You'd better sell before it's too late."

"I'd sell *this* place first," he blurted. Now why had he said that?

Bobby shifted gears. "Why not?" he asked softly. "It's too big. Tony's grown. You know what I can get you for it?"

They had bought their home fifteen years ago, when Tony was five. To redo the house, which clung to the rock by its fingernails, had taken massive loans. He had infused his own sweat to save the plumbing and his cash to build an expensive sun porch suspended over Raccoon Strait. "How much?" he heard himself ask.

"A hundred and fifty, easy." Mitch stiffened. Bobby went on. "Hey, I even have a prospective customer."

"No way," said Mitch. He hung up, feeling oddly nervous. Instead of phoning Tony, he joined Lindy in the living room. Offhandedly, his heart pounding, he told her about the call.

She had been reading the paper. Now she put it down. "Are you serious? Sell our house? What good is the money?"

"It's not the money. Tony *is* leaving someday." He wandered to the window.

She spoke from the chair. "Are you *tired* of the house, Mitch?"

"I don't know," he murmured. "Hell, you know how I am."

"But it's not a camera or a motorcycle! It's home! And I love it! It's *us!*"

"Okay, I *told* Bobby to forget it. Let's us forget it too."

He didn't know, himself, what he'd had in mind. After the trial he'd think it through.

THEIR CLIENT was brought before the bench in her iron lung. The effect on the jury was brutal, and her smile, reflected in the mirror she used to see other human beings, was heartbreaking. As she was wheeled out, Mitch sensed from the jury that it was no longer a question of *whether*, simply *how much*.

Mitch missed Bernie's summation. He was alone in the jury room, lying on a couch to take the strain off his back. He was jumpy and fearful. Something was changing within him. When his back spasm passed, he returned to find that the court had recessed. A note from Bernie lay on their table: "Enemy tried to bail out. We refused eight hundred grand."

He swore silently and limped to a phone booth in the marble corridor. He dialed his office and caught Bernie arriving.

"Listen, are you running this case all alone?"

"We're doing fine," Bernie said placidly.

"Did you explain she might get *less?*"

"I didn't ask her."

He almost dropped the phone. "She's *my* client! What am I going to tell her when she finds out you turned down eight hundred grand? Without even *consulting* her!"

"Tell her you have the Cincinnati Kid for a partner."

"I may not have him," Mitch said darkly, "for very long." He hung up. Now he really needed a drink. He left the courthouse for a bar-restaurant across the road.

As the head waitress led him through the gloom inside, he glimpsed the surgeon eating alone at a table in the corner. He almost turned to leave, but the doctor glanced up and spotted him. He couldn't retreat after that, so he let the girl seat him. He was sipping a Gibson and studying the menu when he sensed someone standing over him. He knew who it was before he looked up.

"May I sit down?"

He took a deep breath. "Doctor, I'd rather you didn't. The case isn't over. It's a matter of propriety."

"Propriety," echoed the doctor, sitting down anyway. "You almost said ethics, didn't you?"

Mitch's cheeks were burning. If one of the doctor's attorneys wandered in, Mitch might be facing an ethics committee within a week. "We've said it all, Doctor. The jury's out."

The doctor smiled. He was a handsome man, a Californian, but a product of eastern private schools. "I'm told we'll probably lose," he said mildly. "I'm facing bankruptcy. Also, a ruined practice. And I have some questions about it, that's all."

"I can't answer them." Mitch searched for the waitress.

The doctor went on: "You're an intelligent man. No matter what you believed when you started, our testimony convinced you that I hadn't caused her paralysis. But you continued. Why?"

"You're presuming you convinced me," Mitch said. "And you didn't." He reminded the doctor that in civil cases the defendant

408

wasn't necessarily innocent until proven guilty. He sounded phony
to himself. "A civil case is built on a preponderance of evidence.
And that we submitted, I think."

"You don't think that at all," the doctor said softly.

"I won't discuss it," Mitch insisted. And then, stupidly: "She's
paralyzed. You couldn't prove *how* it happened."

"She's paralyzed, all right. But we proved how it didn't happen.
To you, I'm sure. To the judge? I don't know. Not to the jury, I'm
sure."

"Doctor," Mitch blurted, "we can't discuss this any further."

The doctor nodded, put his hands on the table. They were
reputedly among the surest in the city. He slid back his chair, but
did not rise. "You know I saved her life."

"I'll concede that," Mitch said hoarsely.

"I'm rewarded with ruin. Have you thought of the effect on
other doctors? They know that what happened to my patient
wasn't overmedication, or a severed nerve, or whatever else your
partner contended. Just bad luck. Maybe psychosomatic! Or a
bite from a housefly who'd been to a stable, or a blood clot ready
to go adrift. An act of God."

"Doctor," broke in Mitch, "if *you're* not going, I will."

"What happens to the next physician with a patient like mine?
She comes out of anesthetic and she's paralyzed, dying. Will he
work night and day to save you a potential plaintiff?"

"What?" croaked Mitch. "You mean he'd let the patient die?"

"Suppose I *hadn't* been able to save her? The issue would now
be a hospital bill, some funeral arrangements, a doctor's bill. Two
thousand dollars. Not enough to make the papers, even if her
husband had sued."

"We'd have *advised* him to sue," Mitch said weakly.

"Maybe," the doctor said, rising. "But a thirty percent con-
tingency fee of two thousand dollars is six hundred bucks. Who
would have taken the case?"

Mitch heard himself say stuffily: "I would have."

"Good. I wondered." He looked into Mitch's eyes and left.

Mitch got up, strode to the cashier's desk, slapped down a
five-dollar bill for the drink, and left without waiting for change.

Chapter Three

He swung in giant arcs twenty-five feet above the water, sitting astride the spreader. The seas were rising. To hang on to the mast, he had to face toward the sail, one foot dangling forward of the mast and one aft. To scan the swells behind him, he had to twist his upper body completely, straining the ligaments in his back.

He checked his watch. It was 6:40 a.m. He was reaching the northern limit of search. If she had fallen overboard just after he had gone to sleep, she was in these waters. She could be no farther up the track. But he decided to stay on course another fifteen minutes, in case his estimated position was off.

The two terns had stayed with him since dawn. He guessed that they assumed he was a *bonnitier*, fishing far from Tahiti, and that they were waiting for him to jettison bait. But through the hours they had become his allies. They wheeled now in intricate climbing turns, as if searching for her in waters he could not see.

He climbed stiffly down the ratlines and tried once more to call Papeete on the radio. Nothing came back but a crackling buzz. The crags of Moorea still blocked him.

He considered clearing out of the area to call for help, but that would take half the morning. Her chances were better if he stayed. He took another quick look for the logbook, but he found nothing. A mystery he had no time to mull over.

He scrambled to the cockpit, disengaged Irwin, and turned the boat to the SSE course. He had been climbing down from the mast every fifteen minutes to drop something overboard to mark his trail and leave debris that might help her. Bunk pillows, spare timbers, lifejackets were all strewn somewhere in his wake. Now he dumped his foam mattress overboard at the northwestern limit of his search. The southeastern limit was already marked with the strobe light and waving flag.

Watching the mattress, he wished instantly that he had not dropped it. It mocked his search. In less than thirty seconds it was out of sight behind the purple swells. He felt that she had no chance, not in these swells. His guard dropped for a moment.

The terns swooped from aloft to inspect the mattress. They discussed it in high piping voices and banked to the east. Something in their purposeful flight told him that they had given up and were returning to Moorea. He felt betrayed. He almost shouted after them to stay. He massaged his eyeballs. He was groggy with fatigue: hardly 7:00 a.m. and he was ready to yell at birds.

He climbed back aloft.

HE SAT miserably in his office high above the city. Neatly centered on his desk lay the file on a three-year-old accident case due for trial next week. His client, a beefy stockbroker, long out of his neckbrace, was still the innocent victim of painful whiplash. Mitch had not the slightest interest in the case.

His back ached. He shifted in his leather chair, squirmed, and tried to concentrate. The telephone on his desk rang. It was Bernie, from the Hall of Justice.

"Mitch, you sitting down?"

"Okay. What is it?"

The jury on the malpractice case had found in full. The young judge, incredibly, was letting the judgment stand. Mitch almost dropped the phone. "Say again?"

"The whole *million five!*"

His hands went clammy. He tried to picture their client, getting the news in her iron coffin, but the surgeon's face intruded.

Bernie began to issue orders like an admiral. Mitch was to call the *Examiner*, then meet him at the airport with Lindy. "What say champagne and lobster for lunch?"

They had flown to Monterey for lunch before, to celebrate lesser victories. This time Mitch did not feel like going at all. But Lindy would enjoy it, so he agreed.

They took off in Bernie's private plane, Lindy in back and Mitch in the copilot's seat. He got Bernie to sweep past the yacht harbor at Half Moon Bay, on the offchance that they would spot the red ketch. Nothing they saw resembled her. They banked and sped south. In Monterey, they rented a car and drove to Lou's Fish Grotto on the pier. They sopped up two quarts of champagne over magnificent lobster. Lindy grew giggly, which almost never happened. Bernie lifted his glass. "To Gordon, Bertelli, et al.—May its clients prosper, and may its name be on all tongues—"

"I didn't call the paper," Mitch cut in.

Bernie stiffened. "*You didn't call the paper?* Why not?"

"That doctor's got enough problems without coming home to a spread in the *Examiner.*"

Bernie's cheeks reddened. He was furious, but keeping it down. He lifted his glass again. "Anyway, to bigger and better things."

Mitch did not lift his glass. "Not bigger."

Bernie regarded him thoughtfully. "What's that mean?"

"We're getting *too* big. And hard." He faced Bernie. "You gambled with that poor gal's settlement—"

"*And* our fee, *and* máde her a millionaire!"

"Well, I don't like gambling. And I'm losing the joy of combat."

"You're never *in* combat anymore," Bernie pointed out. "You run the aid station. I'm the bad guy."

"Then maybe you'd better go it alone."

"Mitch!" Lindy exclaimed. "Not *now!*"

"Sure, now," Bernie said softly. "Let's talk about it now."

"I'm going to pick up my chips and quit," Mitch said tonelessly.

"When?"

"I don't know."

"A year?" Bernie's eyes glittered into Mitch's. "Two years?"

Outside the window, a fishing boat pulled away from the dock. She wore a jaunty red pilothouse and carried her nets hung high.

With an effort, Mitch looked back at Bernie. "Three months?" It came out as if he were asking permission.

SHE SAT NEXT to Bernie on the flight back. Mitch was asleep in the rear. Winging high above the coastal cliffs, Bernie said: "Lindy, what is all this stuff about quitting?"

She hated to admit that it was news to her. "He just got high, I guess. The case was a strain."

"He didn't even *want* it," Bernie complained. "He's not aggressive enough anymore."

"Then you shouldn't mind his leaving," Lindy said hotly.

"Only I *do.* Why's that?"

412

She wouldn't answer, so he did. "I need him," he decided.

"You probably do."

"He's ten times brighter than me."

"He probably is."

"And he's my best friend?"

"So it seems."

Bernie glanced at her. "I'm asking you, Lindy. Is he?"

"How would I know? Look, Bernie, if he leaves, it isn't on account of you. Whatever it is, *that* isn't it."

"Okay, okay," said Bernie distractedly. "But if he doesn't like to win, why'd he study law?"

"He likes to win," Lindy said. "Don't ever forget it."

"When he's interested. If a third of a million five doesn't do it, how do you get him interested?"

She didn't know, and she didn't really care. The victory celebration had turned into a huge cold turkey, and she was tired. "I don't know, maybe you change the rules. Or the game."

MITCH WOKE UP the next morning with a hangover. He left Lindy in bed and sneaked down to brew coffee. Cup in hand, he stared down at the bay, daydreaming that the red ketch, by simple luck, would drop anchor in the cove, and he, with his coming windfall, could make the owner an offer he couldn't refuse.

Lindy padded up behind him. She wore a shorty nightgown. She always awakened beautiful, he thought. She kissed him lightly and nodded toward the water.

"You're still looking for that ketch."

"If we find her," he blurted, "or any decent cruising boat—"

"*Cruising* boat," she repeated thoughtfully. "Let me say it?"

"Say what?"

"You were about to suggest," she said, "that if we find her we buy her. And some day sell out and move aboard."

He was astonished. She was right.

"And cruise away," she added, "leaving all annoyance behind?"

"Honey, we've talked about buying a boat for years!"

"A *racing* boat, off and on. Well, maybe I *would* like us to buy her. But you don't *know* that, do you?"

413

"No. So tell me, one way or the other."

"It's just that you're so darned *unilateral*. A boat might be great for vacations. Actually moving aboard would be another matter." She waved toward Sausalito, with its forests of masts. "Would we want to leave this to cram into that?"

"I was thinking," he said slowly, "more of the South Seas. Marquesas, Tahiti . . ."

"Every couple down there is thinking of Tahiti. They never go. They get divorces instead, from living on top of each other. The guy ends up with the boat, and the girl gets the kids."

"Divorce," he said stiffly, "seems a little farfetched for you and me."

"But selling our house and beach, and leaving Tony isn't?" She managed to smile, but her voice was troubled. "If that comes up, could I maybe have a few minutes on it?"

He nodded. "We both can. Weeks, months, as long as we want."

"And it could still go either way?"

"Either way. One man, one vote."

"That's what I'm afraid of."

"One person, one vote," he promised.

THAT AFTERNOON they began in earnest to look for the red ketch. They sailed her father's sloop to Sausalito and back. They passed through regattas, races and anchorages. They saw hundreds of boats, but not the red ketch.

That night Mitch called a yard in Seattle which still made wooden boats. They knew the Atkins design. They phoned back with an estimate. Bare-hull, unrigged, someone else to do cabinet work, tanks, engine installation, and shipfitting: "Thirty-one thousand, Mr. Gordon."

A bare hull was hardly a start. Rigging and fittings would triple the price and add years to the time they must wait. He put down the phone, defeated. He could never get her built in America. Hong Kong might be cheaper, but the Far East had turned to fiberglass and he did not want glass, or even steel: he wanted a boat that lived. His heart was set on wood.

He wanted the red ketch.

414

SUNDAY AFTERNOON Mitch and his father-in-law sailed the old man's sloop on the bay in a whipping westerly. While Shawn steered, Mitch tuned *Invincible*'s rigging. He attacked the fittings one by one, setting taut a stay, easing a shroud, twanging at another like a giant guitar string.

When he had finished, Mitch took the wheel to test her feel. They headed home with a failing breeze and a fierce outgoing tide. In golden light, with the first wisps of evening fog racing toward the apartments on the crest of Pacific Heights, he steered for the lighthouse at the end of the yacht club quay.

When they were abeam the club, he eased the sloop toward the bouldered seawall, reached down, and started the engine. "Hey!" protested Shawn. Shawn always tried to berth his boat under sail. The drill called for Mitch to sail *Invincible* through the yacht club harbor, then turn over the helm at the last instant so that the owner could bring her in, to the plaudits of some imaginary crowd.

Mitch cut the engine. Sails full, he tacked through the jammed harbor. When the slip was dead ahead, he gave Shawn the helm. The old man managed for once to release his mainsheet almost on time. Mitch leaped for the dock, got a turn on a cleat, and let the line take up the shock. When Shawn hit his usual piling, it left hardly a mark on the hull.

No one was watching anyway.

THEY SHOWERED and dressed in the club locker room, then joined Lindy in the dining room. She was waiting at the old man's favorite table overlooking the bay. She dug into her pocketbook and drew out a message from a yacht broker who was offering an English-built ketch for $75,000.

"Fiberglass or wood?"

"Glass."

Mitch shook his head, and Shawn said: "Okay, you won a big case. You hit the jackpot. You got to spend it on a boat. And it's got to be that red wooden ketch?"

"Not necessarily," Mitch said. "She's disappeared, anyway."

"If you find her, you'll never have time for *Invincible*."

"No, Pops," said Mitch. "I probably won't."

The old man's eyes fell. "If you're tinkering with your own boat, who navigates for me in the next Hawaii Race?"

Lindy was studying her father curiously. "Mitch would go. He wouldn't just dump you."

Shawn sulked. "Have I *seen* that boat?"

"My God, Shawn," Mitch exclaimed, "you almost ran her down!"

"Shh," Lindy cautioned. "Dad, you've *found* her, haven't you?"

Shawn sat back triumphantly. "She's at Cox's yard, Sausalito. They're painting her white. So I guess she's for sale."

Mitch cut in angrily. "How long have you known?"

"A week, ten days." Shawn shrugged. "I forget."

"Forget, hell!" flared Lindy. Her cheeks were flaming.

Shawn ignored her. "If you got her," he asked Mitch, "what would you do? She's too slow to race."

"We'd cruise her."

"Offshore? She's only forty feet."

"Shawn, *Invincible* is only fifty, and Hawaii's offshore!"

"I *race*. With a six-man crew." He shrugged. "Or I did. . . ."

He looked indescribably sad. Lindy reached across the table and took his hand. "You'll still race, Dad."

He did not answer. Lips clamped, he stared stubbornly ahead. They finished dinner and left him playing dominoes at the bar.

Driving back across the bridge, Lindy sat distantly by the car window. Mitch saw that her cheeks were wet.

"It isn't his *racing* he's worried about," he pointed out. "He's afraid I'll sail off with his little girl."

"Then why won't he say it?" she murmured. "Why doesn't anybody ever say it?"

"I love you?" He thought for a moment. "*I* say it all the time."

"When you mean thank you. Why not when you mean I *love* you."

He squeezed her hand. "I love you, I love you, I *love* you."

"Watch it, Romeo, there's a cop." He slowed.

He had sounded tinny as a worn-out tape, and he didn't have the slightest idea why.

Chapter Four

He clung aloft. Earlier, he had been shaded by the mainsail. Now the sun had risen above the sail and there was no relief.

He was plowing seas he had not yet searched by daylight, nearing the spot where he had discovered her gone. In these waters, six hours before, he had tossed in the strobe light and buoy and man-overboard flag. He had an unreasoning hope that he would see them again, once he surmounted the wave ahead.

She, nestling in the horseshoe buoy, holding aloft the strobe.

He climbed the swell. Nothing. The vision fled.

Far below he heard three bells from the cabin. 9:30 a.m. He glanced toward the sun. It was high enough for a morning shot. With that celestial observation and his dead-reckoning track, he would have an estimated position to transmit to Tahiti, if he ever raised them. He could brew coffee, shoot the sun, try Tahiti, and be back on his perch in fifteen minutes.

He crawled down. In the gloomy chaos of the cabin, he gulped water and primed Lindy's stove. He touched it with a match and watched as the raw alcohol went off in an orange puff. He remembered her doing it swiftly and expertly. Her long auburn hair, always close to the flame, never seemed to get singed.

She must be hungry . . . .

Doing the things she would have been doing was agonizing. He pumped water into her kettle, put it over the flame, and glanced at the clock. Three minutes gone from the quarter hour he had allotted. He drank more water.

She must be dehydrating too. . . .

Automatically he began to prepare for the morning observation. He slid his chronometer from a drawer, grabbed the handle of the sextant case on the shelf over his bunk and waited. With its case, it weighed ten pounds. He must ease it over the retaining rail without straining his back. He caught the sea in league with him and hiked it over. As usual, he strained his back anyway.

He opened the case and drew out the polished-brass instrument. With the sextant vulnerable in his hand, he turned cautious as a father with a newborn infant. If he banged its arc or jarred the telescope, he would be lost at sea until he readjusted the whole thing. Their spare sextant was an 1880 antique Lindy had bought for him in Copenhagen. It still worked, but the engraved figures on its silver arc were almost too worn to read.

He reached for his stopwatch hanging from the spice rack in her galley. Lindy insisted on using the watch to time his eggs in the morning. Because tiny things mattered at sea, her attachment was an invasion of his private bubble as navigator. He found himself frozen, remembering the argument they had made of it.

He grabbed the sextant, climbed halfway out the hatch, and braced himself, feet on the companionway ladder, for the morning sun shot. He waited to be carried to the peak of a swell. When he felt his belly grow light at the summit, he lined up the horizon. Then he swung his heaviest filter over the lens and began to search for the sun in his telescope. He glimpsed it, lost it, found it again. When he had the bottom of the great orange ball at the razor edge of the horizon, he punched his stopwatch. He had made his observation.

Cradling the sextant in both arms, he inched back down the ladder and pulled various publications from his navigation locker. He braced all of them on the leeward edge of the chart table. On the chart, he found the shaky circle he had labeled as their estimated position at 0312, when he had discovered that she was lost. He laid the sextant on the bunk, flung open the *Nautical Almanac*, and began working.

He glanced at the clock. 0945 already. He ought to have reversed course again by now. If he couldn't work a simple sun sight after only six hours aloft, he would dissolve completely when real fatigue set in. He stood up, sat down again. Close to panic, he forced himself to concentrate on the figures before him.

When he was finally through, his new position lay within two miles of his dead reckoning. He placed a tiny square around it and picked off the latitude and longitude with dividers. Then he called Mahina Radio, Navy Papeete, finally any ship or station on the emergency frequency. He ended with another blind Mayday. No one answered.

SHE SAW the white speck miles away, and lost it instantly as she sank into the next undulating valley. She felt that it was a sail, that it was Mitch, and that she was too far from him to be seen. She lost the speck each time she dipped into a trough, but every time she thought that it was gone, it would reappear. ·

It was far past whistling range, but she began to wave the jerrycan whenever she would crest a wave and see the boat. Now the low, massive lines of *Linda Lee* were unmistakable. Mitch was probably on the spreader, sweeping the seas with binoculars.

She could not actually see him there, but she was sure that he had seen her. She forced herself to relax. If the boat was approaching, her best chance was to save her strength to help him get her aboard. She lay back and rested. She had already forgotten her fevered head, cracked lips, and the awful thirst.

WHEN THERE was no answer on the emergency frequency, he switched to the yachting channels. The odds were almost zero that anyone docked at Papeete would have his set turned on, but he tried anyway. Finally he hung up the mike.

He was putting the sextant into its case when he heard a faint movement in the forward compartment. He froze, forgetting the instrument. Had he looked in the *head?* He couldn't remember. He lurched through the cabin, yanked open the door. The cat regarded him from the toilet lid, slipped past him, and raced up the steps. He remembered. The head had been the first place he had looked. Then he had stuck the cat inside to keep it below.

A premonition hit him, and he swung toward the chart table. The open sextant case was sliding toward the edge. He lunged too late. "No!" It crashed to the cabin floor, spilling the instrument.

He sat on the floor and lifted it. One mirror was far askew. That he could correct, given time. But now he saw that the arc itself was bent. That he could never repair. Dismally, he laid the carcass away. He was stuck with the ancient spare.

The coffee pot began to wheeze. He had no desire for coffee now, but he poured a cup and babied it to the cockpit. He tried to drink it but it was too hot. It was past time to turn. Lindy could not be farther ahead. He threw cup and coffee overboard, disengaged Irwin, reversed course, and reset Irwin's vane to steer north-northwest. Then he climbed back to the yardarm.

THE KETCH was a mile away perhaps, when she noticed that its shape had changed. She had been lying back, resting, but now she became more alert. She was sure that she could see him, midway up the mast. She lifted the plastic container and waved wildly. He had wonderful eyes and he would never lose sight, now that he had spotted her.

The next glimpse shook her confidence. The boat had changed shape because it had changed course. It was pulling away.

"No!"

Suddenly she was in a screaming, thrashing tantrum. She blew her whistle, waved, shouted, and finally came to her senses only when she sank below the surface and swallowed water, which she vomited. Even then, she took a few strokes after the boat. Then she lay back, cradling the jerrycan and staring up at the sky. She had a great thirst. And she was very tired and frightened.

THEY HAD PARKED outside the wooden fence of Cox's tiny boatyard. An enormous wooden platform stood inside. A marine railway led from the building to a dock.

The ways were almost empty. Mitch guessed that the yard was on the edge of bankruptcy. A bearded youth was sanding the planks of a battered schooner. An ancient Italian tapped caulking into a fishing boat hull.

In the water at the end of the wharf lay his dream. She was even prettier in white than red. Her varnished rails and hatches glittered in the sun. Carved on teak sideboards were gilded letters: *Lorelei.*

"Isn't she beautiful?" he asked.

"*You're* beautiful." Lindy squeezed his hand. "Yes, Mitch, she's lovely, you were right. How do we see her?"

A power saw was screaming inside the building, so they wandered in. Far in the rear, a gaunt figure worked at a carpenter's bench. He wore white overalls powdered with sawdust.

420

"Mr. Cox?" asked Mitch.

The man flicked off his table saw. He had pale blue, steady eyes and was as tall as Mitch, with a tanned lined face that must once have been handsome.

"Mr. Cox?" Mitch asked again.

"Cox," the man said, "died thirty years ago. John Dugan is Cox." He nodded toward a glassed cubicle at the corner of the platform.

They moved toward the office, wondering where they had seen the man before. Behind the glass a man motioned them in. He was older than the other, but he resembled him. Probably brothers. Mitch introduced himself and asked if the ketch was for sale.

"For sale? It seems to depend." He picked up a four-foot steel rod, two inches thick. An area a foot from one end was almost eaten through by corrosion. "Know what this is?" he asked Mitch suddenly.

"Keel bolt," Mitch said. "Somebody pulled it just in time. Who owns the ketch?"

Dugan waved a hand toward the bench. "Andrew. My brother."

That explained why the tall man had looked familiar: from the near collision with Shawn's boat. He wondered if Dugan had recognized them. "Why'd he send us in here?"

"Because *I'm* supposed to be the businessman, I guess."

Mitch was looking at the keel bolt. "Was that drawn from *her?*" he asked. If her keel bolts were going, maybe that meant rotten wood under the paint and he wasn't interested.

Dugan snorted. "This? Hell, no. Don't ask *him* that, he'll hit you with it." He opened the door. "Andrew!"

Outside, the howl of the saw continued for a moment, then died, and the other Dugan entered. He took a clothes brush from a hook and carefully whisked the sawdust from his overalls. His brother introduced them and said that Mitch was interested in *Lorelei*.

"I know," said Andrew Dugan.

"Could we take a look aboard?" asked Mitch. With his coming windfall he should feel like a Rockefeller bargaining in a used car lot. Still, the taller brother made him uncomfortable. "May we see her?" he asked again.

The tall man didn't answer. Instead, he commented: "This isn't exactly the boat show, over here."

Mitch was becoming annoyed. His cheeks began to burn. Lindy, watching him, cut in swiftly.

She said: "We think she's beautiful. Can we see below?"

Andrew Dugan shook his head. "No decor. Old-time, you wouldn't be impressed."

Lindy, pretty, friendly, was seldom rebuffed. Mitch faced the older brother, who sat embarrassed, staring at his desk top.

"We got it wrong," Mitch said. "We heard she was for sale. Thanks for your patience." He turned to the taller brother. "And for yours, such as it was."

He started out but Lindy held back. "Mr. Dugan," she repeated softly, "*could* I see below?"

Andrew Dugan studied her. Outside, the fisherman's caulking hammer plunked and the bearded youth's sander whined. Dugan suddenly picked a ring of keys from the wall. "All right," he said. He indicated the door and followed her out. As Mitch moved to leave, the older brother said, "You're the third couple that's been here, but you're the first to make it to the dock."

LINDY AND MITCH followed Dugan aboard. For a moment the three of them were together on the starboard side of the ketch. The boat refused to roll to their weight. She was very solid.

Mitch glanced around topside. A green tarnish on her bronze winches told him that she had not been sailed recently. He plucked at a mizzen shroud. Plow steel. He would replace it with stainless if it were his boat. He slid his hand under the canvas sail cover and felt the mainsail. Fine Egyptian cotton. Nobody had used sails like that for fifteen years. He happened to glance up. Dugan was watching him. Neither spoke and Dugan dropped down the companionway.

Mitch had noticed the boat's low lines and squat cabin top. She might be a wet boat at sea. But low freeboard and a small deck-house meant safety. Portholes instead of a modern expanse of glass meant security. *Lorelei* was built to slog through heavy weather, to dive and cleave the seas, not climb them.

Mitch took a last breath of outside air. His first sniff below, with the boat freshly opened, might bring him the moist-leaf odor of dry rot. He moved down the steps, sniffing. There was no scent of rot. In the dim light below, he saw Dugan sitting on the port bunk, watching him again.

Lindy was watching Mitch too. He looked up. There was a three-inch clearance between the top of his head and the varnished oak beams.

"Headroom," he murmured.

"I'm six-four," said Dugan. "I built her for me."

They were the first words he had volunteered aboard, and they resounded in the cabin with a strangely hollow tone.

"By *yourself?*" Lindy asked.

Dugan nodded. Mitch looked around the main cabin. An old wood-burning stove crouched by the companionway. On the galley sink were two pump faucets, one for fresh water, one for salt. The ambiance was turn-of-the-century, brass and leather. Kerosene lamps swung from the bulkheads, a clock and matching barometer glittered in the dim light.

Apparently, Dugan was not going to guide them. Mitch wandered forward alone. The two bunks in the fo'c'sle were high, with barely room to crawl under the deck beams. But the head compartment was roomy, and everywhere the joinery work was superb.

He moved aft, past Dugan, opened the engine compartment under the companionway steps. Inside was a big gasoline engine, shining in red paint. It looked new, but was easily thirty years old. The bilges were impeccably white.

"So," Dugan said tonelessly, "how much do I want?"

Mitch seated himself across from Dugan. The transaction seemed suddenly less like the sale of a boat than a child-custody case. If he dwelt on money, the man might stalk away.

"She's priceless," he said. "But let's not talk price yet."

"That's unusual," Dugan said. He seemed interested for the first time. "What would you like to discuss?"

"She must have taken years to build. . . ."

"Five years, part-time. Eight, if you count aging her lumber."

"I don't understand why you want to sell her."

He had goofed. Dugan stiffened and rose.

"Actually, I don't. Just something I was kicking around."

Desperately, Mitch plunged ahead. "I'll pay you whatever you think she's worth." Then the lawyer overcame the man of sudden wealth. "Within reason."

"What I think she's worth *isn't* within reason," Dugan said. He turned to face them. "If you bought her, would you leave her here, or what?"

"We would sell our house," Lindy said suddenly, "and move aboard, and cruise her far and wide."

Mitch's heart thumped. He glanced at her gratefully. Her cheeks were red: she was not happy with theatrics. But she was looking dead into his own eyes: she had *meant* it. "She would be *used,* Mr. Dugan. Believe me."

Dugan shrugged. "Far and wide? That has a nice ring. Where? The South Pacific? People plan. Few ever leave."

"*We'd* leave," said Lindy staunchly. "The Marquesas, Tahiti..."

Dugan was wavering and Lindy had done it. He wanted to know how Mitch would change her. Mitch decided to level. He admitted he'd replace the standing rigging with stainless; he'd substitute dacron for Manila lines, and get synthetic sails.

"Would you put in a diesel? I mean, if I *did* sell."

Mitch nodded.

"She should have a diesel," agreed Dugan. "I never seem to get enough money together. . . ." A breeze set a halyard to knocking. "Shame to leave her tied up another year too." He glanced at the bulkhead clock. "Well, Mr. Gordon, I'll think it over."

In the car, Mitch hugged Lindy. "You really *read* him."

"I read you."

"If he sells, and we do decide to move aboard—"

"You've decided, Mitch. I'm probably lucky to go along."

"Quit that!" he warned. He thought for a moment. "We said we'd vote."

"I just voted."

"You know," he murmured, "I love you very much."

She smiled. "You're welcome."

Chapter Five

Andrew Dugan, perhaps to delay his own decision, had finally insisted that Mitch survey the boat before they talked further. Mitch and Lindy had watched her being hauled from the oily water.

Mitch had given her a quick inspection. He wanted the boat so badly, and showed it so flagrantly, that he had set himself up for the maritime fleecing of the century.

"You figure she's sound?" Andrew Dugan asked tartly.

Mitch was nervous. The deal was not set, and he was afraid to say anything that might give Dugan an excuse to back out. "Beautiful. Just beautiful."

Dugan whirled away suddenly and escaped to the clapboard windlass shack, where his brother was preparing to lower *Lorelei*. Mitch touched his pocket. His checkbook was there. He entered the shack. "Mr. Dugan, what *do* you want for her?"

The carpenter looked down the tracks at his boat. His brother, face frozen, called the yard workmen to their launching positions through a loudspeaker. The winch motor groaned into life. "I better ride her in," Andrew Dugan muttered, bolting for the door.

Mitch grabbed his arm. "Damn it, how much do you *want?*"

"John?" Andrew Dugan pleaded to his brother.

"Go on down," John Dugan said softly. He glanced at Mitch. "He wants sixteen thousand four hundred and eighty-one dollars. And ninety-one cents."

Andrew Dugan, face stricken, strode from the shack. Mitch almost called him back. He had been ready to go thirty, perhaps thirty-five thousand. And he did not understand the odd dollars and cents. But something told him not to test his luck. He braced his checkbook against the winch housing and began to write.

HE HAD grabbed a flood tide of fortune, it seemed. Within two weeks Lindy's brother had sold the house and the beach property. Mitch found himself suddenly a quarter of a millionaire, and he had not yet even sold out his law partnership.

That was the problem he and Bernie avoided. But sometimes Mitch caught Bernie regarding him speculatively from under lowered brows.

In the meantime the list of items to do and get before they could leave for the South Pacific began to grow.

OUTSIDE the offices of Crowther & Son, marine agents, the little group gathered. Andrew Dugan wore a dated pin-striped suit and a dark tie. His brother, John, had an air of unwavering finality, like a good funeral director. John's sturdy, anxious wife was there too, in a shiny pillbox hat.

"Well . . ." began Mitch and John Dugan simultaneously, then they smiled. Dugan continued. "Got your papers, Andrew?"

Andrew nodded without expression. Inside, they stood at an ancient oaken counter while a clerk squeezed a yellow form into a typewriter and began to tap.

"Name of vessel, *Lorelei*," murmured the clerk.

"Hold it." Mitch dropped his bomb. "*Linda Lee*. For her first mate, cook, and co-owner."

"Mitch!" breathed Lindy. "Do you really want to?"

"*I* do," he murmured, searching her eyes. "Okay?"

She nodded uncertainly, then looked at Andrew Dugan.

"I guess you know it's supposed to be bad luck," he said stonily.

"We'll get a brass nameplate," Lindy said, "for the bulkhead: *Linda Lee, ex-Lorelei;* Andrew Dugan, builder: keel laid such-and-such a date."

Andrew Dugan shrugged. "She's only a boat, and she's *your* boat. Do what you want." To his brother he said: "I'm taking a walk on the Embarcadero. I'll grab the ferry back."

THE EVENT, even with Andrew Dugan gone, seemed to call for more than a farewell handshake with his brother. They went with the John Dugans to the Buena Vista Café on the edge of North Beach.

Mrs. Dugan told them that the boat had once saved their lives. She and her husband had flown one summer to meet Andrew in Anchorage, Alaska, to sail down the coast on *Lorelei*.

427

Off the cliffs of Oregon, the barometer had begun to drop.

"We tried to get into Tillamook," said John Dugan, "but it's breaking across the bar at Cape Meares Light. We're hove to under jib and mizzen and the wind's maybe seventy knots and the seas are maybe forty feet. Three nights! Boat saved our lives!"

"How could he sell her?" Mitch wondered.

Dugan looked at him. "*He'd* have to tell you that. I'll say this, but you know it already: you're getting her awful cheap."

"Yes. Why?"

The other day, Dugan said, Andrew had asked him to add up the yellowing invoices he had kept from the years he was building her. There were paid bills for blocks, winches, ten thousand galvanized screws, compass, clocks, cables. "Lead for the keel. And lumber! Mahogany, spruce, teak, cedar, oak for her frames, stuff you can't find nowadays. That's what you paid for. That's *all* you paid for."

"I wondered," muttered Mitch. "No labor?"

"He told me," said Dugan, "he'd already been paid for the labor."

THE SUN climbed higher. He sat on the yardarm like a weight halfway up a metronome forty feet high. It was not yet high noon and his skin was seared. Longing for the cool of the cabin, he glanced at his watch. Eight minutes until time to go below for his noon sight. He felt guilty. She was treading water somewhere and he was looking for an excuse to hide in the shade below.

His eyes stung from sweat and sunlight and his back was weakening fast. But his discomfort was not all bad. In the last hour he had caught himself twice nodding in fatigue. If the needle of pain in his back had not jabbed him each time he slumped, he might have fallen, dooming Lindy too.

Now his back stabbed him again, this time with authority. He clutched at the mast in agony. It was time to go below. He steeled himself, waited for a roll to starboard to help him dismount, and began to hoist his right foot over the spar. The needle exploded in a flash of pain. Somehow he tolerated it long enough to hoist his foot over the spreader. As he groped with his toes for the highest of the rungs, *Linda Lee* reared on a swell and he slipped.

He had a quick image of his body hurtling twenty-five feet to the deck. He hugged the spreader with knees and hands and swung suspended like a giant sloth beneath the yardarm. He probed for a foothold, found a rung with his toes, and climbed down. Safely on deck, he reached to the highest rung he could touch and hung for a moment, feet dangling, to stretch. This had always given him relief, and when he let himself down he found that he could stand erect.

At the hatchway, he saw the cat lying by the lazaret, waiting for the chirping. A midnight scenario flashed through his mind.

The cat is with Lindy below. It hears the chirping rudder cable. It slinks topside. Lindy notices that it is gone. She worries. She puts on her safety harness to go topside. She sees the cat ready to spring on the spray-slickened lazaret hatch. She has no time to clip her harness to a shroud. She lunges to save the cat and slips. She plummets screaming into the wake. She strikes out for the trailing hawser, grabs it, slips astern until her fingers grasp the plastic buoy. It comes off in her hands.

All this the cat observes, bored and uncaring.

"You bastard!" he yelled at the cat. Despite the press of time, he found himself stalking it. Then, aghast, he turned and swung down the companionway to the cabin. What had he intended to do? Toss it overboard? On no evidence? He had to get control of himself.

He reached for his sextant and then remembered. He rummaged for the ancient spare and found it in its antique mahogany case. He remembered vividly the tiny store where Lindy had found it. He felt again her triumph when he had stepped outside to test it, and reported it usable.

He checked it now on the horizon and found it still accurate, although the figures were so tiny and worn that they were hardly readable. He had four minutes left before noon. He began hurriedly to rub the tarnish from the arc.

AT DAWN, three days before they were to vacate their house, he had awakened in their carton-cluttered bedroom. He thought of the decisions he must make that day in equipping the boat. First, self-steering. He had picked important legal strategies with less mental zigzagging than he was spending on the choice between three vane devices. He decided on the smallest and most expensive.

Next, Lindy's galley. He decided to buy a stainless-steel alcohol stove. Third, Lindy was insisting on an electric anchor winch, to save his back. He decided to stick to Dugan's old hand windlass.

Three decisions already and the day had not yet started. Lindy flopped over beside him, close to waking. Asleep, she usually looked eighteen, but this morning her face sagged. For weeks she had been up until 1:00 or 2:00 a.m. packing. She could not believe that you couldn't stuff the contents of a three-bedroom house into a forty-foot ketch. The choice between a favorite pot and an omelet pan would stop her for half an hour.

He eased out of bed and wove through packing boxes to the bathroom. A tiny box marked BOAT and a large carton marked OUT showed that she had intended to be brutal. The trouble was, the BOAT box was full and the OUT box practically empty.

He could not find his electric razor. Finally he found it in the OUT box. Very funny, but today he was not in the mood. Suddenly he realized that they were not only giving up electric razors, but frozen foods and ice cubes, hot water, and the Raiders' games on Sunday. They were stepping outside the normal stream of their culture. All at once he was dubious of his ability to do it, and of Lindy's.

He heard a whine outside the bathroom door. He had forgotten Justice Holmes! Today was good-by to him. He let him in and rubbed his velvet ears. The dog had known they were leaving the moment Mitch dragged the first suitcases from the attic, and had been lumbering brokenly at Lindy's heels every second for a week.

Mitch dressed quickly and slipped down to the kitchen. He made coffee for himself and filled Justice Holmes's dish with Red Heart. The dog ignored it. Mitch backed the car out of the garage and whistled softly. For the first time in a week Justice Holmes came alive. He bounded into the passenger seat, squealing joyfully.

Suddenly, Lindy was at the door of the car. "Mitch, he could sleep topside!" she quavered.

Someone had to be firm. "Honey, we decided."

He reached up and kissed her, then drove away, narrowly missing a car parked at the curb. By the time he turned Justice Holmes over to his sister-in-law, he felt like crying himself.

HE HAD not been to the office for a week. On his desk was a note from Bernie, two days old, suggesting that they have a talk. Well, that was why he was here. He poured himself a cup of coffee and took it to his partner's office.

"You get my note?" Bernie asked innocently, shutting the door. "There's something you have to know."

Mitch regarded him suspiciously. "What?"

Bernie sat down, grinning. "Western Casualty wants to retain us."

Western had insured the doctor. Mitch was ready for almost anything but this. Bernie skidded a letter across the desk. Western had apparently decided to insure themselves against future problems with Gordon, Bertelli, et al., by canning their present firm and hiring the winners.

A year ago Mitch might have considered the offer a stroke of luck. He must not waver now, or Bernie would never quit trying to change his mind. He let the letter flutter to the desk.

"You negotiate with them," he said. "I'm out." He sketched the outline of their dissolution. Fifty-fifty, right down the middle, even though eighteen years ago he had put up most of the cash from his father's estate. Bernie could continue to use his name if he wanted. By the time he finished he had probably cost himself fifty thousand dollars, but he felt as if he had laid down a ten-ton load. "And you'll still get Western."

Bernie was smiling. "You're very generous. The trouble is, it won't go. Not with Western."

"Why not?"

"They want *you*, not me! You're a college man, I'm night school."

It was impossible to tell if he was serious. "There's no problem, Bernie," Mitch said. "Make Hal a senior partner. He's *Harvard*. And he knows case law better than I do."

"Western stipulated no changes in management for two years."

Mitch's hands were sweaty. "No way," he said hoarsely.

"You can't just shove off," growled Bernie, "and let this place go down the drain. You've got to think of Hal, and me, and the juniors. You have an obligation to our clients." Bernie's rising voice was a danger signal. He'd try to drag Mitch into a swamp of Latin passion, and when they were through they would be enemies.

"What are you leaving *for*? What have you got to prove, this alone-against-the-sea stuff?" He sat back. "It's too bad you have to drag Lindy along too."

Mitch gripped the desk. He forced himself to keep down his voice. "We're *going*, Bernie."

"Well, go, dammit, go!" His eyes were glittering with tears.

"I'm sorry, Bernie," Mitch said quietly.

"Will you just get *out*?"

Mitch left him there. It was the first argument between them he had won for twenty-five years. It did not feel good.

THE SUN PEAKED. The cabin was a steam bath. Dripping sweat, Mitch braced himself under the skylight and tried to read his noon shot on the silver arc of the sextant. He rummaged through the navigation drawer and found a magnifying glass with which to read the tiny figures.

His sweat fell onto his sight form, smearing his calculations. He moved his running fix forward on the chart to give himself the first solid position since she had been lost. It was close to his estimate. Good. He was putting pencil, plotter, and *Nautical Almanac* away when the bulkhead clock chimed eight bells. She had been in the water now at least for nearly nine hours: at most, for almost twelve.

The water was warm, 80 degrees at noon. And she had the jacket, and perhaps the plastic container.

Lindy was a fish. She outlasted him on every swim, and she was in perfect health. She had just survived the worst hurricane to hit French Polynesia in fifty years and had put on three pounds in Bora Bora after the storm. Three pounds of fat could add hours to her body heat.

He tried the radio again. He thought he heard a voice through crackling static. He went topside, wiped spray from an insulator on the antenna, tried again, but heard nothing.

As he began to climb the ratlines again he glimpsed the cat, lying on the dinghy. Its eyes mocked him slyly. In its pea brain was locked the secret that could save her: what time she had gone.

He was again impelled to kill it. For a moment he rested his forehead on a ratline rung. The teak was damp and cool. Then he struggled aloft to the yardarm and resumed his watch.

MITCH AND LINDY began to move aboard the boat in an unsteady drizzle. Twice a day he would return to the house to cram their station wagon with cartons of clothes, linens, and canned goods. Trans-Pacific races had taught him that equipping a vessel was not enough: you had to know precisely where everything was stored. So every item was logged in a card file.

The deadline to vacate the house approached. The drizzle persisted. The galley and cabin and fo'c'sle became engorged with pots, books, and tools. Lindy, working below as he hauled more and more gear from the house, could not keep up.

On the third night Mitch drove down the hill with the last load. It was dark and the boatyard was locked as he slithered to a stop outside. He honked for Red-Dog, the bearded young night watchman. Red-Dog slid open the gate and dived into the car next to him, smelling of wet wool and beer. Mitch could barely see well enough through the slanting rain to back down the dock. Then the two of them grabbed armloads and sprinted down the wharf. They tumbled below in a shower of rain.

He almost groaned when he saw Lindy. He had left her exhausted, in jeans, hair tangled, a smear of dirt on her nose. Now, despite the cold, she was wearing a sweeping hostess gown, and her hair was up. The cabin, after days of grime and mud, was scrubbed and glowed warmly in candlelight. On the varnished table, two glasses flanked a bucket of champagne. He smelled *coq-au-vin* simmering on her stove. They had first eaten it on their honeymoon.

"Welcome home," she said. "Mitch, I've been nasty lately.

About leaving the house and all. So . . . " She studied his face. "What's wrong?"

"Honey?" he pleaded, hating the rain, the boat, himself.

"Oh, no," she murmured. "Not now?"

"Red-Dog's topside. We got to get it all below."

She whirled, to hide tears. Later, as he and Red-Dog passed gear below, she changed clothes to help, but though they gobbled the *coq-au-vin* afterward, they were too tired for the champagne and they put it away.

AT 3:00 P.M. he was bearing down for the second time on the spot at which he had discovered her gone. Clinging to the spreader, he was especially alert and very apprehensive. He was entering the area in which he had pitched over the flag and the strobe light. Three hours northwest, he had sailed until dawn: then three southeast. Three northwest again, and now three southeast.

Searching the horizon for the flag, he became conscious of a distant white speck. He raised his binoculars. It was the cabin top of a powerboat. He recognized her as a Tahitian *bonnitier*, a long way from home. She was cutting across his own course, charging southeast to make Papeete before dusk.

There was no way to cut her off at his own crawling speed. He scrambled down the rigging, slid below, and shouted out a Mayday on the radio. He waited, got no answer, and called again. He found himself babbling, in English and French: *"J'ai perdu ma femme! My wife is overboard! Mayday, Mayday."*

He charged topside. The *bonnitier* had not changed course. He had been stupid to think that the fishing boats carried radios. He groped in the lazaret, found the flare launcher. He pointed it straight up and fired. The flare arose whitely, became lost in the blazing sky, and dropped into his wake. He fired all the flares he had. All were unspectacular.

He had one more card to play, a signal mirror stowed in their life raft. He found it and lined up its peephole with the target, but the sun was too low behind him. He was jamming the mirror back into the raft when he felt a small metallic box. He froze, recognizing the shape.

434

It was a farewell gift from Bernie, a tiny transmitter, powered by little batteries. It was supposed to transmit a warbling emergency signal on international frequencies guarded by all planes in flight.

There were two flights a day between Papeete and Bora Bora, and he was hardly twenty miles from their track. And hourly flights too, between Papeete and Moorea. He flicked it on. Its tiny red eye began to pulse, telling him that it was transmitting.

He took it aloft with him, suspended by a lanyard from his neck, along with the binoculars. Once on the yardarm, he began to tremble as the truth struck him. All the inter-island flights were daylight ones. The sun was dropping already.

He should have turned the radio beacon on twelve hours ago.

AS THE WATER warmed, she became more comfortable. She dropped into a rhythm of dipping her head every few minutes to cool her forehead, then emptying the jerrycan of whatever had trickled in, then lying back again and simply waiting. Her thirst was awful, but if only he found her before the water cooled, she would be okay.

She raised her head and heard a distant rumble. Airplane? Boat? She saw nothing, but within five minutes she was hearing it strongly. She knew now that it was a boat engine, but too powerful for *Linda Lee*.

All at once she spotted it. Diving into sheets of spray, it was less than a quarter mile away, much closer than Mitch had come before he turned. And she was in its path.

She jammed her whistle into her mouth and shrilled with all her strength. She lost sight of the boat as she dipped, and then it was almost on her, a hundred yards away. It slewed from its course, rolled, and gave her a view of a cockpit full of glistening gutted fish. If it didn't hit her, she was saved.

She began to yell, waving her arms. She whistled and screamed. The boat was almost on her—no, it would leave her to starboard, but where was everyone? The roar became overpowering.

Then it was passing in a crescendo of power, pounding into the swells yards away. She finally glimpsed the helmsman, a fat

435

Polynesian. Standing next to him was a handsome young Tahitian. The younger man saw something in the other direction. He pointed to port and the older followed his glance and nodded.

"Hey!" she shrieked. "Help! *M'aidez!*"

They thundered on, and she was suddenly immersed in their wake. When she fought free of that, they were far past hearing, but she whistled anyway until they were almost out of sight.

For a long while she lay exhausted. It had taken all day long, but at last she was truly scared.

IN COX'S BOATYARD, Mitch sat in *Linda Lee*'s cockpit with Andrew Dugan and wrote a check for the yard bill. Tomorrow *Linda Lee* would leave the dock and move to a modern marina.

It was the first time Andrew himself had been aboard since he had sold the boat. He took the check, stuffed it into his pocket, and asked when they were leaving for the South Pacific. Mitch told him in a couple of months: there was still lots to do.

"Go now or you never will. Maybe if I'd done that after the gale, I wouldn't have sold her." He rose.

Mitch said: "Your brother told me about the storm. Awful."

"Awful? Well, that's where storms *are*, at sea! But nobody makes you *go* there, do they?" He was silent for a while. "No, I'd been through gales before. Next summer I was headed for Alaska again. Beautiful day, everything perfect. . . . Nice twelve-knot breeze through the Golden Gate. . . ."

He seemed puzzled. "All at once I turned around and came home. Tied her up and hardly sailed her since."

"We'll sail her," promised Mitch.

"Then *sail* her," growled Dugan. "Don't wait." He shambled down the dock. He did not look back.

THE LATE SUN hung brassy on his port beam. He had turned, and was now at the northwest limit of his search. The trades were heavy but gusting, which meant they were losing their strength for the night. He shifted his position up on the spreader, and switched the transmitter to TEST for the fifth time in an hour. It glowed reassuringly. It would be useless after dark, when local flights stopped. Sunset was at 6:55, only fifteen minutes away.

Again he considered leaving the search area to clear himself from the radio interference of Moorea, and trying to call Papeete. But he could not bring himself to leave her.

The sunlight was a golden freeway leading west. His eyes, unable to stand the glare, slipped idly downward to rest. The ketch was immense seen from above, and beautiful! Her sweeping lines were straight from the Vikings, in flowing harmony with the bow wave and the wake. Lindy had always looked tiny from here.

He had to start the engine to charge the batteries. He wanted bright lights tonight. He swung his foot over the yardarm, waited for the pain in his back to pass, then groped until he found a rung. He descended stiffly, wondering how much longer he could overcome his weakening back to climb up and down the mast.

He hesitated. Before starting the engine, he had better plumb the fuel level in the tank that fed it. He raised the hinged cockpit seat to unscrew the fuel cap. He grunted in surprise, then yelled exultantly. The water-stained logbook lay on the tank. She must have stuffed it there to protect it from spray.

Shakily, he began to leaf through it. He found the last smudged page. Her penciled, rounded figures hopped up at him. Her first entry was course and speed for 1230, then 0100, 0130, 0200, then another for 0230, and—he almost yelled again in relief, or pain—one for 3:00 a.m. He had discovered her gone at 0312. She had fallen in less than twelve minutes before he had awakened.

He had been covering three hours worth of track all day when he could have been searching twelve minutes' worth.

Fifteen miles perhaps by one mile, searched over and over, swell by swell. . . . He was at the wrong end of his pattern *now*; she was three hours southeast.

He whirled and started the engine, disconnected Irwin, and took the wheel. *Linda Lee* slowly gathered speed and leaped ahead, straining under power and sail. He caught his breath as a spray hit him full in the face. The water was becoming colder.

The ketch crashed southeast, where he should have been searching all day.

Chapter Six

Tony hitchhiked down from Humboldt to see them off. He arrived as Mitch was preparing to change the engine's oil filter. Mitch laid out his tools while Tony watched.

"Nothing I can do, Dad?" he asked without enthusiasm. There was plenty, but Mitch shook his head. Tony seemed on the edge of a breakdown; he was yawning, his foot was jiggling, his fingers were tapping, and his eyes were shifting.

"You might tell me what's on your mind."

Tony looked up, startled. "Nothing. Why?" There was no way to float the problem to the surface, so Mitch snaked into a hole in the engine compartment that even his son could barely have fitted in—and hadn't volunteered. He began to unscrew the filter. When there was no chance that he would re-emerge to face him, Tony launched his rocket. "Dad?"

"Um?"

"I can't go back."

Mitch dropped the master nut from the filter casing. In the orange glow of his work lamp he saw it roll along the engine bed. He grabbed for it, knocked it off, and heard it plop into the bilge, far below the pan and forever out of reach. "*Dammit!*"

"I'm sorry, Dad," Tony said distantly. "I flunked biology, and soil chemistry, and—"

Mitch's lap felt moist and he discovered that oil was trickling onto his belly. "Oh, hell!" he growled. "Tony, look—"

"I'm *sorry*, Dad. I know how you feel, but—"

"Tony, just hand me in a towel, okay?"

"A *trowel?*"

"*Towel*, damn it! Paper towel. They're above the sink."

Tony's disembodied hand appeared with a single paper towel. Mitch patted at his belly. "All right," he called. "You flunked out. What are you going to do now?"

"Get a job, I guess."

"Where?"

"Filling station? Garage, maybe."

"Pass me my crescent wrench."

Silence without, and then a great clanking of tools, and then silence again. "What's a crescent wrench?"

Mitch squirmed out. On his hands and knees he regarded his son. "Tony?" Mitch said softly, lifting a crescent wrench from his jumble of tools. "See?"

"Oh! Yeah." Tony smiled. He had a great smile.

"Lots of luck," Mitch said, "with the garage."

THEY TOOK Tony and Nancy out for a farewell dinner. Nancy was clear-eyed, with the oval face of a medieval angel. She showed no hint of intelligence, yet she was making straight A's at University College.

He glanced enviously at the two. Tony, unemployed and possibly unemployable, chewed mightily at a $7.50 sirloin: not a problem in the world.

MITCH SAT on his bunk later that night. Lindy was spreading out their sleeping bags. He watched her as she moved, full of grace and youth.

He had loved her from the first, but medical students should not marry. His dad had been telling him that for years. He knew that his dad saw him as a partner someday. He had no intention of becoming another society doctor, but he'd never had to argue that out; his father had died a year after Mitch and Lindy were married, while Mitch was still at medical school.

Lindy had delivered her hammer blow smack in the middle of the midterm examinations. They were in his room, watching the Sid Caesar show. Halfway through he saw that her eyes were moist.

"Lindy? What's wrong?" She had shaken her head silently. "What is it? Come *on*."

She was two months pregnant. She wanted to have the child, was sure it was a girl. But she was scared to tell her father and wanted to finish college. "What'll I do?"

Not *we*, *I*. Mitch knew half a dozen girls her age who would have broken the news in a fit of pseudo-hysteria.

"You could get married." His stupid smile felt frozen.

439

"To who . . . whom?"

"Clem might do it. You're pretty ugly, but your daddy's rich."

"Clem's unfriendly; I'd prefer a friend."

"*We* could be friends," he said.

She shook her head. "We're lovers. I like it that way. And you don't want to get married."

"I *didn't*," he admitted. He hesitated. He decided that he loved her very much, more than his stupid South Pacific dream. He took her into his arms. "I mean I didn't until just now. And I'm not going to let you get away."

They married the next week. For a semester Mitch fought it out in a trailer, while Lindy got bigger. He was still slugging it out when Tony arrived.

Tony screamed for months. Mitch's concentration wavered. He got a D in an organic chemistry final and a C in French, ordinarily his best subject. His father died. The next semester he quit medicine for law.

Lindy could never seem to get it straight that Tony, unborn, had saved him. He would probably have made a lousy doctor, and he was a good lawyer. He should be eternally grateful.

Lindy was smoothing his bunk. "Hey, Tony's known for years about how we got married!"

"I'll be damned."

"He's decided we did it to be polite. He's not that far wrong."

"Oh, come on, Lindy!"

"Okay, I'm sorry. Anyway, don't feel guilty that we didn't ask him along, I know he wouldn't leave Nancy."

"Hell, I don't feel *guilty!*"

"Good." She fluffed out a pillow and kissed his forehead. "You've done your twenty years."

ON FEBRUARY 2, they stood by a beer keg on the dock and played host to their own farewell party. It seemed to be the only way to take care of the friends they had promised to show aboard.

Linda Lee lay deep in the water and Mitch's work list was only two-thirds checked off and he had doubts about his planning. With two hundred charts of the South Pacific carefully stowed, he had a

440

deep conviction that he had forgotten the very one they would need when they were racing toward some coral-fouled pass.

He had an Accutron watch, two bulkhead clocks, and a navy surplus chronometer. Now that they were about to leave, he had a premonition that they would all fail simultaneously, along with the radios, and leave them lost in infinite seas.

Their tiny medicine cabinet was stuffed with pills and antibiotics. Lindy had somehow found time to go to a first-aid class and a latent Nightingale had awakened: for weeks she injected oranges, bandaged his arms and legs, and splinted his fingers. What they would do if *she* were the victim they hadn't discussed.

They had sailed to Raccoon Strait and spent the day practicing nautical emergencies: fire, abandon ship, man overboard, collision, dismasting.

They might founder, but they would surely not starve. There were eight dozen eggs aboard, fifteen gallons of Fresca, a case of beer, nine pounds of margarine, four cases of canned fruit, twenty-four cans of stew, nine canned hams, twelve cans of salmon, one hundred cans of vegetables, a dozen boxes of breakfast cereal, six pounds of pancake mix, six pounds of rice. There were also ten pounds of sugar and forty-five rolls of toilet paper. He had even discovered two cans of grated coconut.

"Lindy, we're going to Coconutsville!"

"They were ten cents off."

They said good-by to Bernie. Lindy hugged her father and brother, and kissed Tony and Nancy, who had a mutual cold. There were tears in her eyes. Justice Holmes, stupidly brought to see them off, began to bark hysterically. They stepped aboard and cast off. There were too many hands on the dock per line, and too much beer in the hands, and Red-Dog fell in.

Shawn's *Invincible* escorted them through the Golden Gate, then turned and departed, hooting madly. The moment she met the ocean swell, *Linda Lee* began to wallow horribly, as predicted. Seasickness hovered. There was a brief, explosive conference between captain and medical officer. Brow furrowed, lips pursed, Lindy tried to recall her shopping, while Mitch flipped through the cards of their magnificent filing system.

In the medicine cabinet, it promised, he would find Dexedrine to wake them up, Seconal to make them sleep, enough needles, drugs, and syringes to interest the Bureau of Narcotics. She had bandages, compresses, gauze, sterile cotton, splints, and slings.

She had forgotten the Dramamine. With the realization of it, she got sick instantly. Then he became sick too.

At sunset, thirty miles south, they remembered that Justice Holmes's rabies shots were due next week. Mitch put through a call to Bobby via the marine operator.

"Mitch?" crackled Bobby's voice. "I've been trying to raise you! I got bad news."

Lindy grabbed the mike. "It's Dad?"

"He almost passed out on the boat before we got back. He's at Stanford Hospital. They don't know what's wrong."

"Did he eat his dinner?"

"Yeah, such as it was. Why?"

"Tell him I love him. And write us what happens to Nuku Hiva."

"Lindy! Did you hear what I told you?"

"Nuku Hiva, Bobby," she said. "Over and out."

She hung up the mike. Mitch protested and reached for it. She grabbed his wrist. "He's *my* dad, it's my decision."

Mitch called Bobby the next day. Shawn had been discharged from the hospital. He was still planning on the Hawaiian race.

He went topside with two beers. Lindy, still seasick, sat huddled in the lee of the deckhouse. He told her about her dad. She did not seem surprised. "He was just trying to tell me something again. He'd rather try to die than learn the words."

PART TWO: NIGHT

Chapter One

She felt the drop in water temperature that dusk was bringing. Her thirst remained. She tried to fend off the night by keeping her face to the setting sun.

Her cheeks were still feverish from the day's heat and her lips were cracked, but her body was chilled. The jacket continually slithered up her sides and had to be tugged down to keep her upper body bearably warm. Her legs grew colder.

Sometime after the *bonnitier* had passed, she had unlocked and let drop the useless safety belt, which had been rubbing her belly raw. She still clung to the plastic container. It was buoyant, while her jacket was becoming soggy and losing its lift.

She played a game which asked little effort and wasted no heat. She would lie back and pretend that at the peak of the next swell she would raise her head and find his sails bearing down on her.

As darkness deepened, the game lost credibility. She tried another. She would lie back and become driftwood, a log, capable of floating forever until she starved or died of thirst. Log or not, she was freezing. She began to shake uncontrollably.

All day long she had cherished the hope that the faraway flash she had glimpsed after she fell in had been the strobe. So darkness was not all bad. She began to look for the flash again.

CLINGING to the wheel, pounding toward the spot he should have been searching for the last sixteen hours, he watched the sun turn quickly into a squashed tangerine and sink below the horizon. Now that he knew where she was, he would use the last evening twilight for a star fix to pinpoint his own position. He turned off the engine, engaged Irwin, and went below to get the sextant. He shot his star fix, then went to the chart table to plot his position.

He let out a yell of joy. He had traced and retraced his path for fifteen hours and was less than a mile from his track. Two hours to go to where the logbook pinned her down. For the second time that day he found himself on his knees. A childhood reflex maybe, but he didn't care. He lurched topside, adjusted Irwin's course one degree, and climbed the mast.

It was pitch-dark. He was still too far from where he had dropped the strobe to see it, but he began to search anyway.

ON THE THIRD day out of San Francisco, under clammy skies, she tried to cook their first breakfast. Mitch said she was still too sick to cook, and that crackers and beer would do for another day.

444

Obviously he needed a hot meal soon. He would be up in the cockpit all day, for she was so drowsy and seasick that she could only stand watch for an hour or so at a time.

She tried to stow away the last-minute gear. The inexorable roll was maddening. Every time she let go of a handhold she lurched across the cabin and got another bruise. Her belly ached from vomiting and her neck was still stiff from scrabbling into bulkhead lockers. Tony had given her his cold, kissing her good-by; it was the first real kiss he had given her for fifteen years, and it had to be laden with germs.

She was miserable. Mitch, meanwhile, had to do the work of two adults, just to keep them sailing. He was so tired he could hardly move. She awakened one night with the wind moaning and the vane in command. The boat was charging due west, in the wrong direction. Mitch was sitting on his bunk in dripping yellow oilskins, staring at a rubber boot he had got on the wrong foot, apparently unable to tackle the job of changing it. She lay there helpless while he changed the boot and climbed topside, moving like a man of sixty.

Their peace of mind seemed balanced on a knife edge. No matter how she goofed—as in the matter of the seasick pills—he would not let her see a reaction, and she knew that the pressure must be building. Every minor error they made held the seed of catastrophe.

Irwin's base needed cleaning and regluing and began to tremble ominously. She volunteered to get a can of acetone. While Mitch squatted in the stern, waiting, she started to lift the can's metal seal with an ice pick in the galley. But she lurched at the moment of truth and speared the top of the can. She had wrecked the container. There was no more acetone aboard, so somehow she must find something for the contents of the can or they would evaporate.

She dug into the liquor locker and found two half-filled bottles of Johnny Walker. She emptied one into the other, capped the first, filled the empty bottle with acetone. She was lurching aft with it when it struck the corner of the stove and shattered.

Mitch heard the crash and came down, tired and carefully

unangry. He was barefoot. She started to warn him and he stepped on a piece of glass. She dug through Band-aids, letting the acetone eat the varnished cabin floor, but got sick from the smell. He bandaged his own foot while she vomited into the john.

She had been sailing virtually all her life, yet she was only five days under way and unraveling already.

She and Mitch seemed to grow apart. Keeping their balance on their lurching little world used up so much energy they had no time for each other. She was more isolated than when he was at the office: at least, then, he was home nights. Now he was completely occupied with navigation, sails, or the engine. And sleep. . . . Once out of the steamship lanes, he slept all the time.

They spoke little, and never discussed their condition. To admit that all the months of preparation had led to misery would have been brutal.

Mitch grew leaner each day and his skin was tinged with green. She knew that he was often as nauseated as she, and wondered when he would finally crack.

And then late one memorable afternoon she awakened from a nap to feel a certain warmth in the damp cabin air. They were six hundred miles off the Mexican coast. She went topside. When she had dozed off, *Linda Lee* had been lurching like a drunken elephant. Now she was gently lifting to immense purple swells off the port quarter. Mitch, stripped to the waist, was sitting in the cockpit facing the late sun. He flashed her a smile.

"Mitch," she exulted, "what's *happened?*"

"The trades." He grinned. His face was luminous. "And this, my sweet, is what it's all about."

They lost the trades that evening, but regained them sometime during the night. She awakened starved. She discovered that she could move without hanging on. She rinsed her face and looked at herself in the mirror. For six days she had looked haggard and drawn. Now she looked great.

She cooked an enormous breakfast: four eggs for Mitch, three for herself, canned sausages, slabs of toast. She could hear Mitch bellowing "Waltzing Matilda" in the cockpit. She glanced through the hatch as she ladled out the eggs. He had disengaged Irwin and was standing on the cockpit coaming, clinging to a shroud. He was steering with his foot, apparently for the joy of guiding *Linda Lee* down the long sapphire slopes.

He looked down at her. The early light etched his face, beneath his battered skipper's cap, with abrupt shadows. His jaw shone with a thick golden stubble, but he looked wonderful. He was the young student she had married.

After breakfast he went below to sleep, and she took over the wheel. She raced alone for hours across a bottomless deep. Her hand on the wheel was light: she let the boat balance the wind and the sea and let her body soak up the sun. She had nothing to do but to lose herself in the rolling ride downwind.

THE NORTHEAST winds were granite-steady and the swells grew mountainous. *Linda Lee* would rise on the slope, curtsy on the peak, and drop into the following trough as the great blue swell rolled on ahead.

Each trade-wind day was like the last. Every morning at ten Mitch would shoot the sun, and again at noon. The path on his pilot chart inched relentlessly south and a little west, toward the Marquesas Islands.

Lindy wanted the track on the chart to stop. Instead, it moved faster. They were logging over one hundred and twenty miles a day. There were not enough hours for all the things she wanted to do. She was studying Polynesian, and reading about Tahiti and the islands to the west. She continued to cook enormous meals, feeling no threat to her figure; even in the trades every muscle in her body was working for balance all day long.

In the afternoons she lay on the foredeck. Sometimes porpoises would frolic in their bow wave. Once a school played with her for an hour, piping to her and listening to her squeak back.

She saw few birds: they were simply too far from land. But one morning a sparrow-sized land bird squatted on deck in the shade of the dinghy. It made no move to escape when she cuddled it. They decided that it must have been blown to sea from Clipperton Island, but there was no way to know. When it was rested it fluttered its wings and thrashed away to the east.

They tried to fish and caught nothing. But a striped pilot fish adopted them and skimmed along in the shade of their hull. His name was Elmer.

Otherwise, they were utterly alone. One glittering night Mitch called her topside excitedly. He pointed out a satellite streaking hurriedly toward the eastern horizon. Lindy resented it. It was man-made, an intrusion on their privacy.

They could not, of course, stay in the trades forever. One day the northeasterlies slackened at noon, picked up, then died again. The following morning the sun rose on lazy, slapping sails. They had run smack into the doldrums.

They were trapped there for twelve days. Boredom gripped like a vise. All work stopped. Each day was like the last, and time was as flat as the sea. To stay below was unbearable. Topside, it was almost as hot, for there was no breeze at all.

A squall raced in one afternoon, creating a cold shower bath which ended just after Lindy had lathered her hair, but before she could rinse.

They grew worried about water and limited themselves to a pint each day. Despite the canvas cockpit canopy, they broiled at noon. At night they slept topside under liquid stars, because the cabin was a hothouse.

When Lindy honestly thought that she could bear it no longer, they were hit by a line of squalls. The breeze freshened, then died. The next day it rose again and, miraculously, held. They had struck the southeast trades. All morning they scooted south under a ten-knot breeze, and by the next day they had crossed the equator. Lindy was cooled enough by the new trades to bake a cake.

Her moods had become puppets of the wind. Despair, boredom, peace of mind, mirth, no longer came from within her; she caught them from the breeze. In the westerlies she had been sick and scared; in the trades, ecstatic; in the doldrums, a prisoner flailing at Mitch. Now, again, she sank into the joy of trade-wind sailing.

Again, she wished it would never end. But inevitably, the curve on the chart arched closer to the minute dots of the Marquesas.

"Tomorrow morning," Mitch announced one day, "if you will

climb to the spreader and look dead ahead, you will see the island of Nuku Hiva rear its head from the limitless deep."

The next morning she clung there, waiting. At 9:28 she raised the peak of the island, 3800 feet high. In half an hour they could smell flowers, thirty miles away. She did not know whether she was happy or sad.

SHE SOARED and plummeted in unseen swells. The sky was black velvet. She was horribly thirsty and her teeth chattered from the cold. Fits of trembling shook her.

"*Through caverns measureless to man,*" she chanted suddenly. From "Kubla Khan". *Xanadu* engraved on a brass plaque on Jean-Paul's boat.

> "*In Xanadu did Kubla Khan*
> *A stately pleasure-dome decree:*
> *Where Alph, the sacred river, ran*
> *Through caverns measureless to man*
> *Down to a sunless sea.*"

Where are you, Jean-Paul, with *Xanadu*, now that I need you? She could hear his voice, faintly accented, quoting the poet.

Her legs were numb. She began to move them. She looked down. Her feet trailed green bubbles of phosphorescence. She had a sudden vision of them as seen from the eyes of a cruising shark. She stopped moving her legs.

She knew she was swallowing too much salt water: it only increased her thirst. But it was hard to time her breathing to avoid whitecaps she could not see. She felt herself suddenly soaring into the featureless night, impelled by a force from below. It rushed her upward, and when she peaked she was hurled under as a breaker curled over her head.

She surfaced, choking and gasping.

Nothing but a swell, larger than the rest. She waited for the next crest and raised her head. In the distance she saw a flash. Her first thought was lightning, since the rising swell must be coming from a squall. If the full strength of a tropical squall swept down on her, she was not sure she could survive it.

In a little while she saw the lightning again, a single flash. Lightning? Or strobe? She thought she remembered seeing the strobe before dawn, a century ago, just after it happened.

Or had she? Tossing in rising seas, there was no way to judge the frequency of the flashes. But the next time she saw the flash, she began to swim toward it.

She found no way to keep her direction. She did not see it again and after a while she quit. If it was the strobe, it would have to find her. In the rising seas he could not expect *her* to find *it*.

Chapter Two

They cut close to the eastern tip of Nuku Hiva, a thousand miles northeast of Tahiti. After a month at sea, where the highest point was the crest of a wave, the island's crags and pinnacles were overpowering. He called Lindy topside again and again to show her formations he found beautiful. Lindy seemed more interested in cleaning the boat for the customs officers.

They passed through the steep entrance of Tai-o-haé Bay, seat of Marquesan civilization, and were back in the world of people.

"Damn," murmured Mitch. "Lindy?"

Lindy popped topside. Seeing at first only the dark green mountainsides and the moss-covered crags leading to the water, she nodded appreciatively. After the long passage, all the colors you never saw at sea came alive. "Beautiful," she said.

"Yeah, but look ahead," he growled.

At the head of the bay lay a gray ship, flying the French tricolor. Above its funnels shimmered a haze of smog. Mitch sniffed the navy smell of baking bread and smokestack fumes. From every mast and deck level antennae poked skyward. She must be a communications vessel up from the nuclear test area to the south. A liberty launch crammed with pom-pommed sailors and officers sped toward a jetty of coral rocks where a village peeked through the palms.

"Well," Lindy said doubtfully, "it's only *one* ship, anyway. . . ."

"One's enough, and look at the yachts!"

Anchored close to the shore were a dozen sailboats. He identified four American boats, a Swede, a French steel ketch with an orange hull, a Dutch yawl, a Dane, two Canadian boats, and one West German. A tired cutter swung alone, an Australian flag hanging downheartedly near her stern and a white-haired man in spectacles slumped in the cockpit.

"Hell," he muttered, "there were fewer boats anchored in front of our house!"

They raised the quarantine flag and found a spot to drop their anchor. On one side lay a fifty-footer from Las Vegas, Nevada. On the other was anchored the famous schooner *Star of Peace*, out of Auckland, to protest the French nuclear tests.

With Lindy at the wheel, Mitch eased the anchor down. He looked around. They were practically landlocked. The mountains should have given him a sense of security. Instead, they seemed sullen and threatening.

A nude toddler in the schooner's cockpit waved at him. On the fifty-footer, a diminutive American, holding a beaded can of beer, wandered topside. He offered his dinghy, advice on anchoring, and a warning: the only bar in town, Henri's, was overrun with French Navy. He offered everything but a can of the cold beer.

Mitch began to pump up their Avon raft. He felt as deflated as it looked. They had just sailed 2800 miles and no one had even bothered to ask them how the trip had been.

LINDY SAT on a plain chair in the white, airy *gendarmerie*. She admired Mitch's performance in French, found it titillating, as if she had sailed in with a stranger; and she had to remind herself that he faked a lot.

The young gendarme, wearing starched white shorts and an open shirt, stamped their passports cheerfully and stuffed them into a drawer. His wife emerged from the living quarters behind the office.

"*Le vieil Australien . . .*" she murmured to her husband.

The gendarme winced. He spoke rapidly to Mitch, who looked surprised, shocked, and finally nodded. He told Lindy that the old Australian they had seen anchored alone had lost his friend, a

451

retired New Zealand dentist. Three days short of Nuku Hiva, the New Zealander had fallen overboard. "Tossed him a life jacket," Mitch translated, "and then couldn't find him again."

The old man shambled in. His face was gray. He nodded at Lindy and Mitch. "Saw you standing into the bay. Very pretty, you were, sails against the cliffs. Nice passage?"

The gendarme began to fill out his report, questioning the Australian in broken English while his wife typed the answers in French. They quickly fell into a swamp of half-understood nuances. Mitch began to translate for them.

When they were nearly finished, the gendarme seemed to brace himself. "Captain," he mumbled, face flaming, "there is one more question, I mus' ask. My superiors, in Papeete, they . . ." He stumbled, spoke to Mitch in French, beseeching help. Whatever question he wanted to ask, Mitch shook his head and sat mute.

The Australian's lips began to tremble. "I'll go through it again. He waved, you see, and laughed, sure I'd get back. But flying twin headsails, it was five minutes before I could get them down . . . alone." He stopped for a moment. "Then the spray, on my glasses . . . I'd wipe them clear, and in thirty seconds they'd be *useless* again. . . . No radio, the wind vane broken—"

The gendarme broke in unhappily. To Mitch he said: "Please, you must h'ask . . ."

The Australian seemed not have heard. He said to Mitch: "In all events, thank this gentleman for everything. They sent planes out, you know, and a helicopter, can you imagine?"

The gendarme gave up and thanked Mitch for his help.

Mitch invited the old man to join them for a beer, but he shook his head. They watched him row slowly out to his boat.

"What," asked Lindy, "was the question you wouldn't ask?"

"Why he quit searching so soon."

"So *soon?*" He had not given up for twenty-four hours. She visualized the ponderous trade-wind seas. And she knew the fatigue that could have you babbling after four hours on the wheel. Impossible to describe, though, to the young gendarme. "Well," she said, "I'm glad you didn't ask it."

"I might as well have asked," murmured Mitch. "He knew."

MITCH SHOWED his driver's license for identification at the *bureau de poste*, and got a little bundle of mail. Lindy's dad was fine, and Justice Holmes was thriving. Tony had a job at Nancy's father's TV station. A postcard edged in black gave him a scare until he read it; it was from Bernie.

> Magellan: Good news first: (1) Western Casualty bailed out, due your leaving. (2) Hal leaving us, taking the only decent law degree remaining in firm. (3) Golden Client died of pneumonia, but after appeal denied. Will write bad news later.

"That's our Bernie," Lindy muttered.

"She died," murmured Mitch. "We *wrecked* that poor surgeon's life, and the net result is to make a millionaire out of an alcoholic husband who wasn't even taking care of her!"

"Don't let Bernie wreck *this*, Mitch. It's been too hard getting here."

A breeze had come up and the afternoon sun had turned golden. The post office was on a rise above the bay, and the tiny yachts clustering below seemed placed there by an artist. Even the Navy ship, in the softer light, looked better. But on the battered cutter, the old Aussie slumped in his cockpit. He made your throat ache. There was truth in every line of his anguish.

Mitch needed a beer badly, so they went to find Henri's bar.

HE WATCHED tiny elves appear in the glow of the binnacle light and march around his compass. They always came when he was tired enough. He trusted them to keep him on course. The engine droned a shanty for them: *heave-ho, heave-ho, heave-ho, heave . . .*

"Lindy!" he called. He needed coffee, or relief at the wheel. Where the hell was she? "Lindy?"

She was not there. As he drifted right, the mizzen boom shot past an inch above his head, and brought up with a brutal *crack*. Instantly awake, he looked around. If he had been erect, instead of sagging at the wheel, he would have been knocked unconscious. He glanced at his watch. Still forty minutes to go to the point at which she'd gone in.

A dash of salt water flung high off the port bow stung his cheek. He was chilled. *God, how must it be for her in the black emptiness ahead?*

He began to sense a change in the sea, a heave and drop to the swells that had not been there before. A line squall was thrashing the water somewhere nearby.

I'm not far off, he told her. There were delays: for one thing, I couldn't find the damn logbook. But I did, and I'm on my way. . . .

Now, on impulse, he closed his eyes and flipped on every light on the boat. He left them on for fifteen seconds, then turned them off and opened his eyes. In a few minutes he did it again. If she were up ahead, she might spot a glimmer and it might give her hope, and soon he would be there.

SHE SAW Jean-Paul for the first time at Henri's. Afterward, his presence vitalized the memory of the place itself, so that she found it difficult to visualize it as it actually was: a grubby little bar on an island the world had forgotten. The building squatted behind bales of dry goods and barrels of fuel and crates of Manuia beer.

A huge white dog lay on the porch and rinky-dinky French Polynesian guitar music rattled in the background. A musty copra smell was everywhere, with the sweet-sour odor of stale beer. They went through the door into a rough wooden bar jammed with sailors, yachtsmen, and Marquesan natives. Mitch, parched and hoarse, asked for two beers.

Henri, a half-Polynesian with sharp Gallic features, reached into a tub and extracted two immense bottles. He set them dripping on the bar. Mitch paid him and Henri asked them to sign his *livre d'or* of foreign yachts, promising that in it they would find news of all their friends.

Lindy turned to look for a place to sit. Her toes were cramped in shoes, and her cut-off jeans, washed for weeks in salt water, felt like iron. She still had her sea legs and the room rolled and heaved beneath her.

There were four round tables in the room. At one sat Frenchmen in civilian clothes, presumably officers from the ship, with a day's purchases of carved paddles, spears, and tikis laid out on the wet

454

tabletop. The next was full of French sailors. A third was for the local orchestra—three sweating guitarists and a spoon clinker—and the last held a collection of weatherbeaten boat people.

None of the tables seemed to communicate with the others. She felt let down and unwelcome. The room was unbearably hot. The beer was warm. She felt like going back to the boat.

And then Jean-Paul stepped through the wooden door. He swept the crowd with deep blue eyes and looked into her own. Her stomach soared and her cheeks turned hot. It had happened when she first met Mitch and never, really, since.

"Lindy?" she heard Mitch say, as if from a distance.

"Um?" she asked, coming back.

"I said, let's sit on the windowsill."

She ripped her eyes from the shimmering blue gaze. "Yeah, oh, great," she said. She wished she had worn a dress.

MITCH SAT watching the black-bearded man limp across the room. He was very, very French. Mitch had not missed the impact of the blue eyes on Lindy. Maybe, after a month at sea with a man she had lived with for twenty years, a woman was as vulnerable as any sailor. He was amused, but not flattered.

Obviously, a presence had entered the bar. The Frenchman, a head shorter than he and barely taller than Lindy, was recharging the air. When the blue eyes smiled, the place came alive. The guitarists were reborn. The man had even white teeth and laugh crinkles, but his eyes were deep and thoughtful. He wore faded cut-off denims, leather sandals, and a carved pig's tooth mounted on a silver necklace. He was solid, with broad seaman's shoulders, and his movements were sure, despite the limp. He might have been thirty, or forty.

A half-dozen natives had crowded into the bar, square-shouldered, lean-hipped Marquesans. They were trying to draw the black-bearded man into their midst, pressing their beer on him. But his eyes were on Lindy's again, then they flicked to Mitch's. They were the deepest blue Mitch had ever seen. The man smiled. Mitch found himself smiling back. The Frenchman moved toward them.

"You are the white ketch, I think?"

He had a faint French accent. Beneath the beard a vicious scar curved from his temple to his jaw.

Mitch stuck out his hand. "I'm Mitch Gordon. This is my wife, Lindy. Are you anchored here?"

The Frenchman nodded and they shook hands. He told them he had the orange ketch *Xanadu*. "And that ketch, I am afraid she is *my* wife."

"That must save you a lot of confusion," remarked Lindy.

Now what the hell had she meant by that? Mitch studied her thoughtfully. The trip had toughened her; she was lithe and golden and very slender. With the Frenchman near, she glowed. He felt uncomfortable, and annoyed.

Blackbeard's name was Jean-Paul, and he sailed with one Tahitian crewman: "Taarii is a carver of wood, and he cooks, also."

The Frenchman was looking into Lindy's eyes as if the two of them were alone. "And your voyage," he said gently, "it was bad, I think, and good, and already you are forgetting the bad, is it not so?"

Her throat was tight. She would squeak if she talked, so she nodded, and he went on. "Some will *not* forget how bad it was, and they will drop out at Tahiti. And some will grow too full of confidence and lose their boats before Fiji. And some will go round the world on the trades—"

"And Jean-Paul will stay in the Marquesas forever," Henri cut in, setting a jug of wine on the windowsill for him.

"Do not count on it, my friend," Jean-Paul said softly.

"You must not leave," said Henri. "Security demands you stay. Who else will teach us to whittle spears and clubs for the tourists?"

"Your *financial* security demands me to stay," rumbled Jean-Paul. He suggested that teaching the natives to carve what the market demanded was simply giving them money to spend in Henri's bar for wine to rot their bellies. Henri snorted, snapped his towel at Jean-Paul's bare chest, and went back to the bar.

With Jean-Paul that afternoon they met people whom they would meet again during the long sail west. They met a shy young girl from the protest vessel *Star of Peace*, and her tiny daughter.

456

They met a French officer from the nuclear test ship, a Dutch couple and their doll-like little girl, and Jack-the-Rip-off, a piratical young American who wore a headband and had gentle eyes and who single-handed a tough little boat he had built for himself.

Everything Jean-Paul said seemed sparkling to Lindy. From a souvenir stand he selected her a beautifully carved tiki: the carver refused payment because Jean-Paul had been his teacher. For a moment they stood on a village pavilion watching lines of beautiful adolescents swirling their hips and wobbling their knees. Jean-Paul identified the *otea*, a Marquesan war dance. But he turned away quickly. "The greatest warriors of all Polynesia, performing like a troupe of seals!"

He took them to the island's only restaurant, a stucco affair perched on the hill above the bay. There was a line of French officers waiting, but the native proprietor slid them in ahead.

Later they said goodnight at the beach and paddled to their respective craft. They had to sleep on deck, it was so hot below.

"What did you think of Blue Eyes?" Mitch asked suddenly.

"Oh, wow!" she said. He had caught her unawares, and she overreacted. "Charisma, I mean."

"A charismatic Frog," he reflected, "in a tiny pond." Exactly the kind of red-necked generalization they both hated.

In fact, she thought, dozing off, a judgment so uncharacteristic as to be interesting. She fell asleep mulling it over. In a few minutes she was awake again, writhing with stomach pains. From then on it was between her and the germs, whatever they were, and she had hardly a conscious thought of Jean-Paul for almost a week.

Her subsconscious was another matter, and it blew the whistle on her, but Jean-Paul would not tell her of that for a long time.

Chapter Three

She had not seen another flash for a long time and now she was racked with uncontrollable tremblings. Her thirst was agonizing. She succumbed, sipped salt water and gagged.

The skies had partly cleared, and she glimpsed stars she should have learned: Mitch had tried to teach them to her. And Jean-Paul had tried, briefly. She made out the Southern Cross, and then lost it under the crest of a swell.

She began to move her legs faster, to ward off the next attack of shivers. She found the Southern Cross again and lay back to study it. She became aware of a sudden stillness. It was the sort of visceral hint that came before a storm. She pictured Mitch striking the mainsail as he felt the wind drop and the oily swell begin.

The Southern Cross flickered out. She had the sense of an immense anvil cloud bearing down. She heard a gurgling rumble. When she was carried to the crest of a swell, she felt wind on her nose and cheeks. As her body sank into canyons, her descents became more ominous. In one trough, she heard a rush of water down the slope. She instinctively sucked in a breath and ducked. She was tumbled in the breaker like a surfer torn from his board. She clung to the jerrycan through the whole wild ducking.

Great waves began to hammer her down. Once, the jerrycan left her hand. She grabbed it again as it began to sail on the wind up the slope of a swell. Then the rain began. For a moment she opened her mouth like a bird and tried to drink, grunting in relief. But it was all too much, it was in her nose, her eyes, her mouth. She began to think that, surrounded by salt water, she would drown in fresh. She was in a liquid maelstrom, strangling and coughing. Finally there was a calm, and when the rain began again, it was more kindly. The dark cloud had moved away and she could see the Southern Cross again, crystal clear.

Her thirst was eased, and she felt more confident and awake. She looked around. Below the Southern Cross she saw a flash. Perhaps lightning—but the storm had gone the other way. She began to move her legs, traveling south imperceptibly but steadily.

She glimpsed the flash again and again. She caught a certain rhythm to it. If it *was* lightning, it was strange lightning, because it was parked below the Southern Cross and not moving.

HER FISH poisoning, if that was what it was, was so violent that everyone was afraid that she might die.

She had awakened on deck, with a thermometer in her mouth

458

and Mitch's hand on her forehead. She had a temperature of 104 degrees. He rowed her in and carried her up the dusty road to the island hospital. Through clouds of fever and delirium she remembered an enormously obese Polynesian nurse in a white uniform.

She shared a stucco-walled hospital room with an injured Marquesan sailor. A brown-skinned nymph, wearing a *pareu* and a flower behind her ear, attended her. Her name was Tiare. She stood for three days by the door, never averting her gaze, never leaving except to guide her to the toilet.

Mitch tried, through the gendarme, to reach the island doctor, but he was treating someone on Ua Huka, beyond radio recall.

In the daytime a horse grazed outside her paneless window, and at night invisible bugs feasted on Mitch, who slept in a sleeping bag on the floor of her room.

When Dr. Clary, the island doctor, suddenly returned from his rounds on Ua Huka, he pumped antibiotics into her. On the fifth day she improved dramatically. She began to get visitors: Henri, then the old Australian. The doe-eyed hippie girl from *Star of Peace* came with her daughter, the Dutch couple, and their little girl. Even Jack-the-Rip-off turned up.

Jean-Paul came the last evening she was there. She discovered that she was hurt that he had not come before. On his entrance, the impassive Tiare took life and grinned for the first time. She began to move swiftly around the room, dusting with a palm frond, her hips rolling.

He ignored the girl. His eyes stayed on Lindy. When Mitch told him that they were leaving, that they had had it with the Marquesas, he nodded. "So beautiful, and so sinister. Not like Tahiti or the Tuamotus. But you must avoid the Tuamotus. Even I, with my steel boat, am afraid of their reefs. It is too bad, for each little island there is a paradise."

Mitch nodded but said nothing. The doctor came in, and Jean-Paul asked him something in French. The doctor looked surprised, shook his head, and left, chuckling. When Jean-Paul was ready to leave, Mitch shook his hand and thanked him. Jean-Paul's eyes widened.

"Mitch, you speak French?"

"A little. And thanks again."

Jean-Paul passed from the room. Tiare subsided, taking her place at the door. Lindy asked Mitch why he was so grateful to Jean-Paul. He moved to the window and looked out over the bay, then he picked up her bag and said, "Let's check out, okay?"

It was wonderful to be home aboard, where she belonged, among her own things. It was cooler too in the cockpit that evening. When they finished dinner, sitting topside, Mitch stared at the purple hills above them. The musky smell of burning copra drifted across the bay.

"You haven't told me why you thanked Jean-Paul," she reminded him.

He seemed embarrassed. "Yeah . . . Well, he tried to get word to the doctor to come back when the gendarme couldn't."

"How did he do that?"

Jean-Paul, he said, had hiked to a village on Comptroller Bay to see a native psychic who had a brother on Ua Huka. "They sent out a message," Mitch said uncomfortably.

She felt a shiver run along her arms. "A message? How?"

"*I* don't know how! Long-distance thought, I guess."

The shiver reached her stomach. "And the brother *got* it? And told Dr. Clary?"

"Clary was already on his way back."

"Does *he* believe in that?"

"He's . . . well, skeptical."

"But Jean-Paul does," she murmured.

He jerked his head toward the mountains embracing the bay. "Well, he hiked eight miles across that ridge to place the call."

She was restless and fascinated. She asked him what *he* believed. "I mean, you fell all over him, thanking him."

"So he's superstitious! But I *do* believe," he said, looking into her eyes, "that he was awfully concerned."

He was asking her something. They were all at once communicating, for real, and it was what she had wanted, but she found that she could not even hold his gaze, let alone answer.

"Or," she suggested awkwardly, "he's just a real nice guy."

THEY SAILED out of Tai-o-haé Bay at dawn. Mitch did not think they would ever return. He had come closer to losing Lindy than she knew. The vibes here were all wrong.

Tahiti lay nearly a thousand miles away, past the Tuamotu Archipelago, stretching like a minefield between the Marquesas and Tahiti. On the chart, they were dots, but in reality they were vast coral islands pounded by growling surf, impossible to see at night. In daytime they hid until the last moment behind a dazzling horizon. Each crouched, more sea than land, guarded by reefs that might run for thirty miles.

Mitch had heard that there was hardly one atoll among them that did not have its wreck, a ribbed carcass baking in the sun. Still, there was the matter of the extra two hundred miles in going around them. If he found the guts, they could pass through the Tuamotus, stopping at Fakarava, and cut the trip in half.

AT NOON, three days out of Nuku Hiva, she was clinging to the spreader, searching the area ahead. It was sunny and very rough. Mitch was chasing the sun with his sextant on deck below. Abeam, a squall was flailing the jagged horizon, but there was no sign of Fakarava. "No atoll at all," she sang down. If he became discouraged, maybe he would backtrack, cut north to the safer course.

While he was working the star sights the night before, she had read the general remarks in the *Sailing Directions:* "Navigation among these islands is dangerous because of the uncertain set of the currents and the still imperfectly charted reefs and islands. . . ."

Imperfectly charted? She believed Mitch to be an infallible navigator, but if the island itself was misplaced on the chart, what then?

He had made his observation and come below. She read him a passage. "'Six-knot current in the pass,'" she chanted. "'The pass into Fakarava is only eighty yards wide at the seaward end. . . .'"

He was busy at the chart table. "Look, I'm trying to figure out where the hell we are, okay?"

The next morning, Sunday, he had told her to look for a cloud-bottom which might be tinted green with reflected light from a

461

lagoon. At 1:00 p.m., despite her hopes, she saw the green cloud formation. As she peered beneath it, she saw a sawtooth fringe of palm trees enlarging with frightening speed.

"Land ho," she sang down mournfully. He popped topside and swept his eye along the length of the atoll. She climbed down and their glances met. The silent question was, Suppose they'd come on it at night?

They dropped the sails and powered for an hour along the reef. Somewhere there was supposed to be a wreck which would give them a landmark for the pass. They stayed well offshore but kept easing in to see better, and then out when they got scared, for they had no way of knowing where the undersea reef began.

At five thirty they spotted the wreck and sighted the pass. Mitch had worked out the tides. They should be slack in another half hour, maybe. "Let's shoot the pass," he decided.

She begged him to stand offshore for the night, hoping they would drift away and never see the islands again. "No, honey," he said. "New moon, too dark. If the current set us *out*, we'd lose the island, and if it set us *in*, we'd lose the boat."

It answered her question but avoided the real one, which was why they were there in the first place. It was on the tip of her tongue to ask it, but she did not want to add to his problems, so she climbed to her appointed station on the yardarm.

From the spreader, she gaped down at the pass. At its mouth ran great seas. Only a narrow notch in the coral seemed free of the rolling surf. Using the hand signals they had practiced at home, she sliced her hand toward the notch. They began to pitch as they nosed into shallower water. If they grounded, she thought, she would be hurled from the mast like a boulder from a catapult.

Through binoculars, she inspected a little village on the left of the mouth of the channel. It seemed deserted. Between the cannon salvos of the surf behind her, she caught voices raised in a hymn. Church services explained the empty street. But on the coral quay was a little black boy, an impish child holding a guitar as big as himself. She waved to him but he did not wave back, so she shifted her attention to the lagoon beyond.

Something occurred to her suddenly. Now, with the sun low at

462

her back, she could spot each of the coralheads in the channel ahead. But when they made the left hand turn into the lagoon, the dazzle would be in her eyes. And she knew that Mitch, at the wheel, was too blinded by optimism to see anything below the swirling surface. Her eyes were the only ones he had.

She would have liked to discuss this, but there was no way, from here, over the roar of the engine.

She wished she were back in the hospital.

HE SEARCHED for her in sultry darkness. The oily swell from the southeast persisted, and now the shuddering mainsail told him that the storm was approaching fast. He had to get the sail down.

He threw the engine into neutral and scrambled forward. He got the mainsail down and furled it. He was so tired he could hardly fight his way forward to the jib, but he struck it too. Then he staggered aft and got the mizzen down.

The rain began with a roar and wind yelled through the barren rigging. His inclination was to ease off, but he knew Lindy was somewhere ahead and he refused to lose ground. He jammed the engine full forward and began to take the waves head-on. *Linda Lee* hobbyhorsed, tossing her head at the peaks and digging her bowsprit deep in the troughs.

The rain terrified him. Earlier, when the morning squalls had hit, he had not been as scared, for he had imagined that she was somewhere far away. But this storm, driving in from ahead, must have passed her very closely. Its rains seemed capable of slamming her under, or drowning her in a sheer cascade of water.

Finally the wind shifted and the squall passed. He churned onward, fighting to stay alert, searching for the flash of the strobe. Tossing it in blindly had, at the time, seemed a mistake. Now it was his only hope.

In the darkest corner of his mind lurked a depressing fact. He had already searched these waters twice today, at the end of each leg, in the morning and the afternoon. And he had not seen the strobe.

But that was in daylight. How could you see a strobe in the sunlight?

It had to be flashing somewhere ahead. He would find it. Before dawn. And she would be waving when he did. . . .

He heard a heavy thump. Suddenly he was on his back, looking up at a dancing moon. He had passed out and dropped behind the binnacle. The thump had been his head on the deck.

He got up and came back on course. He put a foot on the coaming, one hand on his usual shroud, and pulled himself erect. Balancing there, he could hardly fall asleep again.

He had half an hour to go to where the logbook said she had fallen.

AS THEY STEERED through the break in the Fakarava reef, his eyes were on Lindy, perched on the spreader. She had seemed scared at sea, but now that the chips were down, she was apparently calm. He'd concealed from her how crazily his navigation had suffered under the drunken currents. He was lucky to have found Fakarava at all, and an idiot to have tried cutting through the archipelago. But it was too late to get out now.

They were abeam the village and all at once he was moving into the strength of the current. He tapped the throttle forward and inched past the quay. Aloft, Lindy raised her arm, then sliced it down a little to port. He eased the wheel, waited until her hand pointed amidships, and met the swing. She gave him an okay signal.

The village drifted aft. The little black boy with the guitar bounced excitedly, beckoning them. Or warning them? Mitch hoped not. They were well into the chute now and committed.

Lindy began to point toward a danger to starboard, calmly enough at first, then in a violent, jerky motion. He came hard right, and even from his low vantage he could see the huge gnarled hunk of brown coral that had frightened her. Streams of bubbles flowed from its peaks and crevices.

He got the boat back to midstream and jammed the throttle forward. They might as well burn up the engine as be swept backward into the surf.

Imperceptibly, they drew up the channel. Around the turn the lagoon shimmered invitingly, but the turn was the thing, and that was up to Lindy.

He flashed her a smile and the okay signal. She grinned back down. She did not seem scared at all. With a girl like her, a man could sail anywhere in the world.

SHE HUNG, terrified, to the mast. Approaching the turn, she peered down into water which had suddenly turned to cocoa. She tried to read the patterns of the currents and the depth of the water. She could not. She was afraid to signal the turn too soon or wait too long. She glanced back. He was wire-taut, his eyes darting from her to the current. "Now?" he yelled.

She shook her head. Now was too early, wasn't it? Or was it? How could he do this to her, make her lose his boat? The glare of the sun was blinding; the center of the channel could be anywhere. She leaned out to look more closely, lost her balance, stuck out an arm to regain it.

"Roger!" yelled Mitch. She felt the boat begin to swing.

"No!" she screamed. She turned. "Mitch, no!"

He grinned idiotically, made the okay sign, and continued the turn. The bowsprit swung faster and faster. . . . God, he had better catch it now or they would go crashing into the coral to port. . . . She wrapped arms and legs around the mast, closed her eyes, and waited for the impact.

Nothing happened. She heard the engine ease. Cautiously she opened her eyes. They were slipping through emerald water, utterly alone in a lagoon that stretched to the horizon. Even the village was hidden from sight beyond its palm grove.

She climbed down and lurched aft. Mitch was beaming at her. "You are something," he murmured. He kissed her on her forehead. "You are really something."

"Piece of cake." She shrugged. She sat down casually before her knees collapsed.

They moored miles from the village in a crescent cove hardly larger than the boat. For a week they were more alone than they had been in mid-ocean, with none of the strains and worries. They walked the beach and snorkled the lagoon. They hacked clumsily at coconuts and drank the coconut milk, and they learned to eat *pauah*, abalone-like creatures, which they marinated in lemon juice and ate raw.

They swam and dozed and ate and made love. Mitch had, some-how, got back the touch. To ask him why, she would have had to admit that she had missed it, so she did not. Why rock the boat?

She would awaken at dawn and watch a friendly palm which hung over the bow tracing patterns above the hatch in the morning breeze. The rustle of the trades never stopped and the surf drummed endlessly. She wanted to stay forever. She had only two worries: fresh water and Mitch. Very soon, she was sure, he would get bored.

At dawn, on the eighth day, she again awakened to the swishing of the palm. Her gaze fell from the hatch above her bunk, through the open door, to the main saloon. She almost screamed. Sitting on the companionway steps, staring at her intently, was the tiny black imp from the pier. His jaw and snubnose were infantile be-neath a bulging forehead. His chin rested on his oversized guitar. The body was ten; the eyes were forty.

"Mitch!" she whispered. She reached across and shook him. He awakened instantly. He followed her glance and sat up.

"*Bonjour, mon capitaine,*" the child said, with respect.

"Get lost! *Fiche le camp!*" barked Mitch.

The little boy flinched and turned his eyes on Lindy.

"*Bonjour, madame capitaine?*" he ventured.

"*Bonjour.*" She smiled.

A little-boy grin flashed on her like sudden morning sun. "Hey," he said, "you want a guide? I am Louie, *très bon pilote.*"

"Well, I'll be," Mitch muttered. Louie had come to lead them from the Garden of Eden. Lindy's paradise was lost.

MITCH SAT at breakfast in the saloon, next to Louie. Louie had already eaten five bananas and was eyeing a sixth. He was, he told Mitch, sent by the village chief. The chief would like it very much if the pretty yacht would tie up to the town dock, to be properly welcomed.

Mitch doubted that the chief had sent him. Why Louie? He asked him, as delicately as he could. The shoulders went back. "*Mon père,*" he announced solemnly, "*il est Américain!*"

"His father's American?" asked Lindy from the sink.

"Hey, man, *Américain,*" repeated Louie proudly.

The child was spooky. In the high-domed head was a quick mind, and some secret purpose Mitch could not quite define. Louie said his father lived in Bora Bora, farther even than Tahiti. He too was *bon capitaine*, with a yacht bigger than this. Louie had an American friend as well, Jacques.

He reached into his shirt pocket and drew out a Polaroid picture. It was Jack-the-Rip-off, sitting at the wheel of his scruffy ketch. Louie was standing beside him, his frizzled head touching the tip of Rip-off's tangled beard.

Jacques, announced Louie, was going to take him to Tahiti when he returned. And to Bora Bora too. But Jacques had been delayed, *non?* If *mon capitaine* and the *jolie madame* would take him to Tahiti, he would guide them through the reef.

Mitch shook his head. "*Mais non, mon p'tit. Je regrette. . . .*"

Louie's eyes grew angry. The tiny black hand darted for the last banana on the table. His forearm seemed deliberately to brush the box of cereal. It fell and spilled on the deck. Louie gnawed the banana impassively, while Lindy swept the mess.

"*Le quai?*" he asked suddenly.

Well, they did need water. "Lindy," Mitch suggested, "let's have a go at the dock?"

She nodded resignedly. He smiled at Louie and got up to start the engine. He read a crazy urgent hope on the black face. They had better check for a stowaway when they left.

THE QUAY was a huge tan slab of coral concrete with jagged edges, set on barnacled pilings. The instant they docked, Louie took charge, piping orders and waving his tiny arms. His moment of glory lasted only seconds, until half the village swarmed over the rail. A wiry girl pushed him overboard, and began to roll her hips for Mitch, to the twang of a shiny Japanese guitar. Louie scrambled onto the dock, his tiny face contorted, and trudged off.

The rigging sagged with children, the cockpit churned with teenagers, the saloon was instantly jammed with smiling island women, immaculate in clean *pareus*. Chaos lasted all day and into the night.

By 2:00 a.m. Mitch and Lindy were exhausted. Louie had returned to the dock by then and was sitting with great dignity on a piling. Mitch asked him to explain to the people *avec politesse* that *le bon capitaine* and *madame capitaine* were *très fatigués*.

Louie shrugged. Was *le bon capitaine* going to take him to Tahiti?

"Non! C'est impossible!"

Louie reflected for a moment and relented. He got up and delivered a short Polynesian speech to the people in the cockpit. Then he went below and addressed the women in the saloon. Everyone nodded and smiled and got up. They touched cheeks with Lindy and Mitch and in five minutes the boat was clear.

As a reward, they let Louie sleep in the cockpit.

IN THE MORNING Mitch looked at the swirling currents. He turned to Lindy. "Maybe," he said softly, "we *do* need a pilot to get out of that pass?"

"Oh, boy," said Lindy dubiously, "you *are* getting soft. On the other hand, at least you're asking me."

Mitch asked the village chief about red tape. No problem, *monsieur*, he would radio ahead. All would be arranged. The boy's great aunt lived in Papeete. Mitch returned to the boat and told Louie. The boy's eyes were shining, but his face was impassive. *"Monsieur le capitaine?"* he piped. *"Pour le pilotage, je ne vais rien vous prendre."*

Mitch muttered to Lindy, "He says that he won't charge us!"

"Louie," said Lindy, "you are just too much!"

"Too mawsh," agreed Louie. "Jus' too mawsh."

They had signed on their first crewman, and their last.

THEY CAST OFF from the wharf, wreathed in *leis* and loaded with coconuts. Their friends of the night before were misty-eyed: Lindy was touched, until she decided later that they were crying with joy at Louie's departure. Louie blustered around the deck, coiling lines backward, pointing port and starboard as they churned straight through the pass. At the first swell he turned greenish-gray and threw up. He burrowed into the forepeak and defied efforts to drag him out.

Every hour he would emerge, to stagger topside and look for Tahiti, four days' sail away. He became worried that they had missed it the first day, became sure on the second, certain on the third. Mitch seemed amused, showing more patience with Louie in three days than he had with Tony in twenty years.

On the fourth day, when Mitch escaped for a nap, Lindy raised the crags of Moorea, rising majestically off the starboard bow, right on schedule. In a few moments the peaks of Tahiti showed, dead ahead.

She woke Mitch. She thought she knew what the peaks off their bow meant to him. He had done it his way, sailed his boat to some misty dream of garlands and dells and fictional waterfalls. Tahiti, after sixty days of sweat from San Francisco, should have meant just as much to her. What it really meant was a fresh-water shower and getting rid of Louie.

Chapter Four

She moved through the water slowly, heading for the Southern Cross and the rhythmic flash. The deep, visceral attacks of shivering had become more frequent and violent. She envisioned the sun over the eastern horizon, sweeping toward her. Daylight slid across the earth, Mitch told her. It could be leaving San Francisco now, speeding to warm her.

The seas, now that the squall had moved on, were calmer. If dawn found the seas smooth, Mitch might find her very quickly.

Her right thigh muscle knotted suddenly. She grunted in pain. She ducked facedown, grabbed the leg, and began to knead it frantically. When she threw back her head for a breath, she took a mouthful of water and gagged.

Coughing and struggling, she massaged the muscle. It finally eased. She lay back, exhausted. She was afraid that if she moved, the cramp would return. When she felt better, she carefully re-oriented herself and faced the Southern Cross again. She craned, waiting. Finally she saw the flash once more.

Cramps or not, she began to move again.

MITCH AWAKENED from his nap to find Tahiti dead ahead, all purples and hazy greens. He caught a scent of jasmine and the heavy smell of copra. He also caught a whiff of smog. For Tahiti, you were always one hundred years too late, or fifty years, or twenty. Even Cook had complained on his second voyage about the degradation of the noble savages he had corrupted on his first.

They drew close to the entrance to Papeete Pass and shot toward the notch in the sawtooth coral ledges, astern of a giant U.S. tanker. As they entered the slot, a Pan Am jet labored up from a runway and roared overhead in a gut-shaking crescendo. Louie grinned excitedly. When he saw Mitch looking at him, he composed his face. "*Eh bien.*" He yawned. "My father is *un pilote* and flies such aircraft."

But *un pilote*, Mitch pressed him, surely only of boats.

Boats *and* airplanes, Louie insisted.

Mitch smiled and began to look for a break in the long line of yachts tied stern to along the quay.

Lindy standing on the bowsprit, watched the harbor open before her. A Russian passenger liner dominated the wharf. Along her upper deck was strung a banner: CHAMPAGNE AND CAVIAR CRUISE OF THE SOUTH PACIFIC. Ahead stood a simple white church with a red spire. A modern post office sprawled on the waterfront by a park that looked cool and dark.

470

They crept under power along the quay. Several boats down the line lay a low-slung steel ketch, painted orange. Lindy tensed. The name on her bows was *Xanadu*. And waving to Lindy from the forecastle was Jean-Paul, solid, broad-shouldered, tanned.

Again her stomach flipped. Her cheeks felt hot. Jean-Paul swung his hand in an arc along his rail, indicating room to squeeze in, and began to tie bumpers along his gunwale. Taarii, the young Tahitian crewman, climbed to the bowsprit to wait for a line.

Mitch swung the boat's stern to the quay, and flung the youth a looping line. In a few minutes Lindy was grinning like an idiot across five feet of water into the deep blue eyes. The moment lasted timelessly. She became aware that Louie was staring at her and that there was work to do, and still, she could not draw her glance away.

And then came Mahura. The girl popped from *Xanadu*'s after hatch, dressed in the uniform of an Air France stewardess. She was straightening her skirt when she noticed Lindy. She read her face instantly, flashed a look of amusement, and hurried aft. She was Tahitian-Chinese. She made her drab uniform look like a creation of Yves Saint Laurent.

"Wow!" Lindy heard Mitch mutter. He looked as if he had been clubbed. She couldn't blame him. The girl teetered expertly ashore, hopped onto a bright yellow motor scooter, and whipped into the traffic hurtling along the quay.

Lindy supposed she should be thankful. The problem of her strange chemical reaction to Jean-Paul was solved. The girl was possibly the most beautiful woman she had ever seen. But she did not feel grateful at all. She turned away to find Louie's eyes still on her. Abruptly, she went below. With fresh water available, at least she could wash her hair.

MITCH GATHERED their passports and put on clean clothes to go to immigration. Louie, his tiny valise packed, was on the foredeck staring sullenly at the traffic rumbling along the Quai Bir-Hackeim. He had never seen a motor vehicle and had never crossed a city street. Yet, trudging down the waterfront later, he kept his eyes dead ahead, without a glance at what he must most want to see.

They cleared immigration and phoned Louie's great-aunt. She arrived, piloting a belching Vespa. She accepted Louie gratefully, perhaps knowing no better.

Mitch had given Louie their Polaroid as a going-away gift, but you returned a gift with a gift, not thanks. The little boy reached in his pocket and produced the photo he had shown them on the boat. Now, Jack-the-Rip-off had been cut away; Louie stood alone at the wheel of the boat, lord of all he could see.

He handed the picture to Mitch. "*Pour mon capitaine.*"

"*Et aussi pour madame la capitaine?*" suggested Mitch.

Louie's face hardened. He climbed behind the woman on the Vespa, and looked him dead in the eyes. "No!" he said. "She is bad woman."

"What?" Mitch gasped disbelievingly.

Louie jabbed his great-aunt. "*Allez!*" he ordered.

"Wait a minute, you little—" yelled Mitch. Angrily, he crumpled the photo and dropped it in a trash can. He hated to keep things from Lindy, but that was one message she wasn't going to get.

DAWN HAD NOT come. The flash, when she saw it occasionally, seemed no closer. But the cramp did not return. She lay back and looked straight up. A magnificent star was overhead. It shone steadily, like a planet, but there were tiny beams radiating from it, like a star on a Christmas card.

One night at Papeete, under a gold-studded sky, Jean-Paul had shown her how easy it was to pick the star directly overhead. That was how the ancient Polynesians could find an island in an infinite sea. Their navigators would know that a certain star peaked directly over an atoll after dusk. Each twilight they would readjust their course toward the star. When it was straight overhead just after nightfall, they would be at the island.

But how did they know there were islands out there in the first place? Very simple: accidentally. If a fisherman were swept by current to an uninhabited island, he would use the coconut radio. *Eh bien!* A brother or son would dream of the star and the island and *know*, and the whole village would launch their boats and set sail. You see?

472

*Okay, Jean-Paul. Or Mitch. Either one. Winner take all. I am
here, right below the big orange star. Antares, I think. So steer for
Antares, and quickly, before it begins to set.*

Mitch, darling, are you coming, or not?

There was no answer. It was no use. Mitch did not really believe.
Jean-Paul might receive her, but God knew where he was now.

She turned toward the Southern Cross and began to swim again.

THEY ELBOWED into the life of the quay. They were on the outskirts of Frenchman's Row, a relatively permanent gathering of
French yachts. *Star of Peace* and three other long-hair boats
were moored in Hippie Haven, and Hamburg Heights was studded
with the ensigns of West Germany. Kurt in *Kormorant*, an
imperious Berlin carpenter, and his ex-busdriver cook, had
been tied up there for years.

Papeete authorities practised *laissez-faire* with yachtsmen. If you were sober and your finances held up, you got
an extension on your visa.

Within weeks Mitch and Lindy had made many warm
friends. Marriages and crews dissolved, loves were
born, Kurt of *Kormorant* knocked his lifelong friend
into the water and dived in to rescue
him. A doctor on *Mistress* saved a
bungled birth on a Chilean yawl, and a
young millionaire on *Foam* got religion,
donated his boat to Jehovah's
Witnesses, and no one laughed.

You thought of the people as their
boat and the boat as the people.
Within six months Lindy was ready
to stay forever. She was weary of
sailing; she dreaded the day
they must leave.

MITCH SAT at the saloon table,
his typewriter 'before him. Face
down on its right lay fifty pages of

Impossible Dream, a chronicle of their voyage. He had begun it to placate his conscience for six months' idleness. But he was tired of writing. It was time to move on.

He heard someone pounding on the hull. Grateful for the excuse to escape, he went topside. Jean-Paul was pulling himself from the dirty water onto *Linda Lee*'s deck. *Xanadu* was gone from her berth, winched out from the quay. He remembered that she was scheduled for a haul-out across the harbor. She had no engine and had been waiting all day for wind. Now she was floating strangely, bowdown, stern up.

"Anchors fouled?" asked Mitch.

Jean-Paul nodded. He had a diving mask pushed up on his forehead. "Our anchors, they seem mated. *Je regrette*, Mitch."

"My fault," shrugged Mitch. He had anchored last, six months ago. He must have dropped directly over Jean-Paul's chain. Worse, his scuba tanks were empty. So he'd have to skin it in thirty feet of mud.

He put on a mask and fins, and Lindy rowed them over to their anchors in the rubber raft. He slipped into the water and followed the Frenchman down through levels of translucent green, tan, opaque brown, until he lost sight of Jean-Paul's orange trunks in a morass of mud, chain, and anchor flukes.

Jean-Paul, working alone while Taarii winched from above, had somehow managed to dig his anchor free. It hung a few feet above the soupy bottom, a fathom of Mitch's chain twisted around it. Spiraling deeper, Mitch found the Frenchman digging at *Linda Lee*'s thirty-five-pound anchor.

Mitch sank his fins into the mushy bottom and gave a few ineffectual heaves. His heart began to pound. He had a great set of lungs for poolside games. But in Jean-Paul he had apparently met his match. Mitch quit and broke surface by the raft, a good fifteen seconds before the Frenchman.

"*C'est impossible?*" asked Jean-Paul. "Perhaps we must get filled your tanks?"

"No," panted Mitch. "We can do it." He began to draw in mammoth breaths, hyperventilating.

"Mitch?" pleaded Lindy from the raft. "Let's fill the tanks?"

He glared at her. What she meant was, Watch it, Buster, you're forty-five. Well, Jean-Paul was hardly younger. He tugged down his mask and dived.

He plummeted to the bottom, felt for his chain, and followed it to his anchor. *Xanadu's* anchor had apparently been eased back to the bottom. To untangle the mess, they must somehow hoist *Linda Lee's* hook over *Xanadu's* chain three times—once for each twist.

He grabbed the shank of his own anchor. When he had it half over Jean-Paul's chain, he felt the Frenchman helping him. They pitched it over, grabbed it again, and repeated. Mitch felt his lungs convulsing, but the Frenchman showed no sign of letting go. He could feel the granite body next to his own, straining. The anchor was caught, no, free and ready to drop, no, snagged. . . .

He hung on frantically, damned if he'd give up first. He felt Jean-Paul pat his shoulder once, then tug at his arm, urging him to let go too. He shrugged him off, caught a quick glimpse of the orange trunks rising toward the surface. Still he hung on, hauling the anchor over the chain with a last mighty effort.

He hated to let it fall, for then, later, he would have to haul it up and reset it. Reluctantly, he began to ease his grip, then changed his mind. He had a feeling of immense and sudden power. Flippers churning, he powered for the surface, weighted by anchor and chain. He fought upward, through brown water to tan, green sunlight somewhere, he had better let go, *he needed air.* . . .

Clinging to his anchor, he broke surface a foot behind the raft. Desperately, he gripped the handline draped on its side. Jean-Paul and Lindy were at the other end, staring down into the water. They did not see him. Jean-Paul was poised to dive. "Oh, God," he heard Lindy wail. "*Go!*"

Mitch, near fainting, took a deep breath. "Hey, guys?"

Jean-Paul whirled, lumbered down the raft, and gasped: "Your h'anchor?" He plunged his arm into the water, and heaved it aboard. "*C'est formidable!*" he breathed. "*C'est impossible!*"

Mitch could not find the strength to slither aboard. Hanging on to the side, he looked up at Lindy. She stared down at him. She had never looked so angry. "Tell me why you did that!"

"Well, we'd have had to haul it up later to reset it. . . ."

"Do you really," she asked softly, "think that's what I mean?"

He felt his cheeks go hot with shame. "I guess not."

"Then why pretend?"

He winced. Jean-Paul turned scarlet and elaborately checked their anchor shackle. They dropped him at his boat, reset their own anchor, and never mentioned the dive again.

THE THOUGHT of the long slog west became a nightmare to Lindy. When Mitch talked of the Cook Islands, and the Tongas, and Fiji, she projected less and less interest. She was content and never bored with Papeete, though her routine never varied. She awakened each morning to the sound of the first motor scooters blasting past Parc Bougainville.

This was early morning, go-to-market time. The *bonnitiers* would be casting off, bamboo poles slung on cabin tops, gleefully rocking the yachts and trying to awaken anyone still asleep below.

One morning she finished her garden-hose shower in a bikini on the quay, dressed, and strolled down the Quai Bir-Hackeim. Early risers from the *Star of Peace* were up. The battered schooner was here on French sufferance after being slammed, ostensibly by accident, by a French destroyer off the Mururoa test grounds. The clean Dutch yawl was here from Nuku Hiva, and the tiny girl was growing fatter every day. The old Australian had arrived and was trying to sell his cutter rather than face the trip home single-handed.

Most of their friends would be leaving soon on the trades toward the west. Despite her feeble protests, if she read Mitch correctly, they would be with them.

She crossed the street toward the market. A sleepy bartender was sweeping the sidewalk outside the ancient Hotel Scott, a relic of the old Papeete waterfront. He greeted her with a smile and the silent lifted eyebrows of Polynesia.

It was too soon to leave Tahiti: she was just getting acquainted. Tahitians never accepted anyone on sight, and for a month or two she and Mitch had been in social quarantine with the natives. And then everything had changed. A waitress at the Café Vaima, who had always ignored them before, rushed over one evening and kissed her on either cheek. A postal clerk began to set aside their mail. The sidewalks blossomed with smiles from Tahitians they barely knew.

Now she entered the cavernous marketplace, carefully stepping over a shrieking piglet trussed at the entrance. She went to the bread stall, where her friend the Chinese baker had saved her a loaf as long as her arm. Under its iron crust, she knew, beat a heart of moist bread, bursting with calories. She did not care: it looked as if she would soon lose it all again, sailing west.

She found a table in Patisserie Pam Pam, on the Rue Jeanne d'Arc, where she nibbled a croissant and waited routinely for Jean-Paul and Mahura. Outside, *les trucs* began to line up for a post-market exodus to the outlying districts. She studied one. It was bright crimson and fully loaded with passengers. On its roof was a huge new washtub, an immense slab of melting ice, and a crate of breadfruit. From its rear hung a string of yams, two stalks of bananas, and a flopping chicken.

Le truc seemed burdened past all further insult, but as she watched, a giant Tahitian woman waddled grinning to the steps at the rear. She was clutching a monstrous tuna which someone tied to the roof. Two men jumped from the rear and took position behind her, one on each side. The giantess and everyone else howled with laughter as they stuffed her into the bus. *Le truc* sagged on its springs, started with a roar, and moved irresolutely into traffic.

"*C'est drôle, n'est-ce pas?*" Jean-Paul murmured into her ear. Lindy had been the only woman in the patisserie who had not noticed his arrival. After all these months, her stomach still flipped.

Her virtue seemed safe. At 7:00 a.m. Mahura was breathtakingly beautiful, if angry. She wore what Jean-Paul called her tiger look, learned, he said, from pictures in *Vogue*. They were having one of their arguments. The girl sat down and leaned back, staring blankly out the window.

"And a happy good day to you two, too," Lindy offered.

"That one!" she spat, tossing her head toward Jean-Paul.

"Today," he told Lindy, "she is Chinese. I hope tomorrow she will be *Tahitienne* once more."

Mahura touched her heart dramatically. "Here, I am French. Which is more than you. You *Hoopipi!*"

"What's a *Hoopipi?*" asked Lindy.

"Gutter Tahitian for Frenchman," said Jean-Paul. "But she says I am not French. Which shows how logical is her mind." Jean-Paul exploded into laughter. His was the most handsome, honest laughter Lindy had ever heard. "Is she not fantastic?"

Mahura glanced at her watch, stuffed the last of Lindy's croissant into her mouth, and stood up. She touched her cheeks to Lindy's. "I have a flight to Hono, I return late tonight." She regarded Jean-Paul pensively, then wheeled and marched out the door.

He swirled his coffee for a moment and swept his eyes to Lindy's. Her heart jumped. How he did it, she did not know.

"More coffee?" he asked.

She nodded, though it was her third cup. They had never been alone before, probably never would be again, and she didn't want the moment to end.

WHEN MITCH awakened, Lindy was not back from the morning marketing. She was very late. He glanced at the boat next door. Taarii was hacking at an adolescent coconut with a machete. He was after the jellied, candy-like center. Jean-Paul was nowhere in sight. Neither was Mahura, which was too bad: she could make his whole day with one flashing grin. They were probably with Lindy, stuffing themselves at the patisserie.

He crossed the street, picked up the mail at the post office, and took it next door to Café Vaima. He sat at a favorite sidewalk table, shaded by a boxed fig tree, where he could watch the line of boats beyond the traffic. The little Dutch girl was pumping furiously down the quay on her tricycle. *Linda Lee* and *Xanadu*, which had returned from the yard wearing an even brighter coat of orange paint, stirred restlessly side by side.

He found himself yawning. Too lethargic to open the mail, he waited in a trance for the plump waitress, Yvonne, to shuffle out with his coffee.

Suddenly he saw Mahura on her motor scooter rocketing along

478

the quay, heading for the airport. She spotted him and squealed to a stop. He strolled across the sidewalk and she kissed him on both cheeks. "Lindy is at the patisserie," she reported. "They stuff each other with croissants, and you sit here alone."

"I slept late."

"Do not sleep too late in Tahiti," she warned.

"C'mon, Mahura." He grinned. "What are you trying to say?"

"I do not know." She shrugged. "He makes me very angry, sometimes. Hey, she does not make you angry?"

"No. But you might. Sit down, have a cup of coffee."

"I have a flight." She smiled. She had perfect teeth, a short upper lip, a full lower one, a perfect nose, and skin like golden silk. "But you are right, *probablement*," she decided. "With a man like you, how can that little Frenchman compare?"

She squeezed his hand, laughed, and was off in a cloud of smoke. He returned to his table and sipped his coffee. Down the quay, he could see the tiny black figure of Louie, who had once tried to tell him the same thing Mahura just had. The hell with them. He had more confidence in Lindy's fidelity than his own. Especially if Mahura made a pass.

Louie had apparently quit school, and now he haunted the waterfront, a tiny entrepreneur who was everywhere at all times. He would dive for a dropped bolt off a quayside yacht; he would polish portholes or climb your mast to unfoul your halyard. But he was scared to death of Mitch and never came near *Linda Lee*, which was exactly what Mitch wanted.

Lindy and Jean-Paul appeared finally, walking down the quay. He sat for a minute watching them. She was swinging her basket, smiling into the Frenchman's face. Jean-Paul, not much taller than she, seemed to be grinning. Mitch wondered how he kept so trim. As for Lindy, she moved like an eighteen-year-old.

Preoccupied, the two almost passed *Linda Lee*. They stopped in confusion and parted. She stumbled coltishly boarding their gangway, smiled back at Jean-Paul, and went below.

Lindy would wonder where he was, but the hell with it. He paid the bill and strolled to a shaded bookstore on Place Notre Dame which carried nautical charts. He needed maps of Bora Bora, the rest of the Îles sous le Vent, and the Cooks and Tongas, if they had them.

He was depressed. Papeete had finally gotten to him. It was time to head west.

Chapter Five

The flashing light had grown steadier, though no stronger. She rested, floating back in the water, staring up at the great golden star she thought was Antares. It was no longer quite overhead.

Lindy is alive and well, Mitch, and living under Antares. She rang you once or twice, but you never picked up the phone.

Her mind rose from the swells, leaving her body floating there. First she flew east, then north, then south, then in confused circles. Finally she found the pale, starlit sails. He was moving far too slowly.

He slumped red-eyed and half dead at the helm. Now she could not tell him where to go. She was lost herself. *Antares! Steer for Antares before it is too late. Forget the charts, she screamed silently: forget everything but the star. Hurry.*

She opened her eyes. The star twinkled down at her but the others were orbiting it. She was in a whirlpool of them. She kicked upright, avoiding vertigo. Erect and treading water, she stared about, still too disoriented to tell north from south. As she raised her head, the air and sea around her paled for an instant. The impression was so brief that she could not be sure that it had really happened. She lost her fatigue. She pirouetted, searching the rim of her moving canyon. There was nothing.

She must have imagined the flash. Her pace had been too listless to have brought her anywhere near the strobe. She was simply losing her mind from fatigue and fear and thirst.

The rim of her surging valley lit suddenly. A white-plumed breaker, slipping over its crest, posed starkly as if trapped by a flashbulb. She yelled with joy. Thrashing up the side of the swell, she lost the plastic container. She did not care.

All at once she was blinded by an immense white flash directly ahead. Then she was in total darkness. She had lost her night vision and could see no stars, no waves. She squinted, dreading the next explosion of light.

When it came she was ready. The strobe flashed, leaving imprinted on her after-vision its orange cylinder, the man-overboard flag, and the bright yellow horseshoe buoy, all attached to each other by a yellow line snaking up the wave.

She lunged blindly for the buoy, felt its slippery plastic cover, and lost it again in the rush of water. She took two brave strokes into the white foam, snatched the buoy, and lifted it over her head. She worked her arms through the opening and snapped the stainless cable across its open end.

She kept slipping through the horseshoe because her arms were too tired to stay up on the rim. And, relieved of the need to kick, she was cold again in minutes. She had little hope that he would spot the flag at dawn. There was more hope in the flash, if only he would hurry.

FOR FOUR HOURS he had been zigzagging back and forth over his wake. If his navigation and the logbook were right, this was the area where she had fallen. He teetered on the coaming, steering with one foot. The necessity to balance kept him awake.

In an hour the eastern sky would lighten and, he hoped, bring back the trades. He jammed the engine in forward and began a square search: fifteen minutes and a ninety-degree left turn, thirty minutes and another, forty-five minutes and another, an hour and another.

The clock chimed seven bells—0330. She had been in the water over twenty-four hours. One hour, he estimated, to first light. He wondered if the strobe had gone out, drifted too far, or sunk. Until daylight, it was all he had to look for.

THEY LEFT Papeete with a large kitten because Yvonne, at the Café Vaima, heard they were going. Although they said good-by quietly to Jean-Paul and Taarii and tried to slip away before dawn to avoid farewells, the waitress was there with M. le Chat for Lindy before they could warp away from the quay.

"A cat for eat the rat," she said. Yvonne had a little girl to support, as well as three cats and far too many kittens.

They did not see Mahura to say good-by. She had left Jean-Paul for a big blond Pan Am copilot.

They spent a week in Cook's Bay and another in Robinson's Cove where they tied stern to a palm tree under the peaks and could step ashore from the fantail. Then they touched at Huahine Island and at Raiatea, where they rowed the dinghy up the river. Lindy plucked hibiscus from the banks, feeling like a model in *National Geographic*, as Mitch paddled lazily. They cruised to Tahaa, and then, having saved the most beautiful French island for last, headed toward the jagged peak of Bora Bora.

They shot through the wide Bora Bora pass and found two familiar boats. The Dutch ketch, racing for Samoa to beat the hurricane season, was weighing anchor off the beach. The *Star of Peace* was tied to a buoy; they were looking for a leak in its bilges before facing the run to Auckland. Lindy realized suddenly that she was looking for the orange steel ketch. It was not there.

They tied to the ramshackle dock. A young gendarme awaited them there, with a week-old radiogram in his hand. Lindy's father had had a stroke. He was paralyzed and speechless. Bobby begged her to fly home. Mitch pressed her in his arms. She was numb with shock, full of guilt because she could not cry.

"Do you want me to go too?" he murmured.

She stared at him. If he had to ask, the hell with it. Yet he was right to hesitate: they shouldn't leave *Linda Lee* unattended in an open lagoon at this time of year.

She was on a plane to Tahiti in two hours.

HER FATHER did not know her at all, or, if he did, could not convey it. The first evening, Lindy took his hand, drew a deep breath, and began to talk. She asked forgiveness for getting pregnant before she was married, and for forgetting his birthday in 1968, and for being in Paris instead of home when he had a prostate operation in 1969.

He gave no sign that he understood, but it was a great purgative. Then there was nothing to do except to read him Kipling, the only poet he had ever touched. It was like reading to a corpse, but she persisted for a week. Then she kissed him goodby.

Tony and Nancy came to the airport: they were planning to marry in January. Tony had a job pumping Texaco in Sausalito. She hugged Bobby and his wife, and Justice Holmes, who had obviously forgotten all about her. She said goodby to Bernie, bought Mitch a Nikon camera for Christmas at the duty-free counter, and climbed on a plane to Tahiti.

When she arrived, the airport was sultry and jammed, as usual. She made a reservation on the morning flight to Bora Bora, but did not cable Mitch: if he knew she was coming, he would meet the plane, and it was a long boat ride from the wharf to the airstrip.

She did not know why, but she felt strangely disembodied and free. She ignored the taxis and took *le truc* to Papeete. The passengers scrunched together to give her room, and a Tahitian woman offered her a drink from a bottle of beer. She took it. Everyone apparently had seen her before, so they loved her; she was very big on *le truc*. She wished Mitch had wanted to buy property here.

She hopped to the pavement as *le truc* squeaked to a stop on Rue G. Lagarde, and moved through sidewalk crowds to the water. To the right lay the Royal Papeete Hotel—air conditioning, TV, and a shower. To the left lay Quai des Yachts, and the battered Hotel Scott.

She hesitated. Across the street, new boats plugged the holes where *Star of Peace* and the Dutch ketch had been. Louie and a gang of smaller children were diving for something off the seawall. The quay was otherwise the same, but all was bathed in a strange ruddy light. Far down the lane of masts she could see the pitch-black poles of *Xanadu*.

She turned toward it, started to walk toward the Hotel Scott. Her head felt light and her body heavy. The air was full of tension. This was silly: she was tempting fate. She should go back to the Royal, where Mitch would expect her to stay. Not the Scott, above the raucous bar. And above *Xanadu*.

She kept going.

She entered the rickety lobby and asked for a room. She was awarded an immense room with a balcony and a ceiling fan. She bathed, wrapped herself in an orange *pareu,* and stepped to the balcony. Her heart was thumping, and her hands were numb.

She looked down at *Xanadu.* Taarii was topside, doubling her mooring ropes. Something was brewing in the skies or *Xanadu,* with her massive strength, would be the last boat in the harbor to worry. She hoped whatever it was would miss Bora Bora.

If Taarii looked up, okay, but she refused to call out. He secured the lines and started below. Opening the hatch, he glanced idly across the street. She waved. He looked startled, called below, and in a moment Jean-Paul's head appeared.

Her legs turned weak. She turned away so that she would not have to watch him cross the street. His footsteps on the creaky stairs started her hands trembling. They were shaking so badly by the time he tapped at the door that she could hardly turn the old brass knob.

They stood facing each other for a moment. Her eyes filled, and then she was in his arms.

THE STRANGE swell that had been building all day in the Bora Bora lagoon impelled Mitch to row out to *Star of Peace.* He sipped beer while her mate cranked up the ham radio. Graham, the skipper, lounged on his disheveled bunk. He was a steady, well-balanced seaman. But now he seemed indecisive.

There was a squawk and a whistle from the ham rig. A woman's voice crackled through the static. The Canadian yacht *Golden Dragon* was anchored at Nuku Hiva, eight hundred miles northeast. She reported storm clouds—mare's tails—in the northern sky, large swells, and a barometer which had dropped a tenth of an inch in the last hour.

Mitch spotted a copy of Bowditch's *Practical Navigator* in the bookcase. In it he found a table which told him that one tenth of an inch an hour meant that *Golden Dragon* was one hundred miles from the eye of the hurricane.

If there *was* a hurricane. The last tropical cyclone to hit French Polynesia was in 1961. Twelve years, almost. . . .

Graham moved to a chart table, and plotted a position one hundred miles north of Nuku Hiva. From it he sketched a typical southern latitude hurricane path. He did not finish the line, but if it recurved east, as hurricanes often did, Bora Bora would sit astride it. Mitch's tongue felt dry.

Graham drummed his fingers. "Mitch, if it does recurve . . . will you run to sea, or stay?"

Mitch had been about to ask him the same question. Now he couldn't: the kid was as confused as he. He felt sorry for him. At least *Linda Lee* was his own, and insured; *Star of Peace*, financed by donation, was not Graham's to lose, and she couldn't possibly be insured.

Mitch shook his head dubiously and climbed halfway up the ladder to look for signs that the word was out, looking for natives, perhaps, lashing their palm-thatched roofs or boarding up their gaping, paneless homes. There was no activity at all. The lagoon, in the afternoon shade of the crags, was like a mirror.

But the swell was still rolling onto Te Avanui Pass, the only way out; rolling with an authority that indicated no mere local storm. The sky above was clear, but that meant nothing: it might be twelve hours before the *Golden Dragon*'s mare's tails appeared here, and then it would be too late to run.

Here there were no rivers to hide in, no bights or coves. If you dragged anchor to the east, you'd be hurled high and dry, and if you dragged to the west, you'd be splintered on the reefs. A true sailor would probably head for open water while there was time.

If he had the guts. And valued the boat more than his life. Mitch looked at *Linda Lee*, swinging at the dock. He stepped back down. "I'm going to leave the dock, put down every anchor I've got, then row ashore and lash myself to a barstool."

"You've been out in one?" asked Graham. Mitch shook his head. "Well, I have," Graham murmured, "on a yawl in Cyclone Bebe. She hit me dead on. Thought I'd never bloody run to sea again."

"That's what I mean," said Mitch.

"Until," added Graham sweetly, "I got back and saw what had happened ashore."

There seemed nothing more to say. "Thank you, Graham," muttered Mitch. He rowed in and helped Hans, the hotel owner, board up his bar. The gendarme jeeped up with a hurricane warning. Hans begged Mitch to leave the dock. Apparently he didn't want *Linda Lee* as a decoration in his lobby.

Back aboard, Mitch was jittery. He got everything movable belowdecks or lashed down. Then he doubled his lines for the night. He poured himself a drink and tuned the radio to WWV out of Hawaii. The cyclone had just been christened Arlene. Its center was west of the Marquesas. WWV gave its predicted position. Idly, he plotted the curve and extended it. It passed north of Tahiti but very nearly bisected Bora Bora.

He was glad he had not gone to Papeete to meet Lindy, as he'd planned to. Unless Pan Am had held at Honolulu, she was at the Royal Papeete tonight. He walked to the *bureau de poste* and sent her a cable at the hotel, telling her to stay where she was. He would rather have her in Papeete than here when the storm hit.

SHE AWAKENED to the midnight clang of the bell from Temple Paofai. Jean-Paul was on the balcony, silhouetted against the stars. She got up drowsily, tucked a *pareu* around herself, and padded out. He put an arm around her waist and drew her close.

"The stars," he said. "Have you seen this before?"

She had not. They shone with a brilliance that seemed alive.

"The barometric pressure rises, I think, the better to drop after," he told her. "Therefore the clarity." He pointed out Antares and told her how the ancient Polynesians must have used it to navigate.

Her mind jumped to Mitch. "Is he okay at Bora Bora?" she asked.

He shrugged. "He is *homme formidable*. I think he would not fear to run to sea."

"*Run to sea?* Without me? I'd kill him!"

He looked into her eyes. "You need not run to sea." He told her of a shelter at Bora Bora, blasted into coral during the war by the Seabees, a haven against Japanese shelling. It was big enough for a single PT boat. Or a yacht. "There are rings for lines set within the coral. . . ."

"He's probably there now," she said.

He thought not. The natives would not tell him it was there. The Seabees had ignored local protests and blasted it next to a sacred burial ground. "Bad luck, the people think." He spread his hands. "But it is worse luck to run to sea. If you get to Bora Bora in time, you tell him." He smiled into her eyes. "I also have a boat, you know. With no engine. And there is just enough breeze for the pass."

"You're going to sea?"

He nodded. "Papeete harbor I do not trust. Listen?"

He inclined his head toward the yachts. She could hear voices. They were all getting ready to leave the danger of the seawall. Some would run for it. Others would anchor across the harbor in the lee of the Motu Uta docks.

"Lindy, this, tonight, with us, I knew it must happen, and you must not have bad feelings, for then it would ruin it all."

"You *knew?* I didn't."

He smiled. "Nothing is a secret in these islands. The girl, Tiare, in the hospital at Nuku Hiva, she told me that when you had the delirium, you spoke of me. And it is strange, but I had already taken steps, of which you could know nothing."

She told him that she knew about his message to the doctor, and of how far he had walked to try to get it through.

He looked embarrassed. "Of course, you do not believe—"

"I believe," she said. "Where you and I are concerned, I believe."

He kissed her good-by. She watched him cross the street. In a few minutes he and Taarii had hoisted sail. She could see him ghosting toward the pass, then he was gone.

She went back to bed and drifted into sleep.

IN THE MORNING she waited at the Air Polynésie counter for her flight to Bora Bora. It had been canceled, put on again, canceled once more. It was hot and very sultry. Departing passengers for Huahine and Bora Bora were jittery. Suddenly the flight was on and everyone piled into the plane.

Lindy crawled into the seat behind the captain. Then she was startled to see Louie race across the concrete to the plane. He was barefoot, and in his hand he held a ticket. They opened the door and let him in. He took the seat behind her.

She turned curiously. "*Bonjour,* Louie."

His wizened little face froze and his eyes were full of contempt. Shocked, she stuttered: "Where are you going, anyway?"

"I go to help my father. And why *you* h'ask?"

Astonished, she turned back. She tried to lose herself in the beauty of the flight over the Îles sous le Vent. But she could not relax with the ebony eyes drilling the back of her head.

At Bora Bora she found a van to take her to the dock. A hundred yards down the road, they passed Louie. Her impulse was to ask the driver to pick him up, but she conquered it.

Let him walk.

MITCH STEPPED topside for perhaps the tenth time that hour, to look at the sky.

WWV had located Arlene two hundred miles northeast of him, and moving at fourteen knots. She had recurved. Unless she recurved again, she would hit Bora Bora in less than twenty hours.

He made ready to cast off from the pier. He had the vague intention of trying to anchor in Faanui Bay. He would stay aboard until things got too rough. Then, if he had to, he could let the boat fend for herself and try to row into Faanui village.

He was casting off when he heard Lindy's voice. He cleated the line and looked up. She was lugging her suitcase, with her long bronze hair swaying. He had not known how much he missed her. He shut off the engine, jumped ashore, and took her in his arms. He kissed her and looked into her face. She was tired. Below, she told him about her father and why she had come back.

"Honey," he scolded her, "this thing's *missing* Tahiti! And heading here. Didn't you get my cable?"

Her eyes dropped. Something about it jarred him. She looked up and said: "I *had* to come. There's a shelter here! A hurricane hole!"

SITTING on the cabin settee, she almost gagged on the coffee he had made. She was sick with guilt. He was leaning on the navigation table, running his pencil along the Bora Bora chart, looking

488

for Jean-Paul's shelter. "I'll double up lines to the coconut trees, bow and stern, and—"

"*We*," she said weakly. "I'm back."

He studied her for a moment. "Okay." He stretched exultantly. "That lovely, blue-eyed sonofabitch has saved our boat."

"He went to sea," she said. "I hope he saves his own."

The boat trembled to a gust. She heard footsteps creaking along the dock, and bare feet padding aboard. A shadow fell across the open hatch and Louie appeared. His hard black eyes challenged her for an instant, turned to Mitch.

"'Allo, *mon capitaine*," he said. "I have come for 'elp you for cyclone. I show you through the reef, okay?"

Mitch seemed surprised but, as always lately with Louie, curiously cool. "You didn't come to Bora Bora for *that?*"

"I sell camera, yes, for *that!*"

"We're not going through the reef, and you're not going with us." He turned to Lindy and told her, after six months, that Louie's last thanks to her had been an insult.

Her heart began to hammer. She saw it all now, the truth approaching like the hurricane. She tried to beat Louie to the punch, but her throat was so tight that nothing came out.

"*I* will 'elp you. She is bad woman." The little boy drew himself to his full height. "Ees right, what I say before."

"Get lost," grated Mitch. He took a step toward Louie. "Now!"

Louie's eyes bulged with fright, but he stood his ground. "*Non!* She is *bad!* Las' night—" His lips clenched, his eyes filled with tears.

Mitch grabbed Louie's skinny thigh as the child looked down at them from the steps. "Last night, *what?*" he growled.

The boy stiffened. "With the *Hoopipi* of the steel boat . . . the two of them at *l'Hôtel Scott!*"

Mitch moved swiftly. He lifted the child and was up through the hatch in a flash. She lunged after them, and was barely topside as he lifted Louie overhead to hurl him into the water.

"No!" she yelled into his ear. "Damn it! Mitch, it's *true!*"

Mitch froze. Slowly he lowered Louie. Louie leaped to the dock and turned. "Bad woman!" he screamed, then ran.

"So," muttered Mitch dully, "you didn't *get* my cable?"

She shook her head. "No Royal Papeete," she murmured. "No cable. Mitch, I would have told you!"

"And *that* we'll never know." He stepped forward, started the engine, and tossed off the stern line. He ordered Lindy ashore.

"I'm staying. To help tie her up."

"I'm not *going*," he said softly, "to his pen."

"Why not?" she begged.

"The rent's too damn high."

She stayed aboard. If he wanted to anchor out, she would take her chances too. He slammed the gearshift viciously into reverse. The engine, still cold, screamed in protest. He backed off, ignoring Louie watching from the road. They charged full forward, vomiting smoke. *Star of Peace* had left her mooring, heading for the pass. Mitch overtook her in half a mile. He cut his throttle, drew close, and yelled to Graham at the wheel. When he was through, Jean-Paul's hurricane hole was lost to *Linda Lee. Star of Peace* sheered off, heading for Faanui Bay.

Lindy waited for Mitch to head for an anchorage and drop a hook. But the bowsprit stayed granite-steady on the pass. And the seas pounding the reef were huge, onrushing walls. One out of three rollers broke in the channel itself. A mile short of the entrance she grabbed his arm. "Mitch," she cried.

"Sea room," he said tonelessly. His eyes were unreadable. "Shall I take you back?" She shook her head and he gently removed her hand. At last she felt that she could cry, but she was damned if she would.

PART THREE: DAY

Chapter One

He felt himself pitching forward and snapped awake. The clock chimed once, and for a moment he could not remember whether it was a half hour past midnight or a half hour past four. He glanced at his watch. Four thirty. He had been on his feet or aloft and searching for over twenty-five hours.

He checked the eastern horizon for the first faint hint of dawn. It was still pitch-black. He did not know whether to be sorry or glad. He was afraid that the strobe was out, yet he kept hoping for it, as a marker if nothing else.

To stay awake, he began to lay plans. With daylight, Bernie's emergency radio would become potentially useful again as the flights began. He had lashed it to the yardarm for elevation. If the pilots bothered to guard the emergency frequency, he might well have a plane homing on him by dawn.

He swept the horizon. He could see a faint paling of the eastern sky. He tensed. He thought he had caught a distant flash off the port bow. He rushed forward, and began to climb the ratlines. Halfway up the mast he paused. He had seen it again, a momentary gleam somewhere on his port bow, infinitely distant, impossible to pinpoint, but there. He returned to the wheel, heart pounding. *Just one more flash,* he begged, *just once more. . . .*

He came hard aport until he thought he was on course for it. In five minutes the eastern sky had gone gray with morning twilight. He did not see the flash again. Perhaps he'd only imagined it.

SHE KEPT DRIFTING between trance and consciousness, and each time she returned from the void she would find herself half under the horseshoe buoy, slipping into the deep. Her jacket was pulling her down. She wanted to shed it, but it was conserving body heat, and she was very, very cold. Also, it was orange, and if she made it until daylight, it could help him spot her. Also . . . there was something else—what? The whistle. It was tied to the zipper, and she'd lose it.

Her whole world had compressed to the flash of the strobe. Her boundaries were herself, the yellow horseshoe, and the scruffy line that led to the man-overboard pole bobbing twenty feet away.

She had lost the stars and the sense of infinity she had known before she found the buoy; the instant she had touched the horseshoe she had traded vision for security. She no longer looked for the dawn. She had no sense, even, of which way was east.

Now the strobe seemed weaker. But it was not. It was simply competing with the morning light. Soon the sun burst over the eastern horizon, upstaging the light so mightily that she forgot it was there.

She was not sure, but she thought she had been in the water for over twenty-four hours.

Gusts from Mount Pahia raced across the Bora Bora lagoon. She ignored the wind, hypnotized by the surf in the pass. She still wore a dress, from the flight, but did not dare go below to change. If he entered the pass, they would be hurled back, perhaps overturned, and she did not want to be trapped below.

She could not take her eyes off the swells that began far at sea. When they hit the coral below, the boom was visceral. It drummed into her gut before she heard it with her ears.

They were half a mile short of the channel when a strong flurry heeled them over. Mitch spun the boat around, bow to the wind. For a moment she hoped that he had given up. Instead, he hoisted the mizzen sail. Then he strode forward and raised the jib. She was grabbing the wheel to steady the boat when he dropped back into the cockpit and took the helm without a word. He turned west, and once again they were headed for the pass.

She searched for something that would save them. What if she offered to go back now? By the time he dropped her off, the swell might rise so high that he would have to stay too. But no matter how high the surf in the pass, he might choose to leave without her anyway. In twenty years, she had learned nothing that would help her judge his present mood.

She turned and faced him. "Is it to punish me, or what?"

He left the wheel, picked up her safety belt, and handed it to her. "Get it on," he said, cinching his own and snapping it to a shroud. Reluctantly, she clicked on the belt and took a turn around the mizzenmast. There was no question of going forward, as she usually did on leaving a pass: when they foundered, she wanted to be here, with him.

Two hundred yards from the entrance, they plowed into white water. Feeling undertow, the boat slewed to port and picked up speed. The throb of the engine quickened as they rushed toward the pass. There was nothing to do now but hang on.

Linda Lee rose to the incoming surge. The first swell stopped them cold. To either side, the big blue mountains hung curled over the reef and fell in twin bellows of rage. A central crest remained. *Linda Lee* hung tottering on it, her propeller flailing air. Then she was sliding down the other side, sails luffing as they fell into the lee of the wave.

The sides of the pass inched astern. When the next wave broke, she was sure they would be trapped in mid channel. It seemed bigger than the last. She found herself straining against her belt, spurring the boat onward. The incoming swell jarred them, stopping them dead again. *Linda Lee* shuddered and lost way. Mitch tested the wheel for control. If the bow didn't stay straight into the wave, they would tumble broadside and never survive the roll.

A gust of wind filled the jib. The boat came alive and climbed. The wave broke under them and they moved down the reverse slope. To seaward the next swell was gathering. *Linda Lee* climbed that one too, balanced for an instant, then the bow went down and they slid out of the pass.

So far as she knew, they were free of land. Nothing else this side of the Cooks, five hundred miles away, could hurt them. She thought of the hurricane as an overgrown gale. Andy Dugan had survived a gale on *Linda Lee* already. She unfastened her belt and went below to change.

AT THE DOCK he had been numb with shock. The need for action in the pass had saved him from thinking. Now, temporarily out of danger, he groped for things to do, looking for refuge from pain.

Behind them, a fine mist suddenly obscured Mount Pahia and the crags. Bora Bora had been safety, for themselves if not the boat. There was no way to re-enter the pass now. A thrill of fear elbowed the agony farther aside. He caught a stinging slap of spray across his face. The wind had shifted dead south, opposing the swell, and the seas were rising.

He set Irwin and eased the sheets. *Linda Lee* began to gallop at six knots, under jib and mizzen. He wanted to get as far away from land as he could before the wall of the cyclone hit.

A fine drizzle began. He went below to put on oilskins. Lindy lurched from the forward compartment. She looked sick. She had apparently lost her sea legs. She seemed exhausted, but calm. He suspected that she thought of what was coming as simply another storm. Well, he had tried to leave her behind. . . .

"Mitch," she said, "you'll have to talk to me. I'm *here!*"

He studied her face in the gloom of the skylight. There were tiny lines at her eyes that he had hardly noticed before. But she was as beautiful as ever.

If only he had gone to California, or to Tahiti to meet her, or had shown more initiative in Nuku Hiva or Papeete when the danger flags were flying; if only the Frenchman had run a day early for sea room. . . . The hell with that! It was not his fault, or Jean-Paul's, or the cyclone's. It was hers.

"Get some sleep," he said. "You're tired."

"Meaning?" she flared.

"Meaning," he blurted, "you didn't get much last night."

Predictably, her eyes grew wet. She crawled into the leeward bunk, turned her face away, and was still. There was no reason, damn it, to comfort her.

A drumroll of raindrops rattled the skylight. He would have to go topside to relieve Irwin before the vane was hurt. But before going up he leafed through Bowditch for "Tropical Hurricanes". The wind and seas they would encounter would depend on which of Arlene's faces they would see. Her gentler, right-hand side would be lethal enough. But it would have gales forty knots less than on her left side, where her speed of advance would add to the speed of her winds. The clue lay in the trend of the wind topside. If it shifted counterclockwise, he was already on her dangerous side.

He closed the book. It was time to find out. He climbed the companionway ladder. A warm, heavy wind greeted him. It was backing and veering, gusting and easing. But he was very much afraid that it was moving counterclockwise.

He looked back toward Bora Bora. "Oh, God," he breathed. Far past the island, on the northeast horizon, lay a great black mass. It seemed immovable, as if a new continent were growing

494

there. Tiny flashes of orange lightning played against the velvet backdrop. It was the bar of the cyclone, and behind it lay Arlene's eye.

Already the sky above him seemed to be darkening. He glanced at his watch. Just past noon. He reefed the mizzen. Lines he had readied for warps were already tied in coils. He thanked God that he had not changed Andrew Dugan's thick little portholes for the windows Lindy had wanted. He detached Irwin's vane and tossed it below. Then he closed the hatch.

A twelve-foot wave gathered itself from somewhere astern, crested aboard, and slapped his face. He glanced back at Arlene's black heart. "Bitch!" he yelled at it. It made him feel better. He took the wheel. From now on it was him and Arlene.

HE STEERED into the dazzle of the morning sun. This was his first daylight sweep of the area she must be in since he'd found the logbook. The flash to the east at dawn must have been a hallucination, like the elves around the binnacle light, for he had been steering east ever since and had seen nothing.

Where *was* the strobe? The absence of the other flotsam he understood. Mattresses and cockpit cushions were light, high out of the water, and would quickly have sailed downwind. But the man-overboard gear: a little sea anchor attached to the buoy was supposed to hold it against the drift. That was why you carried it in the first place.

He had dropped it very near her, according to the log. She must have found it, be clinging to it now. If she lived. . . . His eyes blurred with tears.

Suddenly he heard an engine. He tensed and looked aft. He saw nothing. The throbbing blended with the rumble of *Lindy Lee*'s diesel. He throttled back, then cut his motor entirely and searched again.

Dead aft, perhaps ten miles away, he spotted a tiny silver dot, an aircraft at about four thousand feet. It seemed to be banking toward him. He dived into the lazaret for the Stars and Stripes. He hoisted the flag upside down on the starboard yardarm, and clambered up the shrouds.

The plane now seemed to be turning back, ignoring him. He screamed, waved wildly, almost fell off.

The plane turned toward him again. It approached swiftly, descending, and passed him in a whoosh of wind, very close by. It was a twin-engined turbo-prop. He glimpsed the pilot, a blond hatless young man, and, staring from the portholes, passengers craning to see. The plane climbed, circled, and made another pass. Mitch swept his arm around the horizon, pantomiming search. *Start looking, damn you. Start!*

Instead, the pilot returned once again, nose high and very slow. When the aircraft was fifty feet from Mitch, the pilot pointed to his microphone, then southeast toward Tahiti.

"No!" yelled Mitch. "No, *you* search! *Yourself!*"

He watched the plane climb and disappear in the haze to the west. It probably had fuel only for Bora Bora and return. But at least the word was out, someone knew, and soon he would see the French navy.

Chapter Two

She awakened crashing to the cabin floor. For an instant she could not recall where she was. She was suddenly rolled across the passageway to the foot of the opposite bunk. A pillow fell on her face. "Mitch!" she yelled.

There was no answer. She sat up. A dim light filtered through the skylight, as if it were already twilight, but time was out of kilter, it must still be early in the afternoon. She struggled to her knees and regarded the cabin. Pillows and sleeping bags had fallen to the floor. A chart-table drawer had come open, spilling pencils, rulers, and old logbooks. A locker to port banged open. She slammed it shut and made her way aft.

She tugged at the hatch ineffectually. She was very weak, and afraid that she was going to be seasick. She could not budge the hatch. He had locked it. Suppose something happened to him and she could not get out to help? Stupid, stupid. He was losing his common sense.

496

She was suddenly aware of creaks and groans she had never heard. *Linda Lee* slewed wildly to port, as if there were no hand on the wheel. Panicked, she screamed for Mitch and began to bang on the companionway hatchboards with a pot.

Finally she heard an answering thump, and the bolt slid back. To a shriek of wind from topside, the hatch opened six inches and Mitch's face appeared. She had a sense of unreality. She could hardly believe today, let alone last night.

"Let me up!" she demanded.

"We're in it," he said tersely. "But just on the edges. It's going to get worse. Stay put!"

"I'm going to be sick," she said. "Open the hatch!"

"Get your gear on first." He slammed the hatch again. She reached into the foul-weather locker. By the time she got everything on she was exhausted, and so nauseated she could hardly make it up the ladder. She banged on the hatch. He yanked it open, pulled her through, and slammed it shut again as a fifteen-foot wave crested behind them and swarmed over the stern.

He snapped her safety belt around the mizzenmast and she crawled blindly for the leeward side where she was very sick. When she finally turned to sit in the cockpit, she could not believe her eyes. He had somehow crept forward and set their smallest storm jib. It had never been hoisted before, except once for drill in San Francisco Bay. He had reefed the mizzen too, and lashed the wheel. His feat was impressive but, she thought, futile. They were inching through the most enormous seas she had ever seen and slipping to leeward like skiers in a turn.

She looked around. There was no sun or even any sky. The scud hurtling by above seemed low enough to touch. And then the sound of it came, a quiet humming from aloft. At first she could not believe it was their rigging, it was so melodious. The note rose and fell and rose in pitch again. A giant wave off their port bow rose in a pyramid, and suddenly the top one-third was ripped loose, flying toward them in a stinging hail of salt. She ducked too late. Her cheeks felt as if she had been struck with splinters of glass.

The wind stopped short. She looked up again. They were climbing, and the pyramid was passing beneath them. They balanced on the top and fell into the following trough. She heard a screech from aloft, a rising crescendo that heeled *Linda Lee* to starboard, heeled her farther and farther, until it seemed that they were going over. She clutched at Mitch's arm, missed, and found herself thrown into the mizzenmast instead. The keening aloft got drowned in the roar of a breaking wave from port. The wave struck, drenching her. Hundreds of gallons of green water swirled calf-deep in the cockpit.

The wind rose further. She could no longer face it. She burrowed into her oilskins in the lee of the deckhouse and looked away. The wind drew her breath from her body. Mitch was crouched behind the lashed wheel, back to the seas.

"How long?" she mouthed. She could not hear her own voice.

He shook his head. He couldn't hear, or didn't know, or didn't care to answer. He locked his eyes on hers, pointed decisively below. She tried to protest, but the wind crammed her voice down her throat. He waited for the next wave, which half-drowned her, quickly unsnapped her safety belt and slid the hatch open. With enormous strength, he lifted her and deposited her halfway down the companionway ladder.

She did not want to leave him and waited too long. The hatch was still open when the next wave hit. Water poured down the ladder, inundating the galley and flooding into the main saloon. She heard the hatch slam shut above her. She was suddenly in another world.

Two inches of solid mahogany muted the tempest topside. Here she heard only the groan of *Linda Lee* as she wrestled with the seas. Wearily, she began to stroke the bilge pump. Since he didn't want her topside, she might as well work below. There was, if they should survive, a dim hope gleaming.

She would never sail again.

HE HUDDLED in the cockpit for hours after he stuffed Lindy below. The wheel was lashed. He had no need to steer, no inkling of why he was waiting it out topside. He simply preferred to keep an eye on the maelstrom.

498

Linda Lee took the seas like a fighter jogging in place. At each gust her rudder forced her into the wind. Her jib would tremble, luff, and then she would fall away from the wind. She moved ahead imperceptibly, avoiding being pushed astern, which would fold her rudder back on itself and leave them truly helpless.

He half rose, staring. A mountain of heaving water rushed down on the port bow. He tried to estimate its height: perhaps thirty feet. It broke twenty-five yards off the bow. *Linda Lee* stopped with a mighty crash. White water filled the cockpit.

But his eyes were on the wave which followed. Dead in the water, the boat was helpless, and this one would finish the job. He yelled a warning to Lindy below, but knew that she would never hear him. He braced for the shock.

When it came, it slammed him against the cockpit seat. He caught his shoulderblade on its edge, but hardly noticed the pain.

For the boat was moving astern now, and her rudder was taking the brunt. Sickened with her anguish, he felt *Linda Lee* shudder. The line he had lashed to the wheel sprung taut. He fumbled for his knife to slash it. Too late. The lashing held, but he heard the rudder cable under the lazaret snap with a twang like a giant guitar string. The lashing went slack and he watched her back down on her rudder, squealing in agony.

The huge emergency tiller was lashed near the cockpit. He cut its bindings and fumbled to jam it in the rudderhead before the next wave gathered. He got it half in, grabbed it with both hands, and hauled to port. He could hardly budge the rudder, but slowly her bow fell off the wind. He found himself cringing. If the next wave should hit now, the tiller would sweep him from his seat like a jousting knight. Somehow he hung on. Slowly she came downwind, gathering momentum. She rose to the next wave and skittered down its face.

On the following wave she was surfing. By the next she was flying. He reached with his knife and slashed the reefed mizzen. The sail disappeared in tatters. Then he sawed at the jibsheet. It snapped, and in the chaos forward he heard the tiny jib flogging itself to death too.

The pale seas had heightened further. But joining them had

eased *Linda Lee*'s motion, and quieted the wind in her rigging. The eye of the hurricane was still to come, and the other wall after it, reputed to be the worst. They would probably not survive it. Without sails, they were committed to run before the wind, and running would keep them in the storm. He saw no way to leave the tiller long enough to let out the weighted lines astern to slow them down and keep them from broaching.

So they would simply surf each wave as it came, until he no longer had strength to fight the tiller. When the ultimate wave caught them, he was damned if Lindy was going to be caught below like a rat in a trap. He unlocked the hatch and pounded on the deck with his boot. She peeped out. He signaled her to come topside.

In five minutes she was up, wearing one of his watch caps under the hood of her slicker. She stared at the seas astern, snapped her belt to a shroud, and looked into his face. "Mitch?"

Her voice was faint in the howling wind. He nodded, keeping his eyes on the oncoming seas.

"I love *you*. Nobody else. I want to stay your friend."

He handled the wave, tore his gaze from the next, and regarded her nut-brown face. Fleetingly, he saw it on a pillow, cupped in Jean-Paul's hands. The image faded, but he found that he could not speak.

He felt the surge of the next sea. He hauled at the helm. She put her back into it too, and they slewed left, avoiding a broach. *Linda Lee* soared, gathered herself, and hurtled to the southwest.

He began to hum "Waltzing Matilda".

HE COULD search the glare to the east more easily as the sun rose higher. The line of squalls bearing down on the rising trades still worried him, but he put Irwin in charge. He was leaving the cockpit when he heard the radio burst into life. It stunned him. "Yacht *Linda Lee! Star of Peace* here. . . ."

Star, having barely survived Arlene, even in the pen, was still at Bora Bora. Mitch dived down the hatch and grabbed the mike. "Graham! Go ahead!"

Air Polynésie, Graham said, had arrived in Bora Bora. Papeete had been informed that *Linda Lee* was in distress. Two search planes were on their way, and a French destroyer. *Star of Peace* herself was limping out to help. "What is it, Mitch? Somebody sick?"

Mitch regarded the mike. He choked and could hardly speak. "Lindy," he croaked finally. "Overboard."

"*When?*"

He could not bring himself to tell Graham that it had been almost thirty hours. "Long time," he managed. "If you raise Papeete, tell them hurry, okay?"

A young American voice cut in, faint but perfectly readable. "*Linda Lee,* this is the yacht *Windrift,* clearing Papeete Pass. The word is out on the quay. *Westerly* and *Kialoa* are following. Also *Zen,* no radio, *Xanadu,* likewise. Estimate ten hours to your area."

"Thanks, *Windrift,*" Mitch muttered.

A heavily accented German voice spoke up: "Here is *Kormorant,* coming also, Mitch. For information, two fat French airplanes have just took off from Faaa. So, here is Kurt, on *Kormorant,* over and out."

That call he could not even answer. Tears in his eyes, he climbed the companionway and mounted to the spreader again.

WHEN THE EYE of Arlene arrived, the wind slackened and they could see, for an instant, a patch of mottled blue in the tortured sky. Lindy became elated, thinking that the worst was over, and he did not tell her what was coming. He would not let her go below to try to get crackers and cheese, for he was afraid of a knockdown. So he kept her topside and tried to protect *Linda Lee* as best he could at the tiller. He waited for the wind to shift and the trailing wall to hit.

He was unready for its brutality. It turned the air to foaming water. He could not see or breathe. He fought it as long as he could, trying to surf again in the chaos, but his back gave out. Lindy was half dead from fatigue, and was more hindrance than help. Arlene had beaten them completely. He sent Lindy below, lashed the tiller to leeward, and crawled for the hatch.

Linda Lee lay untended. A forty-foot rogue wave pyramided

and crashed to the deck. He dived through the hatch and slammed it closed above him. She took another monstrous wave, heeling to her beam ends. He was flung across the chart table and jammed against the bulkhead. Very slowly she came erect.

Below, the boat was a sodden tangle of all they owned. Every wave that rolled down threatened to capsize them. They were rolling 40, 50 degrees, dead in the water, and it was impossible to hang on. The cabin floor was strewn with cans, oilskins, boots, and towels. Oily water sloshed up from the bilges through the floorboards.

The bunks were too precarious, so they crawled forward and lay on a littered floor in the narrow passage between the head and the hanging locker. He enveloped her in his arms to protect her from the wildest rolls.

The electrical system shorted and left them in the dark. He heard a scuba tank, lashed in the engine compartment, go adrift and begin to smash itself to pieces. He was too tired to move. He was sure they would die. A galley locker sprang open, and the crockery went in a roaring crash. Somehow, *Linda Lee* avoided capsize. They did not speak at all.

He finally slept. When he awakened, the motion had eased. He crawled to a porthole. The eastern horizon was banded in a steel-gray cast. He crawled back and slept some more. When he awakened again they were in fast-clearing weather. He could see Lindy's profile against the gray skylight.

"Are we okay, Mitch?" she murmured.

He knew what she meant, what she wanted him to say. He couldn't say it. Later, maybe, but Jean-Paul was too close. "Sure," he said. "It's clearing."

He slumbered again. When he finally awoke, his mouth tasted of acid and his face was stubbled with a two-day growth. He had slept almost eighteen hours. He moved topside. *Linda Lee* was still jogging, going nowhere. The sun was rising upwind in a mess of orange squalls, harmless camp followers of Arlene.

They had taken the worst they would ever see. He would never fear weather again, not on this boat, not with Lindy. After repairs, there were the Cooks, the Fijis, New Caledonia. Then? Why not?

Through the Indian Ocean and around the Cape of Good Hope. Around the world?

Buoyantly, he made sail. He set a course for Bora Bora, where they could make repairs and rest awhile. Lindy dragged topside. She was pale and haggard. He knew he himself looked like the tail end of a two-week drunk. But her eyes were lifeless, and though she smiled when she saw the pretty sunrise, she saw none of her cloud people in it. She wanted to help with the tiller but could not seem to keep her mind on the course. He sent her below for more rest.

They reached Bora Bora in three days. The pier was now just a pile of timbers.

Mitch cleared out the chaos below, repaired the steering cable, and patched up Irwin. He could have sailed then, but Lindy was not ready, so they found an isolated cove. They dived and swam and fished. They made love. He exorcised Jean-Paul in his mind and, she swore to him, in hers.

It became almost impossible for him to recall the details of Arlene, or the fear he must have known huddled on the cabin floor. It was all lost somewhere in the triumph of surviving. It seemed equally impossible for her to forget. A great question hung between them, and he could not bring himself to ask it.

One night in the cockpit, sipping Scotch, she brought it up herself. "Let's level, Mitch. What are we getting ready for?"

"Well, Raro, the Cooks—" Something in her face stopped him. "What is it, Lindy?"

"Alone?" She gulped. "All by yourself?"

"Of course not."

She began to cry softly. His gut felt cold. He knew, and there was no use dragging it out of her. "You're through?" he asked.

"Finished, Mitch. While it balances out for me. The gales for the days in the trades, and that pass at Fakarava for the lagoon inside, and Arlene for . . . I don't know."

"For Jean-Paul?"

"No. Arlene for the look you had when you found the boat."

The surf boomed into Te Avanui Pass, gently now but still with the voice to move him. She had been trying to tell him this for a long time, and he hadn't let her close enough to hear. "Okay," he said thickly. "We'll beat back to Tahiti and sell her."

"Mitch, it's awful! I wrecked *one* dream."

He thought of her at eighteen, in the trailer, pregnant, trying to stay out of his way while he studied. "Hell, no! You've wrecked nothing. And I'm not going to lose you over a boat."

"When," she asked softly, "did this cruise really begin?"

"When we spotted the boat," he lied. He reached for her glass. "Another drink?"

She did not believe him, or maybe she did. Early next morning they winched up the anchor and powered out the pass. Lindy could recall every detail of the last mad passage through it, outwardbound. Mitch could barely remember breasting the breakers.

They began to beat back to Tahiti.

Chapter Three

Three separate squalls were sweeping in from the east. He hung on the ratlines, studying their paths. He was so intent that when an aircraft came up from astern, it caught him unaware. It roared past, wiggled its wings, banked sedately, and was back again, this time almost flicking the mast above him.

It apparently had no radio channels he could receive, for it dropped a long red ribbon across his deck with a waterproof bag at its end. He opened it and found a note. In schoolbook English he read that the plane's wingman was already searching five miles astern. A destroyer was less than an hour southeast. The destroyer had the proper frequencies, if he wished to speak, and could relay messages to the planes. If they saw anything, they would drop flares and return to lead him to the spot.

When he finished reading, the plane was already distant, sweeping the water near the squalls. As he watched, it disappeared in scud, reappeared, and dropped lower. It could have missed her as it passed through the cloud, and it would obviously not search that area again.

For all the squalls and infinite valleys they would need ten planes, scores of ships. The sun was peaking, and even if she was still afloat she would not last another night.

He called the destroyer. A voice came back immediately, in perfect English. Mitch explained that his wife was a good swimmer, that she was wearing flotation, and had probably found a lifebuoy and flag he had left.

"And how long, Captain, has it been? She has fallen in, when?"

"Thirty hours," he admitted. He became verbose, repeating his list of the things which were saving her. Drunk with fatigue, he finished by promising that she was still alive, and guaranteed that she was within ten miles of his own position. He begged the destroyer to send for more ships. Perhaps, but later. For now, the destroyer promised to search as long as was necessary.

He fought down his fury. He thanked the destroyer again and climbed to the spreader. A fast-moving squall enveloped him suddenly, drawing a white curtain between him and the world of planes and ships. For ten minutes he simply clung to his perch, peering into driving rain. He could not see five hundred yards.

The squall passed. The plane that had dropped the message seemed even farther away; his wingman, now visible astern, was droning east. He had felt less lonely with the two white terns.

WHEN THE SUN had climbed high enough, it warmed her forehead, but did nothing for the chill in her legs. She was continually slipping through the horseshoe and having to fight her way back. It slid away again, and now she was too tired to care. She realized it suddenly and looked up. The buoy was five feet away. She paddled after it and somehow got herself in once more. If she lost it again, she would not find the strength to reclaim it.

She had forgotten why she was in the water and wondered where Mitch was, and if he were swimming beside her. But that was stupid. She had fallen in, all by herself, at night. Last night? She thought so. But why had he left her? He should have turned back and picked her up; she had hidden his new Nikon behind the Chunky Beef soup, and he'd never find it by Christmas.

It rained. Somewhere in the squall she became aware of the drone of engines. She glimpsed a gray aircraft breaking from wispy clouds. It flashed through a shaft of sunlight. She was too tired to wave. It was instantly swallowed in mist. She wished she were flying it: she'd look for the boat.

She floated for hours. She sensed the sun at its zenith, and in its descent. She dozed. She had a vivid daydream. A great red ketch bore down on her, and its figurehead was Mahura, and Jean-Paul was at its wheel, and Taarii was poised in her bows, harpoon held aloft. She screamed at them silently. She was not a fish, or a whale, she was Lindy. . . .

A whitecap slurped into her face and up her nose, strangling her. She coughed and retched. She had to have air. She struggled erect.

Down-sun emerging from a squall, she saw *Linda Lee*. Then it was gone. She fumbled for her whistle, coughed out the last of the water. She blew with all her might.

The whistle was silent. She spluttered it dry and got out three feeble shrills before she ran out of air. Then she flopped back into the horseshoe. Nothing was left at all.

FROM THE SPREADER, he watched the next squall approach. His bare right foot, braced against the yardarm and slimy with sweat, slipped. He almost pitched from the mast. He glanced downward. Twenty feet below, *Linda Lee* knifed heedlessly through the swells. She took a special roll and almost flung him off again. Her mainsail chuckled softly.

To port, he heard the sudden shrill cry of a bird. It was very weak. The terns? A whistle? He struggled to his feet on the yardarm. Bobbing in the water, one hundred yards down-sun, he saw the man-overboard pole. He saw nothing else, but that was enough.

"Lindy!"

He heard nothing, saw nothing, in the glare beyond the crest of the swell, only the top of the pole and the fluttering flag.

"*Lindy!*" he screamed. He slid down the shrouds, letting go to drop the last ten feet. He dropped the jib, loosed the mizzen, and grabbed the wheel, yanking Irwin out of command. He started the engine, and spun the wheel into the plummeting sun.

He lost the flag in the glare. He spotted it again, and then the horseshoe buoy, and her face turned skyward, and the spill of bronze hair on the rim of the buoy.

He brought the bow into the wind, and let the boat go dead. Lindy was twenty feet away. He cut the engine so that she could hear him, for she showed no sign of knowing that he was here. He tossed her the orange life ring, attached to the boat with a long floating line. It dropped within five feet of her. "Lindy!" he shouted. "Grab it!"

She raised her head. She seemed dazed. He yelled again. She seemed to see the ring. She slipped from the horseshoe and tried for it. It was not three feet away from her when she reached out, floundered, and went under.

He dived in. The coolness shocked him. He surfaced. He saw her face, contorted with effort, on the face of a swell. He reached her, slid his hip under her back and his arm across her breasts, and plowed for the orange ring. It was drifting downwind fast. He barely reached it. He jammed an arm through it, rested for a moment, holding her high. Her eyes were closed.

"Lindy," he begged. "Lindy?"

She opened her eyes. They were very dim. "I fell," she murmured. "Mitch—"

Her mouth went slack. She seemed to strangle. Panicked, he squeezed her nose shut, found her mouth with his lips, bent her head back, and tried to breathe into her lungs. The life ring yanked at his crooked elbow, almost pulling free. He grabbed convulsively, got his arm back through it, and found that he was forcing her head beneath the waves. He quit the mouth-to-mouth; he had to get her aboard. The ring tugged again. He glanced at the boat. His heart almost stopped.

Linda Lee was hobbyhorsing. The jib had eased from its furlings and was filling with wind at each crest. As the sail bellied, it began to climb magically up the headstay. The ketch's bow was turning downwind now, and with every swell the sail grew fatter.

The life ring jerked again, almost pulling his arm from its socket as it began to tow them both. His back, supporting Lindy, clenched with a shock of agony.

The boat was gathering speed. A tiny bow wave formed at her stem, like a smile. His arm slipped again. *Linda Lee* heaved forward, towing them faster. He hung on, a link between Lindy, the life ring, and the boat. The flag, the horseshoe that had saved her, and the light were already lost astern.

The ketch began to draw a wake, half drowning him. Across thirty feet of water he heard a burst of static from the radio through the open hatch. Water was shoving against his face, tearing Lindy from his grip. He tried to shift her weight. She planed under and slithered from his grasp.

He was suddenly light in the water. If he pulled himself aboard and came back . . . he would find her dead, if he found her at all. He twisted to look back. She was already fifteen feet away, limp on her back in a cresting swell. He glimpsed her cheeks, bronze in the late sunlight. Her eyes were closed, but her mouth was open and her teeth gleamed whitely.

He let go and stroked for her. "Lindy!" he called.

Her eyes opened once. She saw him. A cresting wave hung over her head. She seemed to try to speak, and then she was gone.

He filled his lungs and dived. He sliced downward. He saw nothing but shards of brassy sunlight lancing the depths. He heard a low-pitched throb and cleared his ears: the beat remained, and he recognized the drum of distant screws.

He curved deeper. The agony of airlessness was brief; he was already through the level of no return. He recognized the edge of narcosis: for a while he was gloriously happy, soaring in a cobalt void, and then he glimpsed a pale form drifting below him.

Languidly, he spiraled down. Her body was blurred and ghostly until he reached for it. He brushed her arm and she seemed to come alive. Her skin was soft and pliant; he felt her hair sweep across his cheek. He clasped her around the waist and let her guide him down. Suddenly the depths exploded in a chaos of sapphire and gold.

And then he finally saw it all: his own body writhing in agony, hers at ease and quite content. He saw it from outside himself, with her.

Hank Searls

Like Mitch Gordon, Hank Searls was brought up in San Francisco and he too fulfilled his dream of cruising the South Pacific aboard a wooden ketch. His boat was the *Berna Ann*, named after his wife, Bunny. "But on our trip," Hank is quick to explain, "no one was swept overboard, and Jean-Paul never appeared!"

"A three-year cruise by a couple alone on a forty-foot boat is, however, an acid test of marriage. Every year hundreds of couples cast off, usually westward-bound across the Pacific. Some marriages don't survive Tahiti. Some marriages survive, but the dream dies. Few marriages and dreams survive together."

Hank and Bunny Searls are among the lucky few. They clearly enjoy each other's company. "Hank is home all day, writing," says Bunny, "and I love it." He has written six books now, including *The Big X*, which was also a Condensed Book selection.

On their own idyllic cruise, they made many landfalls, including all those described in *Overboard*. They stayed in Bora Bora for three months, but French Polynesia's climate was enervating and Hank's writing went too slowly. So the couple sailed for New Zealand. "En route we encountered gales so violent," Bunny remembers, "that I thought the boat was going to fly apart." After seven months in New Zealand they sold the *Berna Ann* and flew home to California.

Now that *Overboard* has been published, Hank and Bunny plan to set off again, this time aboard a slightly larger boat. And they can't wait. "The feeling of freedom is fantastic," says Bunny. "When you're on your boat, you've got everything— your man, your sails and your food—and you can go anywhere in the world."

EXCELLENCY. Original full-length version © David Beaty 1977. British condensed version © The Reader's Digest Association Limited 1977.

CHASE THE WIND. Original full-length version © E. V. Thompson 1977. British condensed version © The Reader's Digest Association Limited 1977.

THE BADGERS OF SUMMERCOMBE. Original full-length version © Ewan Clarkson 1977. British condensed version © The Reader's Digest Association Limited 1977.

OVERBOARD. Original full-length version © Hank Searls 1977. U.S. condensed version © The Reader's Digest Association, Inc. 1977. British condensed version © The Reader's Digest Association Limited 1977.

© The Reader's Digest Association Limited 1977.
© The Reader's Digest Association South Africa (Pty) Limited 1977.

All rights reserved. No part of this publication may be reproduced, stored in a retrieval system, or transmitted in any form or by any means, electronic, mechanical, photocopying, recording or otherwise, without the prior permission of the copyright holders.
® "READER'S DIGEST" is a registered trade-mark of The Reader's Digest Association, Inc., of Pleasantville, New York, U.S.A.

KK93